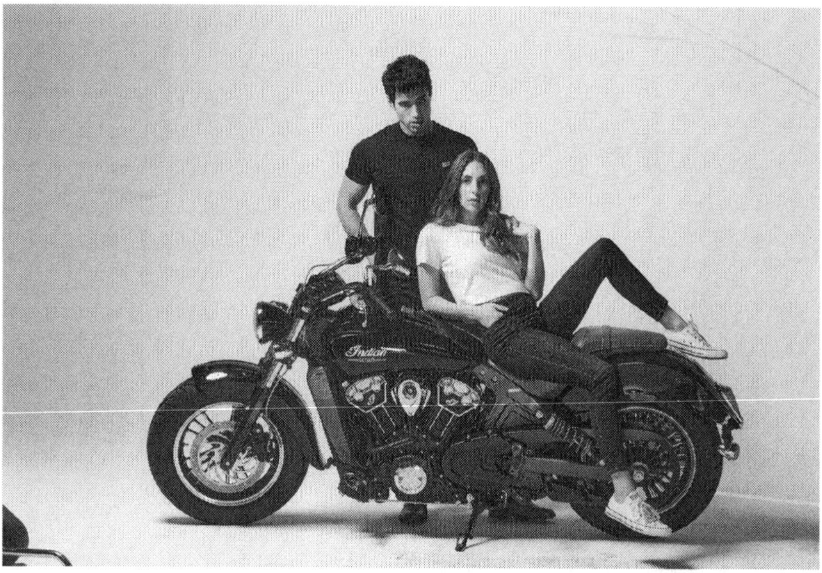

RECKLESS AT RALEIGH HIGH

Copyright © 2020 by Callie Hart

All rights reserved.

No part of this book may be reproduced in any form or by any electronic or mechanical means, including information storage and retrieval systems, without written permission from the author, except for the use of brief quotations in a book review.

*Yea, though I walk through the valley of the shadow of death...*
*I will fear no evil...*

# PROLOGUE

"It's like *Star Wars*, Mom. All the little white flecks flying toward the window are like stars. This is what it looks like when you're traveling through space, y'know."

The woman sitting in the driver's seat of the people carrier smiles affectionately at the young boy sitting in the back seat. Her back hurts from all the driving, but they're on the homestretch now. Well...not the homestretch. Home's an hour in the other direction, where the roads are a decent size, people are civilized, and you can buy a cup of coffee that doesn't taste like piss. Raleigh is the worst kind of backwater, podunk, nowhere town there is, and if the woman had her way, she'd never visit the damn place again.

Soon, perhaps. The wheels are in motion. One day not too far from now, she'll gain custody of the little boy in the backseat and it'll become official: she'll be his mother. Legally. She won't have to flinch every time someone overhears him calling her that. It was wrong to ask him to use that title before everything's been ironed out in court. If things don't go according to plan and the boy's brother does somehow manage to gain custody of the kid, then it'll end up being very disruptive for the boy. He needed a mother, though. He's never had anyone solid and stable in his life to call Mom. She *wants* to be that maternal figure to him. Hell, the first time he called her by that title, she locked herself in the downstairs bathroom by the utility room, the washing machine midway through its loud spin cycle, and she squealed like a giddy teenager into the new Ray Dunn hand towels she'd just bought from Target. She could have corrected him. If she'd had more self-control, she could have told him it wasn't a good idea to use names like 'Mom' just yet, but it had felt far too good for that. The precious little boy, small for his eleven years, with his mop of black, wavy hair, and his dark, expressive eyes wanted her to be his mother, and there was no way she was going to turn down the role.

She'd immediately started planning the trip to Hawaii for the holidays, knowing that the time away together would drive a wedge between the boy and his brother. An escape from all the cold, the rain and the snow. And surfing? Sunshine? Christmas Day dinner on the beach, with a colorful lei around his neck, and the sound of the ocean waves crashing on the shore to rock him to sleep each night? It was a trip that would stay with him forever. Something only she could give him. Something that useless piece of shit brother of his would *never* be able to give him.

Everything had been going so well. The woman knew it in her bones; each evening, when she kissed the boy goodnight, pressing her lips to the crown of his head, smelling the salt in his thick confusion of hair, she *felt* it working. He was forgetting about his brother, talking about him less, thinking about him less, growing closer and closer to *her* instead.

And then it had all come crashing down. Surprise, surprise, the brother had found a way to interfere with her plans. He always did. The phone call came in just after dinner, when she and the boy had been cleaning up in the kitchen of the Airbnb she'd rented. She'd let the old-school answering machine catch the call, which had been her biggest mistake. If the boy hadn't heard the social worker's voice projecting from those shitty speakers, she could have hidden the news from him until they'd returned to Washington.

*"Hello, Jackie, it's Maeve Rogers from CPS. Sorry to be calling so late and I'm sorry to leave this kind of information in a message for you, but it's kind of urgent. Alex has been arrested...for shooting a boy from his school. I know. I know that sounds bad, but believe me...it's not what you're thinking. He's being held at Stafford Creek. He could really use a friendly face right now. Is*

there any way you can bring Ben back to Raleigh to see him? I'm confident this is all going to blow over quickly, but still. Stafford Creek's no walk in the park. Even a short stay in a place like that can change a person, and Alex has been doing so well. He needs Ben right now. If he knows his brother's close by, I know he'll do his best to stay out of trouble. You know I wouldn't suggest it unless—"

The message had ended there, the machine cutting the social worker off, but it was already too late. The damage had been done. Ben had heard those magical words—his brother needed him—and that was it. Final. There was no way she could have kept him in Hawaii without alienating him. She'd tried, even knowing that would probably be the outcome. For another week, she'd delayed traveling back to the mainland. Put it off. Told the boy that his brother would call himself if he wanted Ben to come back. In the end, there was nothing else she could do, though. Reluctantly, she'd purchased the tickets back to Seattle, viciously stabbing at the keyboard keys as she'd entered the digits of her credit card into the booking form. And now here they were, eleven o'clock at night, driving through a godforsaken blizzard on their way to Raleigh, when they should be tucked up, sound asleep in their own small little Hawaiian paradise.

The woman sets her jaw, staring straight ahead, trying to breathe around her anger. "Prisons are pretty scary places, y'know, Benny. Even for adults. You sure you wanna go there tomorrow?"

The woman knows it's a low blow, but she has to try. The boy blinks owlishly at her from the dark recesses of the backseat. "I'm not afraid," he says. "I'm excited. I've only seen prison on TV. And I get to see Alex, too. He's been waiting for me."

"He doesn't know you're coming, remember? We kept it a secret, so it would be a surprise." The woman convinced the boy that it'd be fun, a sort of game to show up at the prison unexpectedly. The dirty truth is that she's still hoping to persuade him that the visit is a bad idea.

The boy nods thoughtfully in the rearview. "I know. But he'll be excited when I get there. I bet he's missed me. Now we can all spend Christmas together, can't we. We'll be able to take him home with us from the prison, and everything will be okay."

"It doesn't work like that, buddy. Your brother did something really, really bad. That's why they're keeping him at the prison. He'll have to stay there until they can decide what they want to do with him. We've talked about this, remember? There's a chance Alex'll have to stay in prison for very long time. Maybe even years."

*Wouldn't that just be fan-fucking-tastic?*

Where has that sour taste in her mouth suddenly come from, though? Tastes like lies and deceit. The woman swallows it down, doing her best to ignore the rotten tang. She didn't lie to the child. His brother shot someone, for crying out loud. *Shot* somebody, a good boy from a wealthy, well-to-do family. She's done her research. She's read the news reports online. There are plenty of rumors and mistruths flying around, but the woman's been dealing with the boy's brother for years now. She knows him inside out. He's a liar and a thief. He breaks everything he touches. There's no way he shot an ivy-league candidate because he was trying to murder that ditzy little girlfriend of his. She probably came to her senses and cheated on the brother with the Weaving boy. That was more likely. The brother had probably found them in bed together, fucking like the horny teenaged morons that they were, and he'd lost his temper. Pulled the gun and shot Weaving in a fit of rage.

"I just want to see him," the boy says quietly. "I know he didn't mean to hurt that other boy. Alex isn't bad, Mom."

Urgh. Poor, naïve, innocent, sweet child. Maybe the realities of a prison will scare some sense into him. She'll go with him in the morning, and she'll do nothing to shield him from the horrors of an underfunded penitentiary. There's every chance—

*SHIT!*

Red.

White.

Startled, wild brown eyes.

The impact rocks the car, the sound a deafening roar.

The windshield...gone.

Glass, shattered, raining down like diamonds.

The woman wrenches at the wheel, stunned, reacting blindly, steering the car, left, left, left...

Weightlessness...

Darkness...

The desperate, frightened, thin scream of a child. *"ALEX!"*
So much fear. So much terror.
White, spiraling into the black.
Another impact. Jarring.
Breathless, winded, jagged, sharppain... pain... painpainpain...p...p...
Ticking metal.
Hissing steam.
They...they're off the road. In a ditch. Accident. There's been an accident. A deer...out of nowhere. It came out of nowhere.
"Ben? Benny, are...you okay?"
Nothing.
The woman tries to turn and sees the shard of metal protruding from her chest. It doesn't make sense, that piece of metal. It's a part of the car's fender. How? It shouldn't...be inside the car. It shouldn't be inside *her*.
"Ben? Ben, answer me, baby? Can you...hear me? Are you okay?" It's impossible to spin in the seat; the twisted piece of fender won't allow for that kind of movement. Instead, the woman has to use the rearview, angling it to the left and down, in order to find the boy on the back seat. His head is open, blood pouring down his face. It looks bad enough that when she opens her mouth and tries to cry out, no sound comes. His eyes are open. He silently blinks at her, his small shoulders shaking...
Oh god.
The boy's shoulder's dislocated. And she can see white showing in amongst the beautiful thick waves of his hair—the kind of white that should *never* be showing.
A small, voiceless whimper comes out of his mouth.
"Oh god. Oh...god, Benny. Hold...on, son. I'll...I'll get...help." Each word is harder to form. Each breath is harder to take. Her insides feel wet. It feels like she's breathing water. With both hands, the woman takes hold of the sharp metal pinning her to her seat and she slowly begins to pull. There isn't much time. If she tries... If she really tries... If she hurries...
The pain nearly robs her of her last moments of consciousness. If she was alone, the pain would be enough to force her into submission

right here and now. She would gladly throw in the towel, admit defeat and sigh out her last breath, knowing that it'd be a reprieve from the staggering wall of agony that's slamming into her. She isn't alone, though. There's Ben. He's hurt, and he needs her. If she doesn't make it back onto the road, then he isn't going to make it...

The broken piece of fender, slick with blood, makes a hollow clanging sound as it falls into the footwell. Warmth spreads down the woman's chest, staining the *'Aloha Kākou!'* sweater she bought at the airport a dazzling shade of red.

The door won't open on her first try. It won't budge on her second attempt. The third time, the woman lays her shoulder into the busted plastic housing of the door, and the metal groans, swinging open, depositing her out onto the ground in the snow.

*Get up.*
*Save him.*
*Save your son.*
*Your son...*
*Your son...*
*Your son...*

With her life pouring out of her into the cold, relentless night, the woman manages to crawl halfway up the slope that leads up to the road. Dizzy, disoriented, fighting for breath, her brain feels so damn muddled all of a sudden.

Why was she climbing up the slope again?

She rolls onto her back, dazed and numb, and laughs silently as she coughs up blood.

Wow. The night is so beautiful. The snowflakes, swirling down from the heavens, so thick and fast...they really look like *stars*.

# 1

## SILVER

Guilt's an unpredictable beast. It doesn't behave the way you assume it will. When Kacey Winters was still undisputed queen of Raleigh High and I was yet to be cast out of the Sirens, she encouraged us to be as hateful as she was. The meaner we were, the more arrogant, the more we established our dominance over the lower echelons of the socio-economic student body, the more we pleased Kacey. The pursuit to win her approval was a full-time job that required a level of dedication and determination most high school students are unfamiliar with. But I was never as cruel or unkind as Zen was.

Fiercely competitive, Zen was always willing to take things that one step too far. By rights, she should have been Kacey's favorite. It never worked out that way, though. I laughed along with the jokes, I made spiteful comments under my breath whenever Kacey prodded at me to tease someone, and I made sure to mock the girls on the cheer team whenever one of them fucked up. In hindsight, I was the John Lennon to Zen's Colonel Gaddafi, but that was irrelevant. *I* was Kacey's favorite.

I never felt guilty about the malicious acts I participated in under Kacey's reign of terror. Not until long after, once Jake and his bastard friends held me down and hurt me.

This morning, however, I'm choked with guilt. I haven't done anything wrong. I haven't constructed a fake body in my bed out of lumpy pillows and a wig and snuck out of the house in the middle of the night. Mom and Max are in Toronto for the next six weeks, visiting my Aunt Sarah. Dad gave his permission for me to stay at Alex's apartment. I don't have to be home until midday, but...*it's Christmas morning.* It feels like I'm breaking some kind of rule, waking up here in bed with Alex, blissed out and deliriously happy.

We spent last night with Dad, decorating the entire house, arranging our gifts by the fire place, wrestling ornaments out of Nipper's mouth and drinking eggnog, but I still feel bad that my father's going to wake up this morning to an empty house for the first time in twenty something years. It just doesn't seem right.

The sun ekes in through the window next to the bed, washing my skin in cool winter light. It's still early, just after dawn. If we get up and get dressed now, there's still time to make it back to the house before Dad's finished with his morning shower. God knows what Alex is going to say about leaving his warm, comfortable bed, though. His arm tightens reflexively around me, his body hot as a furnace, his smooth, hard chest rising and falling beneath my head as I lay nestled into his side. For the past fifteen minutes, I've been lightly tracing the tips of my fingers over the lines of the extensive ink that covers his torso and spreads down his arms, admiring the complexity and the beauty of the work, and he hasn't even stirred. Once he passes out, there's very little that can wake a sleeping Alessandro Moretti.

I take the opportunity to study him. Usually, I'm careful about the length of time I allow myself to stare at his handsome, artfully drawn features. When he's awake, he's highly sensitive to the weight of another person's eyes on him; he knows the moment he's being watched, and he isn't afraid to call me out on it when he catches me scrutinizing him. Plenty of times I've done it unwittingly—risked a sidelong glance at him, just to see what expression he's making, or to gauge the look in his eyes—only to wind up mortified when he curves one of his dark eyebrows and angles his face toward me, smirking like the bastard that he is.

*"Thirsty, Argento? Need something to quench your appetite?"*

I shiver against the mere memory of such a suggestion. I *always* need him. I *always* want him, his hands on my waist, roughly kneading my breasts, his sharp-edged, filthy tongue between my legs…

Moments like this, when Alex is asleep and dead to the world, are the only times I get to feast on the sight of him without having to fend off hot embarrassment, so I seize them with both hands.

His eyelashes are so long, ink-black and perfectly curled. They look like they've been drawn on individually by hand. The deep dimple in his cheek is missing. His mouth, the tool he uses most to convey his amusement courtesy of that damned smirk of his, is relaxed, his full lips slightly open. The cupid's bow cut from his top lip is so pronounced that scores of women have likely envied it since he was old enough for them to notice him.

And boy-oh-boy do they notice him. He doesn't play on it, or really acknowledge it, but the truth of the matter is that Alex turns women's heads wherever he goes. In the grocery store; at the gas station; in line for popcorn at the movie theater. Even at school, I sometimes catch the eyes of the female faculty members inadvertently following after him as he walks down the hall or across the cafeteria.

Basically, he's sexy as fuck. Good looking, in a rough-cut, edgy, overtly dangerous way that turns people on and scares them at the same time. And, somehow, *I* am the one he's decided to claim as his own. The math doesn't quite add up.

His pulse throbs evenly in the hollow of his throat, making his tattooed, vine-covered skin tick there. His nose, arrow straight and in perfect proportion to the rest of his face, wrinkles slightly as he swallows, turning his face toward me in his sleep. It's as if he can tell I'm assessing the individual parts of him that make him whole and he's trying to give me a better view.

God. How have I ended up so entangled in this person? I try to play it cool as often as possible, but I'm sure he sees right through me. I'm addicted to him. Obsessed. I never wanted to be that girl, the girl who loses herself in her high school crush, but I find myself unraveling day by day. If someone asked me to find the thread where I end and Alex begins, then I honestly wouldn't be able to pinpoint it. It's too interwoven with him now. I'm lost to his dark eyes, and the gravel of his voice, and the callouses on his hands that match my own.

I go very, very still when his breathing hitches. It's weird that you can tell when a person wakes and their consciousness comes flooding back in, even if their outward appearance doesn't change. Alex looks like he's still asleep, his eyelids closed, facial features relaxed and loose, but he's awake. I can *feel* him there, like the answer to a question that I've been asking for a really long time, reaching out for me.

Bracing, I wait for the caustic comment that's about to come out of his mouth. He'll tease me any chance he gets, especially if he's caught me swooning over him. Seconds pass, and then a minute. But Alex remains silent. I begin to think that maybe I'm mistaken and he isn't awake after all, but then his eyelids flutter and he slowly, languidly opens them. The dark pools of his eyes meet mine, and my breath catches in my throat. He doesn't smile. Doesn't say a word. He stares back at me with the intensity of a thousand burning suns, his gaze searching and curious, his expression fierce, and for the millionth time since I met him, I have to steel myself, forcing myself not to look away. He's so damn serious. I'm eaten alive by his thorough examination, stripped bare and left stupefied.

The crisp cotton sheets whisper as Alex turns onto his side to face me properly, sliding himself across the pillow so that his forehead is little more than an inch away from mine. Still, he doesn't say anything. We face one another, chests rising and falling, hearts beating in time, locked in this weird staring contest that's both intimidating and incredibly satiating. I'm dying of thirst, and Alex is an ice-cold glass of water. I'm burning alive, and he is the flood that douses the flames. I'm falling so fast, so hard, so dangerously out of all control, and Alex is the one who reaches out and catches me. This man, who has been nothing to so many, is absolutely *everything* to me.

Suddenly, I can't bear the silence anymore. Dad can make it through breakfast without us. I have to have Alex. I have to absorb him into me somehow. In the very least, I have to press myself against him and feel his heart quicken. We move at the same time, sharing the same thought, needing the same thing. His mouth meets mine, and it's as though my soul's just been cut loose and is flying free. His lips press against mine, not rough but firm and insistent, and he blows out a long, hot breath down his nose, sighing softly. Our bodies gravitate toward each other, closing the small space between us, and Alex slides his free arm around me, pulling me up against him.

He isn't like other guys our age. They're all still transitioning into manhood. Their bodies might have filled out and made it through the other side of puberty, but they're still swamped in confusion and uncertainty as people, trying to figure out what part they are going to play in the theaters of their own lives.

Alex isn't confused. He knows himself. He's confident in his beautifully decorated skin. When he holds me the way he's holding me now, kisses me the way he's kissing me now, he's so sure of himself that he leaves no room for doubt. I belong to him. He's staked his claim, and he isn't planning on relinquishing. Ever.

He forces my mouth open, slipping his tongue past my lips, not caring that neither of us have brushed our teeth yet, and the bed feels like it's tilting, tipping sideways, my head spiraling out of control. Only he can unbalance me like this when I'm fucking horizontal.

Winding his fingers into my hair, he cradles my face in his hands, pressing his hips against mine, and any kind of chill I might have been cultivating up until this point flies out of the window. His morning glory really is fucking glorious. I can't wait for him to thrust it deep inside me. If that's not where this is going, then there's gonna be fireworks...

Pulling the duvet down, I slide my hand up Alex's side, relishing the delicious shift of the muscle beneath his skin as I stroke up his back, between the flat blades of his shoulders. From there, I don't have far to reach for the back of his neck. I dig my fingernails into his skin, savoring the prickle of the freshly shaved, close cropped hair at the back of his head, and Alex groans breathlessly into my mouth.

"Fuck, *Argento*. You're sure you wanna be pulling that shit this early in the morning? You're gonna get yourself into trouble."

I love the sound of that. I've learned from past experience that trouble with Alex always ends in an orgasm or three—the kind of brain-melting orgasm that leaves you boneless and sated. I laugh, pulling my bottom lip through my teeth. "What if I like trouble?"

Alex grins, arching his back like a cat as I scratch the back of his head again. He reacts the same way without fail whenever I do this. He can't help himself. His eyes, dark as midnight pools, roll back in his head as he angles his chin up, exposing the column of his throat, and I have to refrain from sinking my teeth into the curve where his shoulder meets his neck. Like me, my Alessandro isn't averse to a little pain every now and then. He'd enjoy the press of my incisors against his jugular, I'm sure, but we're going to be seeing Dad soon and my old man has G.I. Joe grade eagle eyes. He'd spot a hickey a mile away.

Alex's hand snaps up out of nowhere, grabbing hold of me by the wrist and wrenching my hand up high over my head. His eyes open lazily, traveling up and down my face, his gaze finally settling on my mouth.

"You woke up feisty, *dolcezza*. Careful. I could get used to this." In a split second, he shoves me onto my back, pulling me away from the cold wall so that my body is in the center of the bed and he holds himself directly above me. The arm I was lying on gets repositioned, my other hand joining my one already above my head, and Alex bears down, burying his face into my neck. Apparently, *he* has no aversion to using his teeth on areas of *my* body that my father will likely see.

"Alex! *Alex!*" I pant, wheezing the words out, squirming underneath the satisfyingly heavy press of his body, but I'm only making things worse. The more I writhe, the more fired up he's going to get. No way will he leave me unmarked with me responding like this. Once upon a time, that thought would have scared the ever-loving shit out of me. Pinned to a mattress, hands locked over my head, restrained, with nowhere to go and no way of getting out? My body would have forced me to bolt and run, as memories of Jacob Weaving's leering face assaulted me from all angles.

But Alex isn't Jake. He's nothing like any of the sick, twisted, evil fucks who trapped me in that bathroom. One word from me—*stop*—and he'll stop. He'll be on the other side of the room before I can even register that he's let me go. I participate in this kind of roughhousing with Alex, because I know without question that he'd never do anything to hurt me.

"I wanna fucking eat you," he huffs into my hair. "I want to devour every last piece of you. You taste like fucking sugar. I can't get enough..."

Gasping for air, I bow away from the bed, crushing my tits against his chest, willing for him to take more of me. The thin material of the shirt he let me sleep in last night rubs against my nipples, causing them to stiffen painfully, and my imagination runs away with me. I'm picturing him licking and sucking at the tight, pink buds of flesh. I can already see the white flash of his teeth as he takes them into his mouth one at a time and bites down until I cry out his name.

Alex pulls back, chuckling darkly as he hovers over me. "You wanna get fucked, don't you, Silver Parisi." Not really a question. He knows it's the truth just as much as I do. His grey sweats are riding low, exposing his hip bones and the beginnings of the maddening vee that dips down lower, between his legs. The sight of the tensed muscles in his chest and stomach is the final straw; a girl can only take so much provocation before she outright loses her mind. I place my feet flat against the mattress, bending my knees, and I grip him between my thighs, squeezing tight, silently begging him to tear my shorts off and plunge himself inside me already.

A jolt of pain lances through my side, my still-broken ribs complaining bitterly about all of the movement, but the discomfort doesn't compare to the promise of the pleasure that's just around the corner.

The bruises still blooming all over my body like morbid flowers are a grim, ugly reminder of recent trauma, but it's as though Alex doesn't even see them. He stares down at me, wide-eyed and wonderous, like I'm the most beautiful thing he's ever seen. Sitting back on his heels, he straddles me, hooking his fingers beneath the waistband of my shorts, almost giving me what I so badly need. His erection tents the material of his sweats, perfectly outlining the head of his dick, and I reach down, about to close my hand around him, and—

*DUM! DUM! DUM!*

Three loud bangs echo through the apartment, bouncing off the walls. Alex's head whips around, looking back over his shoulder, frowning deeply at the interruption. "Seven am, Christmas morning? You sure your dad was cool with you crashing here?"

I nod, need still pulsing around my nervous system, waiting for his hands to return to the waistband of my shorts. "You were there when I asked him."

Alex grunts. "Then whoever that is can fuck right off."

Normally, I'd be the voice of reason. It's early, so maybe it's important. Could be Henry from downstairs, needing access to a breaker board or something. Perhaps my mom found out where I was and lost her fucking mind. Today, I'm throwing caution to the wind, though. I don't care who's at the door or what they want. Alex was about to strip me naked and fuck me, and that's honestly all I care about...

He grabs my shorts, yanking them down over my hips, and I whimper in anticipation. Jesus, when did I become this needy? It's all because of him. I'd still be at the hand-holding stage with anyone else, but it's impossible to cultivate that kind of control with Alex. My body craves him like a junkie craves their next fix. I've forgotten what restraint even looks like these days.

"You wet for me, *dolcezza*? You think you deserve my tongue on your clit?"

Heat explodes across my face and down my torso, shooting in between my thighs. Holy fuck. A handful of words and a piercing stare and I'm ready to implode.

*DUM DUM DUM!*

"Alex! Open the door. It's Maeve!"

Maeve? What the hell? The name sets alarm bells ringing in my head. Fuck, it sets alarm *klaxons* ringing in my head. Social workers don't clock in on the biggest holiday of the year. I'm assuming they don't, anyway. Dad's always complaining about civil servants and how they're hardly ever available during normal working hours. Today's Christmas Day. Maeve should be spending time with her family. I don't like the panicked note I heard in her voice through three walls and across an entire apartment. Makes me think worrying thoughts.

A cold, unpleasant sensation creeps its way up my spine. "Don't answer." I grip Alex tighter between my legs, holding him in place. "She can't just show up here whenever she feels like it. You're allowed some privacy, right? Don't I deserve some undisturbed time alone with you?"

I sound like a petty little bitch, whining at her boyfriend to pay attention to her, but that isn't what's going on here. Maeve's advocated for Alex on numerous occasions. She was standing up for him the very first time I saw him in the hallway outside Darhower's office. She squared away the fact that he was a minor living on his own, even though he was still supposed to be under Monty's care. Without her, Alex would never have scored this apartment. And she promised she'd help Alex with his custody case for Ben. Not to mention, if she hadn't been standing by his side when he went into court after shooting Jake, then chances are he'd probably still be in jail right now. Alex verbally swipes at her all the time, but I know he appreciates her. I do, too. I think the woman's a badass.

No, I don't want him to go and answer the door because something *bad* is waiting for us on the other side of it. And once we've let it in, we won't be able to shut it out again. I rarely have gut feelings about anything, but this…this is different. A sense of dread crushes me in its jaws. This is the kind of foreboding that perches on your shoulder moments before something comes along and destroys everything you hold dear, and you right along with it.

"Needy little Parisi. Don't worry. I've been a good boy. I haven't broken any laws. That I know of, anyway." He smirks, amusement sparking like the embers of a fire in his dark eyes. "The weirdest things turn out to be illegal sometimes. I'll see what she wants and get rid of her. The woman's persistent as fuck. If she thinks I'm home, she won't lea—"

"*Alex! I'm not messing around! You need to answer this door right now!*"

Dark hair tumbling into his eyes, Alex cants his head to one side, his expression rueful. "*See.*" He climbs off me, and that icy dread sinks it's claws deeper. I want to grab hold of him and *make* him stay. Locked away here in our little bubble, whatever madness exists outside can't affect us. Can't hurt us.

Glancing down, Alex notices the fact that his hard-on is still tenting his sweatpants. He laughs breathlessly as he reaches down the front of his pants and tucks his dick into his waistband in an attempt to hide it. "Don't look so sad, *dolcezza*. No chance this thing's going anywhere any time soon. I'm harder than fucking reinforced steel. Give me two seconds. Here." He takes hold of me by the wrist, guiding my hand down in between my own legs. "I want you shaking and trembling by the time I get back. No coming, though. I'll punish the shit out of you if you rob me of that."

I watch him put on a t-shirt, frozen in place and in time. Later, this moment will replay itself on a loop in my head. I'll recall the way the muscles in Alex's broad back shifted so beautifully as he worked his arms into his shirt and pulled it lazily over his head. I won't be able to forget the slow, confident smile he throws over his shoulder at me as he steps over his guitar case and leaves the bedroom, drawing the door half-closed behind him. I'll still be smelling the rich, doughy, enticing aroma of fresh bread emanating from the bakery across the road, and it will still be turning my stomach...

Mechanically, I inch myself toward the edge of the bed. My arms and legs are wooden and uncooperative as I tug on a sweater and a pair of jeans. Basic manners dictate that it'd rude to follow after him, I should give him space to have a private conversation with his social worker, but manners and etiquette don't seem important right now. I need to be with Alex. I can feel it. I know it.

The air in the hallway is a solid ten degrees colder than in the bedroom. A gust of biting wind snakes its way past the two figures standing in the doorway up ahead; it knifes straight through the black hoody I just pulled on, making my skin break out in goosebumps.

A high-pitched ringing sound mutes my hearing as I take each step forward.

*You're wrong. You're being fucking paranoid. Stop overreacting. Offer to make a pot of coffee or something. Seriously, chill the fuck out, girl...*

My little pep talk falls on deaf ears.

Three feet away, Alex reaches out and takes a hold of the door, his knuckles turning white as he grasps at the wood. *"What?"*

"I know. I know, Alex, look...let me in, okay. There's a lot of information to unpack here. You should be sitting—"

"You're lying." Alex's shoulder blades knit together beneath his t-shirt. The tension he's radiating is even more shocking than the cold. "This is her, I know it is. Jackie's concocted this bullshit story to cut ties with me for good. She wants to make sure I never see him again, and you...you're going along with it for some reason. Why...*why the fuck would you do that?*" His voice is soft, but he's tripping all over his words.

Right behind him now, I peer around his arm, making eye contact with Maeve. I've only seen her the once, that time at Raleigh. She was wearing an elegant grey pantsuit, the collar of her shirt pressed into a sharp fold. Her dark hair was swept back into a practical bun. This woman looks nothing like the person who argued Alex's case with Darhower. She's dressed in track pants and a massive sweater with the words, 'SPIRITUAL GANGSTER' emblazoned across the front. The messy top knot on the crown of her head looks like rats have been nesting in it, and the tell-tale black smudge of yesterday's mascara beneath each of her eyes implies that she didn't wash her face this morning before she rushed out of the house.

She shakes her head, her voice, rough with emotion, catching in her throat. "You think I'm *that* cruel? You don't think I'm on your side? After everything that's happened?"

Alex notices that I'm behind him. He moves an inch to the side, making room for me, but his eyes don't break away from Maeve. "If you're not complicit, then she's fooling you too," he says gruffly. "You know how bad she wants to keep him. She'll do anything to make sure I don't get Ben back."

Maeve drops her head, her eyes closing for a beat. When she opens them, she doesn't look up. She stares down at the keys in her hands, rubbing the pad of her thumb against a gold disc that's attached to the fob. "I wish...that were true. If that were the case, it'd be simple. We'd track them down and find them. But...I was just at the funeral home, Alex. I...I saw Ben. It *was* him. He's been there almost a week now. There was some kind of admin mix up. They couldn't figure out who they needed to call."

Alex backs away, shaking his head. He stumbles, barely bothering to correct his footing as he attempts a hasty retreat. "Bullshit," he hisses. "Fucking *bullshit*. Jackie...she found a way to...I'm telling you, this is just Jackie..."

"This isn't pretend, Alex. I'm not making it up." Maeve sounds like she's on the other side of the world, speaking down a really bad telephone line. My ears are trying to block out what she's saying. "She was at the funeral home, too, okay? Her injuries were catastrophic. She...she didn't make it, either."

Alex stops, slumping sideways against the wall. He looks at me, a tiny frown marring his brow, his chest not moving, and my heart fucking shatters and breaks. I haven't heard Maeve say it. I haven't heard him say it, either, but the words are there, like an IED I've unwittingly stepped on, blowing up, and blowing up, and blowing up, the explosion never fucking ending.

*Ben's dead.*

*Something awful has happened.*

*Alex's brother is gone.*

# DAY ONE

Idon'tknowwhattodoDadhejustkeepsstaringatthewallIcan'tdoanythingforhimIcan'thelphimpleasetellmewhatI'msupposedtodo…

# DAY TWO

"Please, Baby. You've got to eat something. Can you just try? You're gonna make yourself ill. Alex? *Alex?*"

## DAY THREE

"They asked what you want him to wear. I can…I can go to the store and get a suit or something? What do you think? I'm sorry. I know you don't want to deal with this, but they say they need to know…"

# DAY FOUR

"I DON'T WANT A FUCKING PIECE OF TOAST, OKAY! JUST PUT...PUT THE BREAD DOWN, SILVER!

Fuck.

I'm sorry. I'm sorry. God, I'm so fucking sorry. I shouldn't have snapped at you. Jesus fucking Christ. I'm...you shouldn't be around me right now. You really need to go."

# DAY FIVE

"When will we have given enough? When will we have lost enough? There's no one out there, keeping track of how much pain we're dealt...how much we're asked to bear...and that's the most terrifying thing, Silver.

'Cause if there's no one keeping track...

*...then there's no one out there to make it stop.*"

# DAY SIX

"I love you so goddamn much, *Argento*. I know you're trying to help, but…please. *Please* go home for a while. I'll be okay, I promise. I just need a little time to think."

2
---

# ALEX

*One Week Later*

I jerk upright, the sound of loud, obnoxious punk music splitting my head apart. For a bewildering moment, I'm so fucking turned around that I have no idea where I am or what the fuck is happening. The trailer's popcorned ceiling isn't where it's supposed to be. The window to my right wasn't there last night, when I collapsed on top of my bed sheets and descended into oblivion. The door opposite the bed has moved three feet to the left of its own accord...

Only...

...wait...

The trailer. I don't live in the trailer anymore. I have an apartment now. I live above the hardware store. And Silver—

*Silver.*

The moment I think of her, other dangerous memories begin to creep back in. Truths that shouldn't be faced right now. I sit bolt upright, the room see-sawing like a pitching ship as I try to get up from the bed and realize, belatedly, that I'm more hungover than I have ever been in my entire fucking life and I'm about to throw my guts up. "Holy...*shit.*" Scrambling, I'm all arms and legs as I try to make it to the bathroom. Luck ain't on my side, though. I retch, bile blazing a pathway up my esophagus, and I am out of fucking options. I grab the first thing I lay my hands on and double over it, capturing the vomit that erupts out of my mouth.

It feels as though I've been repeatedly donkey kicked in the stomach by the time the spasms in my diaphragm quit and I can finally draw in a ragged, burning breath. Which is when I see that I've just hurled in my empty fucking guitar case.

*Fuck.*

*Fuck, fuck, fucking fuck.*

I grit my teeth, wincing as the raucous, pounding music playing somewhere in the apartment intensifies to a deafening crescendo. There can be only one explanation for any of this madness. Somehow, I pull in a second, shallow breath, and roar at the top of my lungs, "ZAAAAAAANDER!"

A jarring screech interrupts the thrashing punk tune—the sound of a needle being egregiously dragged across the surface of a record— and the music cuts off. Steady thumping sounds follow. I can't tell if it's footfall or the reluctant, labored pumping of my own heart, but a second later Zander Hawkins appears in the bedroom doorway, clad in a pair of black boxers and bright red silk robe—the kind of robe bored housewives wear in soap operas while lazily considering whether or not they should try and seduce the pool boy.

Zander's broad, shit-eating grin dissolves into open disgust when he lays eyes on me. "Dude. You desecrated your gig bag. Fuck's wrong with you? You're sitting next to a perfectly good trash can."

I look to my left, in the direction that he's pointing, and he's right. I could easily have grabbed the trash can instead of my case a second ago, but I was too preoccupied with the fact that it'd felt like I was about to die on my bedroom floor. Still feels like I might expire any second now.

"What the fuck did you do to me?" I press a hand to my face. Fuuu- uck. Breathing is *so* much easier with my eyes closed.

*Alex? Where were you? I don't like it here. Can you come and get me?*

God...

Nope.

No fucking way.

A spiderweb of pain spreads its fingers across my chest. Quickly, I chase the sound of that voice right out of my head.

Zander lets out a scathing, "*Ha!*" I sense his approach, but I don't bother cracking my eyelids. "You did this all by yourself, my friend. I told you to stop after your tenth shot, but would you listen? I'm gonna let you guess the answer to that one. Boy oh boy, you look like expertly hammered *shit,* my friend."

I swallow, tamping down the urge to vomit again. "Tequila?" I already know— can *taste*—the answer.

"You took down that sexy Latina mistress like she'd just *begged* you to fuck up her shit," Zander confirms. "I barely got a look in. Lucky for me I brought my friend Jack Daniels along to your sad sack one-man pity party. Otherwise I'd have had to watch you drink yourself into oblivion totally fucking sober. That would have been really lame, dude. It was bad enough watching it all go down while buzzed."

I groan, which I instantly regret. The vibration of the air traveling over my vocal cords makes me feel like I'm about to implode. Or explode. Not sure which. "Pity party?" I pant.

Zander's pronounced shrug is practically audible. "Don't ask me. I haven't got a clue why Alessandro Moretti, Destroyer of Worlds, came out to play. Not my job to pry. I'm only good for vague, surface emotions and drinking games. You did mention something about your little brother? And that woman who's taking care of him. You called her…what was it? An evil, vicious cunt?"

Yeah. Evil, vicious cunt sounds about right. I clench my jaw, grabbing hold of my own wrist and squeezing it as hard as I can. I have to get the fuck out of here. My stomach complains resentfully as I heave myself into a seated position, leaning my back against the side of my bed. "Phone? Have you seen my phone?"

Zander chuckles under his breath as he slumps down beside me on the floor. "Oh yeah. I've seen it all right. Here."

The light stabs at my eyes when I crack them open. Zander reaches into the pocket of his red silk robe and takes out a mangled piece of bent metal, placing it unceremoniously on top of my chest. I haven't had the iPhone for long. Couple of months, maybe. I'd held out on buying a cell phone for the longest time, convinced I was never going to need one and the mere purchase of such a piece of technology was going to make my life infinitely worse. Then I'd met Silver and all that had changed. The phone quickly became one of my most treasured possessions, because it was my direct link to her. Now, its screen is shattered. The whole thing is warped, bent into a worrying curve. No way it still works.

"You were laying into it with a hammer when I got here," Zander supplies, sticking the end of a vape pen into his mouth. He pulls on it, his cheeks hollowing out for a second, and then a thick cloud of white smoke pours down his nose and out of his mouth. The smell of cherries fills the bedroom, sweet and noxious. "I've seen some stupid shit in my time, but that particular act of wanton destruction topped the list. Those things are fucking expensive. How the fuck you gonna watch porn now?"

"I need to call Silver," I groan.

"Unless you have her number memorized, I'm afraid you're shit out of luck," Zander says in a sing-song voice. His cheery disposition is hurting my goddamn teeth. "I could drive you over to her place, since you're clearly in no fit state to operate heavy machinery," he offers. "But I only just got the Thunderbird and you still look barfy. I'm not having you tossing your cookies all over the leather. It's original."

I can't voice my displeasure at his comment in real words, but the guttural, wolf-like growl I force out does the trick. Zander sucks on his vape pen again, blowing out of the corner of his mouth, purposefully aiming the sickly-sweet billow of white smoke at my face. "Do that again, and I'll shove that thing where the sun don't shine."

"All right. Touchy touchy."

"Aren't you supposed to be at Raleigh, anyway?"

Zander assesses me coolly. "Not unless the powers that be are now expecting us to attend that shithole during the Christmas break."

"So you thought you'd blast the most offensive music I own as loud as you could, just to *really* piss off the neighbors?" I grumble.

"It's six forty-five in the morning. There won't be anyone downstairs for another two hours. At least that's what you told me last night. I thought some upbeat tunes might help you wake up in a good mood. Gotta say, you've rudely dashed my hopes. And you used to be such a morning person."

That is a blatant lie. Back in Denney, the juvenile detention center where Zander and I met, I was a walking zombie until I'd managed to bribe one of the screws into giving me a double serving of coffee. And Zander just said it himself: he sat and watched me put away a bottle of tequila last night. He knew full well I was going to have a sore head this morning. I calculate the energy it'll require to twist around and thump him squarely in the jaw, but then decide the satisfaction of hearing him yelp isn't worth it. "Help me up. I need a cold shower. Then I'll be able to take the bike—"

"It's too dangerous to ride, man. Fuck! It's like an ice rink out there. And anyway, I took your keys off you last night."

"You're gonna give them back."

"I'm not, actually. Friends don't let friends do stupid shit."

This time, I don't bother to do the math. I spin on him and launch my fist into his side, grinding my teeth together as I make contact. Zander huffs out a winded breath, his silk robe slipping off his tattooed shoulders as he doubles over, groaning.

"Do I need to ask again?" I snap.

"No, no," he wheezes, his eyes rolling up into his head. "That should do the trick."

## 3

## SILVER

It's amazing how many times a person can stave off death and still not feel like they deserve to live. Every morning, I wake up with the same question burning in my mind: Why? Why me? Why have *I* escaped death, when there have been so many times I could easily have bitten it.

Leon Wickman's Spring Fling party.

The shooting at school.

Being kidnapped and hung from the rafters of the Raleigh High gymnasium roof.

Eighteen people died at Raleigh the day Leon decided enough was enough. *Eighteen.* Sarah Gilbert did charity work every weekend. Charisma Wells spent last summer in Ghana, teaching English to children in poverty stricken remote villages. Lawrence Harding was one of the smartest kids in school. He'd already scored himself a full ride at Duke. He was going to be a doctor. Chances were he was going to cure cancer or something, but his bright and promising future was snuffed out with the simple compression of a random fucking trigger.

I'm nothing special. I'm averagely smart. On a good day, I'd say I'm not too hard on the eyes, but the world sure as hell isn't going to change for the better because I'm not hideous. I won't grow up to make the world a better place because I am in it.

So…why? How have I survived so many disasters and dangerous situations, when there are innocent eleven-year-old kids bleeding to death in the back of cars with five-star safety ratings?

*Careful, Silver. Don't fall. Don't slip down that rocky slope. Don't imagine his face. Don't imagine his pain. Don't imagine his fear. You won't survive* that.

The only thing frightening or shocking enough to pull me back from the brink of the dark precipice yawning open in my mind is the face of the boy who raped me. Sick that I have to resort to picturing *him*, but it works. The moment his smug, cruel smile flits through my mind, I shut it down, all of it—every tender and aching thought that's been swirling around the inside of my head for what feels like an eon.

I'm left standing in my room, hovering in front of the full-length mirror by my bathroom door, staring at a black dress in my hands. God knows how long I've been clutching it to my stomach. God knows how long I've been standing here in my underwear, hip bones jutting out a little too far, face a little thinner than it ought to be, drowning in thoughts of death and misery.

I'm a sight to behold. Day by day, my body's been repairing itself from the litany of injuries Jake inflicted upon me…but I'm far from healed. The sickly pale ghosts of my bruises still linger, a myriad of unsettling colors that stubbornly will not fade no matter how much arnica I slather on them. My ribs protest violently whenever I cough, sneeze, or breathe too deeply. I can't laugh without having to double over and grit my teeth while I ride out the pain. Not that I've had to do that over the past week, of course. There hasn't been much to laugh about.

I shake out the dress in my hands, stepping into the fabric and pulling it up my body, eager to cover up all of the marks and blemishes that still mar my skin. If I can't see them, I can pretend they aren't there. If I can pretend they're not there, then I can pretend none of it ever happ—

"Sure you don't want me to come with you?"

"Jesus Christ!" I slap my hand to my chest, bracing myself against my chest of drawers. "Dad! Quit sneaking! You're gonna give me a heart attack."

My father stands in the doorway, dressed in a formal black button-down shirt and heavily pressed suit pants. The thin black tie knotted around his throat shirt looks like it's trying to strangle him. He's never exactly been tan, but his cheeks usually hold a little more color than they do right now. At his feet, Nipper sits, his black coat scruffy and wiry, his dark eyes sad. He whines softly as he gets up and limps across my room, giving my foot a little lick with his raspy pink tongue. Like me, he's recovering from his ordeal with Jake, but he will probably bear the scars of his injuries for the rest of his life.

"I sang Sweet Home Alabama all the way up the stairs to let you know I was coming. You were in your own little world," Dad says.

Jeez. Poor guy. He could have been blowing into a tuba and banging a drum as he approached my room and I probably wouldn't have heard him. The world's been slipping away a lot recently. "I don't think it's right, you two heading over there on your own. I think I should come with you," he says, propping himself up against the door jamb. He looks like he dressed accordingly this morning, just in case.

I huff down my nose, trying to smile and failing miserably. Reflected in the mirror, my face looks comically contorted. If this is the best I can do at forging a simple smile, then it's a good job I never wanted to pursue a career in acting.

"Stay here, Dad. Get some work done. I feel bad that you haven't been able to make any progress on the book in, well, weeks now."

"Book? What book? Fuck the book." He laughs quietly. "This is big, Sil. You're so grown up, way too grown up, but this is bigger than you. It's definitely bigger than Alex. Maybe...I don't know. Maybe having me there will help."

My eyes prick, burning the way they've been burning for the past week, every time I think about the knock on the door that echoed through Alex's apartment. I'm barely holding onto the strands of my sanity right now. I've unwittingly found myself participating in an unwinnable game of tug-of-war, and every second I have to fight to keep my hands wrapped around the rope, to keep pulling, to drag myself back over an imaginary line in the sand, where I might be able to think and breathe and exist without feeling like I have a knife plunged into the fragile meat of my heart.

Sometimes minutes, even hours will pass in a day, and the pain will dim. I won't forget. I *can't* forget. But, for brief snatches of time, my exhausted nerves become numb, anesthetized and I trick myself into thinking I can handle this. That I might finally have my shit together. And then someone will say something about Alex, or Ben, or offer me help, and the rope will tear through my hands, drawing blood, dragging me off my feet and pulling me into the chaos again.

And Alex…god, Ben wasn't even my brother. It goes without saying that Alex is a train wreck. I know it's stupid, he'd never do it, but I get scared at night, when I'm alone and he's sent me away, that I'm going to wake up to a text message telling me that he's fucking killed himself.

Dad doesn't mean any harm—he's only offering to come with us because he loves me more than life itself, and he cares about Alex, too —but his kindness has inadvertently taken me out at the knees. I close my eyes, blowing out a steady breath, pleading with myself.

*Don't.*

*Don't do it.*

*Don't you fucking dare, Silver Parisi.*

*You are* not *going to fucking cry.*

I've had to reapply my make-up twice already; if I start crying again now, I'm still going to be bloodshot and sniffling when I arrive to pick Alex up, and I can't. I can't fucking do that to him. He's been strong for me so many times before. I need to be strong for him now.

Absently, I collect the black headband that's clipped over the top of my mirror, running my fingers over the cluster of small black silk flowers that adorn it. My throat throbs as I look up, finding my own eyes in the reflection. I don't look at Dad. If I do, I'm definitely going to lose my shit. "Alex didn't even want me to go. I think…" God, damn it. This is so hard already. How the hell am I going to get through today? How am I ever going to be able to look my boyfriend in the eye again without bursting into tears?

Not too long ago, he said something that stuck with me. *"I can't bear for anything to happen to you. I can't see you hurt and not feel it. I can't see you suffer and not have something wither and die inside me. I can't see you wounded and not feel like I'm fucking failing you."* The emotion in his voice had startled me. I could see that he really meant what he was saying, that he was suffering because I was suffering, but I thought it was a gesture, some token of affection. An attempt on his part to try and shoulder some of the misery that was crushing me. I understand now, though. I wasn't entirely wrong; I want to take on the crippling burden that's grinding Alex into the dirt, but this feeling inside me is more than that. It's *worse*. I feel like I'm dying. I feel like I *am* failing him, because nothing I can do or say will ever temper this pain. Whatever measure a soul is weighed in, I feel like mine is seeping away, piece by piece, ounce by ounce, whisper by whisper. Every second that Alessandro Moretti has to live with the knowledge that his little brother is dead, I feel like I will die from the hurt of it.

From the moment I met him, Alex has been the light that has lifted the shadows. He's been the strength that's held me up. He's been a sheer force of nature, incomprehensible in his complexity, who has astonished and amazed me at every turn. When his mouth crooks into that lopsided, suggestive smirk, I fall in love with him all over again, and I can't bear the thought that perhaps he'll never be able to smile again.

*If Max died...*

Christ. No. No, no, no. I can't entertain the thought, not even for a second. There's no room left inside me for any more hurt, theoretical or otherwise. I'm already brimming over, too full and swollen with grief to house one drop more.

Steeling myself, I place the band of black silk flowers onto my head, quickly arranging my hair around it. I look so fucking normal. Even with the bruises, I still look like me. How is that even possible, when I feel like I've morphed into someone completely not myself? "I appreciate it, Dad. I really do," I say stiffly. "But Alex is... he's..."

What is he, exactly? Traumatized? Mourning? I can't tell. I've been searching for all of the usual signs of grief a normal person might exhibit when they lose someone close to them, but it's been hard to pin-point signs of anything with Alex. He seems empty. Null. Hollowed out. When he looks at me, he doesn't see me. He stares through me, into some dark, forbidden void. He was sucked into that void a week ago, a place where I can't follow after him, and he hasn't been able to find his way back out of it ever since. I'm beginning to think, beginning to worry, that he might not *want* to surface from the inky black depths of it.

"Okay. You know him best. If it has to be just the two of you, then it has to be just the two of you. But..."

I turn around and face my dad. "But you're worried about me? You're scared that this will be the final thing that sends me spiraling into a nervous breakdown?"

He huffs out a laugh on an exhale, looking down at his feet. "Nah. You're stronger than the rest of us combined. A wrecking ball couldn't put a dent in you, kid."

He's playing. I know this, because I know him well, and I also know that he *is* worried about me. "All you need to do is call, Silver," he says. "You know I'll come. You know I'll be there if either of you change your minds."

My chest pinches tightly, not with pain this time, but with love. To look at my father, you wouldn't peg him as the knight-in-shining-armor type. His glasses are always just a fraction lopsided, the lenses perpetually smudged by fingerprints. His hair typically looks a little wild, his waves refusing to lay flat and be tamed. The beard he's been sporting of late isn't the well-manicured hipster kind that he believes it to be, nor is it the beard of a woodcutter or some sort of cabin-dwelling lumberjack. It's the kind of beard a writer grows when he's been crouched over a laptop keyboard, hammering away, living off caffeine and bagels for six months, trading in every spare second of the day in return for a handful of precious words.

That violent, hard spark inherent in many other men doesn't exist within him. It isn't in his nature to lose his temper or throw his fists, which is why it's all the more impressive when he leaps to the defense of those he loves without a second thought to what it might cost him, or how much it might hurt. I know what he was planning with Alex the night Jacob Weaving came to the house and took me. We haven't spoken about it, but the truth has lain heavily between us all the same. He went with Alex to hurt the bastard who hurt *me*. He went to draw blood...and he went there carrying a gun.

Cameron Parisi, the architect.

Cameron Parisi, the novelist.

Cameron Parisi, the father.

Cameron Parisi, the would-be executioner.

"Love you, Dad," I croak out, rummaging in my jewelry box. I'm already wearing a pair of simple gold studs and the fine gold chain that Gram gave me for my birthday last year. I don't need any more bling. I just need to be busy. I can't stand straight-backed and motionless and tell my father that I love him without falling to pieces.

"Love you, too, kiddo." His voice is soft and warm, and I feel like I'm floating, like I could fall into his words and be cushioned by them, protected and safe and eight-years-old again. "All right. Well...it's nearly time. The car'll be here in five. I've already made sure the driver knows you're stopping at Henry's on the way." My father's feet make shushing sounds as he crosses the carpet in his socks. He kisses the back of my head lightly, laying a steadying hand on my shoulder, and I'm overwhelmed with gratitude. I'm so grateful for him. So grateful, lucky and blessed that I have him here, ready for me to lean on if I need him. Having a father like mine is basically like winning the lottery. I'm so fucking lucky to have him in my life...which only serves to remind me that right now, the guy I love is alone, without either of his parents to lean on.

∽

The engine of the black Lincoln town car purrs like a cat as we glide across Raleigh. The world outside is crisp and white, shrouded with snow. The sky is a leached duck egg blue, practically devoid of all color. In the front seat, the driver adjusts his trim chauffeur's hat and tries to make eye contact with me in the rear-view mirror. I avoid doing so at all costs, however my carefully crafted blank stare out of the window doesn't deter him. "Well, then? What you got planned? A party? Some sort of girly sleepover?"

My eyes snap up and to the left, locking with his watery blue irises in the small expanse of mirror. "I'm sorry? What?"

The driver—now that I'm looking at him, I see he's older than I originally thought—grins at me. "Yeah, y'know. New Year's Eve? Bull*shit* if you high school kids don't celebrate New Year's anymore. I know you do. I was cleaning puke out of this car for a week after last year. Gotta say, that get-up's a little depressing for a party, though. Figured you kids were all still into neon and shit. Looks like you're going to a fucking funeral."

I almost laugh. Almost. I've clean forgotten that it's New Year's Eve.

The car was Dad's idea. He didn't think I should have to drive today, and he knew Alex wouldn't be capable, so he forked out for a professional driver to transport us to the church and then on to the cemetery. Clearly whatever agency Dad used hasn't passed on the particulars of today's journey to their driver.

I'll break into pieces if I have to fill him in. I lean my head against the window beside me and the glass is cold and wet, anchoring me into place. "Yeah, well. You know how it goes," I mutter. "Fashion's a fickle thing. One week it's electric pink. The next, it's black lace and *memento mori*."

"What's that? Latin?" He grunts. "You Raleigh kids are fancy. Didn't teach us no Latin at Bellingham." All of a sudden, he doesn't sound too impressed. I think I've offended him with my use of a foreign language, and a dead one at that. He thinks I'm being pompous. "What are *memento mori*, anyway? Three-hundred-dollar sneakers?" he grumbles.

I'm so drained, wrecked from night after night of insomnia. I dig deep for the energy necessary to explain that *memento mori* have nothing to do with sneakers, but I come up empty. For the remainder of the car ride, I close my eyes, head tilted back, resting on the seat behind me, and I pretend to be asleep. Weak, yes, but I've realized that sometimes you have to play dead in order to survive.

When we reach Raleigh's main street, a deep cavern of sadness pulls at me; swarming the snowy sidewalks, gathered in front of the decorated store fronts, the residents of Raleigh are rosy-cheeked and smiling, still drunk on the holidays and the fact that most of them didn't have to show up for work this morning. The town's small enough that I recognize a number of faces loitering on the corner in front of the hardware store. They recognize me as I climb out of the Town Car, too, and their festive smiles tactfully fade as I sidle past them, heading around the back of Henry's to the fire escape that leads to Alex's front door.

When I was raped in that bathroom, I didn't want to broadcast what had happened to the world. I told one person, Principal Darhower, who summarily dismissed my accusation as, in his words, a *'storm in a teacup. Something and nothing.'* I kept my mouth shut after that. No one knew what Jake, Sam and Cillian did to me. They know now. It was impossible to keep the information quiet once I was hospitalized, Jake was arrested, and people started to talk. It came out, all of it, every gory, hideous, ugly detail, and now everyone within a twenty-mile radius of Raleigh knows who I am: Silver Parisi, seventeen years of age, raped, kidnapped, assaulted, attempted murder victim.

*Victim. Victim. Victim. Victim. Victim. Victim.*

I hate that word. No matter how hard I reject it, people keep trying to pin it to me like one of those red and white, *Hi! My name is_____!* stickers. They want me to be broken. If I'm a mess, whimpering and crying in public, then they can get behind my story. They can make sense of it. I was bullied, kicked, punched, spat on, embarrassed and humiliated too many times before Jake dragged my unconscious body out of my house, though. I'd already learned to set my jaw, lift my head high, and dole out a look of defiance that screamed 'FUCK YOU' very loudly whenever I felt judgmental eyes on me. That defiance doesn't sit well with people. It gives them the impression that whatever happened to me couldn't have been that bad…which is so untrue it's almost funny. This morning, I keep my head down, avoiding making eye contact with anyone in the first place. No sense in fueling gossip or feeding the rumor mill.

The studded metal steps that lead up to Alex's place are slippery. I hold onto the handrail nice and tight as I ascend the stairs, and dread seeps into my veins. Alex has been a supercharged magnet over the past week; I'm pulled toward him so fiercely that it sometimes feels as though it physically hurts to be apart from him. At the same time, it also seems like Alex has been doing his level best to push me away. I've been both drawn to and repelled by him so badly since the news about Ben that I barely know if I'm coming or going anymore.

I knock on the door—the doorbell hasn't worked since Alex moved in—and tuck my chin into the collar of my thick wool coat, waiting nervously for him to answer. It's nine thirty in the morning. The service doesn't start until ten, but we need to get across town and settled into the church, so we need to leave pretty much immediately.

The door remains closed.

"Come on, Alex," I mutter under my breath, knocking again, this time with a little more force. If he's in the shower, we're going to be late...

Just as I'm about to knock for a third time, the door flies open, sending a cloud of weed smoke and red light billowing out into the early morning. Zander Hawkins greets me with a flat, bored smile. He's wearing a Chicago Bulls basketball shirt underneath a red silk robe that looks like it belongs to a forty-five-year-old woman named Maura. "'S'up Parisi?" He brings a pipe to his lips and takes a deep pull.

This is becoming a really bad habit. Why, whenever I show up at Alex's place, does Zander Hawkins end up answering the door? He's like a bad fucking smell that will not go away. "Where is he?" I shove past Zander, making my way down the hallway toward the bedroom, briefly scanning the living room through its open doorway as I pass. Alex might be a hard ass, and he might give off the impression that he will gladly punch a hole through someone's head so much as look at them, but he's not what most people expect him to be. He's meticulously clean—tidy, to the point that even I get embarrassed by my own messiness whenever I'm around him. He needs his environment to be controlled. Everything has its place, everything has an order, which is why I'm so confused when I see the state of the apartment. The place is a fucking shit show.

"What the fuck, Zander? How has this place gotten so trashed? I was here *yesterday*, for Christ's sake. It did *not* look like this then."

Empty beer bottles; pizza boxes; actual pizza crusts discarded on the coffee table; a pool of something dark red and sticky-looking, half-dried on the hardwood floor outside the bathroom. The place reeks of cigarette smoke.

"Don't blame me, sweetheart." Zander smirks, holding up his hands as he follows me toward the end of the hallway. "Our boy got himself a little sideways last night. I only came by to watch the fireworks."

A stab of anxiety, cold and piercing, knifes into my chest. "Alex did *not* do this by himself." My tone's confident, like I'm one hundred percent sure that my boyfriend would never trash his own hard-won apartment like this, but in truth I can believe it. I've been waiting for him to blow for days. There was no way he was going to be able to maintain his flat, sketchy, *I-feel-nothing* level of detachment forever. He was bound to snap. I was hoping I'd be there when it happened, so I could do some firefighting, try to minimize the damage both to Alex and to his surroundings, but it looks like I got here a little late.

I should never have left him in the first place. I should have refused to leave. He was so adamant that he was fine, though. He swore he just wanted to sleep...

"You're wasting your time," Zander calls after me. I walk through Alex's bedroom door, and inside his room, the bed is unmade, a welter of tangled sheets hanging half off the mattress, showing the shiny silver fabric of the pillowtop underneath. Piles of clothes have been dumped all over the room, the odd shoe, separated from its partner, abandoned on the polished wood like a forgotten landmine, waiting to be tripped over or trodden on. Alex's bedside table is crowded with crushed cigarette packets, pens, loose change, scraps of paper, receipts, and small plastic baggies—empty, bar a faint white residue that tells a disturbing story all of its own.

Alex is nowhere to be seen.

Spinning around in the three-inch heels I borrowed from Mom's designer shoe collection, I lock onto Zander with a laser beam focus. He immediately retreats, backing into the doorframe. "Whoa, now, sweetheart. I really had nothing to do with this. Alex was on a tear when I got here. He didn't stop until his eyes rolled back in his head and he hit the deck somewhere 'round three this morning."

"*Where is he now?*" I'm not used to hissing at people. I don't think Zander's accustomed to people speaking to him this way, either. He scowls, a disdainful dimple punctuating his cheek.

"Who the fuck knows? Haven't got a clue. He woke up at six-thirty, threw up in his guitar case, took a cold shower, and then he left. And before you accuse me of being a shitty friend, I *did* ask where the hell he thought he was going. He declined to part with the information."

"You should have gone after him," I snarl, pushing past him out of the bedroom.

He follows me, bare feet thumping against the floorboards. "Ha! Yeah, right. I make questionable decisions all the time, but I'm not that stupid, darlin'. I don't have life insurance and chasing after a category five hurricane does not sound like a good time to me."

God, I could throat punch him. "You should have called me, then. Told me what he was doing. I would have come." My cell phone's already in my hand. I'm already pulling up Alex's contact info on the screen. A second later, I'm hitting the green call button.

"Sorry, but again…I wouldn't bother." Zander gestures to something on the floor. I stoop down and pick up…oh, that's just fucking great. It's his cell phone. Smashed beyond recognition, the metal warped and flattened.

"What the hell happened?" I look up at Zander, expecting a reasonable explanation for this, but then I see just how ridiculous he looks and realize I'm not going to get anything sensible out of him. "Urgh, never mind."

Where the hell would he have gone? Did he run out of booze? Maybe he went out to grab some more. But no…Zander said he threw up in his guitar case. He couldn't have been feeling well. More alcohol was probably the last thing he wanted. So then what? I stand by the front door, pressing my fingers against my brow, trying to think. "It's his brother's fucking funeral this morning, Zander. I can't believe you'd let him do this. Not today."

The music stops, the song that was playing coming to an end, and for one second a complete, consuming silence floods the empty spaces inside the apartment. It feels alive and angry.

*"What did you just say?"*

I give Zander a withering sidelong look, surprised when I see his expression. He looks stunned. I've seen him arrogant. I've seen him amused. I've seen him annoyed. But I've never seen him like this. The swagger is gone, and suddenly he doesn't look like a member of a potentially very dangerous motorcycle club. He looks like the seventeen-year-old high school student that he is. "What do you mean, it's his brother's *funeral* today?"

Oh, this just gets better and better. "He didn't tell you? Of course he didn't tell you." Makes perfect sense, really. Alex has been so shut down, getting him to speak to *me* has been a labor of love. Alex's friendship with Zander is clearly complicated, but I can see it for what it is—a love/hate relationship. It didn't even cross my mind that Alex would have kept this from him, though. Sliding my phone back into my pocket, I sigh, the weight on my shoulders far heavier than it was a moment ago. Telling this story isn't something I relish.

"Ben and the woman who was fostering him, they were in a car accident. They...neither of them made it." I keep it as simple as possible. I can't talk about Jackie's perforated lungs. How she drowned in her own blood. I can't talk about Ben's brain bleed, or how he slipped away from this world without anyone sitting on the backseat beside him, holding his hand.

Zander's face is ashen. "That isn't funny, sweetheart."

"You think I'm joking? Christ, what kind of person would joke about something like that?"

"Tell me you're fucking with me," he persists. "That's why he destroyed himself last night? That..." Shaking his head, Zander slumps back against the wall behind him, pressing the heels of his hands into his eyes. "Ben *died?*"

I sympathize with him. It doesn't feel real to me, either. I *still* can't wrap my head around any of this. "Zander, you gotta think. Did he say anything about where he was going? Anything that might tell us where he is. I don't think he's in his right mind. I'm really fucking worried."

When Zander drops his hands, his eyes are red and bloodshot. He clears his throat. "Yeah. Yeah, um..." Frowning, he shrugs. "He said something about going to see his mom. He stormed out of here without a jacket. He said he wouldn't need it. He took the Scout."

"*He rode the bike?*" I look around, surveying the chaos and destruction that is Alex's apartment, trying to mentally add up how many units of alcohol are still churning around his system. I throw my hands up in the air, turning toward the door, then turning right back again. "He's fucking dead," I whisper. "He's probably driven head-on into a Mack truck and now he's fucking dead, too."

Tense, and with a face whiter than a sheet, Zander shoves away from the wall. "No need to get melodramatic, Parisi. If we're lucky, he might have just paralyzed himself from the waist down. You said the funeral's this morning?"

I nod, fighting the urge to dash into the kitchen and throw up in the sink; I could have done without the thought that Alex might ironically share the same fate as Cillian Dupris. "Yeah. In twenty minutes."

"Then that's where we're going. He wouldn't miss Ben's funeral. Come on, I'm coming over there with you," he says, shaking his head. "Jesus fucking Christ, I can't believe this is even fucking happening."

# 4

# SILVER

The driver doesn't say a word about Zander's robe, or the fact that the jeans he quickly put on are shredded beyond all functionality. His lips remain sealed in a tight, disapproving line as he drives us to the church. Greenwood Presbyterian is on the outskirts of Raleigh, set high on the side of a hill that overlooks town. It was the very first structure erected here, before the quaint stores on Main Street were built, or the warehouses and factories, owned by the Weaving family for generations, began to monopolize Raleigh's modest skyline. The four families who founded Raleigh decided that the town's people would need God more than anything else, and so they made a house of worship their first priority.

When we pull up outside the church, Zander and I bolt from the Town Car, hurrying inside the building. The large solid wood doors crash open, startling the figure dressed in white, standing in front of the lectern in the church's apse. My legs nearly go out from underneath me when I see the small, half-sized coffin at the head of the pews, festooned with sunflowers.

Zander grabs my hand, pulling me behind him up the aisle, head sweeping from left to right. "He isn't here."

"Mr. Moretti?" the priest calls from the apse. "Welcome. I took the liberty of—"

"Nope. Not Alex," Zander replies. "He hasn't been here?"

Closer now, I see that the priest is ancient, in his late seventies, his bald head freckled with age spots. His eyes are clouded by cataracts and watery, giving him the look of a man permanently on the brink of tears. He shakes his head. "You're the first to arrive this morning, I'm afraid," he says.

"Fuck." Zander claps a hand over his mouth. "Fuck, sorry, father. I didn't mean to—damnit, I'm just going to stop talking. You take over," he says, pushing me forward.

"I'm sorry, Father. We've kind of *lost* Alessandro. Is there any way the service can be held for a while? Just an hour, while we look for him?"

The priest's face crumples into a maze of deep lines—a mourning mask, a face that has creased in sympathy too many times to count. "I'm so sorry, my dear. If it were any other day of the week, I would of course say yes. Today's Saturday, though, and New Year's Eve to boot. We have two weddings this afternoon. The first guests arrive in an hour. If Benjamin is to have a religious service, then I'm afraid we really must start now."

"I can't be here without him. I can't…" Shit, it wouldn't be right to sit here through Ben's funeral service without Alex. Selfishly, I don't think I can *make it* through the service without him. I'm not…I don't feel that strong.

"If you don't stay, then Ben's not going to have anyone here with him. No one that he knows," Zander says, his voice pitchy and uneven. He's battling with his emotions, though he's doing a stellar job. His cracked voice is the only sign that he's struggling. And he's just said the one thing that will enable me to get through an entire funeral service for a little boy on my own: *Ben won't have anyone here with him*.

It's been eating me alive, the fact that he was alone when he died. There's nothing I can do about that now, but I can stay at the church and be here for this. I can stay with him so that he's not alone for this part of his final journey.

"Okay, you go then," I say to Zander. "Go. Find him. Bring him to the cemetery as quickly as you can. He can't do this. He needs to say goodbye or he's never gonna heal." Even if Zander can find Alex and he *does* get him to the cemetery in time for Ben's interment, saying goodbye isn't going to be enough. I know that. Alex can say goodbye to his brother a thousand times over, every morning and every night until his lips are chapped and bleeding from the repetition, but it won't help him heal. Only time will do that, and I have no idea how many weeks, or months, or years will be enough to accomplish that. Still, he has to be there. He's going to hate himself for the rest of his life if he doesn't show up for this.

5

## ALEX

They used to play stupid games back at Denney. There was little to do besides work out, watch the same family game shows on repeat, and pretend to study in the library, so to appease the mind-numbing boredom, my fellow inmates bombarded one another with a litany of pointless questions. *'Would You Rather'* was a favorite. Would you rather get your dick sucked by a Kardashian or fuck Taylor Swift in the ass? Win the lottery and die at fifty or live 'til you're a hundred but be broke as fuck? During one of the last rounds of *'Would You Rather'* I played before I walked out of Denney, Harrison Ash asked me would I rather be deaf or blind?

At the time, I'd thought it was an easy one. A no brainer. I'd told him I'd rather go blind. For months, I'd been dying to play my guitar, my fingers itching to fly up and down the neck of the instrument I'd had to leave in Gary Quincy's garage. All I'd had to stare at were bland grey walls and the ugly-as-fuck faces of the other dumb bastards I'd been locked away with. I'd forgotten that there was beauty in the world. It seemed that without music I'd lost a piece of my soul, and the concept of losing it forever was pure fucking torture to me.

Amazing how quickly a mind can change when the world starts falling apart. Sitting in a pew of Raleigh's Holy Trinity Catholic

Church, the depth of the silence that cloaks the darkened alcoves and recessed confessional roars. The pressure of it butts up against my eardrums, a smothering quality to it...and I can't help but feel relieved.

No one asking me if there's anything they can do.

*I dunno. How 'bout you bring my dead kid brother back to life?*

No one giving me stupid fucking advice on how to navigate the hazardous terrain of grief and loss, and how this too shall fucking pass.

*You don't think I've been here before? You don't think I've sat down and dined on the same bitter food as the Grim Reaper himself? We're best fucking friends, asshole.*

No one asking me if I'm okay.

*No, of course I am not fucking okay. What the fuck is wrong with you? On what planet would I actually be fucking okay?*

If I'm deaf to the endless questions and the sickening pity in their voices, then I don't have to keep my temper at bay. I don't have to force myself to swallow my angry responses down, where they burn at the back of my throat like acid-filled blisters.

I've gone so long with people pretending I don't exist, that now they're all wracked with sympathy and guilt, going out of their way to check in on me, I don't know how to handle their attention. I don't want it. I don't fucking need it. I need for all of this to go away, to have never fucking happened in the first place. I need...god, more than anything, I just need Silver.

A stab of guilt pinches in my chest. I should be with her right now. She would have already gone to the apartment, looking for me, but I just couldn't be there. If I'd stayed, she would have talked me off the ledge. Those beautiful blue eyes of hers would have met mine and I would have gone with her, if only to stem her hurt during the ordeal of yet another goddamn funeral. I had to get out of there before I could see her dressed in her mourning clothes and my own sense of duty kicked in.

I could not fucking sit in a pew at the front of a depressingly empty Presbyterian church, staring numbly at a coffin, knowing that Ben's lifeless, cold body was inside it. It would have taken my very last energy reserves along with what little remains of my will to live to make it through a service like that, and I need both to ensure I don't throw myself in Lake Cushman tomorrow morning.

How simple would it be to let the clear glacial water flood me, fill me up, and drag me down into the darkness? Seems like such a logical solution to the problem that I'm currently faced with. I'm hurting. I'm suffering beyond any measure I've previously experienced. If I sank below the still, mirrored surface of the lake and let the patient waters take me, then it would be done with. No more pain. No more suffering.

Except…

Suicide's never going to be an option for me. Not while Silver draws breath. I know what it is to be left behind, tossed and turned in the wake after someone you love punches their ticket on that one-way journey. It's a fate worse than death to exist in a world where the person you love decided it was better to die than stay behind and love you back. It isn't that simple. It's never that simple. But that's how it fucking *feels*.

My mother was haunted by her ghosts. In the last two or three years before she died, she never knew a moment's peace. The black dog was always crouched over her, baring its teeth, refusing to let her up even for a second. And through it all, she tried. She woke up every morning and made herself get out of bed, and she *tried*. Most days, she failed. She was angry. She was manic. She hallucinated, and she kicked and screamed. Exhaustion drove her to put the muzzle of that gun in her mouth, and despair made her pull the trigger. It took a long time for me to accept that what she did that day didn't mean that she didn't love me enough. It was just that the pain and the endless, bottomless agony of being alive was too *big* for her to overcome in the end.

If I took myself out, eventually Silver would come to the same realization. Before that, she'd know the same brilliant, blinding kind of pain that I felt as a six-year-old boy, and I could never fucking do that to her. Ironically, I'd die before I ever put her through something like that.

A trickle of incense hits the back of my nose, bringing me back into myself—I've been so absent for days now that I'm always kind of shocked when I snap out of my reveries and realize that I've somehow found my way across Raleigh, or, in this instance, to Holy Trinity. A

Catholic church, because my mother was Catholic. That's how Ben and I were raised. Ben should have been brought here for his funeral service, but I wasn't thinking straight when the funeral home informed me that Jackie's will stated all services should be conducted as per her Presbyterian faith. I should have demanded the arrangements be changed. Jackie had no right to include Ben in her will in the first place, but it had already taken everything I had to make sure Ben was buried here instead of back in Bellingham.

Holy Trinity is soaked in the same rich, velveteen sublimity that all Catholic churches share. A humble reverence that's momentarily calmed the restless void in my chest. People mistake the healing atmosphere inside buildings like this for the presence of God all the time. It's awe-inspiring, to feel the soul salved simply by walking inside a specific building and sitting quietly for a while. That's the thing, though. Madness grips people's lives at every fucking turn. Kids; bills; work; financial stress; the expectations and hopes of others. Everywhere they turn, there's so much noise and chatter and fucking insanity that the first moment they get to sit in the silent dark and breathe, they're bound to feel like they're communing with the sublime.

That's why I came here, after all. Because this is a good place to think.

*Eterno riposo, concedere a loro, o Signore, e lasciare che perpetua risplenda ad essi la luce. Maggio le anime dei fedeli defunti attraverso il ricordo di Dio, riposa in pace, Amen.*

The words aren't welcome. I haven't searched them out, but they push to the surface of my memory anyway, shoving aside my other thoughts. I remember the susurrus of *her* voice, catching on the consonants and vowels, creating a melody out of the prayer every All Souls' Day in November. I knew Thanksgiving was only a few weeks away when my mother decked our apartment out with chrysanthemums, set three extra places at the table, and lay out food for people I'd never met before. Nor would I, since they were all dead. My grandparents were long gone by the time I was born. So was my uncle, her half-brother, who managed to fall from the third-floor balcony of a hotel room in Rome when he was drunk and landed on his head.

She'd cook every single Italian recipe she could remember from her childhood, and then she'd wrap me up in my thickest winter jacket, and we'd go knocking on our neighbor's doors, offering them *dolci dei morti*—the sweets of the dead. She'd told me that the small white biscuits were supposed to sweeten the bitterness of death, and that in Italy, children would knock on doors for them along with other candies and treats in return for a prayer for the dead.

*Eterno riposo, concedere a loro, o Signore, e lasciare che perpetua risplenda ad essi la luce. Maggio le anime dei fedeli defunti attraverso il ricordo di Dio, riposa in pace, Amen.*

All Souls' Day is long behind us now, but my mother's voice chants her prayers regardless. The door to the church groans, and a rush of cold air makes my arms break out in goosebumps. Someone's just come in. Part of me is irritated that the silence is going to be marred by someone else's presence. Then again, I'm glad I'm not alone anymore. Another second of solitude and I might never have resurfaced again...

"Thought I might find you here," a gruff voice says behind me. Not the voice of a priest, that's for sure. Far too whiskey-soaked. The hairs on the back of my neck stand to attention, an alertness returning to me that's been gone ever since I answered that stupid fucking door to Maeve.

For a second, I think it's Zander, come to drag me to the funeral at Greenwood, but then—

"Heard you were living here in Raleigh. Guess I didn't really believe it. Not 'til now."

Being tased is a unique experience. Hard to describe. Your body locks up, screaming in pain, jaw clenched, hands clenched, asshole clenched, fucking everything clenched, and your mind is screaming at you to *MOVE! Get. A. Way. From. The. Pain.* But you can't. You're frozen in place, lungs seized, and all you can do is lay there and take it. I've never felt anything like it before. Until this moment right now.

If the best memories of my childhood are of my mother, then the worst, without a shadow of a doubt, are of my father. Even when she was manic and hysterical, making wild, outlandish threats, he was still worse...because he was indifferent, and then he was fucking *gone*. Over the years, I've tried to erase the stain of him from my head, but Giacomo Moretti has always been paradoxically indelible.

And now, it seems as though he's standing right behind me.

I don't turn around.

I hear him—the scuff of old, worn boot soles against the stone floor. The huff that comes out of him as he sinks down onto the pew behind mine. I smell him, too. Cold winter air, and snow, engine grease and clove cigarettes.

"You're bigger than I thought you'd be." He says it casually, like he's commenting on unexpectedly good weather to a stranger. "You were a scrawny mite when you were little. Way shorter than the other kids at school."

*Alex...*

*Do not...*

*...turn around...*

Giacomo—Jack—is quiet for a moment, as if he has every right to waltz in here and destroy my peace, and he isn't planning on losing any sleep over it. Meanwhile, my synapses are firing so rapidly and randomly that I can't formulate a single thought beyond '*KILL HIM.*'

A tapping sound breaks the silence—the toe of his boot, knocking against the underside of my pew, directly beneath me. "I came because...well, you know why I came. I came because of Benny."

My first words to my father in over ten years are this: "I'm surprised you even remembered his name."

The stranger behind me sucks on his teeth disapprovingly. "C'mon now, A. That's not very fair. Of course I remember his name. He was my son."

"No."

Somewhere outside, a car horn keens.

Ten seconds later, a young woman enters through a door at the head of the church and dips to her knees before the life-sized depiction of Christ on the cross. She prays, quickly crosses herself, and then hurries down the aisle toward the exit. The sound of the heavy door closing after her echoes for what feels like an eternity.

Giacomo's had plenty of time to stew on his response. "I'm sorry? What do you mean, *no?*"

"You weren't his father. You were the guy...who lived with our mother for a couple of years…knocked her up twice…cost her the national debt of a small country in lost fucking bail money…sold our television…then fucking disappeared off the face of the planet." I don't mean to keep taking breaks before each statement. I just can't speak properly. I never thought an emotion would be able to eclipse the grief I've been experiencing the past few days, but I was wrong. The fury hurtling along my nerve endings and forging fires within my bones is like white lightning.

Giacomo laughs under his breath. "Alessandro. You have no idea what you're talking about. I didn't just up and disappear. No, she *made* me leave. You were too young to remember the fights. The screaming. I wasn't perfect, son, but your mother was fucking cra—"

I could give two shits about being in a house of God. I twist, spinning around, hurling myself at the back of the pew, practically throwing myself over it. Suddenly, I have a handful of t-shirt material in my left fist, and my right is raised high above my head, ready to come crashing down into the miserable fucker's face, which is…

…so much like my own.

He doesn't blink. Doesn't even react to the fact that I've grabbed hold of him and I'm about to knock his front fucking teeth out. His eyes, dark as midnight in the gloom of the church, pierce through me in an unsettling way that seems all too familiar. There are lines on his face, bracketing his mouth, across his forehead and at the corners of his eyes, but his hair is still jet-black, not a grey hair in sight. He looks fit, too. Like he's kept himself in shape. He always was a vain bastard.

"If you're gonna hit me, get on and do it, A. We've got a lot to talk about, an' I don't see any point in wasting time posturing."

"Posturing?" Laughter bubbles up the back of my throat. That's what he thinks this is? Some sort of pissing contest between a hormonal teenager and his hard-done-by old man? He was about to call my mother crazy but *he's* the one with the fucking screw loose. I let him go, shoving him roughly as I get to my feet. "You shouldn't have come back here. You're not wanted. You're not fucking welcome."

I walk away before I can do something stupid. I've dreamed of this moment so many times over the years—how I was going to take great pleasure in beating the ever-loving shit out of him for everything he did to us—but now that the opportunity has presented itself, I see it for the bad idea that it is. If I give myself permission to hit the sack of shit today, in this state of mind, I'm not going to be able to stop myself. I'll fucking kill him, and where will that leave me? Rotting in a jail cell for the rest of my life, unable to hold Silver in my arms again? Yeah, fuck that. He isn't fucking worth it.

I'm halfway to the church exit when it dawns on me that he's following me. "Don't you wanna know how I knew you were here?" he asks.

"No."

"The bike out front. The Scout. It's just like the old Indian I used to have. First motorcycle you ever rode on, Alessandro. Who else would have a bike like that around here? And who'd be dumb enough to actually ride it in this kind of weather?"

"What, you think it's some kind of homage? Some kind of sign?" I slam through the doors, out into the sheet rain that's started to fall while I was inside. "I barely remember you being at the house. Why the fuck would I remember what kind of bike you had?"

"You're full of shit, kid. You remember just fine." He grabs me by the shoulder, attempting to spin me round, but I knock his hand away. I'm genuinely surprised that he'd even try and touch me.

"Don't. Don't do that. Don't call me kid. Son. A. None of it."

He rubs at his bottom lip, grinning broad as you like. He's soaked from head to toe already, the shoulders of his leather jacket turned dark with the rain, the front of his t-shirt plastered to his chest. "What you want me to call you, then? Fucking Sparkles?"

Hah. So funny. He's actually fucking enjoying this. I lunge forward, getting up in his shit. I tower over him, four inches taller than he is. I'm bigger than him, too. Much, *much* bigger. He's forty-five years old, and he hasn't been in a fight in a very long time. At least not a proper fight, with someone who truly hates his stinking guts. I could tear him limb from limb and I am *this* fucking close to doing it.

Giacomo shakes his head, feigning disappointment. Can't tell what he's disappointed about, and I don't really care. All I know is that I need to get away from the piece of shit before I lose all sense of reason and logic. "In case you forgot, they're burying Ben today," I grit out between my teeth. "Over at Greenwood. How about you do me and him both a favor and you stay the fuck away, yeah? There's too little too late, old man. And then there's *this*."

He doesn't follow after me again. He stands in the church parking lot, hands in his pockets, his eyes following me as I storm over to my bike, jam my helmet on my head, start the engine, and I tear away through the rain.

It isn't until I'm halfway to the cemetery that I process the fact that my father's leather jacket bore a Dreadnaughts M.C. patch on its sleeve.

# 6

## SILVER

I'm doubled over with worry, heartsick and miserable as the priest begins the service. It's so wrong that *I* am the only person here. Ben had lots of friends at school in Bellingham. A few of their parents reached out, asking if it would be okay if they brought their kids along to say goodbye, but Alex shut them down. He made the excuse that funerals were no place for eleven-year-old kids, and he was right, but many of Ben's teachers had wanted to come, too. He'd flatly refused to have any of them at the church or at the cemetery. I'd had to fight tooth and nail to be able to come myself, and now...*this?* An empty church, and a dour, tufty-haired old coot mumbling distractedly over Ben's coffin, doing his best...but not doing good enough? Ben deserves so much more than this.

I haven't stopped crying since I sat down and the priest began to speak. My eyes feel clogged with grit, which is why I don't notice the person sidling their way down the pew toward me until they're almost on top of me. It's Dad, of course. He smiles sadly as he sits down, wrapping an arm around my shoulders and pulling me into his side. "Didn't feel right, sitting at home," he whispers.

I'm so relieved to see him, I could cry. I'm already crying, though, so I give in and cry a little harder. How many times did I tell him not to come? At least five times this morning, and double that last night.

He's my father, though. He didn't listen, because it's his job *not* to listen sometimes. He knew I'd need him, so he came even though I explicitly told him not to.

The service is brief, and I float through it without having to think too much now that I have Dad by my side. The priest finds his stride eventually and says some really beautiful things about Ben, stories I never knew about him. How he liked to dance, of all things. That underneath his shy exterior, Ben loved to sing and play the piano for people once he got to know them a little better. He was good at math, and he was top of his class in English. He loved to write fantastical stories about pirates and wizards that made anyone who read them laugh.

When the priest announces the end of the service, he tells us in his quiet, soothing voice that Ben's coffin will be taken directly to the cemetery, where another, short bible reading will be read over the gravesite. I listen, nodding my head like a demented puppet, holding my breath to avoid sobbing out loud in the church. The word 'gravesite' nearly causes me to collapse into a heap on the floor at the priest's feet.

Every time my heart beats, it feels as though my sorrow is chipping away at me from the inside, a chisel and a hammer slowly whittling me down to nothing. It doesn't matter how many funerals I've been to. I've never been to a child's funeral before, and it's just… it's fucking harrowing. How any parent can lose a child and still draw breath is beyond me.

Dad takes me by the arm, guiding me down the aisle toward the grim, rain-drenched winter morning that awaits us outside. When we reach the exit, we both come to a stop at the top of the slick stone steps. Halfway down, Alex is sitting there, alone, his shirt plastered to his broad back, his dark hair soaked, ignoring the rain that's furiously pelting his shivering body.

"Here." Dad pops open the large, black umbrella he brought with him, passing me the handle. Immediately, the rain drums against the taut fabric, roaring like thunder. "I'm gonna go wait in the car," he tells me. "If you need anything, give me a wave."

Once again, I'm reminded that Cameron Parisi is one of the good ones. Countless times, he could have looked at recent events and decided Alex wasn't a good influence. He could have looked to the future, seen where my association with Alex might possibly lead me, and he could have pulled the plug on my entire relationship with him right there and then. The boy sitting on the steps in the rain has been broken so many times before. He *keeps on* getting broken, over and over, despite the fact that all he wants is to live his life and be happy. He's angry, and he's hurt. Right now, he isn't the very best version of himself. There's every chance he's about to derail himself in a spectacular way and take half of Raleigh down with him, but that isn't what my father sees when he looks at him. He sees a guy who's lost so much and doesn't need to lose one more thing.

Alex's head stays bowed when I sit down next to him on the steps. The seat of my dress is immediately drenched, but I don't care. I hold the umbrella over the both of us, sheltering Alex from the rain, and a small, solemn smile tugs at the corner of his mouth. His eyes stay closed, but he knows I'm here. The loud rumble of the raindrops striking the umbrella is hard to miss.

"Thought about coming inside. Wanted to. Couldn't seem to make myself," he murmurs. "I heard all of it, though. The guy did a good job." A bead of water drips from the end of a wet strand of hair that's hanging down into his face. I want to catch it, like it's a part of him that needs saving. I want to catch all of him, to keep him safe and somehow carry him through this, the way he's carried me before. I don't know if I'm strong enough, though. I also don't know if he'll even let me. Since he found out about Ben, he's become harder and harder to reach every single day.

I lean my elbow on my thigh, resting my chin in my palm, turning to look out over the snow-capped mountain range in the distance. Such savage sentinels, looming over Raleigh. Sometimes they make me feel safe here. Protected. Sometimes, they make me feel trapped.

"When Max first learned to read, he brought his book into my room every night to read it to me. It was cute at first, but I started getting annoyed by it after a while. He tripped over all the words, and he always wanted to read the same damn thing. The Hungry Caterpillar. After two weeks, I could recite the entire thing from cover to cover by memory. I wanted to stick that book in Dad's document shredder."

Alex opens his eyes and looks at me. I'm so accustomed to his self-assuredness that the desolation I see in him now makes me feel like I've been knifed in the chest and I'm bleeding out.

"I let myself be irritated and frustrated by Max ever since he was born. I used to hate having to run around after him all the time. I've loved him, but I've never really appreciated him the way I should. I know that now. Alex, I am so sorry. This isn't right. None of it. If there was something I could do to…" *Turn back time. Fix this. Fix Ben. Fix you. Make it all go away.* It's pointless even saying it. There's nothing I can do and we both know it. Alex clears his throat, turning to face the mountain range in the distance, shadowed by the curtains of rain that are still falling.

"Don't say you're sorry, *Argento*. Don't say you wish things were different. This is the way things are. I have to learn to accept that." Carefully, he reaches out and traces his fingertips down the side of my face, featherlight and gentle. I try to lean into him, but he drops his hand, huffing under his breath.

In a broken voice, he whispers, "Careful, *Argento*. Everything I love turns to ashes. Everything I touch falls to pieces in the end."

Firmly, I shake my head. "That's not true. What happened to Ben had nothing to do with you. None of this is your fault. You're not *cursed*, Alex."

He drops his head again, smiling bitterly. "I am though, aren't I. Come on. Let's go say goodbye to Ben."

# 7

## ALEX

The small boy standing on the stool in front of the kitchen counter is me.

I'm aware of that. I'm also aware that this is a dream.

Neither shard of awareness allows me to separate myself from the fact that the sun-soaked, warm bubble in which I find myself appears totally real. I exist both within my seventeen-year-old body and that of the much smaller six-year-old version of myself, who sings in soft, breathy melodies as he digs his hands into a fat ball of dough. He grins as he splays his fingers wide, grinning at the thick sticky mess that cakes his skin and shores up beneath his fingernails. I can feel it under my own nails, covering my own hands.

The hands of a boy.

The hands of a man.

I see from two very different vantage points, through two different pairs of eyes. One pair observes the world as a place filled with wonder and hope; the other can't help but see the promise of hurt and pain in every direction as he casts his gaze.

"Are you ready, mi amore? Have you made it just right?"

I smell her first. The scent of lilies and fresh summer fields floods the cramped space, overriding the bright, saccharine tang of the icing sugar that floats on the air, and my stomach twists in both excitement and bitter pain. My mother enters the room in a whirlwind of music and energy. Her dark, thick curls are wild, reaching in all directions like vines reaching for the sun. Her warm, brown eyes are bright with an electric, contagious energy. The smile on her beautiful face lights up the entire room so brightly that I'm almost blinded by it.

I'm completely in love with this woman. This is the type of unconditional love that sons bear their mothers before they discover she has flaws, and the illusion that she's the most perfect creature to ever walk the earth is eventually shattered.

Joy washes over me as she rushes up behind me, tickling her fingers into my sides, burying her face into the crook of my neck. I squeal as she pretends to gobble me up. "Who cares about pizza, passerotto? I think I'll just eat you. Little boys taste the best, I think."

Six-year-old me gasps for breath, fighting to get his words out around his high-pitched laughter. "No, Mama! No, no, no, don't eat me! Don't eat me!"

The older version of myself only rumbles out half of the sentence, his words thick with misery. "No, Mama. No, no, no."

The smell inside the kitchen evolves, the dream twisting, evolving around me like a shifting painting, and now we are sitting down at the kitchen table, all three of us, staring down at a pizza big enough to feed an army. My mother folds her arms in front of her, leaning toward my younger self across the worn grain of the wood, whispering conspiratorially. "What do you think, mi amore? Is it perfect? Should we eat and eat and eat until our bellies burst open and our guts spill out like little red snakes?"

Young Alessandro giggles, deep dimples marking both of his cheeks. His smile forces his eyes closed as he laughs at the prospect of such gluttony. "Yes, Mama. Let's eat the whole thing. And then dessert!"

My mother, in her floral print wraparound dress, sits straight up in her seat, jerking to attention. "Dessert? Who said anything about dessert?" She opens her mouth wide in pretend shock. "Did you look inside the fridge, little sparrow?"

The little boy covers his mouth with his hands, trying not to laugh even harder. He turns to me, the older version of himself, sitting next to him at the table, and he cups one hand around his mouth, whispering loudly. "There's panna cotta in there. Did you see it?"

I nod slowly. Sadly. "Yeah, buddy. I saw it."

I saw it just now, when I snuck a peek inside the refrigerator, even though

Mama told me not to. I saw it eleven years ago, before the darkness, and the suffering, and the broken bones, and the prison bars.

"You cheated," Mama cries, addressing both of us. "That was very naughty." Her eyes dance with delight. "Dessert is only for birthday boys, you know. I don't think I know any birthday boys."

Two voices fill the kitchen, loud and excited, quiet and withdrawn. "It IS my birthday."

My mother continues to feign surprise. "It is?"

"Yes!"

"Oh, my goodness, little sparrow. I had no idea!"

"You did, you did!" I insist.

Her smile makes me light up on the inside. "All right then. I suppose, in that case, then there might be a little something sweet in the fridge for you after dinner. But first, mi amore, I need your help with something, okay? Do you think you can help your mama with one small job really quickly?"

I never feel more special, more needed, than when she asks me to help her. Excitement blooms in my six-year-old eyes. My seventeen-year-old heart beats a little faster. "Of course, Mama! I can do anything!"

"I know you can, my precious boy. You can slay dragons, and save the princess, and make the whole world right again. That's why I love you so much. You're the strongest little sparrow in the whole entire world. Come on. Come upstairs with me. This won't take a second." She holds out her hand to the small boy, and he accepts it happily without a second thought. The woman in the wraparound dress with the wild brown curls avoids looking at the older version of me as she takes her young son and begins to lead him up the stairs.

"Don't go up there, Alex." My voice is so cracked, so broken. Excruciatingly quiet. I feel like I'm screaming the words, but the little boy doesn't hear me over my mother's soft humming.

I follow them because I have to. I'm pulled up the stairs behind them, the smell of lilies and fresh summer fields flooding my head, intoxicating and terrifying. My legs are heavy as lead weights, resisting the pull of time and what has already come to pass, but cannot be avoided.

This isn't how it happened...

This isn't how it happened...

None of this is right.

The kitchen was a sun pocket, warm and bathed in the happy memories of my childhood. When I step onto the landing, completing the climb up the tight, carpeted stairway, I walk right into winter. There are no happy memories up here. Only fractured shards of grief that bite sharp teeth into my skin, twisting in the pit of my stomach, a cold sense of trepidation filling me from head to toe. Blue and grey, black and heavy.

My mother guides me into her bedroom, the room where she used to swaddle herself up in her depression, only tossing back the covers on her bed when she wanted to scream and curse at me—hate-filled words that never sounded right spewing from her mouth

I enter behind her, and fog forms on my breath. The place is as icy and frigid as a meat locker. As a morgue. My mother is no longer holding my hand. She's lying on the floor, legs contorted and splayed at odd angles, the hem of her beautiful dress soaked red.

In her hands: a shining, silver gun.

Her eyes find mine, swiveling in her head. "What are you waiting for, baby? You know what you have to do. It's okay. Quick and simple. Let's just get it done."

"N—no, Mama. No."

Her eyes roll, too much white showing, like a terrified horse rearing before a snake. "Everything's going to be okay, baby. It'll all right. Pull the trigger and you'll see. We can go back downstairs and have dessert afterward. That's what you want, isn't it? We can celebrate your birthday."

Hot, metallic fear climbs up the back of my throat—the taste of death. The small boy reaches out for the gun, wanting to make his mother happy. To stop her from hurting. His small hand shakes with uncertainty.

The older version of myself steps over my mother, crouching down between the little boy's slender frame and my mother's prone body, but it's too late. He's already touching the heavy steel. He's a second away from taking the gun from her. I clasp my older, wiser hands around his, holding them fast in place, preventing the moment from happening.

"Don't listen to her," I whisper. "This isn't the help she needs. This...this never should have happened."

I'm invisible to the little boy now, though. I'm a future he cannot foresee. Only I can look back on what was and see him, trembling, afraid, wanting to give the brightest light in his world the only thing she has ever begged him for.

His small hands cut through mine like my grasp is so much smoke, the irreversible action already pressing forward, appeasing the gods of time.

What has already passed cannot be undone...

"Don't," I plead. "For fuck's sake, listen to me. Hear me. Don't do this. We can still make it right. We can change everything. We can set it all right! If we save her, then we can save Ben!"

I'm lying to myself. There's no fixing this. There was never a way to fix any of it. When I look down at my mother again, her face is a bloody ruin, half her jaw ripped away. A pool of blood soaks into the threadbare carpet, thick and viscous, so dark it looks black.

No longer capable of asking me with her words, she begs me with wide, panicked, fearful eyes. Do it. End it. Make it stop. Pull the trigger, passarotto.

What happens next was written in stone eleven years ago, but I can't stop myself from hoping for a different outcome. I wait for the little boy to drop the gun. I hold my breath, lungs seizing in my chest, hope soaring as I pray for him to drop the terrible weapon in his grasp and call out for help.

He whimpers, tears chasing down his cheeks, catching on his dark eyelashes. My vision blurs. I can barely see...

The recoil nearly takes my arm off.

I stagger back, the kick of the gun everywhere all at once. I feel the impact of the bullet in my chest, and suddenly I'm lying on my back in a library, the sound of screaming in my ears.

"Oh my god, Alex, Alex! I'm so sorry! I didn't mean to! I didn't fucking mean to, I swear!" A girl with long black hair and ruby red lips stands over me, her hand fluttering at her chest. Her pale Snow-White porcelain cheeks are spattered red. Pain spreads through my chest like the roots of a tree, burrowing deeper, taking hold, wrapping around my bones...

The girl with the black hair takes hold of my younger self, pulling him tight to her chest, wrapping an arm around him protectively. "It's okay, Alex. It's okay. You did what you had to do. You did what you had to do. You did what you had to do. You did what you had to do. You did what you had to do. You did what you had to do..."

# 8

## ALEX

"You cleaned the carbs out? Air filter, too? And it's still not turning over?"

The trailer's a fucking bomb site. I never spent a fortune on the furniture or decked it out real nice, but I kept it fucking clean and tidy. Since Zander moved in, it looks like he's made a few changes. Plates and dishes clutter the counter tops in the kitchen, and mugs of half-drunk coffee are busy growing mold at random spots all over the place. Piles of clothes litter the floor, along with empty cartons of greasy Chinese food and crushed beer cans. In the hallway in front of the bedroom door, there's a piece of toast sitting on the hardwood, covered in peanut butter and dust bunnies. *A piece of fucking toast.* He's only lived here for fourteen days. This level of destruction is kind of impressive.

"Can you get it on a trailer? If you can bring it over here, I can take a look at it. I don't have time to drive out there today, though."

Zander's voice is muffled and echoey, like he's conducting his phone call inside a tin can. Lord, who talks to someone on the phone while they're sitting on the shitter? It's obvious to all parties concerned that you're defecating. I wait in the living room for him, back up against the wall, tire iron in my hand. It feels good to have something heavy and solid to fuck around with while I bide my time.

Saves me from repeatedly driving my fist into a wall instead, just to feel a different kind of pain.

"What are you doing, Alex? I don't even like it here. Let's go."

Ben's voice has joined my mother's, it seems. My mind tortures me at frequent intervals throughout the day now, adding Ben's imaginary thoughts and feelings to my inner monologue as it sees fit. Before too long, there'll be so many dead people talking to me that my own voice will be fucking drowned out by all the chatter.

In the bathroom, Zander ends his call and flushes the toilet, confirming my suspicions. Dirty bastard. The door opens, making the same creaking groan it made when I lived here, and the son of a bitch trundles through to the kitchen, slamming about as he rifles around for god knows what. When he staggers into the living room in a vest and boxers, his hair all over the place and a fresh cup of coffee in his hand, I push away from the wall and step out in front of him.

His reaction is violent. Dressed head to heel in black, my face concealed behind a ski mask, I don't look like I came here to try and sell him home insurance.

"Hell fucking *no!*" Zander hurls the cup of coffee at me, launching its steaming hot contents at my face. I'm ready for him. Ducking neatly to one side, I avoid the projectile, which explodes against the wall above his television. A quarter of a second later I have him by his throat, pinned against a rickety bookcase, and I'm hefting the tire iron above my head.

"What the fuck!" Zander shoves me in the chest, but I ain't going nowhere. Gouging my gloved fingers into his esophagus, I keep on digging until I feel something pop. Only then do I ease back. End of the day, I don't want to destroy his vocal cords. I want the fucker to talk, and that isn't going to happen if I render him mute for the rest of his miserable life.

"S'up, Hawk," I snarl. "Thought I'd bring you over a housewarming gift."

Zander hacks and splutters, wheezing as he attempts to scramble away from me. "Alex? What the *fuck*, man? I thought you were gonna kill me. Why the hell are you wearing a ski mask?"

I keep a hold on him, slamming him back against the bookcase again. "It's cold out," I say flatly. "Plus, I wanted to scare the living shit out of you." I pull the ski mask off, throwing it into his face.

Zander's expression is priceless. He's a strong guy. We're matched in a lot of ways. He knows how to fight. He taught me plenty in juvie. Right now, he can feel the rage rolling off of me, though, and it's put him on the backfoot. He scowls, throwing a half-hearted jab into my ribs. When I lean forward, putting all my weight against his throat again, he quits any ideas of fighting back. "You've been a whiny little bitch ever since I showed up in Raleigh, Alex. What the fuck's your problem now?" he grouses. "Let me guess. You got yourself a papercut and it's somehow my fucking fault, right?"

Hah. So much attitude. He won't be sniping at me in a motherfucking minute. He'll be lucky if he still has all of his fucking teeth. "Ahh, y'know. Spent a lot of time at the cemetery yesterday," I reply. "We buried my little brother. He was in a car accident. Bled inside his skull until he died. It was a whole thing—"

"Jesus, Alex. I know. I'm sorry! You should have fucking told me the other night. Just...let *go!*" He wrenches himself free at last, lurching away, holding his hand against his neck. A pair of baleful, dark brown eyes glare at me from across the living room. "I know shit's been tough, okay. I know you've had the worst run of all fucking time. But Christ, dude. No need to break into my place and murder *me* for it."

I hold a set of keys aloft, jangling them in the air. "Didn't break in. I forgot to mention I kept a spare set inside one of the breezeblocks around back." He catches them when I toss them to him. "As for murdering you, I don't know yet. I'll admit, I've been thinking about it. See, someone paid me a visit yesterday. Someone I suspect you're well-acquainted with."

He looks at me like I've lost my mind, eyebrows arched, top lip curled in confusion. Slowly, he paces to the old couch I left here when I moved out and collapses down onto it. "Spit it out, man. I have no idea what you're talking about."

"My old man. Daddy Dearest. Giacomo Moretti. You might know him as Jack? He waltzed back into my life for a friendly little chat like he'd never even been gone. And d'you know what he was wearing when I set eyes on him for the first time in ten years? Care to hazard a guess?"

Zander's face blanches white. He isn't looking too well. Leaning forward, he grabs a can of beer from an open case on top of the coffee table and cracks it open. "Alex. I had no idea your old man was a Dreadnaught. Not until I came out to Raleigh. I'd never even heard his name until he showed up a couple of weeks ago at the club house. I've never even spoken to the guy." He tips the beer back, chugging the liquid, and doesn't stop until the can's empty. Wincing, he discards it on the floor, rubbing at his throat. "You really fucked up my shit, dude. You could have broken my neck."

Ignoring his pussy griping, I grab a beer from the case and sink down into the armchair opposite him, searching his face. "I don't believe you. You've spoken to him plenty. And I'm betting you knew him before, too." I pop the tab on the beer, holding the rim of the cold metal to my lips. "You know him before juvie, Zander?"

"Look, I just told you—"

"Zander."

He curses under his breath. "Fine. Yeah. Fine. Jesus. I've spoken to Jack. I know him. But I didn't know he was your old man until we'd already become friends at Denney. I pieced it together based on the stuff you said about him, okay. And it didn't seem like a smart move to let on that we had ties when you obviously hated the guy so fucking much."

I swill the beer around the inside of my mouth, hoping it'll wash away the metallic taste of blood that's been lingering on my tongue for days now. When I swallow, it's still all I can taste, though. "You contacted him? Told him I was inside with you?"

"Sure. He already knew though, dude. It wasn't news to him."

"He asked you to keep an eye on me?"

Zander laughs, letting his head fall back onto the couch. "He didn't say much of anything about it. Just grunted on the other end of the line. He didn't tell me to do shit. I had your back because we were friends, man. For real. That had nothing to do with Jack."

I don't know if I can believe him. It all seems a little too coincidental to me. I don't have the emotional wherewithal to unpack unimportant bullshit friend stuff at the moment, though. I just need to figure out what Jack's game is and put an immediate stop to it. Because there is some sort of game here. There has to be. "And now? You show up at my place of work? You're enrolled at the same school as me? This is all because we're friends and you wanted to come hang out? I don't buy it."

"I told you why I came to Raleigh," Zander replies wearily. "Q owed Monty a favor. He wanted me to register at Raleigh and figure out who's been taking a chunk out of his coke business ever since that stuck-up Kacey bitch got sent away. That's it. The end. Jack was never even near this deal. There's bad blood between him and Monty. As far as I was aware, you couldn't pay Jack to come to Raleigh, no matter how much you offered him."

"So then what? He just shows up out of nowhere of his own volition one day? That's a load of shit."

"Like you said, man. You buried your little brother yesterday. He was Ben's fath—"

I hurl the beer can across the room, roaring at the top of my lungs. "*I WISH—*"

*Deep breath. Take a deep breath,* mi amore. *That's it. Shhhhh. Breathe....*

I pause second, waiting for the tidal wave of anger to subside. "I *wish* people would stop calling him that. Giacomo was *not* Ben's father. He's not my father, either. He's a scum sucking piece of trash that uses and abuses things until he breaks them. He never cared about us before. He didn't give a shit about us when my mom died. He didn't care about us when we were thrown into the foster care system. There's no fucking way in hell he showed up yesterday because he was affected by Ben's death. So, don't give me that *'he was Ben's father'* bullshit. It won't fucking wash."

Zander lets out an exasperated sigh. "What the hell do I know, man? I'm just doing what I'm fucking told, trying not to get my ass handed to me by dudes with way more clout than me. My dad kicked it three months before I was even born, so all *this*," he says, gesturing angrily at me, "makes no fucking sense to me anyway. I'm sorry about Ben. I know how bad you wanted him to come stay with you. For what it's worth, I know you'd have taken awesome care of him. But I don't know anything about Jack coming here. I don't keep tabs on the man. I was hoping things'd be cool with us if I came here. So long as you don't try and snap my neck again, I still think that'd be dope. But that is literally all I got for you right now."

I swallow, regretting that I hurled my beer across the room. Feeling a *tiny* bit bad that Pabst Blue Ribbon is currently running down my old living room wall.

However, this is all grade-A bullshit.

Zander sounds genuine. I mostly believe what he's just told me, but even if it is all true, that still means he spent six months in juvie with me, knowing way more about me than he let on. He knew where Giacomo was when I didn't. I bitched, and I griped, and I told him things about my family that I hadn't told anybody before, and he didn't say a fucking word. It wasn't as if he didn't have the opportunity. I mean, all we did was hang out all day, lifting weights and sparring, for fuck's sake.

I twist the tire iron around in my hand, watching it spin as I run my tongue over my teeth. After a second, I stop it abruptly, jumping to my feet. "Fair enough."

Zander follows me with his eyes as I make my way to the door. "That's it? Fair enough? Where the fuck are you going, man? I feel like you need a zanny or something."

"I don't need a *zanny*," I spit. "I need to make sure Jack's fucks off back to wherever the hell he came from."

~

Monty and my father are *not* friends.

That's what Zander said.

When he petitioned to become my legal guardian, Monty told me he owed it to Jack to look out for me, which means Monty's been lying to me, keeping secrets...

My temper's on a high simmer as I slam through the entrance into the Rock. For a Saturday, the place is uncharacteristically quiet. Barely anyone hanging out by the pool tables. The booths in the back by the rear bar are all empty, which is super weird.

Paulie, the bar tender, looks like he's seen a ghost when he clocks me storming toward the 'employees only' entrance that leads to

Monty's office. "Alex, man! What are you doing here? Boss said you were gonna be off for a couple of weeks?"

I flip him the bird and a cutting grin at the same time, then enjoy watching him trying to figure out the greeting as I push open the door and disappear through it into the dark hallway beyond.

"Alex! *ALEX!*" The door opens again and Paul calls after me. "Hang back, brother. He's got someone in there with him. Alex, are you listeni—"

No, I'm *not* listening. The moment I saw the other gleaming black Camaro out in the parking lot, I knew my sneaky bastard of a father had shown up here, bad blood or no. If my sperm donor's having a tête-à-tête with the boss, then I want to know what the fuck they're talking about. I'm *so* done with this bullshit. Dispensing with formality I don't bother to knock, barging right into Monty's office… only to find Monty pinned face-down on his desk by a man who most definitely is *not* my father.

The guy's head whips up, and I'm met with the cold, dead eyes of a killer. I don't even think. I fucking duck, because that's what my fight or flight reflex screams at me to do. There's a swift *thunk* overhead, followed by the sharp, juddering sound of wobbling metal, and…*holy fucking shit*…I look up and there's a mean-looking serrated hunting knife buried an inch deep in the staff notice board, right where my head was a moment ago.

"Wait, wait, wait! Fuck's sake!" Monty hollers. "Relax, okay! He's just a fucking kid. Alex, get the fuck out of here. NOW!" There's genuine concern in his voice. For a split second, I almost believe that he does actually care about me and this hasn't all been some kind of game to him.

The guy grinding Monty's head into his computer keyboard hasn't even blinked. He's a monster of a dude, built like a line-backer. I've been confronted with some dangerous motherfuckers in my time, but this guy looks like he'd put a bullet between my eyes without even flinching.

"Zeth! Zeth, I mean it, man. Just…*don't*. Alex, get back in the bar and wait for me there."

Hmm. What to do, what to do. Part of me wants to bolt down the hall and get the fuck out of here. But then there's the part of me that's craving chaos and destruction. The part of me that's still reeling from everything that's happened recently. It's the dangerous part of me that wants to break open like rotten fruit and bleed out all of my pain, spilling my tangled guts out onto the earth...

I unfurl myself like a cat, straightening up with care, never taking my eyes off the guy. "If I walk back that way, I'm coming back with a shotgun," I tell him.

"Better kill you where you stand then," the other guy rumbles. His voice is so deep and rough, it sounds like he eats a side of glass with every meal.

"Jesus Christ, this is fucking ridiculous. Quit it, both of you. Zeth, sit back down," Monty commands. "We can discuss this like the proper business-minded gentlemen that we are."

The stranger, Zeth, runs me through with sharp, angry eyes, still staring me down. "I'm not business minded. I'm not gentle. I'm *pissed*. Sitting down ain't gonna change that."

Squaring my shoulders, I take a step forward into the office. Monty grits his teeth, baring them like a rabid dog. "Are you fucking deaf, kid? I told you to go."

I look him dead in the eye—sharp, cold, and hostile. "I just had an interesting chat with Zander. He shed some light on your relationship with my father."

"God's sake, Alex. Now is not the fucking time! If you wanna be useful, go find Q. Tell him—"

Zeth tuts under his breath, leaning his weight forward onto Monty's head. The added pressure of such a huge guy bearing down on his skull must be pretty spectacular, because Monty quits handing out his instructions and opens his mouth, yelling silently.

"Ever cracked someone's head open, kid?" Zeth asks. "Seen inside their brain pan? Poked around in their grey matter? Pretty fucking fascinating stuff."

Damn it. I'm not happy with Monty, but I don't necessarily want him dead. Not yet, anyway. There are still a bunch of pressing questions that I'd like answers to. I take a step forward, ready to snap out a right hook, but Zeth's eyes narrow a fraction, barely a millimeter, and I know it would be a bad idea. He sees me coming. I can attempt every trick I know to try and throw him off, but this guy's a professional.

He's played all the plays. He's wise to any deception I might try and throw at him. "The brain's an interesting thing," he continues. "Shielded by bone, floating around in all that cerebrospinal fluid, it has the power to create worlds. Build empires. Inspire nations. But poke at it with something sharp…in just the right way…"

"I didn't come here for an anatomy lesson."

He cocks his head sharply to one side. "I didn't come here to teach one. I came here for a bag. Wouldn't happen to know where it is, would you? Black? Kind you might take to the gym?"

Monty winces, hissing through his teeth, spit flying everywhere. "Keep your goddamn mouth shu—"

In a black blur of movement, startlingly fast, Zeth reaches around, grabs something silver and shining from the small of his back, and—

CRACK!

A hail of splinters explodes into the air. A curl of smoke, bitter-smelling and acrid, rises from the muzzle of the gun in Zeth's hand. He just shot Monty's desk, barely an inch away from the old bastard's face.

"It occurs to me," the man in the leather jacket says, "that you're not taking this situation very seriously. Forgive me for not making myself clear. This isn't a business meeting. It ain't a friendly negotiation. The bag belongs to me. If I don't get it back, I am gonna get fucking medieval on your ass. By all means, decide how the rest of your day is gonna look. No skin off my nose. I *will* find what I came here for…and I've always wondered what it'd be like to hang, draw and quarter someone."

Monty's as still as a marble statue, blinking like crazy. God knows what having a gun go off right next to your face will do to a man's vision, but it can't be good for you. "I—I—" he stammers. God, he's a stubborn piece of shit. He nearly just took a bullet to the face, for fuck's sake, and that shot wasn't an empty threat. It was a reminder of what comes next if he doesn't start playing ball.

Suddenly, I'm far too tired and bored by this whole situation to watch it spiral any further down the rabbit hole. Fuck Monty. Fuck this job. Fuck Zeth and his stupid fucking bag. "I have the duffel, asshole," I announce. "It's at my apartment. You want it, you're welcome to it."

"You little shit. You're fucking dead!" Monty hollers.

He can be mad all he wants. He's about to learn just how little I like being manipulated. If Zeth's surprised by my claim that I have his bag, then he keeps his thoughts well hidden. "Take me to it," he demands.

Monty kicks out, trying to hit Zeth in an attempt to wrestle himself free. "Alex. You're gonna cost me a hundred Gs—"

Zeth picks Monty's head up and smashes it back down onto the desk. "Your life worth more than a hundred grand to you, asshole?" When Monty doesn't respond, Zeth scoots down and bends over him, getting up in his face. "That wasn't rhetorical. *Is your miserable backwater pimp existence worth more than one hundred thousand dollars to you?*"

"Y-yes!"

"Then shut your fucking mouth, stand up straight and head out to the parking lot. Cause trouble and I'll bury a bullet in the back of your head, and the rest of your staff will be dead before your out-of-shape carcass hits the deck. Got it?"

Monty's eyes are full of fire and brimstone as he reluctantly pushes away from the desk and stands ramrod straight. He puffs his chest out like he just fought and won the right to stand instead of being told to get up. An angry muscle ticks in his jaw. The cold, hard glare he gives me as he slowly walks out of the office conveys plenty with its leaden weight. *This is betrayal. You're fucking dead to me, Moretti. Don't expect to be forgiven for this...*

In all the time I've known Montgomery, he's ruled his little empire with an iron fist. There's a measure of pride he takes in his work and a level of respect he commands from the people who deal with him. He's never been disrespected like this before, and certainly not in front of one of his subordinates. Even if he could forgive me for handing over this bag so easily, he'll never be able to forgive me for seeing him bettered like this. His shame will turn to vengeance, even though my actions have probably just saved his life.

His intentions are irrelevant now, though. I don't want to be forgiven. I want to burn his world down to its foundations.

Zeth gestures with false benevolence for me to go ahead of him. In a grim, sour tone, Monty insists on having the last word. "Do whatever the fuck you like, Mayfair. You are *not* putting me in the fucking trunk."

## 9

## SILVER

"Wait. You're supposed to be a woman. My mom said you cut some sort of deal in court when Alex was released." The man on the front doorstep spreads his hands out in front of him, palm-up, and shrugs.

"Maybe your mom wasn't actually there. Maybe she just read the court transcript. There's...there *was* another Detective Lowell. My sister. Clerks mix us up all the time when they type up their reports."

Sounds like a lie, but I just inspected his ID and it looked perfectly legit. "This won't take a minute," the detective says. "We have everything we need for our case. There are a few small details I'd like to go over before submitting *my* report. That okay with you?" He's tall and clean-cut, wearing a North Face puffer jacket. The hair on the sides of his head has been shaved to a tight, fashionable fade. He's dressed casually but there's something militaristic and severe about him. He doesn't give off the impression that I could decline to answer his questions. His authoritative, no-nonsense tone makes it clear that I don't really have a choice in the matter, which sucks because I could really do without this shit right now.

"I've gone over my statement at least six times already. This weekend's been really shitty, Agent Lowell. Can't this wait until next week or something?"

The guy smiles tightly, not meaning it. "Call me Jamie. And unfortunately, no. I have to present the information I've gathered to my boss tomorrow. If there are discrepancies, we won't be presenting our strongest case to the judge when the time comes. And I'm just guessing here, but I'm pretty sure you don't want Weaving let off with a caution and some community service for the shit he pulled in that gymnasium, right?"

*Weaving.*

Nausea rolls through me in a never-ending wave. Hearing that name said out loud makes me flinch. "Oh, no. I'd love it if he got off with a caution, *Jamie*. I think it'd be great if he gets released and then tries to murder me again. Hopefully he'll be successful next time."

Agent Lowell grimaces, rocking on the balls of his feet. It's freezing cold out. The rain turned to snow a couple of hours ago, and the wind is howling across the porch. I probably should have invited him inside, but so what? Fucking sue me. I'm exhausted. My manners have taken a sabbatical.

"Listen, Silver. I know this is all really overwhelming. Talking about what happened must bring up a lot of bad memories, but I wouldn't be here if it wasn't important. What if Jake gets out and it isn't *you* he comes after? What if he hurts someone else, and another assault could have been prevented if—"

Rolling my eyes, I head back into the house, leaving the door open behind me. "Stop. You've made your point." I just want this whole fiasco to be over. Sending Agent Lowell away only to have to deal with him another time is tantamount to putting off the inevitable; I might as well just get it out of the way.

In the kitchen, I pour coffee into a filter, dump it inside the machine, slam the lid closed, and hit the brew button. In the corner, lying in his bed by pantry door, Nipper bares his teeth and growls at the stranger in his house. Agent Lowell—doesn't look anything like a Jamie to me—curls a lip up at the dog, then leans across the kitchen island, resting on his forearms. He's in his mid-twenties, probably. With his dirty blond hair, neat stubble, and his ice blue eyes, he's good-looking and he knows it. Confidence oozes out of him like he's been nailed by buckshot and he just can't stop the flow. Women of all ages melt when he turns that roguish, half-apologetic smile on them,

I'll bet. Jake was good looking too, though. I've learned that good looks don't make you a good person. Your appearance doesn't mean shit if your soul's as black as tar. I lean back against the oven, folding my arms across my chest.

Agent Lowell doesn't seem to know what to do with my blank stare. "Like I said. There were a few things I wanted to clarify…." He trails off.

"Go ahead."

"You told the officer who interviewed you at the hospital that Jacob Weaving raped you earlier this year. I'm a little confused. If you were sexually assaulted by Jacob, why was there no report on file?"

My nerve endings prickle, a thousand tiny fire ants biting the flesh between my shoulder blades and down the backs of my arms. Seriously? He's gonna pull *this* shit? "I didn't file a report. I was too scared of what would happen if I did. Girls get judged when the use the word *rape*. In my experience, that word makes a lot of men uncomfortable. I'd already been violated enough by then. I couldn't have handled the endless questioning and probing. I told one person and he downplayed the whole thing. Tried to make out like nothing unusual happened. Yes, I've come forward now, and, no, I don't think that it's convenient timing, when Jake's locked up for other crimes. I don't think any of it is *convenient*. I did what I had to in order to make it through one day, and then the next. And then the next. That's all there is to it."

Lowell pouts, his mouth pulling down at both corners. It's a *'sure. Maybe I can see that being true'* face. I want to make this fucker bleed. "Okay. After the incident, you said you went shopping for some items from the pharmacy?"

The expression slides off my face. Shopping? Fucking *shopping*? "I went to get the morning after pill, because I didn't want to end up pregnant after three different guys forced their dicks inside me. I wasn't stocking up on lip gloss and hair products."

"Logical," he says, chewing the inside of his cheek. "Very logical. I've dealt with a lot of rape cases. Most girls don't show that level of forethought. They're usually too distraught to think that clearly—"

The coffee maker pings, noisily bubbling away as it begins to pour the brewed coffee into the carafe. Meanwhile, a stunned calm has fallen over me. "Why are you really here, *Jamie*? What do you gain from questioning me like this? Zen was attacked. You've seen those photos, right? They don't leave much room for conjecture. She's given her statement, too. Jake's already locked up for his involvement in his dad's smuggling ring, not to mention breaking most of my ribs and trying to hang me in the school gym. Like I said, I gain nothing from reporting the attack now. Jake's gonna rot behind bars for a very long time…"

Agent Lowell smiles broadly, looking down at the covered plate of cookies by the fruit bowl to his right. "Precisely." He shrugs. "Apart from the fact that people are fawning over your friend. They're very sympathetic toward her. Her hospital room looks like a high-end florists. But you…" He makes a show of looking around, hunting for the flowers that I *haven't* been sent. "They're less sympathetic to your story, Silver. People seem to think you might have had reason to target Jake. Some sort of high school vendetta. You used to have a crush on him, didn't you?"

A high-pitched, endless tone rings in my ears, muting my thoughts. *I can't…he can't really be…fucking* serious? I scramble to form words, to refute the implications that he's making, but I can't even remember how to speak.

Thankfully, I don't have to. "You'd better have a damn good reason for being in my kitchen, questioning my underage daughter without an adult present, Detective."

I didn't hear Dad pull up in the driveway. Didn't hear the front door open, either. My father charges into the kitchen like a thunderstorm, exuding a dark fury that has Lowell pushing away from the kitchen island, the smug look on his face morphing into a mask of professionalism.

"Mr. Parisi. Silver agreed to talk with me. She's a smart girl. She knows that if she's got nothing to hide, she—"

Nipper launches out of his bed, hackles raised, barking loudly as he darts back and forth in front of the detective, showing him his teeth. Dad doesn't say a word to call him off. I'd say I've never seen my father look so angry, but I've seen him riled like this too many times of late. He grabs Lowell by the shoulder, fisting his jacket, shoving him toward the hallway. "Nothing she just said to you is admissible.

You do *not* have my permission to be in this house. Get the fuck out before I accidentally shoot you for trespassing." He pushes Lowell, and the detective staggers back, nearly tripping over his own Nikes. He runs his tongue over his teeth, straightening out his jacket as he backs away toward the door.

"Not smart to threaten a DEA agent, Mr. Parisi. But not to worry. I won't take it personally. I can only imagine how stressful it is, trying to raise a problem teenager on your own."

Dad takes off his glasses, setting them down on the countertop. "I don't give a shit who you are or who you work for. I swear to god, if you're not out of my house in the next three seconds, you and I are gonna have issues."

Lowell's arrogant sneer doesn't slip. Not even for a second. Glancing over Dad's shoulder, he locks eyes with me and winks. "We're not done, Silver. Next time, I'll be asking these questions in an interview room, and there'll be cameras pointed in your face. I'm sure the truth will come out then. Meantime, you two make sure you enjoy the rest of your weekend, okay?"

## 10

## ALEX

"L*et....me...OUT, you fuck!*"
  I know how to drive *my* Camaro, but Zeth puts me to shame. His car—a mirror of my own in nearly every way—is like an extension of his body as he drifts it around the bend, sliding perfectly in the snow, forcing the contents of the trunk to slam and loudly roll around. The hammering from the back gets louder as he jumps on the breaks at a red light so abruptly that I have to brace myself against the dash.
  This whole thing, Zeth purposefully tormenting Monty, and Monty losing his shit so badly, would be funny if it weren't for the fact that, best case scenario, my boss is going to fire me, worst case scenario murder me, and my little brother was lowered into the ice-cold earth twenty-four hours ago. Every time the fucker in the driver's seat next to me coasts through the snow a little too recklessly, all I can see is Jackie's supposedly extra-safe people carrier hurtling off the road and smashing into a tree, killing Ben in the process.
  "Little tense?" Zeth asks, the suggestion of a smile twitching at the corner of his mouth. Kind of surprising; I wouldn't have thought the guy capable of such a thing.
  I brush off his comment, pulling my pack of smokes out of my

pocket. "What's the big deal with this bag, anyway? I've seen everything inside it. Nothing irreplaceable."

"I'm sentimental about my tools," he replies. "Had some of them for well over a decade. And besides..." He drifts across the double yellow line, crossing onto the wrong side of the road as we hurtle through yet another bend. "It doesn't matter what the bag contains, what it's worth, or if it can be replaced. It's *mine*. It belongs to me. I don't let two-bit con artists from the middle of fucking nowhere steal my shit, kid. You let one person take something small one day, they're trying to take that which you hold dearest the next. Bad for business."

"Didn't think you were a businessman."

"I'm whatever the fuck I wanna be when the moment takes me, shithead. And you light that cigarette in my car without asking, you're gonna wind up with a broken hand, you feel me?"

I've already sparked the lighter; the flame hovers two centimeters away from the end of the smoke that I've already put in my mouth. I consider holding the wavering yellow flame against the cigarette and pulling on it hard, just to defy him, but I meet his dark, flat stare and think better of it. *"You mind?"* I ask, laying the attitude on thick.

Zeth turns to look straight ahead out of the windshield again. "Be my guest."

The smoke burns at the back of my throat, making me feel sick, but I pull on it hard again and again until I hit the filter. Shame I don't have any Jack on me. I could really use a drink. Across Raleigh, Silver's waiting for me to come over for dinner. Cam's in the middle of making lasagna or some shit. There's a girl who loves me, ready to hold me, and kiss me, and make all of this godforsaken shit feel a teeny, tiny bit better...but I'm happy to be headed in the opposite direction. I don't *want* to feel better. I want to feel worse, because that's what I fucking deserve, isn't it? If I'd gotten my shit together a little sooner and not been such a fuck-up for so long, then perhaps I could have convinced CPS to give me custody of Ben early. If I hadn't been so damn fixated on teaching Gary Quincy a lesson for treating me like garbage, then I might have been able to devote my energy towards the things that really mattered. Ben could have been living with me a goddamn year ago. Then he would never have been in that car with Jackie, driving through the night...

*To see you. Because you'd landed your ass in prison, Alex. They could have been safe and sound, enjoying Hawaii, but no...*

"You alright there, princess?" Zeth rumbles. "You're looking a little peaky."

Taking another cigarette out of the pack, I light it, scowling deeply. "I'm giving you what you came here for. That's all you need to worry about. My general wellbeing's none of your concern."

He laughs under his breath. "So much drama. I forgot what seventeen was like."

"Fuck you, prick. What, you think you're gonna Doctor Fucking Phil me now? You kill people for money, old man. Let's not forget that. And I'm a teenager. So what? I've had to deal with far more shit than most adults do in their entire lifetimes. I stood over my Mom when they buried her. I stood over my little brother when they buried him yesterday. My girlfriend thinks I'm an unfeeling piece of shit because I can't mourn properly. And, oh, she's recovering from being attacked and nearly fucking murdered as well, just to really ice that cake nice and good. Now I'm here dealing with your hostile ass. So…I get to be a little shitty, yeah? The past month has been fucking brutal."

The cherry on the cigarette flares as I pull on it angrily. Bracing myself, I wait for the pain to arrive. A guy like Zeth doesn't let people talk to him like he's something they scraped off their shoe just because they're having a hard time. There's always retribution for that level of disrespect.

But the pain never comes.

I shoot him a casual glance out of the corner of my eye. He's focusing on the road, his brow furrowed, but other than that he doesn't look like he's about to smash my face into the console. "I know what it's like to lose a sibling," he says softly. As softly as his gravelly voice allows, anyway. "I had a sister…" He trails off, the front of the car filling with an unspoken tension. The mention of his sister's brought back painful memories, by the looks of things.

Not my problem, though. Just because he can put himself in my shoes and comprehend what's going on in my head doesn't mean we're gonna be best fucking friends. "Just drive," I grumble, flicking the smoke out of the open window. "No point in dredging up pointless shit anyway."

Zeth follows closer than my shadow as I run up the fire escape to the apartment. The fucker should have waited down by the Camaro—I'm hardly gonna try and bolt, what with Monty locked in the trunk of his vehicle—but I keep a civil tongue in my head. Better to refrain from antagonizing the bastard at this stage in the proceedings. Once I've handed over the bag, he'll disappear from my life and I'll never have to see him again. From everything Monty told me about the owner of his precious duffel bag, Zeth's a big fucking deal in Seattle. Unlikely that he'll need to come out this way again any time soon.

"Nice place," he comments, following me down the hallway. Admittedly, I've let things slide ever since Maeve showed up to deliver her life-shattering news; the apartment's a mess, clothes lying in crumpled piles all over the place. No dirty dishes or take-out cartons, though. I haven't eaten properly in days so that's a bonus, I guess. I intend on heading straight for the bedroom, but Zeth has other ideas. He sidles past me into the kitchen, his sharp eyes taking everything in.

Leaning against the door jamb, I watch as he opens up the utility closet and stares intently at the bucket of cleaning products on the shelf inside. "What? You think I got someone lying in wait for you?" I ask.

"Who fucking knows." Satisfied that there's no one in the cleaning closet, waiting to jump out and spritz him with Windex, Zeth kicks the door closed and turns to face me. He sees my shattered cell phone sitting on the counter and quirks an eyebrow at me. "You run that thing over or what?"

"Sure." I don't need to explain *shit* to him.

"Cool. Where's the bag, kid?"

It's still sitting in the bottom of the walk-in closet in the bedroom, right where I dumped it the night I moved in. "This way."

He follows on my heels again as I enter the bedroom. I head straight for the closet and grab the bag for him, thrusting it into his chest. "It's all there. Apart from the gun, of course."

Zeth doesn't look too stoked about this. "Where's the gun?"

"Police lock-up. They confiscated it."

"How the fuck did that happen?"

"What do you think? I shot someone with it. They took it away from me." Zeth lets out a surprising bark of laughter that catches me off guard. "That's *funny*?" I ask.

He nods, just once, a curt, efficient movement. "Sure. Why the fuck not. I can picture you shooting someone and getting away with it. You're a hellraiser, huh, kid?"

I don't know if I'm supposed to take this as a compliment; it's hard enough trying to figure out if he's fucking with me. Bitterly, I agree with him. "Looks like I'm turning out to be my father's son. Giacomo Moretti would be proud, if only he knew how."

Like a slowly deflating balloon, Zeth's amused expression wilts. "You're Jack Moretti's boy?"

*Oh.*

*Fucking.*

*Great.*

Juuuuuuust fucking great. Why am I not surprised that a stone-cold killer like this guy knows my father? "Not voluntarily," I tell him.

Zeth grunts, hoisting the straps of the duffel bag over his shoulder. "Looks like you just lost your job at that shit hole Cohen runs. You got money?"

I still have close to seventy grand in a pillowcase under the floorboards in the bedroom, courtesy of all the runs I did for Monty. Not that it's any of this fucker's business. What, am I supposed to believe that he feels sorry for me? He hurled a hunting knife at my head thirty-five minutes ago. "*Plenty*," I tell him.

Zeth nods, sticking his hand into his pocket, taking out his iPhone. In a matter of seconds, he's produced a paperclip from somewhere, popped out the SIM card, and then he's tossing the device up in the air.

I catch it before it can hit the floor, frowning as the strange bastard turns and walks down the hallway, toward the door. "I know all about shitty fathers, too," he rumbles over his shoulder. "You seem like you might be smart, Alex. Keep it that way. Stay away from guys like Montgomery Cohen and Giacomo Moretti."

"Hey! Don't you want your phone back?"

"Keep it. It was a burner."

# 11

## ALEX

I don't go to Silver's. After Zeth leaves with Monty still kicking and screaming in the trunk of his Camaro, I sit in the car, turning the keys over in my hand, trying to pull my shit together. I can't make head nor tails of what's been going on lately. It's all just too fucking much, and I don't think I can trust myself to be the person I need to be. How am I supposed to be good for Silver, help her recover from her ordeal with Jake, when I'm too fucking broken to hold myself together? How can she comfort me, when she wakes up clawing at her throat every morning, trying to free herself from a noose that isn't there?

We're both so bruised and battered that it feels as though we're both going to try and support the other, only to break and unintentionally let them fall. I don't want to do that to her. I love her so fucking much. The last thing I want to do is let her down. I need her more than I need the air in my lungs, but I also need her to be okay… which leaves me in a complicated, confusing situation. She won't be okay with me around. Currently, she's sacrificing her own sanity for the sake of mine, and that's not healthy. For her *or* for me.

In the end, because I'm a weak piece of shit, I do drive over to the Parisi's place. I don't go inside, though. I sit on the curb, at the end of their driveway with the engine idling, watching the lights go on and off in the house as Silver and her father move from room to room. The snow that paused earlier returns with a vengeance, and for a little while I feel cocooned inside the car. With the air vents blowing hot air on full blast and the steady, throaty purr of the engine vibrating the entire vehicle, the world falls away and nothing exists apart from me, the Camaro, and the promise of Silver, safely tucked away in the house at the top of the driveway.

She texts me eventually.

SILVER: You thinking about coming inside?

She must have spotted me out of a window. Slowly, I type out a response and hit send.

ME: Will you still love me if I say I can't?

SILVER: No matter what.

Cursing myself for being such a weak fuck, I start the Camaro's engine and I drive off into the night.

## MESSAGE RECEIVED

*Message received from...Maeve Rogers...on Sunday, January second at eight twenty-two pm.*

'Hi Alex. Me again. I'll stop calling if you actually pick up, y'know. Listen...I know this is tough. You miss your brother. I can't even imagine how much you miss him. It'll help if you talk about it, though, believe me. I'll be here, when you're ready. Just...just please, call back, okay?'

*Press one to save this message. Press two to—*

*Message deleted.*

## 12

## SILVER

"Good morning, students of Raleigh High! Principal Darhower, Ms. Gilcrest, and the rest of the Raleigh High faculty would like to wish you all a bright and happy new year! We hope you enjoyed the Christmas holidays and made the most of your time with family and friends. After a long and well-earned break, we now return to Raleigh to create, learn, and excel in all fields of academia. The date is Monday, January the third, students. Let's make today excellent in every way!"

As one, the entire student body stands in stunned horror, heads cricked at weird angles, staring at the brand-new PA speakers that have been mounted in the hallways, classrooms and changing rooms of Raleigh High. Shiny and new, the speakers have metal cages around them, bolted to the walls, as if Darhower and his cronies think we might object to the new additions and rip them from the walls.

"While our under-the-sea theme has been a big hit for numerous successive years, a new initiative at Raleigh means that we'll be opening up a ballot box outside the cafeteria this week, where suggestions can be made for this year's senior prom theme. Please note, all suggestions must be sensible and within reason. Any inappropriate, vulgar or offensive suggestions will be dismissed out of hand without discussion. Thank you for your attention, students. Go, Roughnecks, go!"

Confused chatter breaks out in the hallway as a loud, cheery chime blares out of the speaker, signaling the end of the morning's announcements. We've never had a PA system at Raleigh before, never needed one, but this new addition to our small, controlled eco-system is a welcome one in my eyes.

See, for the time being, no one's looking at me as I shove my books into my locker and rummage through my bag, trying to find a working pen. They're all too astonished by the weird, old-new technology that's invaded our little world to be thinking about Silver Parisi. I embrace the moment, reveling in an anonymity that cannot last. Raleigh's a small town, and people gossip here like mother hens. Everyone knows what happened during break. Jacob Weaving's larger-than-life presence is noticeably missing already, and it won't be long before my fellow students begin to ask questions.

I have a few questions of my own. Namely, where the hell is Alessandro Moretti? He texted me the other night, so obviously he has a new phone. He hasn't made any attempt to find or talk to me since then, though. Hasn't shown up at the house. I dropped by his apartment yesterday, but he didn't answer the door and the Camaro was gone. It's as though he's just fallen off the face of the earth.

This was *not* how the start of the year was supposed to go. Alex and I were supposed to come back to Raleigh on top of our game, ready to buckle down, get through the remaining months before graduation, focus on getting good grades so Alex could apply for custody of Ben. Now it feels as though none of it is worth it. College doesn't even seem like a consideration anymore. Further education's more of an afterthought at the moment. Without Ben…Jesus, I don't know what Alex will have to work towards now.

I take the long way around to get to my first class of the day, walking the outside perimeter of the building in order to avoid the long hallway that leads to the gym. I can still hear the wet slap and squeak of my bare, bloody feet fighting for purchase against the linoleum whenever I close my eyes. At some point, I'll have to face my fears and walk that hallway. Worse, I'll have to actually go *into* the gymnasium. For today, however, I'm showing myself a little kindness and making an exception. Not to mention, taking the outside route to class also has the added benefit of avoiding all of the senior prom posters that are already covering every free inch of wall space inside the hallways of Raleigh High. A year ago, I would have been so pumped up about our last hurrah as seniors before graduation, but I was an entirely different person back then.

The wind claws at my jacket, trying to rip it from my body as I hurry toward the south entrance of the school where the English labs are located. My hand's on the ice-slick handle, bitingly cold, when someone grabs me by the shoulder...

I react without thinking.

I twist and launch my right fist into the air at the same time, half expecting it to hit nothing. Pain jangles up my hand, into my wrist and then my shoulder, letting me know that my aim was true, though.

"Ahh, *fuck*! What the fucking...!" A guy in a leather jacket dances back, nearly slipping over on a patch of ice, holding a tattooed hand to his face. When he removes the hand, his palm is spattered with blood...and my heart stops dead in my chest.

At first, I think it's Alex. A much older, worn version of him that's been left out in the wind and the rain for a couple of decades. His eyes, a deep, chestnut brown, are so similar to Alex's in both color and shape. His dark hair, and the cut of his jaw, and the way his nose juts uncompromisingly from his face...all of it seems so *Alex* that for a second I can't make sense of what I'm seeing.

Then the guy turns his attention to me, our eyes meeting, and I realize my mistake. His eyes are nothing like Alex's after all. They're harder. Unkind, unforgiving and flinty, in a disturbing way that makes my blood run cold. The resemblance is undeniable—I even see Ben in the man standing before me—but he isn't the Moretti I fell in love with.

I pull my jacket tighter around my body, stepping back toward the door. "What the hell do you think you're doing?"

"Didn't mean to startle you, darlin. I should have called out or something. Don't worry, I'm not some creepy pervert. I'm—"

"I know exactly who you are. What do you want?"

The man in the leather jacket looks taken aback by this. "Really? He told you about me?"

"No. But I have eyes in my head, don't I? It's pretty obvious you're his father. What can I do for you, Mr. Moretti?"

"Oh, Jack, please," he says, waving me off with his bloody hand. I see where I broke the skin now—a small cut just below his nose.

"Mr. Moretti's just fine," I answer stiffly. "We're not friends. I've never even met you before."

"Surely Alex *has* told you about me, though?" He sounds so certain of himself. As if there's no way his son wouldn't have regaled me with all kinds of stories about his notorious father.

"He did tell me he thought you might be dead once," I inform him in a chilly tone. "He also told me how you skipped out on your family when they needed you most."

The cock-sure smile on Giacomo's face sags, the assertive spark in his eye guttering out and slowly dying. "Yeah, well. Everything's so cut and dried when you're a kid. He was too young to understand what was going on at the time. Things were complicated, weren't they. His mother was a difficult woman. You understand how these things go."

Taking a step back, halfway through the door, I meet his eyes. I think he's trying to cow me with his direct gaze—poor, timid little girl, unsettled by the magnetic, overwhelming presence of a grown man in a motorcycle club cut—but he's got another thing coming. I know a bully when I see one, and I know every underhanded trick in their playbook. I've stared down death and I didn't look away. I sure as hell won't be subjugated by a washed-up, powerless old man like Giacomo Moretti. "No, actually," I tell him. "I don't understand. I know that your wife was sick and you ducked out on her and your two young kids when things got hard, rather than staying to figure out how to help her. Seems pretty cowardly to me."

Giacomo smiles, emotionless, devoid of any humor. "Well, shit. Aren't you a little spitfire? I can see why Alex likes you—"

"I'm sorry, I'm confused. Is there something I can help you with? Because you're on Raleigh High property, y'know. I have to get to class…and I'd hate for a member of staff to see you and get the wrong impression. *I* know you're not a pedophile, prowling around the English block, looking for kids to lure into the back of a van, but Principal Darhower might not give you the benefit of the doubt. Things have been kinda crazy around here lately." Sarcasm drips from every word; I've really outdone myself on the passive aggressive front. On its own, my statement was polite enough. A friendly warning offered to a stranger. My tone, however, is anything *but* friendly, and paints a very vivid picture in which Giacomo is arrested and carted off Raleigh property without so much as a by-your-leave.

Alex's father runs his tongue over his teeth, flaring his nostrils as he glances down at his worn leather boots. "You're protective of him. I like that. It's good that he has you in his life."

"We're good for *each other*," I correct him.

"I just wanted to know if he was doing okay."

"In that case, no, Alex is doing pretty miserably right now. His little brother just died. He'll come through the other side eventually, though. He has me, and he has my dad. We'll both be here to help him for as long as he needs us. Now, if you don't mind, the bell's about to ring and I don't wanna be late."

*Keep your damn mouth shut, Giacomo. Just keep that stupid, filthy, lying trap closed...*

He doesn't, no matter how hard I wish it. I've almost managed to turn away from him before he calls out after me. "Silver? Hey, Silver. That wasn't *all* I wanted."

Sighing heavily under my breath, I spin back around. "Why am I not surprised?"

"I want to make things right with Alex. With Alex's mom gone, and now Ben, too, it isn't right that there be should be such a massive divide between us. He's my son, Silver. I'm his father. I appreciate your dad for looking out for my boy, but it ain't his job. All I'm asking for is a chance. Just one chance to fix things and be there for him."

My emotions riot, bouncing all over the place. No way in hell should he be trying to pull the old, *he's-my-son, your-dad-should-mind-his-own-damn-business* bullshit. He has absolutely no fucking right. I marshal my face into a blank mask, tamping down my thoughts. I can be mad all I want on Alex's behalf. In the end, none of this is up to me. "Then you need to say all of that to Alex, Mr. Moretti."

"He won't listen. He has a shitty temper. He won't sit still long enough for me to get the words out."

I'm sure he's right. Alex hates this man. He probably wouldn't piss on him if he was on fire. "What do you want *me* to do about it?"

"Just...talk to him. Play devil's advocate for me. Make him see that

I'm genuine an' I've changed. Convince him that I only have his best interests at heart. You can do that for me, can't you?"

There he goes again, wheedling, turning on the charm, treating me like a naïve little girl who can't see right through his bullshit. I laugh harshly, clouds of fog forming on my breath. "No, I can't do that for you. I don't know anything about you. I sure as fuck don't know that you're genuine. I don't know the first thing about your motives. I'm guessing they have very little do with Alex's best fucking interest, though. I won't try to convince him of anything. If you're serious about everything you just said, then you're gonna have to *show* him that yourself."

Giacomo doesn't like my answer. He shoves his hands into his jacket pockets, slowly shaking his head. "Such a foul mouth on such a pretty little thing," he muses.

This time, I *do* turn around, and I *do* walk away. "Oh, Mr. Moretti...you have *no* fucking idea."

# 13

## ALEX

It's pathetic, really, stalking Silver. I'm her boyfriend for fuck's sake. I'm done with the part of our story where I have to duck my head and hide every time she pauses in a hallway and glances over her shoulder. I definitely shouldn't be trailing her out in the cold, hood pulled down low over my eyes, creeping around after her like I'm about to drag her into the forest and kidnap her.

We've been through so much shit since we met; there's nothing I can't talk to her about. Nothing I can't say to her. But I was supposed to get stronger as time passed by, things were supposed to get easier for us, not harder, and after Ben's death…

Fuck, I'm not the guy I'm supposed to be right now. I've always prided myself on knowing who I am and knowing what I want, fighting for my goals no matter how deep the shit I had to wade through became, but this version of me? This shattered, cored out, broken man, bereft and without even the smallest glimmer of hope? What good am I like this? I'm useless. I'm a fucking train wreck.

She's broken and hurting, too. Today's the first day back at school, and she'd rather face the sleet and the cold than walk fifty feet passed the gym, for fuck's sake. I don't even know how she's mustered the strength to show up here today after all of the shit that's gone down inside this school. She's a fucking miracle, this girl.

Remarkable, and so much stronger than anyone can possibly realize...

The icy wind blasts into me as I carefully tread through the frosted, brittle blades of grass, staying close to the building's perimeter. Rolling my feet, heel-toe, heel-toe, heel-toe, I try not to make too much noise, but I don't really need to worry. The snap and crunch of the undergrowth giving way beneath the soles of my boots is loud, but the low, mournful howl of the wind is louder.

Up head, Silver's hair stirs, creating a halo of blonde and copper around her head as she turns the corner at the end of the building. One last look at her before she disappears inside the school. That's all I really need. Somehow, that will be enough to sustain me until I can drive by her place later on tonight. Hurrying, I jog the remaining distance to the end of the brick wall, sucking in a breath and holding it in my lungs, as if that will somehow render me invisible. I'm two long strides away from turning the corner myself when I hear his voice.

"I didn't mean to startle you. I should have called out or something..."

WHAT. THE. ACTUAL. FUCK.

Anger sizzles up my spine like a spark chasing along a fuse. He shouldn't be here. He...he has no fucking *right* to be here. Approaching her like this...the bastard's lost his fucking mind. My hands have already made fists. My feet move with a mind of their own, propelling me forward, urging me to run around the corner and make the fucker bleed for this outrageous intrusion, but...

*Hush, Passarotto. Let him speak. Then you'll know what he wants...and how to make him leave.*

It goes against every scrap of sense I possess, but I manage to still myself, planting my feet into the frozen earth. Paralyzed, too afraid to move a millimeter in case I snap and lose all control, I lean against the wall, closing my eyes, straining to hear what's being said against the rustling of the leaves.

I almost chip my teeth when my father starts to make excuses for his past behavior. I break the skin of my palms, fingernails gouging into my flesh, when he comments on how protective Silver is over me. Hot bile burns at the back of my throat he tries to worm his way into her good graces, asking for her help to get me on side. Pride and *relief* wash over me like a winter squall when she basically tells him to go fuck himself.

*That's my girl, Silver. That's my girl.*

The door to the building slams closed behind her when she goes, sealing her inside the light and the warmth of Raleigh High, and a deadly calm settles over me. The anger's still there, but it isn't the searing brand it was a moment ago. No, this is a different kind of anger altogether—the kind that cools to tempered steel and runs soul-deep, woven into the very fabric of a man's being. I shove away from the wall, rounding the corner just as my father begins to walk away.

"What the fuck do you think you're doing?" I growl.

He stops in his tracks, his head whipping in my direction. A calculating smile forms on his lips as he looks me up and down. "Well, well, well. The man himself. Didn't think I was gonna see you today, son."

"Bullshit. You know I'm enrolled here."

He stifles a laugh, tipping his head back to look up at the stark, winter sky. "Yeah, well…you have to be enrolled somewhere. There's a difference between being on the books and actually showing up, right? And us Morettis, we're hardly the *further education* type, are we?"

He says 'further education' like it's something to be embarrassed about—a dirty, shameful secret that guys like us would ever consider being associated with such a lame concept as learning.

"You don't know shit, old man. Just because you were happy to remain ignorant the rest of your life, doesn't mean the rest of us want that. You kept yourself stupid. And to what end? To look *cool*? Hate to burst your bubble, Giacomo, but flunking out of high school, not even bothering to get a GED? That's not cool. That's the dumbest thing a guy can do."

He grimaces, his mouth pulling down at the corners. "I got plenty of money, kid. A solid roof over my head. Food in the cupboards—"

"That's more than you left Mom with."

He slowly blinks, visibly side-stepping the comment. "What did I need math and science and fucking theater class for, huh? It's all fucking pointless. You'd do just fine if you turned around and walked out of this place right now. Waste of fucking time if you ask me."

"No one did ask you, though, did they. No one's asked you for anything at all. You're the only one wasting your time. I'll never forgive you for what you did. You could have hurt me all day long. You could have rejected me and Ben and I would have found a way to make my peace with it. Men like you have been disappointing their kids since the dawn of fucking time. But the way you hurt her? It was *unforgiveable*. She was convinced you were gonna come back, y'know. She used to talk to you all the time, like you were standing on the other side of the front door, about to come through it any fucking seco—"

"That's because she was fucking *crazy*, Alessandro!" The words explode out of his mouth, echoing out across the dell, the deep cavern behind the school repeating them back to him like the report of a gunshot. Rooted to the spot, I stand perfectly still as he rushes toward me, jabbing a finger angrily into my face. "You have *no* idea what it was like, boy. She was unstable when we met but it was cute back then. Kinda exciting. You never knew what she was gonna do next. The unpredictability was fun. But when you were born, she..." He shakes his head, disgust carved deep into the planes of his face. "She lost her fucking mind, Alex. And not in a fun way. She tried to stab me, for fuck's sake. How's a guy supposed to handle a bitch when she's fucking certifiable like that?"

"If you refer to my mother as *bitch* again, I will personally see to it that you never eat solid food again." There's an electrical storm building in my chest, and any second I'll crack open and unleash it upon him.

Jack holds out his hands in a placating gesture. "Alex. This is exactly why I came to see your girl first. I hoped she'd help you see that I didn't come here to cause problems. That all I wanted was to build a relationship between us finally, after way too many years—"

I lunge forward, slamming my hands into his chest. "Where were you when they locked me and Benny in that group home, huh?" A current of fury bristles just beneath the surface of my skin. "Where were you when I got kicked out of my first foster home?" I push him again, grinding my teeth together. "Or the second?" He does a good job of standing his ground, but when I push him again, he loses his footing, slipping in the rotten snow. "What about the third home, Jack? Did you know the guy in my third home wouldn't let me wear underwear? He used to strip me fucking naked and lock me in a dog crate in the garage. He thought it was funny to piss on me through the bars when he came drunk every other night."

The miserable fucker's eyes round out, like I've just said the most hurtful thing I could possibly think of. "I…I didn't…know, Alex. I wouldn't have…"

Fuck him. Fuck him and his fake guilt. "Right. You wouldn't have done a thing," I spit. "You didn't even check on us."

"Ben?" he whispers. "Did…they hurt him, too?"

Manic laughter bubbles up the back of my throat. Stepping away from him, putting a healthy amount of space between us, I let my head rock back and I unleash it: howling raw, insane laughter up at the sky. "No. *No, no,* y'know, Ben was actually pretty fucking lucky. How ironic is that? I fought tooth and nail, and I railed against Jackie, but at least she fucking loved him. She never would have *hurt* him. Not on purpose. He had a stable home, which is more than I can say I ever had. Not that any of it matters now, of course, but BEN IS FUCKING DEAD AND YOU CAN GO TO FUCKING HELL!"

I hurl myself at him, letting it all go; the lightning inside me needs out and won't be told no a second longer. Jack throws up his hands, shielding his face, but I'm not out to break his nose. A broken nose is painful, but it's not the end of the world. I home in on a more fragile part of his body: his chest, and his stomach. If I can break a few of his ribs, I might be able to do some more serious damage underneath. Deflate a lung. Stop his heart. I don't know…just *something*.

I drive my fists into his sides and his chest with as much force as I can muster, blow after blow raining down…and he immediately topples over onto his ass. Not what I was expecting. I wait for him to get up, blowing hard, switching my weight from one foot to the other, ready to fucking end this…but then Jack rolls onto his side in the dirty snow and hacks, wheezing as he tries to sit himself up…and all I see is a pathetic loser in a leather jacket, pretending to be something he's not. Pretending that he still fucking matters.

"*Goddamnit.*" I drag my hands through my hair, pulling on it out of frustration. "Just…get the fuck out of here, Jack. I'm sick of looking at your face. For the last time, do us both a solid and leave Raleigh in your rearview, okay? I don't want you here."

Huffing, my father gets to his feet, straightening out his t-shirt and his jacket. His face is sheet white, the same color as the bleached-out sky. His bottom lip is busted open, staining his teeth bright crimson. "Would if I could, son," he pants. "But I'm gonna be here for at least another couple of weeks. I'm staying at the Motel 6…if you change your mind and wanna…talk."

I watch him hobbling off toward the parking lot, amazed that those few hits I got in didn't miraculously make me feel better. During the long nights and the endless days when I've imagined laying into my old man, I was so fucking sure that they would.

~

I haven't brought a bag with me. No notebooks. No textbooks. No pens. I basically came to Raleigh to observe Silver from a distance, but after what just happened with Jack, my plans have changed dramatically. Jack dropped out of school the moment he could legally get away with it. He took shitty construction jobs, never rising above the lowest paid shit-kicker position, because he was never willing to put the hard yards in. He gave up on everything before he even got started, and that went for my mother, too.

If I bail on school just because Ben's not here anymore, and I walk away from Silver because things have gotten hard, then how am I really any different than him? Ben would be disappointed in me if I quit on everything now, when I was the one who was always encouraging him to do better, be stronger, to put his head down and focus on his education and the life he was going to build for himself.

When I enter the classroom on the first floor of the English block, Ms. Swift squints at me over the top of her iPad, frowning. She's a mousy, quirky looking woman, and her bangs are permanently in her eyes. "Mr. Moretti, I don't believe you're in this class?"

At the mention of my name, Silver's head snaps up, her brightly shining eyes searching me out. It kills me that her go-to reaction is immediate worry; I can read it on her face from a mile away. Her cheeks are still flushed from the cold outside, the end of her nose adorably pink. She's so damn beautiful, it makes me breathless to even look at her. I smile in an attempt to quash the look of panic she's wearing, hoping that her mind will stop racing quite so much. "I requested a class change, Ms. Swift. I don't feel adequately challenged in my current English class."

"Uhhh…" Ms. Swift looks down at her iPad, flitting through a couple of screens. "I don't see a transfer notification from the office here, Alex. You can't just show up to an AP class because you feel like it. Making it into an AP class is…well, it's kind of a big deal. So…"

The students on the front row avoid eye contact with me, staring down at their open textbooks like they're afraid I'm about to hulk out and trash the place. A couple of the kids on the second row brave a glance or two at me while also watching Ms. Swift, waiting to see what she'll do.

I'm not really paying attention to any of them, though. I'm too focused on Silver, trying to communicate a stumbling apology to her with my eyes. "I won't bring your class average down," I inform Ms. Swift tightly. "I'm here to learn."

"You're sure? Because it looks like you came to make eyes at Silver Parisi rather than open your mind to the brilliance of the English language."

I turn my full attention to her now, my gaze drilling into her face. "I swear. I won't cause any trouble. I'll sit by the window. I won't even be near Silver."

She doesn't look too convinced. Doesn't sound it either. "All right. By the window it is. Waste our time and we'll boot you outta the room quicker than you can say *'Geoffrey Chaucer who?'* And I will be checking with Karen after lunch to make sure you put that request in. Sit your butt down, Mr. Moretti."

I go and claim the only available seat left in the room—third row, directly under the AC vent, which is churning out cold air despite the fact that there are icicles dangling from the top of the casement on the other side of the window. "Uh, great. Umm, I actually need to borrow a pen. And some paper. And a textbook."

Ms. Swift eyes me balefully. "Ah. You clearly *did* come here to learn, didn't you?" Her frosty smile doesn't affect me. I'm chilled to the bone and only getting colder with the AC continually blasting me, and I've just seriously screwed myself over by electing to bump myself up a class—the workload's bound to be way harder than my regular class—but that's all background noise. I'm breathing the same air that Silver's breathing. I feel the proximity of her, and the wild, frenetic beast inside of me that's been bucking and pulling on its chains finally calms, finally breathes a massive sigh of relief. This is where I'm supposed to be. And if joining yet another AP class and burning my brain cells to a crisp means that I get to be near her, then so fucking be it.

## 14

## ALEX

I tell her about Zander's confession concerning my father. I tell her about my run-in with Monty. I tell her I won't be working at the Rock anymore. Once I've reassured her that I won't be struggling to pay rent for a long while yet, she seems to take everything in stride. Predictably, she's not too happy that I vanished on her, though.

"You get to be sad, Alex. You get to be lost, and hurt, and turned around. What you don't get to do is ghost me. I'm not okay with that. We don't do that to each oth—"

She deserves to chew me out for the shit I've been pulling over the past couple of days. I owe her better than I've been giving her, and she has every right to tear me a new one for vanishing on her so spectacularly, but in this moment, the air shivering with snow out of the Camaro's window and everything so peaceful and quiet, all I want to do is kiss her.

I hold her by the nape of her neck, quickly pulling her to me, and I bring my mouth down on hers before she can finish her sentence. She tastes of cinnamon, and mint, and the ginger tea she likes to drink sometimes; I consume all of it, all of her, plunging my tongue into her mouth with a wild abandon that halts her breath in her lungs.

I guess she wasn't banking on being kissed like she's about to get fucked. It takes her a second to respond. When she does, it's with a shuddering sigh that makes the hairs on the back of my neck stand up straight.

Her fingers wind into my hair, tracing down the sides of my face, running over my collar bones until she's driving her nails into the tops of my shoulders, panting out sharp blasts of air down her nose. She's so fucking bitable. I suck her lower lip into my mouth, tugging on it with my front teeth, and Silver lets out a little whimper that has another part of me altogether standing to attention.

Reluctantly, I break off the kiss before we go too far. Sure, I want her real bad. Goes without saying that I want my dick inside her, with her shivering out an orgasm on top of me, but this is more important than sex. I need to make things right with her. If we apologize and make up, communicating only through sex, we'll forget how to actually talk about our shit, and I'm no genius when it comes to emotions but I'm pretty sure that'll end in disaster.

I cradle her face in my hands, committing the dazed, heated look on her face to memory. Then I gently stroke the tip of my index finger down the length of her nose, rubbing away the wet sheen of her mouth so I can't be distracted by how hot she is, all pouty and swollen like this.

"I let you down," I whisper. "I'm fucking sorry."

Her eyes still unfocused, she shakes her head, swallowing. "You didn't let anyone down. That's the whole point. No one expects you to just get up, dust yourself off and move on like nothing happened. You lost him, you lost *Ben*, and—"

The words, sharp as knives, flay me to the bone. I've been trying to outrun them ever since I found out Ben was dead, but this time I settle into my seat and I face them, I *feel* them, and I try not to flee from the truth.

Ben's dead.

My brother is gone, and he isn't coming back.

I'm never going to sit across from him at the diner and dip French fries into a milkshake with him. We're never going to watch scary movies together. The sound of his incredibly rare laughter is never going to fill the spare room of the apartment I got just so he could come and live with me.

These are hard realities to face. I don't want to accept any of it, but that's the thing about death. It can't be ignored. You just have to find a way to live with the hand it deals you, and that sucks more than I can bear.

Silver clears her throat, plucking at the collar of my t-shirt, worrying at the stitching. "I'm not mad at you for disappearing. Not really. I don't know how you're supposed to handle any of this, okay? There are no guidelines for coping with grief."

"There are actually. There are millions of them online, and every single one of them is horseshit. I'm gonna be okay. I just need to figure out how to put one foot in front of the other, and…"

She rests her chin on my shoulder, curling my hair around her finger. "And?"

"And…I'm supposed to go to college, then get a good job, right? Pay off my loans over the next twenty fucking years and get a mortgage. Become a responsible human being who regrets covering himself in tattoos. That's what comes next."

Leaning back, Silver's disturbingly quiet for a very long time. After a while she rests the back of her head against the frosted window behind her and lets out a long breath. "What would your Mom say about that? What did she want for you when you grew up?"

Well, shit. I could really do without unleashing my mother on the inside of this car. To remember her is to give her life, and she's just too big and overwhelming to deal with right now. Silver asked the question, though, and she looks like she's expecting an answer. "She… she wanted me to make music. She wanted me to be an artist like Giacomo. She wanted me to be an arctic explorer. A deep-sea diver. She wanted me to be happy."

Silver smiles softly, brushing the pad of her thumb along the line of my jaw, making my stubble rasp in the silent car. "She wanted you to be *free*…" she says in a hushed tone. "None of the things she envisioned for you involved office jobs, mortgages or regrets. You're not made for that world, Alessandro. You were made for colorful ink and the rumble of an engine, and an open highway, full of possibilities and uncertainty. That's what your life looks like after high school."

The oxygen rushes out of my lungs in a winded, long exhale. "I'm not interested in a future that doesn't feature you in it, *Argento*."

"Who said anything about that? I've told you once already, I'm not going anywhere. We'll weather whatever storms come our way together, I promise. We have so far, haven't we?"

Man, when did I turn into such a little bitch? When did I start feeling this swollen ache in my chest any time Silver talks about the future? It feels like I'm holding something fragile in my hands, delicate beyond measure, and the slightest twitch will cause it to shatter. My whole life, I've had to be forceful and brash in order to make it from one day to the next. This entire thing with Silver requires finesse, though. It requires a gentle touch that I sure as shit wasn't born with. As the bell rings inside the school, across the other side of the parking lot, I find myself praying that I can figure it all out before I end up *permanently* breaking something.

## 15

## SILVER

*Three Weeks Later*

"I heard she got busted sucking Jake's dick and the new kid lost his temper. What kind of psycho carries a gun around anyway? I've been saying there's something off with that Moretti guy ever since he walked through the front door."

"God, you are such a dipshit. If that was true, how did she end up in the hospital with broken ribs and a rope burn around her neck?"

"What the fuck, dude. How the hell am I supposed to have all the answers? What am I, a bad daytime TV detective? All I know is, Jake's s'posed to come into some of his inheritance after his eighteenth birthday. Watch this space. That bitch is gonna be knocking on his door, holding out her unmanicured hand, looking for a payout. Seriously, have you seen her hands? They are gross. Her fingers are actually calloused like an old man's."

"Oh my god, Leah, you're such a *bitch!*"

An eruption of laughter bounces off the tiled walls of the changing room—a pack of hyenas cackling over a fresh kill. I roll my eyes, marveling at how stupid the girls sound, tittering to one another on the other side of the lockers. The past three weeks have been fine.

With both Kacey and Jake gone, no one's bothered openly attacking me. What would be the point? There's no one left to impress with their random acts of cruelty, and so I'm mostly ignored. Every once in a while, this kind of bullshit takes place, though. Tall tales and sharp words crafted to entertain at my expense. The girls know I'm here, which means their little gossip session's being conducted with the specific purpose of fucking with me. Sucks for them that I've heard way worse. Nothing they or anyone else says can hurt me now. I'm literally fucking *untouchable*. Bored by the whole affair, I finish tying my chucks, straighten out my Raleigh sweatpants, and sit myself down on the bench next to me.

"Olives," I say loudly. The girls on the other side of the locker fall auspiciously quiet. "In the forties, after the war, my gram married my grandpa. They were young and in love, and they wanted to move away from their parents, so they bought a patch of old farming land in Toscana and decided to start growing olives."

A head pops around the side of the locker: blonde hair blown out to perfection; black cat-eye liner and heavy mascara; ridiculously overdrawn lips that look kind of clownish. It's Leah Prescott, in the spray-tanned flesh. She was always a low-ranked member of the Sirens, but with Kacey gone all sorts of powerplays have been set in motion as a number of the girls jostle for the position of Queen Bee.

"The fuck are you talking about? Olives?" She lets out a disgusted sigh. "You're that desperate for attention now that you just start rambling about fucking *olives*?"

I give her a saccharine-sweet smile. "They're one of Italy's biggest exports. Gram and Pops built up themselves an olive empire. When they moved to America in the seventies, they outsourced the management of the business and lived off the profit. Gram sold the business in the mid-nineties when my Pops died. I won't go into specifics, but let's just say the Parisi family did damn well for themselves. We're what some people might call *obscenely* well off. I'm set for life. I sure as fuck don't need Jacob Weaving's inheritance money. But even if I were planning on extorting cash out of that piece of shit, I'd have a tough time. He's a *psychotic rapist*. He's gonna spend the next thirty years rotting in a jail cell with all of his assets frozen. Now. Do you want to head into the gym and actually practice, or are you gonna hang around out here, pulling your kick shorts out of your ass crack and popping pineapple Hubba Bubba like the basic bitch that you are?"

Leah's jaw drops. Low and behold, there, wedged into the side of her cheek, is a wad of bright yellow gum. "Eww," she grouses. "Have you been staring at my ass? Gross. Don't even think about it, okay."

God, seriously. Yawn. I make mention of her ass and suddenly I'm *hitting* on her? "If I were into girls, Leah, *you* would not be on my radar. I'm only interested in creatures with a soul, and you're a fucking vampire."

"Rude! Wait, what kind of vampire? Like, a Bella Swan kind of vampire? Or the dusty old hag kind out of one of those old black and white movies?"

"*GIRLS!*" Coach Foley's voice roars into the changing room, causing one of the girls still loitering on the other side of the lockers to scream out loud in surprise. "I can hear your bickering from my office on the other side of the damn hall. What in God's green earth is wrong with you?" Coach Foley used to work at Raleigh, but she retired a couple of years ago. Darhower enticed her away from her gardening and her cross-country mountain biking to cover for Coach Quentin while he takes a leave of absence.

I'm glad it's Foley who'll be coaching the Sirens during my first term back on the team. She always kept Kacey in check whenever my ex-best friend used to haze the new girls who joined the team. I wasn't strong or brave enough to shut Kace down myself, no one was, to do such a thing would have been social suicide, but Coach Foley didn't give a shit about Kacey's ice queen routine. She was immune to every single one of Kacey's powerplays, and she'll be immune to Leah's brand of bullshit now, too. "Get your asses into the gym right now. And if I hear any of you say fuck one more time, you're all gonna wind up in detention. Get moving! Silver, hang back a sec. I need to go over some game dates with you."

"Bitch," Leah mutters under her breath. "You've been off the team a long time, Parisi. Don't think you're just gonna waltz back in and claim your old place at the top of the Siren food chain. It won't be that easy."

I smile tightly, pressing my lips into a thin line. "Siren politics don't interest me in the slightest, Leah. I'm only here for the college application credits. Believe me. The floor's *all* yours."

Her mouth opens and closes like a fish out of water, gasping for air. If I stand still long enough, I'm sure she'll come up with a cutting come back about how she doesn't need my permission to jostle for role of Siren's head bitch, but I'm already walking past her, heading for Coach Foley's office. Leah's friends chitter and mumble quietly behind me; I can't tell if they're gossiping about me or their beloved leader. Can't bring myself to care, either. They're so *high school*, clinging on to the unimportant, unnecessary stuff. They still think that surviving at Raleigh is tough, but they're so fucking wrong. Surviving here is easy as hell once you've been raped and nearly strangled to death.

"I know I've been gone a while, but I read the papers. I still have friends on the faculty here, and I have to say, I'm surprised you haven't transferred out to Bellingham, Silver. What you've had to deal with..." Coach Foley puffs out her cheeks, eyes wide as she shakes her head. "It's unconscionable that the situation wasn't dealt with properly before it could come to a head like that. Principal Darhower should have investigated the matter and taken the appropriate steps to make sure you were safe. I'm sorry that didn't happen. Truly, I am."

My eyebrows hit my hairline; it takes a second to register that a member of Raleigh's staff just *apologized* to me for what happened. Foley's the first person to openly acknowledge that it even happened in the first place. The other teachers have all been making an obvious effort to avoid eye contact; there must have been a staff meeting held in my honor, detailing how little attention should be drawn to my existence.

"No need to look so surprised." Foley steeples her fingers together. "The school administration's been woefully corrupt for the better part of the past decade. It's part of the reason why I retired early in the first place. My position here's temporary now, though, so I can say whatever the hell I like. The Weaving family are evil incarnate, and they deserve everything coming to them. I doubt the board's going to replace Principal Darhower mid-way through an academic year, a regime change like that might be too upsetting to the status quo, but believe me...it's on the cards. It'll be too late to right the wrongs he's done to you, but next year hopefully there'll be someone a little more competent in the driver's seat."

I'm astonished that she'd say all of this to me. She's talking to me like I'm...well, like I'm not only an actual, real life person with real feelings, but like I'm an adult who is due an explanation. I remain mute, uncomfortably gripping the sides of the metal chair I'm sitting on, waiting for this unexpected moment to be over.

"All that aside, I won't be bringing this up again. And I won't be going easy on you, Parisi. Mollycoddling does more damage than good, and I'm guessing you might want things to be as normal as possible for your remaining months here as a senior. Am I way off base?"

"No, Coach Foley. You're right *on* base."

"Good." Perfunctory. All business. I like this about her. She shuffles a bunch of papers, organizing them into one neat stack, which she places in the *'out'* tray on her desk. "There are only so many spots on this team. You were a good cheerleader once upon a time, but you were always deferring to Kacey, dumbing down your own talents so she could shine. I knew you could be better, and now I'm demanding it from you. There won't be any in-fighting. No backstabbing. No arguments, and no drama. If I see things going south with the Sirens, I will confiscate your damn uniforms and disband this shit quicker than you can say *'Go, Rebels, Go.'* Do we understand each other?"

"Um...you mean Roughnecks?"

"No. I mean *Rebels*, kiddo. This football team was called the Raleigh Rebels for twenty-two years before Caleb Weaving showed up and made Jim change their name. He wanted an all-new brand for his son to rule over, but Jake isn't here anymore, and neither is his fucking father. It's about time this school remembered its roots. We're going back to the Rebels. Now, I repeat. Do we understand each other, Silver?"

For someone who just reprimanded us for cursing, her language choice is a little colorful. I nod, though, answering her question. "I'm here to train and nothing else. You won't get any trouble out of me."

"What about that boyfriend of yours?"

"Sorry?"

"The new kid. I haven't even seen him yet, but I've heard plenty. Sounds like he's got trouble tattooed on his back."

"The tattoo on his back actually says '*Unbreakable*'," I tell her, my mouth aching around the smile that's trying to bully its way onto my face.

Coach Foley gives me a wry sidelong look. "He's been caught up with the cops before. And now he wants on the football team? I wanna know what to expect from him."

I hide my surprise well. Nearly a month has passed since Ben's funeral and things have been...well, they've been hard. Alex has dipped in and out of that scary dark recess in his mind, floundering every once in a while, as he struggles to overcome his grief. But at the same time, he's been trying. He's been studying ferociously, acing all of his assignments. Every day, he runs five miles in the cold sleet and snow before school. He works on his bike in the small garage at the back of the hardware store. He's even started picking up some shifts when Henry needs to drive down to Seattle for supplies. He might not be working at the Rock anymore, but he's found plenty of other ways to fill his time. Every single moment of his day is full. He's always moving, always busy, always keeping his mind occupied. And now he wants on the football team again? He tried out at the beginning of the year, but Caleb Weaving had him booted not long after. I assumed he didn't really give a shit, but that can't be true if Coach Foley is right about him requesting his spot back.

"Uh...Alex is determined. Passionate. He works hard," I tell Coach Foley. "He's still a mess after his brother's death, but...he probably needs this. He's trying to stay afloat. He's not gonna cause any issues for you, I promise."

～

*Creeeeaaaak.*

"*Quit flailing, Silver. It's done. It's fucking* done."

Jake's vicious words taunt me on my approach to the gym. I've been walking around the outside of the school for long enough now; I know I can't avoid the it forever. That doesn't mean that my anxiety isn't riding high, though. The last time I walked, or rather I was *dragged* down this hallway, I had broken ribs, my face had been mashed to a pulp and I was about to be hung by the neck from the rafters. Such violent memories are enough to make even the strongest person break out into a cold sweat.

*Creeeeeeeaaaaaak.*

"You want the pain. You want the humiliation. You want to be degraded, hit and kicked and spit on. It's all you know now. It breeds inside you like a plague."

I can't differentiate between my heartbeats. My pulse pounds at my temples like a drum. It throbs in the soles of my feet, *dum, dum, dum, dum,* out of control.

But...wait.

The pounding, it isn't my pulse. It's a *sound*, outside of my body. A repetitive banging, stomping...and it's coming from inside the gym.

"Oh my god, he's gonna fucking kill him!"

Coach Foley frowns, quickening her pace. "What the *hell*?"

I have a bad feeling about this. Too cold and snowy to practice outside right now, the Sirens and the Rebels are having to share the gym for their training sessions, which makes for seriously close quarters. A high-pitched scream splits the air in two just as Coach Foley slams the gym doors open and storms her way through the knot of students who have all formed a tight circle around—

Oh, *great*.

Around a very familiar looking senior with vine tattoos tangled around the column of his neck, and another student with a Dreadnaughts MC badge inked onto his upper right arm.

It's Alex and Zander.

Of course it fucking is.

Coach Foley scowls at me over her shoulder. "No issues, huh? I'm assuming one of these morons belongs to you?"

My face hot with embarrassment, I nod, pointing to Alex. "The one who's about to—" Ahhh crap. Too late. Alex slams his fist into Zander's jaw, and his friend topples over backwards, landing hard on his ass.

"Next time he gives you a message to pass on, you know where you can tell him to shove it!" Alex roars.

Laboring for breath, Zander collapses flat on his back, hands resting on his ribcage, laughing at the top of his lungs. "One of these days, I'll be done letting you use me as a punching bag, man. You're not gonna like it when I start hitting back."

"*Please.*" Alex looms over Zander, his face red from exertion. "Don't act like a little bitch on my account. Feel free to fight back anytime."

"As far as I can see, you're *both* being little bitches," Coach Foley snaps. Thirty heads turn in unison toward the sound of her voice, including Zander and Alex's. The look on my boyfriend's face when he sees me standing behind Coach Foley says plenty: he knows he's fucked up, he knows I'm disappointed, and he immediately regrets the stunt he just pulled in front of an entire gymnasium full of our classmates. He scrubs his face with his hand, grimacing as he turns away from Coach Foley and begins pacing up and down like a caged lion.

"The Lord only knows what the hell this was about, but violence will not be tolerated here, and especially not in this goddamn gymnasium. You hear me?" Coach Foley hisses. "I'd have thought you'd know better, Alessandro, considering what went down the last time you were in this space."

Alex shoots a pained look at me out of the corner of his eye, like he's just remembered what happened here with Jacob himself and his guilt is eating him alive. "*Alex*," he mutters softly.

Coach Foley shakes her head in confusion. "I'm sorry?"

"My name's Alex."

"I don't give a good god damn what name you prefer to be called, Mr. Moretti," she splutters. "Only people who act like civilized members of society get any respect from me. At this rate, I'll be calling you fucking Susan for the rest of the year if I decide it fucking suits you."

Still on the floor, except now with his hands beneath his head providing a pillow, Zander chuckles maniacally—probably a bad idea, since the sound draws Coach Foley's attention. "And what the hell are *you* doing? Taking a siesta? What's *your* name, princess?"

Zander's smile dies. "Judging from the look on your face, it's probably gonna be Mavis."

"Perfect. Mavis and Susan. Off you go, ladies. Suicides. You stop when one of you can give me a good enough explanation for the carnage I just walked in on. What the hell are you still lying there for? Get your ass up off that floor right now!"

On the other side of the gym, Leah and her crew snicker behind their hands, giving Alex dirty looks. Their disapproval is a show put on especially for me. They're terrible actresses, though. Alex, with his brand new Raleigh Rebels Crew t-shirt pulling taut across his chest, and his dark, unruly waves mussed like the devil himself just tousled them, looks so sexy that I could drop down fucking dead. The girls squint down their noses at him and sneer to try and make me feel bad, but they can't help their treacherous hormones from softening their spite. I see their hunger as their eyes cut him down, and it brings me a savage satisfaction to know that they're never going to get to eat at *that* table.

Zander and Alex shuttle up and down the gym, glaring mutinously at one another every time they pass. The football team and the Sirens disperse, plainly disappointed that the fun is over, and each team heads to their respective ends of the gym. Meanwhile, I duck my head, praying that I'm not as red in the face as I feel.

"Sorry, *Argento*." Alex slows a little as he passes me. "Couldn't help it."

I'm not *mad* at him. It would have been nice to commence my first day of training with the Sirens without a spectacle. "Jack?" I ask quietly. "He asked Zander to try and get you on side?"

Alex is too far away to respond now, but from the steely, unhappy flare of acknowledgement in his dark brown eyes, I know I'm right. It's surprising that Giacomo hasn't tried to elicit Zander's help before now. I've waited with bated breath every single day since Alex's father approached me outside of the English block, bracing myself for the next Giacomo Moretti-related incident. It's a miracle that it's taken this long to arrive.

I stretch quickly, warming up my muscles, trying to ignore the lancing pain in my ribcage every time I twist, or just how generally stiff and sore I am all over my body. The doctors recommended I wait at least six weeks before I attempted any kind of physical activity. It's almost been that long now, but my injuries still aren't completely healed. If I have to sit out on the sidelines, missing my chance to catch up with my own life, then I'm going to lose my mind, though. I'll tolerate the pain. I'm going to have to.

The mat area set aside for stretching is small, but the other girls give me a wide berth as I sit down and fold myself over my legs, easing the tension in my hamstrings. Things are going to be really interesting if they don't find a way to get over themselves soon. Cheerleading is all about trust. You have to trust the person next to you to move in sync with you, and you need to trust the person at the bottom of the pyramid to catch you when you leap. Without trust, the whole thing literally falls apart in the blink of an eye. Usually with very painful consequences.

"Silver?"

I look up, and a pair of white Adidas sneakers with pink laces fill my vision.

Huh.

The sneakers are brand new, the same as style as all of the other Sirens' footwear, but I only know of one person who wears pink laces. One person, who used to dive bomb into Lake Cushman with me during long, hot summers, and who used to giggle and laugh about boys with me in the back conservatory of her parents' house.

Slowly, taking a second to prepare myself for whatever's about to come next, I lift my head and look up. "Hi, Hal."

Her thick strawberry blonde hair is longer than ever. Her Sirens uniform is perfect as always, her skirt pleated in a crisp, sharp way that always used to piss Kacey off because she could never get hers to look as good. A couple of years ago at an away game, Kace even made Halliday switch skirts with her because it was her 'duty' as captain of the Sirens to look better than everyone else. Halliday had given up her skirt without flinching, but when Kacey had tried to put it on, it had been a size too small and she couldn't get the zipper up. Suffice it to say, that had not gone down well. Not at all. Kacey had given Hal a week to put on five pounds or she was going to have to find somewhere else to sit at lunch. Again, Halliday hadn't flinched. She'd happily gorged herself on donuts and grilled cheese while the rest of us picked at our salads morosely, and by the end of the allotted time, Halliday had in fact gained six pounds. On her tits.

I still remember Kacey's rage when she realized Halliday was still a dress size smaller than she was but that her rack had become significantly more impressive. She'd told Hal she looked like a blow-up fuck doll, all the while jealously eyeing the boys on the football team, who all seemed to appreciate Hal's new curves.

Now, Halliday warily eyes the other girls; they've all stopped their own stretching routines to surreptitiously watch our exchange. "Um. Hi. I...I..." she stammers.

The last time we were this close, I'd just pieced together that she was on her way to the Rock to strip, and things had gotten pretty fucking weird. At the time, I'd thought things couldn't have gotten any more uncomfortable between us, but it looks like I was wrong. She shifts anxiously from one foot to the other. "Glad you're back on the team," she says. "And...I'm glad you're doing better, after..."

"After Jacob hung me from that rafter and made me swing?" I point to the specific rafter in question. Better to avoid any confusion.

Halliday ducks her head, twin spots of red burning on her cheeks. She looks many things: ashamed; afraid; mortified; remorseful. I could ease up and try not to be so confrontational, but I'm feeling spiky and her meek approach hasn't made me feel very merciful. She was my friend, one of my best friends. She was the one who found me, shell-shocked and covered in blood, wearing nothing but one of Mr. Wickman's dress shirts and a pint of my own bloody at Leon's party. She'd panicked, scared as hell, because she'd known something terrible had happened to me, and yet she'd still let Kacey spurn me from the group. She could have taken a stand that night and left with me. She could have picked me over Kacey, right over wrong, countless other times during the months that followed, when the other students at Raleigh made my life a living hell. So, no. I could go easier on her, but I'm not feeling that benevolent.

Halliday swallows thickly as she looks up, eyes fixed on the rafter over our heads. I've been doing a damn good job of avoiding looking at it, but I can't stop myself now. To my horror, there's still a piece of police tape fluttering away, high over our heads, snagged on the beam.

"Fuck, Sil," she whispers. Her hand goes to her throat, as if she's picturing what it must have felt like to have that noose biting into *her* skin, tightening, tightening, tightening... "I—I—I don't know what to say."

"So say nothing." I bend back over my leg, grabbing onto my foot so I can pull myself lower into the stretch. "It won't change anything."

A long, awkward moment passes, where Halliday stands silently over me, watching me, and I do absolutely nothing to set her at ease. Inevitably, she speaks again. "Look…I know you probably hate me, and I don't blame you for that. I've hated myself for the way I treated you. I hated myself when I was doing it…"

The question burns on the tip of my tongue: *So then why the fuck did you do it, Halliday?* But it's a question that I already know the answer to. She did it for the same reason I did so many shady, shitty things over the years. You never went against Kacey. Not if you wanted to survive. I bite the inside of my cheek, waiting for her to continue.

"I don't expect you to forgive me, after everything that's happened, but…I kind of need your help." She says the words like she knows just how ridiculous they sound coming out of her mouth.

She needs my *help?* I misheard her. There's no fucking way she just told me that she needs my help.

"What could you possibly need from me, Halliday? Seems like Raleigh life's been working out for you pretty well since Kacey was banished to Seattle." I see everything, and I hear everything, two skills I picked up quickly once I became Public Enemy Number One at my own high school. Being hyper aware of my surroundings helped me stay ahead of the curveball when Jake and his idiotic buddies on the football team were plotting new and interesting ways to embarrass or humiliate me. When Alex arrived at Raleigh, I began to let things slip, though. I have no idea how Halliday is faring at school now that, for better or worse, there's a Kacey Winters shaped hole in all of our lives. She could be the new Silver 2.0 for all I know, spit on and laughed at in the hallways, abandoned by anyone and everyone who ever called her a friend. But I doubt it. Halliday's way too likeable for any of that.

She makes a distressed, choking sound that would have made me jump to my feet and hug her once upon a time. "You can tell me to go to hell if you want to, but I was hoping you'd come with me to the hospital after school today. If you're not busy," she hastily adds.

I'm intrigued. Against my better judgement, I look up again. "The hospital? Why?"

"Because Zen..." Again, she makes the distressed sound, pulling a face at Leah Prescott, who is studiously pretending not to listen to our conversation. Halliday tucks her long curls behind her ears, stoops down, and cups her hand to shield the words that come tumbling out of her mouth. "Zen tried to kill herself. She's not right, um, *mentally*. And I figured...I *hoped* you might be able to help her."

"And why would I be able to do that?"

Halliday's eyes shine like wet glass, like she's hating the fact that I'm actually making her say this. "Because she went through what you went through. And *you* were strong enough to endure it."

# 16

## SILVER

The smell always hits me hardest—the burn of bleach and hand sanitizer, coupled with the sickly-sweet fragrance of flowers that have begun to decay in vases of stale water. I stopper up the back of my nose, careful to breathe through my mouth as I follow behind Halliday, our sneakers squeaking cheerfully against the linoleum. As always, the strip lights overhead are slightly too bright. As always, their inaudible hum buzzes irritatingly against my eardrums, unheard but definitely felt.

Nurses pass us as we make our way through the hospital corridors. I know many of their names. Tracey, fresh out of nursing school, whose fifteen-year-old brother stole her car and drove it to Tacoma, where he sold it to buy heroin. Lindsay, who loves birds and hates winter because all of the Ospreys, Caspian terns, and tufted puffins migrate to weather the cold elsewhere. Mitch, who sounds like Michael Bublé when he sings but can't dance to save his life. Phillipa, the sternest RN on staff, who strikes fear into the hearts of her subordinates, but who also makes sure to swipe extra pudding cups from the cafeteria for the sick kids on the cancer ward.

My face is healed now, the bruising faded and gone, and the nurses' eyes skate over me as if they don't even recognize me, which is a relief. I hated my time here, confined to my uncomfortable hospital bed, unable to go anywhere or do anything. I hated their pity the most, though. I despised being Poor Silver Parisi, the weak, vulnerable girl who nearly died at the hands of a mad, spoiled rich boy.

Halliday slows as she nears a set of double doors at the end of the hallway, wringing her hands anxiously. "The woman on the desk never lets me through," she says. "Zen's mom's put a block on visitors. She told me I couldn't see Zen until she comes home…but then I heard the doctor saying it was going to be weeks before they'd consider releasing her. And she shouldn't be alone in there, Silver. She just shouldn't. This place…it's too surgical and cold. It's—"

"*Hell*," I finish for her. I'm lower on sympathy than I ought to be, but I know all-too-well what it feels like to stare at the tile of a hospital room ceiling and feel like time has ground to a halt. If my parents hadn't come to see me with Max, I would have lost my ever-loving mind. Setting my jaw, I push my way through the double doors, holding my head high. "Just follow me. Don't look at the nurse on the desk. Just keep close and loosen up, for fuck's sake. You look guilty as fuck and we haven't even broken any rules yet."

"I'm not good at breaking rules," Halliday mumbles behind me.

This isn't true. I doubt her mom signed off on her stripping at the Rock for one thing, but I keep my mouth shut. Now isn't the time to bring that up. Once we're through the double doors, I beeline for the secure-access door that leads to the ward where Zen's room is located.

Holy shit. I hesitate when I read the sign taped to the wall.

PSYCHIATRIC ICU WARD

*Sharp Objects Restricted Beyond This Point. Med Carts Must Be Locked And Keys Kept With The Duty Nurse On Call.*

I knew Zen tried to kill herself, but she's being kept on the psych ward? On the same ward as potentially dangerous patients and people who still pose a risk to themselves or others? I think I've grossly underestimated just how bad Zen's situation is.

"The door doesn't just open," Halliday whispers. "They have to hit the big green button on the wall by the desk to let you through."

"Shhh. Come on." I recover myself, pressing forward toward the door, knowing how this kind of thing works. The nurse at the psych ward desk is harried, drowning in paperwork, and she's hungry. She won't have had a chance to stop for lunch, which was five hours ago now. She's also tired because the department is massively under-staffed and she's doing the job of three people. If we walk right up to her and try to appeal to her humanity, we're going to be met with short shrift. If we waltz right up to the secured-access door and punch in the code—a code that could very well be wrong for this part of the building or might have changed since I was discharged before Christmas, then she isn't going to bat an eyelid. During my time here, I learned fast that if you looked like you were supposed to be somewhere, no one really questioned it.

My hand shakes as I punch the five digit code Mitch, the nurse who could sing but couldn't dance, gave me when he told me to go and fetch my own damn blanket from the supply counter on the third floor; I'd refused to walk for a long time after I was admitted, and his tough love, coupled with the freezing ass temperatures in my room at night, were the only things that got me moving.

*Seven...three...eight...zero...zero...*

I'm *so* close to fist pumping in the air when the small green light at the top of the keypad flicks on and a whirring, mechanical sounds buzzes out of the lock. That really shouldn't have worked. The hospital's security protocols should be way tighter than this. Access codes should be changed regularly, or at least vary from one section of the building to another. Not complaining, though.

Hurrying Halliday through the door, I follow after her, marshalling my expression into a mask of calm. If anyone was really paying attention, they might have asked why two teenaged girls wearing cheerleading uniforms were letting themselves into a restricted area, but no one makes a goddamn peep.

The psych ward's different to other wards I've been on in the hospital. For starters, there are no bays with curtains around them, drawn closed for privacy. We find ourselves in a long, broad corridor with pale blue walls. Doors line the corridor on either side, with small white boards tacked to the walls, detailing patient information and stats, plus any relevant medication information.

The bleach smell, overpowering everywhere else, is absent here. The plush, thick cream carpet underfoot makes it feel as though we're walking down the hallway of a five-star hotel, not the mental health ward of a public hospital.

"I have to admit, this is way, *way* nicer than I imagined when I saw where we were heading," I mutter under my breath. "God, are they piping in *elevator music?*"

Halliday squeaks, almost walking into the back of me in her attempt to stay close. "Dad used to say that elevator music was designed to *make* people crazy," she says.

I have to agree. The bland tinkling piano notes are little too condescending for my liking. I'd probably torch the place and burn it to the ground if I had to listen to this bullshit all day long.

"Come on. She's down here," Halliday says, rushing down the hallway.

"I thought they wouldn't let you back here?"

"I was allowed to sit with her for half an hour last week. Zen got really agitated when I started talking about school and they kicked me out. That's when her mom told me not to come back for a while."

We reach the very end of the hall, and Hal stops in front of the last door on the right. Sure enough, Zen's name has been drawn onto the whiteboard beside the door, along with a handful of stars and smiley faces that are probably supposed to make this whole experience somehow seem less terrifying.

*Self-harm risk.*
   *Intermittent hysteria.*
   *Catatonic intervals.*
   *Cognitive Behavioral Therapist: Dr. Ramda-Patel (on-call)*
   *100mg Zoloft every 6 hours.*
   *Nembutal as needed.*
   *Next of kin: Angela MacReady 360 545 1865 (MOTHER)*

They tried to put me on antidepressants after my last encounter with Jake. The first few nights in the hospital, I woke up screaming every few hours, gulping like my airways were being closed off all over again, and Dr. Killington recommended Zoloft. I'd agreed without really thinking about it, willing to try anything if it meant that Jake's face would be banished from my mind. The meds made me sluggish and foggy, though. They made me sweat like crazy. They also gave me insomnia instead of helping me sleep. I refused to take them after only a few days. They'd made Mom explain to me that the meds needed time to settle in my system and that usually those side effects dissipated as time went on, but I'd stood my ground. Feeling that way, so detached from the world, wouldn't have been worth it, even if the meds had helped me sleep.

"D'you think they locked her in?" Halliday asks, staring down at the door handle like it's a venomous snake.

"Doubt it. This isn't *prison*." I'm hesitant, though. Maybe they *have* locked her in. If the doctors consider her a self-harm risk—which she definitely is, if she tried to kill herself—then why wouldn't they keep her under lock and key? It'd be bad press for the hospital if she managed to find her way up to the roof and throw herself off it. When I try the handle, however, the door opens easily and swings open. There, on the bed beneath the window, Zen, with her hair cropped unbelievably close to her skull, lies fast asleep under a dusky violet comforter, propped up on thick, fluffy pillows that I know from first-hand experience are not hospital issue. Her mom must have brought stuff from home for her. The posters on the walls; the stylized family photos in the silver frames on the windowsill; the cute stuffed elephants on the nightstand; the stack of books on the desk against the wall: all of these little touches make the room feel less sterile, but also make it seem like Zen might have moved in for the foreseeable future.

The television, mounted to the wall, is turned to some soapy teen drama, the volume down low. Halliday stands by Zen's bedside, her eyes roaming up and down her still, almost lifeless figure, and a stab of jealousy knifes through me.

Hal never visited me in the hospital. She and Zen were friends obviously, but they were never as close and she was with me. The look of pure misery on her face now makes me want to scream at her for being absent when *I* needed her.

"She looks so tired," Halliday whispers. "Maybe we shouldn't wake her."

It's true that the delicate purple shadows beneath Zen's closed eyes make her look exhausted, even in rest. I remember the weeks that followed that night in Mr. Wickman's bathroom. All I did was sleep. I locked myself away in my room as often as I could, refusing to interact with the world. I sank into the oblivion that unconsciousness offered me, and I did everything in my power to stay that way. Sleeping eighteen hours a day, checking out of reality, was far easier than facing it. Depression affects people differently, though. Zen might struggle to pass out at all; without the drugs to keep her under, she might be plagued by insomnia.

"We'll sit and wait a while," I say, moving to stand by the window. I'm on edge. No way I'm going to be able to relax. My own time here aside, I'm dreading the moment when Zen stirs and wakes up. The last time I saw her, she was fighting with Rosa Jimenez, who was sawing hanks of her gorgeous afro off by the handful—settling an account between them that was long overdue. I'd felt sorry for Zen, but I'd also felt vindicated. I'd decided that she deserved the punishment, served up to her in front of the whole school, because of the way she'd treated me at Kacey's behest. Her dogged pursuit of Alex had made me despise her even more than I already had, and it had seemed about time for karma to leap up and bite Zen in the ass. I hadn't known then that she'd suffered the same violence at Jake's hands that I had. When I'd found out what he and his asshole buddies had done to her, my initial response to that information still brings me a deep and harrowing shame. For one awful moment, again, I'd thought...*serves her right.*

She knew what he'd done to me, and she'd shunned me for it.

She'd mocked and harassed me along with the rest of the school and done nothing about the pain they'd inflicted upon me.

She'd stood by while Jake and his friends got off scott-free for assaulting me, leaving them free to do it again to someone else.

For one awful microsecond, when my anger and my hurt had gotten the better of me, it seemed only fair that they *had* ended up hurting someone else, and that someone else had been *her*.

The moment had been so fleeting that it barely even registered as a complete thought, but I knew my mind had gone there. The rank taste of such a vile, unkind thought left a sourness in my mouth that's never really disappeared, and standing here in Zen's room this afternoon, understanding exactly what she went through and how badly it must have scarred her, it feels like she's going to take one look at me and know that I wished this misery upon her in a moment of weakness. No one, not even the lowest, shittiest person in the world, should have to cope with the horrors that haunt her whenever she hears the names *Jacob, Cillian, Sam*.

I stare out of the window, watching the dim glow of the sun fade over the forest on the other side of the hospital parking lot, trying to unravel the mess I find myself tangled up in. When did we stop supporting each other? When did it become more important to bow and scrape to the likes of Jake Weaving than to have each other's backs? When did our friendships lose their value so dramatically that we were willing to overlook heinous, brutal crimes simply to maintain our status in the pointless, short-term eco-system that is high school?

Halliday sits on the edge of the chair by the desk, watching me intently. The weight of her gaze on my back burns through the fabric of my cheer uniform. I know she wants to talk to me, but I'm not interested in a catch-up session. Not right now. My mind's racing, too full, too many thoughts chasing around one another in a maddening dervish; it's taking all my strength just to stand quietly at the window without screaming at the top of my lungs.

A long time passes. I grow numb as I watch the dusk creep over the horizon. All of a sudden, it's fully dark outside and there are pinpricks of flickering white light scattered across the clear night sky. "Beautiful, huh?" Halliday murmurs beside me. God knows when she came and stood beside me, but I get the feeling from the way she's dejectedly resting her forehead against the glass that she's been there a while. "Remember when we were little? We used to try and count them all. We thought, if we closed one eye and worked our way from left to right, we'd be able to keep track."

"*I remember.*" The croaky voice on the other side of the room startles both of us. I must have been really zoned out, because Zen is awake and she's sitting up in the bed, hugging her knees to her chest.

"Kacey used to laugh at us," she says quietly. "She said we were stupid for even trying, but we never listened. We used to sit outside in our sleeping bags in middle of winter and stuff our faces with marshmallows."

Four young girls, still children, huddled together for warmth and laughing up at the sky: those memories seem so distant now that it comes as a shock to even recall them. We were innocent once. We weren't always this selfish, unkind, lost.

"Othello pooped in your hoody," I say, smirking a little. Othello, Zen's old family dog, had come with us on a number of trips up to the cabin. He always looked like he was grinning, tongue lolling out of the side of his head. Usually meant he'd shit somewhere he wasn't supposed to. The hoody shitting incident had been particularly unforgettable, because Zen hadn't noticed the present Othello had deposited in her clothes and had put *on* the hoody in question. It'd taken at least half an hour for the smell to become unbearable, at which point we'd discovered the smeared dog shit caked deep into the back of Zen's tightly curled hair.

She huffs sadly, rubbing her hand over the back of her bare skull, her eyes gazing unfocused out of the window. "Yeah. I guess I don't need to worry about getting shit in my hair anymore, huh? I'm going for a more minimalist look these days."

"I think it looks cool," Halliday offers very seriously, heading over to sit on the edge of Zen's bed. "Edgy, y'know. Very Demi Moore in G.I. Jane."

Zen hides her face behind her legs, so only her eyes are peeking out over the tops of her knees. "Come on. We all know it's more of a Britney, post meltdown look."

"No. No way." Hal shakes her head firmly. "Britney was fucking crazy."

This elicits a hard, derisory bark of laughter from the bald girl in the bed. "In case you haven't noticed, I'm being held captive in a hospital psychiatric ward. That's usually where they put the crazy people, Hal."

Halliday growls, shoving at Zen until she grudgingly shifts over in the bed, making room for her. Once she's settled and she's made herself comfortable, her back bolstered up against the pillows, Halliday puts an arm around Zen's shoulder and forces her to snuggle. Zen—always loud, always confident, always brash and larger than life—looks like a broken and frail little girl tucked into Halliday's side. "There's a difference between crazy and sad. You haven't lost your mind," she whispers.

"Feels like it." Zen's eyes close. She folds her arms into her chest, curling up tighter against Halliday, and for the first time I notice the white dressings wrapped around both of her wrists. I assumed Zen had taken a bunch of pills or something. I imagined herself getting comfortable in bed and relaxing, tossing a bunch of Vicodin down her throat and polishing it all off with a bottle of Malbec. Seemed like a very *Zen* suicide attempt. Slitting your wrists is another level. From the way her dressings are taped, she cut vertically, not horizontally. She meant business. This wasn't a cry for help. She wanted to purge her blood, like letting it out would release all of her pain and the poison inside of her at the same time. *Holy shit...*

Zen takes a shuddering breath and opens her eyes, slowly turning her head to look at me—the first time she's looked at me without open hatred on her face in nearly a year. "What did she have to say to talk you into this? Or was the chance to say *I told you so* too good to pass up?" she asks stiffly.

I have to push around the block in my throat in order to speak; it isn't an easy task. "I only came for the food. Wednesdays are meatloaf night in the cafeteria." Zen pulls a face, smiling a little, but the wariness in her eyes lets me know that my presence here is putting her on edge. I'm right there with her. Suddenly, this all seems too much, and I'm too tired and rundown by everything to stand up a second longer. I slump down into the chair Halliday was occupying before, sighing heavily. "I'm not here to make you feel bad, Zen. I'm not here to make you feel better, either. I'm just...*here*."

That's what I needed, back then. To not be alone. I didn't want the fuss, and the blame, or the pity and the questions. I just wanted to feel like I wasn't tumbling down into the murky black depths of a bottomless pit all by myself. It would have been comforting to know that I could have reached out at any point and somebody would have taken hold of my hand.

There have been many wrongs committed over the past twelve months. Zen's far from free of blame, but it serves no purpose to cling onto that at the moment. If she needs me, then I'll be here for her, because right here, right now, that's the *right* thing to do.

∽

At seven, a nurse busts us in Zen's room and shoos us out before evening visitation hours. She could cause a real stink, since we broke into the ward and flaunted a number of the hospital's other rules in the process, but she does the kind thing and advises us not to do it again. Halliday and I hurry away from the psychiatric ward like there's a fire licking at our heels.

As we cut through the emergency room to make our way out of the hospital, a familiar face halts me in my tracks. The woman smiles broadly at me, weaving her way across the crowded E.R. "Hi, Silver. Great to see you up and on your feet. Tell me you haven't been performing any split lifts, though," she says, eyeing my Sirens uniform. "'Cause that would *not* be smart."

"No, Dr. Romera. I'm starting off slow. Keeping my feet on the ground until I get the all-clear from you guys."

Behind her, a tall guy in a black sweatshirt and black jeans approaches, sliding a cell phone into his back pocket. The very embodiment of intimidation, he looks like he's about tear one of the waiting room chairs out of the ground and start trashing the place. A deep, unhappy frown marks his brow. I'm about to warn Dr. Romera that a dangerous-looking inked-up psychopath is about to lynch her, but then the guy slides his arm around her waist.

Well, fuck me.

How ironic is this?

I took one look at Dr. Romera, and I took one look at the guy, and I decided there wasn't a realm or plane of reality in which they might possibly be together. Which is exactly what other people do when they see me and Alex walking down the street together, holding hands. I look wholesome, the same way Dr. Romera does. Our men both look like they just got spat out of hell because even the halls of the damned couldn't contain them.

Beside me, Halliday squeaks nervously, plucking at my sleeve. "I'll meet you by the car. I need to make a phone call."

*I hope to god she's not calling 911.*

"All good?" the huge guy asks, giving Dr. Romera a smile that borders on frightening.

The smile the doctor returns to him is far sweeter. "Just saying hello to a previous patient. Silver, this is Zeth. He's my…well, he's *mine*," she says laughing awkwardly.

The guy, Zeth, turns his attention to me, nodding just the once, and I almost mimic Halliday and make a run for the door. "Pleased to meet you," he tells me, in a deep, rough-edged baritone.

"Likewise."

He brushes a hand possessively over Dr. Romera's hair, smoothing down an errant strand. "I have something I need to take care of. Be back for you in an hour?"

She nods, and I have to look away from them, embarrassment coursing up and down my spine. The expression on his face is so openly sexual that I nearly burn up from the heat of it. Shit, is this how people feel when they're trapped at close quarters with me and Alex? I seriously hope we're not *this* fucking obvious.

I'm contemplating how best to back away from them without being noticed when I see someone on the other side of the E.R. that makes my pulse spike through the fucking roof. Narrowing my eyes, I glare at the bastard talking to the nurse at the desk with all the intensity of a thousand burning suns. "*Lowell.*"

"What the fuck did you just say?" Zeth isn't looking at Dr. Romera anymore. He's looking at me, and I really wish he wasn't. His eyes are sharper than daggers and glint very dangerously indeed. "Did you just say *Lowell?*"

Dr. Romera's eyes are on the verge of bugging out of her head. She looks at Zeth, then back at me, tightening her hand around the white lab coat she's holding.

I've said something wrong, somehow, and I have no idea how to fix it. "Yeah, um… A detective with the DEA."

Zeth's back straightens. "*Here?*"

Nervously, I point over to the Detective, unsure if I'm doing the right thing. "He questioned me about what happened when I was attacked. He implied that I'd made it up or something. I accused him of taking a bribe from the Weaving family and things got a little ugly."

The rigidity in Zeth's body eases. Even Dr. Romera seems to relax. Zeth's dark eyes bore into the detective, though, still just as cutting as they were a moment ago. "No such thing as a coincidence," he growls. "I'll go talk to him."

"Hey, don't," Dr. Romera pleads. "Go. Run your errands. I'll make sure the guy doesn't cause any problems here. It's all good. Seriously. Please."

I wouldn't have thought a freight train could stop this guy once he gets an idea in his head, but that one word from Dr. Romera—*please*—has him pumping the brakes hard. "Fine. Okay. Let me know if you need me." He nods to me again, giving me an approximation of a smile. Reaching into his pocket, he takes out a wallet and produces a plain card from inside. "That fucker causes you any more trouble, you call this number." I take the card from him, noting that there's no name on it. No address. No business information. Just a Seattle number, printed on the face of the card stock in stark, unassuming characters.

"Uh…thanks?" I'm worn-thin from spending time with Zen, and this weird interaction has officially fried my brain. I need to get the fuck out of here. Bidding the doctor and her *whatever* he is goodbye would be the polite thing to do, but I'm too turned around to come up with the words. I hurry out of the hospital, ignoring the cold wind that slams me right in the face as I step out into the lot, and I don't stop walking until I reach Halliday's car.

"What was that all about?" Hal asks when I throw myself into the passenger seat.

"I have no idea. I really don't *want* to know. Come on. Let's get out of here. I've had enough of this place to last me a goddamn lifetime."

Halliday turns the key in the car's ignition, bringing the vehicle to life. She puts the car in reverse…only she doesn't execute the maneuver. When I look at her, fat, unhappy tears are streaking down her cheeks. "Jesus. What is it, Hal?"

She sniffs, aggressively rubbing at her nose with the back of her hand, like she's mad at herself. "I wasn't supposed to say." Her voice is thick and clogged up with emotion. "You know me, though," she says, smiling brokenly through her tears. "I don't hold up well under pressure. Zen...things are far more complicated than they seem. She's fucking *pregnant*."

My blood runs ice cold in my veins. At the same time, Sam Hawthorne's voice whispers at me from the grave. *"If you wind up pregnant, that'd probably be really bad, don't you think? You'd have to explain that you went whoring around with not one but three guys..."*

Detective Lowell suggested I was thinking too logically when I walked in that pharmacy after Leon Wickman's party and downed a Morning After pill. Sam planted the seed in my head, though. He'd painted a picture, and I'd wanted to avoid that terrible outcome at all costs.

Doesn't look like he had the same little chat with Zen.

## 17

## ALEX

The week passes by and things settle into a weird, off-kilter routine. I pick Silver up in the Camaro, waiting in the driveway for her to come flying out of the house with her guitar case clutched under one arm, her hair flying all over the place in the wind.

On the way to Raleigh, I make a point of discussing what's going on inside my head, even though it's dark, and fucked up, and I don't want to. I'm no good at talking about my fucking feelings like a little bitch in therapy but sharing things with Silver is different. She doesn't judge me for whatever I'm thinking. I don't feel any less *Alex*, the unstoppable, undefeatable rebel of Raleigh High, for revealing the tender, raw parts of myself to her. If anything, I feel like I'm beginning to understand myself better by looking inwards instead of burying everything down and ignoring it the way that I normally would.

Giacomo maintains his distance. I teeter on the brink of forgetting that he's even here, poisoning the Raleigh air with his toxicity, but I don't quite manage to pull it off. A part of me can sense the fucker lurking in my peripherals, just waiting for another opportunity to swoop in and turn my shit upside down again. I vow to myself that I won't let his presence affect me, though. For the most part it works.

After our pseudo fight in the gym, Zander gives me a wide birth, though he does jam the odd Post-It through the vent of my locker, bearing highly creative, colorfully offensive names that I assume are all aimed at me.

*Goat Ball Licker.*

*Gooch Stain.*

*Jizz Monkey.*

Occasionally (and disturbingly), the name-calling is accompanied by a diagram depicting the name in question. At first, I screwed up the Post-Its and tossed them in the trash, making sure Zander could see me do it, but I gave up halfway through Wednesday and started collecting them instead. The inside of my locker door is covered in pink, orange and lime-green sticky notes with doodles on them that would make a sailor blush.

When Friday rolls around, I wait for Silver in the driveway like usual, but when the door swings open…it isn't my girlfriend who comes stomping down the steps. Wearing a thick black puffer jacket over his red and black flannel pajamas, Cameron evidently hasn't spent much time prepping for his day yet. His hair is a fucking nightmare. I cringe as he makes his way around the Camaro, opens up the passenger door, and climbs on in like it's totally fucking normal.

He looks out of the windshield, back up toward the house. When he lifts his mug of coffee to his mouth, the steam from the hot liquid inside fogs up his horn-rimmed glasses. "Asshole," he says into the cup.

"I'm sorry? Did you just call me an asshole?"

He nods. "You bet I did."

I mull this over. "Well…I'd say *you* were the asshole. Where's *my* coffee?"

His stupid puffer jacket rustles when he turns his head to look at me. "It's in the pot. In the kitchen. Inside the house. You remember how that works, right? You actually get out of your car. You walk up the stairs. You knock on the front door. No, wait, y'know what? Fuck it. You don't even need to knock. You already know you don't. We moved past that stage a long fucking time ago, didn't we?"

"Are you mad that I haven't come over to say hi, Cameron?" I ask flatly.

"It's more of a *manners* thing," he counters, his voice weirdly trailing up at the end. Blowing into his coffee, he leans forward and turns the radio on, scrolling through the channels until he finds some CCR. "You and I went on a mission to make another man bleed. You'd think that might earn me the odd hello every once in a while."

"This is cute. You've missed me. It's my charming, sunny outlook, right?" I slouch down into my seat, breathing down the front of my jacket, trying to spread some warmth into my torso. My nipples are so cold, they could cut glass.

Cameron scowls, his lip curling disdainfully. Grumbling, he holds out his mug of coffee. I accept it, taking a deep slug. The liquid inside is scalding hot and bitter as hell, and I almost cry from how beautiful it feels, thawing out my insides. When I go to pass the mug back to Cam, I notice the curly black script that wraps around the white ceramic.

"You'll always be my *Daddy*?" I read out loud.

"Silver gave it to me on Father's Day when she was six. It's my favorite mug."

"Can I keep it?"

"Stop talking, Moretti, before I rip your tongue right out of your head."

He saw my, '*she calls* me *Daddy now,*' joke coming a mile away. "Okay, okay. That might have been a little on the nose."

Cam glowers at me out of the corner of his eye. "My fist'll be on your nose if you're not careful."

"You trudge out here in the snow and the cold just to call me names and threaten me, old man? You need to get out of the house more often."

He takes a sip of coffee and then hands me the mug again. I drink from it and pass it back without comment this time.

"I know you don't wanna talk about Ben," he says quietly. "At least not with me. I wouldn't want to either. But I have this cool architectural software I wanted to show you. Figured you might be interested in it. It pisses all over CAD. You can build these 3D liquid surfaces that make buildings look fucking crazy." He chuckles, sipping again, and I try not to feel like he's just punched me in the fucking gut.

I'm so used to most men being monumental let-downs on the father figure front that I'm always taken aback and surprised by how consistently *good* Cameron Parisi is at this. Sure, he might not be my father—I don't want him to be—but he makes a pretty fucking epic friend.

Before I can change my mind, I lean across the other side of the car and I pull the dumb bastard into a quick, tight sideways hug. I release him right away, returning to my side of the vehicle, clearing my throat as I grab his mug from him again. It's easier to drain its contents than it is to meet his eye. Cam sits in stunned silence for a second before he says, "All right. Well. Cool. I guess we won't talk about that either, then."

"Probably for the best. I finished your coffee." Fidgeting in my seat, I lean on the car horn, willing Silver to hurry the fuck up and come outside so that this tragically uncomfortable moment can be over. "I s'pose I'll come up and grab my own on Monday. Just to be polite."

Cameron smiles, his eyes creasing in the corners, but he does a magnificent job of holding in his laughter. Opening up the passenger door again, he gets out of the car. "Sounds like a plan. See you then."

The door slams with a *thunk*, dislodging a chunk of snow from the Camaro's roof which slides down the windshield, onto the hood. Silver's dad ambles back up to the house, his mug dangling from his index finger. Just before he disappears back inside, he turns and flips me the bird, grinning from ear to ear.

## 18

## ALEX

"Class, this is Detective Lowell. He'd like to ask a few of you a couple of questions. He's assured me it won't take long." At the front of the room, Dr. Harrison looks nervous, like he's secretly been cooking his own meth in the science labs, Heisenberg style, and he's afraid that this DEA Agent might smell the crime on him. The Agent in question—a shortish guy with a wolfish look to him, doesn't look like he works for the Drug Enforcement Agency. From his slicked-back hair, black bomber jacket, and his Nike high tops, he looks like he'd fit right in at a men's clothing store. The kind where hipsters pay through the nose for vintage Gucci fanny packs and secondhand Versace jeans.

I already fucking hate him.

I hate him even more when Silver passes me a slip of paper that reads:

*That's the guy who made out I was lying about Jake.*

My knuckles crack spectacularly when I crush the slip of paper in my fist, eyes narrowed at the greasy punk standing in front of the class.

He radiates smugness in a way that makes me want to take the heel of my fucking Stan Smiths to his face.

"Thanks, man," Detective Lowell says. Dr. Harrison recoils, stepping behind his desk, probably unsure how to proceed since no one has ever called him fucking *'man'* before. He's just not that type of guy.

"Before any of you start freaking out, I wanna make it clear that no one here is in trouble," Lowell announces. He twists a gold ring around his pinkie finger, his eyes skipping over the faces of the students on the front row. "There have been some accusations made against one of your fellow students, and I'm just here to try and get to the bottom of the whole thing. No stress. No drama. This whole thing is gonna be dealt with nice and quick."

*Asshole.*

It isn't until Silver boots me under the desk that I realize I've hissed the word out loud and at least three other people have heard me. Still, I stand by my accusation. This piece of shit is trying to make light of what happened to Silver. By the way he's speaking, you'd think he was here to investigate a missing fucking skateboard.

I don't care who he is, or what government agency he works for. If he causes problems for Silver or even thinks about pulling some dodgy shit to get the charges against Jacob dropped, then I will end this cunt myself.

"First up, I'd like to talk to, uh…Cillian Dupris?"

*This…mother…fucker…right…here.*

"Uh, I'm sorry, Detective Lowell. You may have your paperwork mixed up. Cillian Dupris isn't in this class anymore. He ended up with a severe case of hypothermia last year and unfortunately he's taking a while to recover—"

*Unfortunately? Hah. That fucker got what he deserved.*

"He probably won't be coming back to school for a while yet," Dr. Harrison continues. "My colleagues and I are taking his work to him and helping him out at home whenever we can, though."

Lowell smirks. His gaze passes over the kid sitting on the other side of Silver, but then he lingers on her, pausing a second too long for comfort. It's as though he's taunting her. Teasing her with the name of one of her attackers. If this had happened a month ago, I would have launched myself at this bastard and torn his fucking face off. My temper's cooler now. I know better than to be so reactive, when my ass has only just been released from fucking Stafford Creek. This guy will pay, that goes without saying. I'm just going to be a little smarter about it than declaring all-out warfare in front of thirty other witnesses.

"Nice to know Raleigh's faculty are so accommodating," Lowell says slyly. "I heard about Cillian's injuries. Such a shame that an athlete in his prime was paralyzed like that. I played high school football. I know how hard it'd be to lose a career under such tragic circumstances."

Oh yeah. I can totally see it. This prick on a football team, calling the shots, lording his power over his teammates and terrorizing the other students. I bet this shithead was as bad as Weaving. Maybe he didn't try to rape or kill anyone. Maybe he fucking did. Either way, he's the type of guy to bully and manipulate, and that's precisely what he's doing here, in this classroom. This is all a show, supposed to get under Silver skin. From the way she's nervously tapping the end of her pen against her notebook, I'd day his little performance is working, too.

"Does the DEA sympathize with rapists now, Detective?" I call out.

"Mr. Moretti! We haven't suspended common decency in class just yet. If you have a question, raise your hand." Dr. Harrison's face is purple. Hilarious that he's taken exception to the fact that I spoke without being given permission first, and not because of what I said.

"You people know Cillian hurt Silver. You all fucking do," I growl. "You're all just too chicken shit to hold your hand up and admit you threw your weight behind the wrong fucking team."

No one says a word. Members of the chess club and the theater club alike all look down at their hands. Track stars, trendsetters, and teacher's pets: their heads all hang in shame, looking anywhere and everywhere but at Silver. They know what they did. Every last one of them knows the pain and humiliation they put her through, and not a one of them has the nerve to face her and apologize for it. Motherfuckers.

"Alex, if you don't curb your language, you're going to find yourself on your way to see Principal Darhower. Now, Agent Lowell, is there someone else on your list that you'd like to speak to?"

Agent Lowell's forgotten about Silver; he's turned his gaze onto me, a curious smirk lifting up one side of his mouth. "Ahh yeah. Moretti. The trigger-happy kid. I heard they'd let you out."

"Why would they keep me locked up? I saved someone from being murdered."

His smile spreads. "We don't know that, though, do we? We can only go off your testimony, along with what the girl said." He nods in Silver's direction. "You love this kid, sweetheart? You'd lie for him? Say something that wasn't true to get him out of trouble."

To my left, Silver looks like she wants to jump out of her chair and carve this guy's face up. My fiery, fierce *Argento*. Her cheeks burn bright red. I watch the color spread down her neck, feeling my own ire rising. Dr. Harrison, at last, remembers who he is—the adult in charge of this situation—and speaks up. "I don't think this is an appropriate conversation to be had in front of the rest of the class after all, Agent Lowell. Sorry, but I'm going to have to insist that you talk to any students you wish to question individually. We'll have to call their parents in first as well. I didn't realize what kind of topics you were going to be covering, and without a legal guardian present—"

"It's okay, Doc," Agent Lowell says, cutting him off. "That won't be necessary. I don't think I need to ask those questions after all."

*Shhh, mi amore. Breathe. Nice and deep. If you do something stupid, they'll shut you away again. How will you protect her if you're behind bars?*

Been a while since I've heard my mother's voice in my head. I heed her, even though it requires monumental effort. My jaw cracks. I've been clenching my teeth so hard that my pulse is strobing in my gums. It'd be *so* satisfying to lay my fist into that fucker's face. I can already feel it now—the pop of the connection. The blister and sizzle of pain in my knuckles. The rewarding thump of his body hitting the deck. I savor the thought of it, turning it over in my head again and again.

I'd sit here for hours, happily caught up in the process of mentally beating the shit out this guy, but Silver snatches me out of the violent loop; her hand grasps mine underneath my desk, and the image of Lowell's teeth exploding out of his head blinks out in a flash.

"Don't," she pleads under her breath. "He's not worth it. They're just clutching at straws. Jake's guilty. The cops know that. There's no way they're gonna let some asshole like Lowell stab holes in their case."

Lowell's still smirking like he knows better. He gives Dr. Harrison an arrogant bow of his head before slipping his hands into the pockets of his jeans and slowly sauntering out of the classroom. Forcing my body into submission, I ease the tension out of my shoulders and sit a little straighter in my chair, shaking free of my anger. Gripping onto it so tightly isn't going to make me feel any better. No, I need to save it for later, for a more opportune moment. Lowell needs to let his guard down at some point. There'll come a time when he gets distracted and he forgets to watch his six…and by then I'll have figured out where he lives. I'll have picked the lock on his front door. I'll be waiting for him in the dark.

Smiling, I squeeze Silver's hand, which is still gripping mine tightly under the desk. "No worries, *Argento*. My shit's on lockdown. Nothing to worry about here."

*For now, at least.*

~

The rest of the day, I'm wound so tight I'm on the verge of snapping. Silver's none the wiser, since I make sure to maintain an ease around her that requires an obscene amount of energy, but on the inside I seethe away like that storm on the surface of Jupiter that's been raging for hundreds of years. I fidget in my seat in the last class of the day, anxious to get the fuck out of school.

"*Students of Raleigh High, we're pleased to announce that your votes have been counted and a theme for this year's senior prom has been chosen,*" Karen, Darhower's assistant drones over the P.A. system. "*By popular demand,* James Bond: Spies and Villains *will be our party motif. Principal Darhower would like me to mention that all dresses worn by our female student body should be modest, with no slits above the knee, and shoulders should be covered at all times.*" Karen huffs wearily. "*It's ludicrous that I should even have to read this part out loud, given the year we've already had, but please note, no weapons, real or fake, will be permitted on school property during senior prom. Anyone found in possession of a weapon of any kind,* even as part of a costume, will be immediately expelled from this establishment of higher education without discussion. That is all."

The bell rings once Karen's done speaking. My fellow students are all too excited about the prom theme announcement to realize that they're free. I, on the other hand, am already out the fucking door.

I drop Silver off to teach her first guitar lesson of the evening, and my blood is still churning with irritation over Lowell. I spend three hours on the internet, trying to bully my way into the DEA's personnel files, but hacking is not my forte and so I don't get very far. A simple google search reveals that Agent James Lowell is from Index, an hour east of Seattle. He went to Holcombe High, then on to USC, at which point it becomes difficult to find any information on him at all. The DEA probably don't appreciate their agents splashing their personal lives all over the internet, which explains why he doesn't have a Facebook or an Instagram account.

I make myself some food, all the while boiling away, replaying the bastard's targeted words as I down a beer and try to distract myself in front of the television. It's no use, though. I can't soothe the maelstrom of emotions that are tearing around the inside of my head. I need to get into the DEA personnel database, and to do that I need to engage the services of someone far more proficient at hacking than I am.

I used to know plenty of people at Bellingham who could breach government level cyber security, but here in Raleigh my options are pretty thin on the ground. Thin on the ground meaning one person, and that person being Zander fucking Hawkins. *No chance I'm asking that douchebag for a favor. I'd rather drive all the way over to Bellingham and drag one of my other contacts out of their beds than owe* him *shit.*

I pace the apartment until nine, at which point I realize that I'm gonna go out of my fucking mind unless I do something, so I throw my ass into the Camaro and drive over to Silver's place. I'm a man about it this time. I park in the driveway, right behind Cam's van, and I march right up the porch steps. The door's open, just as Cam said it would be, so I let myself in. I haven't even texted Silver to let her know I'm coming over. If I had, she probably would have given her dad a head's up. Halfway through the door to his office, Cameron looks back at me over his shoulder, one eyebrow curved into a question: *what the hell are you doing here?* His surprise only lasts a second.

"Shoes off," he commands. "Cleaner's just been. No dirty footprints on the hardwood 'til Tuesday at the earliest."

"When d'you turn into such a mom?" I toe off my sneakers, though, kicking them under the mail stand beside Silver's Chucks. "Is that grilled cheese I can smell?"

"It's mine. Make your own."

"Fair enough."

"Harry asked me if you and Silver would play a couple of songs at the diner next week. Don't look at me like that. She told me you could play."

I hit the stairs, flashing Cameron a shit-eating grin over the handrail. "I'll think about it."

"I'll tell him you're in."

"I said I'll think about it."

Cam grumbles under his breath as he heads into his office. I resist the temptation to turn around and follow him in there just to torment him some more. He makes it too damn easy and giving him shit just took my mind off Lowell for a clear ten seconds. My mood's already improved dramatically because of it.

I concocted another plan to relieve my tension on the way over here, though, and I'd much rather follow through on that one. Silver's door is closed when I reach her room; I can hear music playing softly on the other side of it, along with the rhythmic tap, tap, tap of typing on a keyboard. The tapping stops the moment I knock lightly on the wood.

Silver stands in the open doorway a second later, drowning in a huge Raleigh High sweater, her hair tied up into a messy knot on the top of her head.

*Lord have mercy on my soul…*

The temperature outside's bordering on Arctic, but it's plenty warm in here. Her legs are exposed, the tops of her thighs barely covered by the tiny little grey shorts she's wearing, and my dick stirs treacherously in my pants. I hadn't planned on getting hard until I'd convinced her to take a drive with me but looks like my cock has other plans. She's so fucking delectable. I want to strip her down, lift her up, pin her to the wall and drive myself up inside her right here, right now.

"*Alessandro.*" She tries not to smile.

"You expecting someone else?" My voice is a rough growl. My expression—brows drawn together, head lowered, eyes blazing—probably seems a little sinister, but fuck it. I'm feeling a little sinister. I have a number of intentions and none of them are good. I step into Silver, my hands claiming her hips, guiding her back into her room, and her eyes go wide.

"Oh. It's like that, is it?" she whispers, lifting her arms to wind them around my neck. I kick the door closed behind me. "You could have messaged. I would have shaved my legs." She stands up on her tiptoes, trying to plant that delicate, pale pink little mouth of hers on mine, searching for a kiss, but I lean back out of reach.

"I didn't want you to shave your legs. I didn't wanna give you the opportunity to clean yourself. I wanted to taste you just the way you are, Parisi. Your sweat. Your pheromones. Your come. I wanted to bury my face between your fucking legs and savor every last bit of you without you smelling like soap."

Two tiny little dots of pink blossom like shy flowers high on her cheekbones. "What's wrong with smelling like soap?" she asks in a high-pitched voice.

"What's wrong with smelling like yourself?" I walk her backwards, my fingers digging into her skin through the thin fabric of her skimpy little shorts, until the backs of her legs hit the edge of her bed. "I want your sweet, sweet cunt, *dolcezza*. If I wanted a mouthful of perfume, I'd have stayed home and rinsed my mouth out with body lotion."

I trail my fingers over the hollow of her neck, my gaze tripping over the red mark that still lingers there from Jacob's noose. The doctors say it'll fade to nothing eventually, that it'll disappear altogether in time, but for now it's still there—a reminder of the fact that I almost lost her. I pretend like the sight of it doesn't make me angrier than I've ever been in my life. I pretend like I don't see it at all. Silver's oblivious to what I'm thinking, her heart already flying, her pulse visibly jumping in the graceful sweep of her neck. "Jesus, Alex..." she whispers.

"Get changed, or I'm not gonna be welcome in this house," I command.

She feigns ignorance. "What do you mean? What are you talking abo—"

I'm not letting her pull that shit. "You know exactly what I'm talking about. I'm talking about you panting and pleading in my ear, '*Please, Alex, please.*' About you screaming my fucking name. About you digging your fingernails into my ass cheeks as I fuck the living shit out of you, and you begging me to go deeper. About my teeth on your collar bone, and my tongue in your mouth, and all of me fucking *taking* you, and your father trying to knock my fucking teeth out for it. For God's sake, Silver, put some fucking pants on at least. I'm going out of my mind…"

She silences me as quickly and effectively as a bullet to the back of the head. Her hand…ahh *fuck!*…she reaches down between our bodies and places her hand right on top of my erection, which is straining against the zipper of my jeans, squeezing fucking hard.

"Shh. Shh, calm," she murmurs. "I'll be a good girl. I'll give you what you need." Her cheeks are still bright pink, but she seems to have overcome the initial shock of me coming on so strong. Again, she stands on her tiptoes, demanding my mouth, and this time I give it to her. I'll give her *anything* she wants if she continues to squeeze and rub my cock the way she's doing right now. I drive my tongue into her mouth, past her soft, pliant lips, kissing her more roughly than I ever have before, and she lets out a low, needy whisper that sets my blood on fire. Quickly, I grab hold of a fistful of her hair, yanking it back so that the sensitive, pale skin of her neck is exposed. I bite down on that delicate skin hard enough to draw blood. Almost.

"Alex! *Fuck!*" She tears at my belt, frantically trying to get it open…

"Get dressed right fucking now," I snarl.

She looks up at me, eyes the color of a winter stream, sparking with defiance. "Don't…tell me what to do." Before I can say another word, she's unfastened my jeans, pushed them down over my hips, freed my raging hard-on, and she's down on her fucking knees.

"*No.*" I step back, trying to cover myself, forcing myself away from her.

God.

*Fucking...*
*The sight of her like that...*
*On her knees.*
*For me.*

Shame spills through me, hot, dark and slick. It's one of my favorite pastimes, imagining fucking her pretty little mouth, driving myself down her throat to the very hilt of my shaft, until she's fucking choking on me...unable to breathe around me...until I can't take it anymore and I unload in her mouth...

I want it. I want it too fucking much. I can't have her take me into her mouth and not be rough with her, though. I'm barely in control of myself as it is. I'll have no hope of reining myself in if she closes her lips around my hard-on, and that makes me feel like a goddamn monster.

After the way Weaving, Sam and Cillian treated her, Silver deserves to be treated like a fucking queen. She doesn't need my filthy fantasies sullying her. Trouble is, Silver has a mind of her own and she doesn't seem like she's going to give up on the idea of blowing me too easily.

I must be the only guy in high school to try and *stop* a girl from shoving his dick in her mouth. Silver shoots a baleful look up at me, grabbing me by the leg of my jeans, which is kind of hilarious. "Why?" she demands. "I've given you blow jobs before."

"It may sound hard to believe, but I'm actually trying to be the good guy here. You don't need to do anything for me. I just wan—"

"Hell no!" she scoffs. "*You* don't get to bust in here turn me on in the space of five seconds flat, and then limit what I can and can't do because you think you're somehow doing me a favor. Has it ever occurred to you that the thought of going down on you makes me wet, Alessandro Moretti? That I think about it sometimes, feeling you getting harder and harder in my mouth, shaking because you need to come so bad, and it makes me want to storm into *your* apartment and demand that you fuck me immediately?"

*Fuuuck.* She fantasizes about blowing me? I fantasize about eating her pussy, so that doesn't come as such a huge shock. Before Ben died, we were dancing around Silver's desire to test the boundaries of our sex life. She wasn't shy about going after what she wanted, then, and now is no different. Hearing her say this out loud is too fucking much, though. I swear to god, if I don't have her naked really fucking soon, I won't be held accountable for my actions. She's still on her knees, still holding onto my jeans like she's determined to get her way no matter fucking what.

A primal desire boils in the pit of my stomach, ordering me to take action. Unlike the anger I've been wrestling to get out from underneath all day, there's no getting out from underneath this. Because it *is* me. I could sooner grow a third arm than overcome this churning need.

Stooping down with a deliberate slowness, I take hold of her by the arms, gently but firmly bringing her to her feet. "Pants, Parisi. I'm not fucking joking. Don't say another word. I'm fucking begging you. Put on some pants and let's go."

∼

Silver

I assume he's going to drive us back to his place but Alex burns past the hardware store, gripping the steering wheel, staring intensely out of the windshield, his body locked up and rigid, barely even breathing as he coerces the Camaro through turn after turn into the night. The engine screams as he flattens the gas pedal to the floor, and I sit as still as can be in the passenger seat, trying to process the want that's burning inside me. I've never felt anything like it before.

I've needed Alex's touch plenty of times, but this kind of searing heat between us is all new. We haven't had sex since before we found out about Ben. Since then, it's as though there's been an unspoken agreement between us. Alex has needed space to recover from his grief, and I've agreed to give it to him. That space is eating us alive now, though. The air between us is so charged with sexual tension that I'm worried one of us will say something, accidentally touch one another, and the whole damn car will go up in flames.

Alex must feel the same way; his eyes remain fixed on the road ahead, the muscles in his arms flexing and unflexing over and over again as he drives. Twenty minutes after we leave the Raleigh town limits, I realize where he's taking me: to the place where we first kissed. To the place where we first had sex. *My grandfather's cabin.*

It's perfect.

Friday night, no responsibilities over the weekend, no appointments to attend to…but then, my curiosity forces me to break the silence. "What about the store? Don't you have shifts this weekend?"

He shakes his head stiffly, as if even doing that too enthusiastically might send him hurtling down the face of some great cliff. "Henry doesn't need me," he says through his teeth.

By the time he pulls down the long driveway that leads toward our destination, the pressure between us has built to a fever pitch of insanity. He doesn't even kill the engine when he screeches to a halt in front of the cabin. He kicks open the driver's side door, and then he's charging around the front of the vehicle, briefly illuminated by the twin pillars of white light cast off by the headlights that spear out into the night across Lake Cushman.

I fumble to open my door, but Alex is already there. He almost tears the damn thing off its hinges as he wrenches it open. Before I can even take a startled breath, he leans into the car and lifts me out of it, carrying me through the frosty grass that's grown long front of the cabin.

"Alex. God, Alex…"

He sets me down at the top of the porch steps, tearing and ripping at my clothes. He's an animal possessed and I'm no better. I'm trembling from head to toe as I grab hold of the bottom of his hoody and pull it up over his head. His t-shirt goes with it, leaving Alex's torso naked in the cold night air, but he doesn't complain. I don't think he even registers the fact. There's enough heat between us, sizzling and crackling like a hungry open flame, that I don't flinch when he rids me of my sweater and the camisole I'm wearing beneath it.

Three feet away, the cabin's front door stands easily within reach, but it might as well be a mile away. We've already waited too long as it is. Another minute to get inside, another second even…it's just not possible. Alex lets out a low, guttural growl as he dips down and grabs my winter boots, tearing them from my feet. He rips my socks off, hurling them away one at a time, leaving me to stand barefoot on the icy wooden deck that wraps around the building.

The piercing cold robs me of my breath. Hands working of their own accord, I unfasten the belt at Alex's waist for the second time in the space of an hour, ripping the leather from the loops of his jeans. Alex helps, shoving his pants down, kicking his way out of them. His dark eyes stay fixed on me, never leaving mine for a moment.

I strip out of my own sweatpants—the pants he insisted I put on back at the house—and then I step out of my panties, leaving them in a puddle of black lace on the deck by my feet. My bra is the last item of clothing to go. Fully naked and painfully erect, Alex watches me with a dazed adoration on his face as I tease the straps of my bra down over my shoulders, reaching behind my back to unfasten the hook.

He sucks in a sharp, agonized breath when I let my underwear fall to the ground and my breasts spring free. We've been frantic for the last thirty seconds, lost to a fierce, carnal insanity, but now we both fall still, looking at each other, eyes roving over hip and shoulder, stomach and thigh. Fog plumes on Alex's breath as he swallows, taking a tentative step toward me. His huge frame towers over me, dwarfing me in a way that makes me feel incredibly small.

His dark hair hangs in his face, hiding his eyes. He brushes it out of the way with the sweep of a hand, and the simple gesture makes my heart swell in my chest like never before. I love him so fucking much, every small, beautiful, broken, incredible part of him, and it's all too, too much.

The black ink that creeps up his arms, snaking its way around the collar of his throat in a tangle of rose and thorn, looks like it's shifting in the moonlight that cuts through the clouds overhead, painting his torso silver.

It'd be easy to say that he's the most amazing thing I've ever seen and leave it at that, but such a simple description wouldn't do him justice. He isn't just magnificent. He's beyond words. Beyond imagination. Beyond dreaming. If I live to be a hundred, I'll never be able to fully explain just how spectacular Alessandro Moretti is naked. He stands tall and proud, unapologetic of the fact that his dick is hard and brushing up against his stomach in a way that draws the eye down…

"*Argento*," he whispers, sounding almost reproachful. He reaches up and trails his fingers lightly over the side of my face. "I haven't been taking care of you, have I? I've been so wrapped up in all of my own shit, and all that time you've been hungry." He doesn't pose it as a question. He knows it's true, just as well as I do. He can read it on me, the need vibrating off my skin like an electrical charge.

On the other side of the lake, a bird calls, its cry cutting the silent night air apart. The sound reminds us both of us that we're standing outside, naked as the day we were born, in the middle of winter. "I want you here," Alex rumbles, his voice rough as whiskey and smoke. "I want you under the stars, with the moon on our backs and the cold air in our lungs."

I take him by the hand and lead him back down the porch steps, heading for the jetty that thrusts out onto the lake. Stones and sharp shards of wood bite at the undersides of my feet, but it doesn't take long to cross the clearing. Then the jetty's smooth, frozen planks of wood replace the rough ground, making it much easier to walk.

Halfway down the narrow pier, Alex takes hold of me from behind, his hands on my hips, turning me around. "You're a witch, aren't you? You're gonna steal my soul and leave me to drown, love-drunk, in the cold black water."

I close my eyes, smiling. "Ha. So, you love me, then?"

Alex's lips brush lightly against mine, a bristling heat passing between us despite how gentle he is. "You know I do," he murmurs against my mouth. "How could I not? You're quicksand. The more I struggle against you, the deeper I sink."

His chest brushes up against my nipples and a delicious shiver runs through my body. Strange that the ice and the frozen breeze feel like nothing to me, and yet the warmth of Alex's breath skating over my skin has me breaking out in goose bumps. God, I want him so fucking badly. The insides of my thighs are slick, my pussy aching for him to reach between my legs and touch…

Finally, I'm done waiting. I've had *enough*. I can't take it anymore. "I did what you asked, Alex. I got dressed. Bolted out of the house without even telling Dad when I was gonna be back. I came all the way out to the cabin with you. It's time I took charge for a while, and you…"

"Me?" he asks, raising his eyebrows.

"You aren't going to say a word. You're going to lie on your back,"—I reach out for him in a bold move and take hold of him by the dick—"and you're going to stay still, and you're going to let me do whatever the hell I want."

Eyes feverishly bright, mouth parted a little from the attention I'm currently showing his cock, as I firmly pump my hand up and down the length of his shaft, he treats me to a scandalous smile. I'm sure I'm the only person in the world who's ever seen him smile properly, like he actually means it. "And what makes you think I'd sign off on that, *Argento?*"

"Well." I squeeze him tight, enjoying the way he hisses out a curse word through his teeth. "You just said it yourself. You love me. You'll do anything to make me happy, won't you?"

He tips his head back, groaning, and the sound that comes out of him is a mixture of pure ecstasy and pure misery. "I'm doomed."

"You are." No point in disagreeing with him when he's right. "But so am I. You're my Achilles Heel, and I'm your kryptonite. Lucky for us, our weaknesses are also our strengths. Now do it, Moretti. Lie down, before I squeeze *these*." I have him by the balls. Literally.

"Whoa now." He takes hold of me by the wrist, but he doesn't pull my hand away. A playful, crooked smile tugs at his mouth. "I'll obey you always. I'm yours to command. Better be careful if you ever want kids out of me down the road, though. I think you'll find that part of my anatomy is crucial to the baby making process."

He's playing around. He nearly keeled over when I told him about Zen's current state. But hearing him talk about kids, our kids, later on, when we're both ready...it makes me dizzy in an intoxicating, very pleasing way.

Squeezing slightly harder, pressing the tips of my fingernails into his skin, I arch a cool eyebrow at Alex, giving him an open-mouthed smile. "Down," I order. "Before I decide not to fuck you at all."

He drops to his knees like he's just been downed by an arrow. He looks up at me, exposing his throat, baring himself to me. The night sky is clear and full of stars; I can see them reflected in his eyes as his gaze meets mine, and the very sight of him takes my breath away. Slowly, he reclines, sinking onto his elbows first before settling onto his back. The muscles in his throat work as he watches me step toward him. Steeling myself, I take a deep breath, refusing to be embarrassed by how completely and utterly naked I am right now.

It's tempting to cover myself up and hide from Alex's intense gaze, but that's not how we operate. We've never operated that way. No matter how vulnerable we make each other feel, emotionally or physically, we've never hidden from each other, and it isn't time to start doing so now. Stepping over him, I take a moment to enjoy the sight of him, tattooed and fucking magnificent, laying prone beneath me.

"If you're wondering if it'd be impolite to sit on my face," Alex rumbles, "then the answer's no. It would not. In fact, you'd make me a very ha—"

"Stop talking." The words belong to someone else. Someone far braver than me. I don't know what possessed me to make such a forceful command, but Alex immediately obeys, closing his mouth. He breathes out hard down his nose, making his nostrils flare, his hands twitching at his sides. He wants to touch me. The way his fingers keep curling inward makes that perfectly clear. I won't let him yet, though. I want to torture him a little first.

I touch my own fingers to my stomach, lightly trailing them over my skin, moving them down, down, down. Alex's eyes widen as he watches me…

"Fuck, *dolcezza*…"

"*Shhh*." I try not to gasp when I slide my hand between my legs, parting the folds of my pussy so that he can see all of me. I'm plenty wet and plenty ready. The moment I skate the tip of my middle finger over my clit, a violent shiver slams into me, making my whole body lock up. "*Fuck!*"

Alex huffs, but he doesn't say anything. He's learned his lesson. He knows I won't be happy if he speaks again, and so he clenches his jaw tight, staring at the point between my legs where I'm slowly moving my hand, rubbing myself. I feel powerful, looking down at him lying on the frozen boards beneath me. Alex is a fucking hurricane, strong and wild at heart, and somehow he's permitted me to leash him. He could break free of my will at any moment. But he won't. I have hold of him by the *soul* now, and the knowledge that he trusts me that deeply is me a heady, heady thing.

A wave of pleasure rockets through me as I slide my finger back, dipping it inside myself, and Alex growls dangerously through his teeth. He moves his hand, not toward his rock-solid cock, but over the edge of the dock. He lets it fall over the side, disturbing the thin sheet of ice that's formed on top of the black water. Wincing against the cold, he keeps his hand there, submerged up to his wrist, his dark eyes burning holes into my naked skin.

I catch my bottom lip in between my teeth, wrestling to even out my breath before I speak. "Take your hand out of the water. You're going to freeze," I pant.

Alex's eyes shine defiantly. "I need the pain," he grinds out. "I'll come before you even touch me without it."

Another tremor of pleasure chases up my back, this time sheer satisfaction that I'd have this kind of effect on him. I let him keep his hand in the water. For now. Slowly, I sink down so that I'm kneeling over him, straddling his hips. With my free hand, I cup my own breast, kneading my flesh, rolling my nipple between my fingers, making myself whimper a little at the brief jolt of pain that relays between my tits, then down to my swollen clit. Alex growls, screwing his eyes shut, angling his head back. This is pure torture for him…and he's enjoying every second of it.

His eyes snap open when I lower myself down another few inches, planting myself directly on top of his erection. He lifts his head and shoulders away from the deck, staring down the length of his body, at the point where my pussy is pressing down on his rigid dick. I roll my hips, grinding myself forward against him, now cupping both breasts with both hands, and Alex falls back against the deck again, tensing all over.

"*Fuuuuuuuck*," he groans breathlessly.

Instead of chastising him, I repeat the motion, rolling my hips back and then forward again, enjoying how easily our bodies slide against each other. The head of his cock rubs hard against my clit, and I let out a hoarse moan of my own. The tendons in Alex's neck and arms stand proud as I rock again and again, pushing both him and me closer to madness. I can already feel it, blurring my senses and robbing me of all thought. My brain is aware of nothing but the sensation of Alex's taut, hot body beneath mine. He's panting just as heavily as me by the time I grab him by the wrist and pull his hand out of the water, placing his palm against my hip.

"Pull me down on you," I tell him. "Feel how wet I am."

As if the restraints that were holding him down have been broken, Alex snarls, raising his other hand, placing that on my hip, too. His fingers gouge into my chilled skin and he follows my order, pulling me down against him as hard as he can. The pressure and the sensation when he angles *his* hips up, thrusting his cock forward and up against my pussy, is too much to handle. I cry out, arching my back, finding myself suddenly looking up at the stars, and a bright snap of pain lashes between my nipples.

"Shit!"

Alex has risen up, his core supporting his weight, and my left nipple is in his mouth. I see the white flash of his teeth pressing down on the small, tight bud of flesh, and I can tell he's going to bite down again.

I'm prepared for it this time. I grind myself forward, winding my fingers into his hair, driving him down onto my breast as electric, delicious, addicting agony zips up and down my body, pooling in the pit of my belly.

He isn't supposed to be taking charge yet, I was going to make him wait, but the feel of his erection butting up against my pussy has me weak and boneless, so ready to cave and give myself over to him, and I can't help it.

"Do it. Please, Alex. Oh my god, *please*."

Just like in the hospital when Dr. Romera used that word on her terrifying boyfriend, it has an immediate effect on the man I'm riding now. Alex curses, his hot breath skating over my bare chest, and the next thing I know, I'm on my back. The cold of the icy wood underneath me is shocking for a moment, but then Alex is driving himself up inside me, and suddenly the cold doesn't matter anymore.

He fills me to breaking point. He stretches me, and he molds me to him, and then he fills me up some more. I claw at his back, clinging onto him like my life depends on it, and the world begins to spin too fast.

With every deep, possessive thrust of his cock, Alex squeezes me tighter, on the brink of crushing me. I lean into it, letting myself go. It feels too good to make him stop. For a moment, I exist only on the air that Alex allows to slip into my lungs.

"Fuck, Silver. Fuck!" He sinks himself into me over and over again. I wrap my thighs around his waist, desperately begging for more. "You should have put all of me in the water, *Argento*," he growls into my ear. "No way I can stop this now. Come for me. Come hard so I feel it."

I don't need to be told. He's grown so hard inside me that it *is* unavoidable now. I let myself stumble and fall into my orgasm, gulping at the freezing air, unable to even whimper as a wildfire of pleasure rips through my body. Alex leans into me, pressing his forehead against mine, roaring as he climaxes along with me.

Despite the bitter cold, the heat between us has doused us both in sweat. We lay panting, blissfully tangled up in each other's limbs for a moment, while we both try to catch our breath.

"You're dangerous to my health, Silver Georgina Parisi," Alex whispers against my throat. "You're enough to make a man laugh as he gladly dies of pneumonia."

"Are you dying?" I smile into the lush thickness of his hair.

"Any second now," he mumbles.

"We'd better get you inside, then."

It's *him* that carries *me* inside the cabin, though. He's the one who gets a fire going while I shiver in the living room, bundled up in the thickest throw he could find. I call Dad from the cabin's ancient Bakelite phone to let him know we're going to be spending the weekend at the cabin. And once we're warm, the frigid chill thawed from our bones, I snuggle into Alex's side and I give him the news that I've been stewing on ever since this morning, when Dad placed my mail in front of me at the breakfast table.

"Alex?"

"Mmm?" He sounds half-drunk and half-asleep from the heat.

I try not to panic as I rush the words out. "I got a final acceptance letter. They've offered me a place at Dartmouth."

## 19

## ALEX

I never dared to have dreams when I lived with Gary. Life hadn't been particularly generous with me and seemed content to continue kicking me in the balls every chance it got, so what was the point in cultivating hopes for the future? A career? A family? A life in which I didn't wake up every day, waiting for the next big thing that was going to take my feet out from underneath me? Imagining these things felt like asking for trouble. Trouble already knew where I lived and came knocking on the regular, so why risk inviting it in with things like goals and ambition?

The only thing I ever wanted was Ben. Nothing was more important to me than making a home for him, where he walked through the door after being at school all day and his flesh and blood would be there, waiting for him. I wanted to show him how to grow into manhood. I wanted to be a good role model to him. I wanted us to stick together, for him to know that at least *I* loved him, even if our mother opted out on life and our father opted out on *us*. I dared to dream *that* kind of a life…and in a screeching of tires and a crunching of metal, that dream was stolen, snatched away forever.

I'd take back all of the shit I gave Jackie if it meant that my brother hadn't died in that stupid fucking people carrier. I'd rescind any claim I had over Ben. Fuck, I'd agree to never even fucking speak to him again if it meant that he was alive, and safe, and well away from Raleigh. Away from *me*. Instead, my little brother's lying in a grave, cold and alone, and I keep trying to conjure up a way to fix it, to bring him back from the dead, but all I seem to summon are ghosts.

I lost my mother.

I lost my brother.

And now I know how dangerous it is to dream.

Silver wriggles back in her sleep, snuggling into my body, the soft sounds of her slow, even breathing punctuating the deafening silence of the cabin, and I lie very still, trying to wrap my head around the future she proposed in front of the fire earlier this evening.

A life at college together. A small house with a white fence and a little yard for Nipper. A room that gets the afternoon light, filled with stacks of sheet music, a worn old upright piano by the window, and photos of us on the walls. A small kitchen, where we learn how to feed ourselves without setting fire to the pots and pans. A bedroom that we share together, where we fall asleep tangled up in each other's bodies every night, no matter what.

It sounds peaceful.

It sounds magical.

It sounds like a fucking *dream*...and that scares the living shit out of me.

None of the tragic events that I've endured since I was born came about because my existence is ill-fated. My mother was a troubled woman, plagued by depression and manic swings that made her life unbearable. Giacomo left because he was weak. Ben died...

...*fuck*...

I screw my eyes shut tight against the darkness, allowing the pain that comes crashing down on me a moment to settle. The teeth of Ben's loss are still so sharp, they're probably never going to dull. They're impossible to avoid, though. They bite down hard and deep. All I can do is brace myself and wait for the breathlessness they cause to pass.

Ben died because a deer leapt out in front of the car when Jackie was driving, and there was no time for her to react.

There were reasons for these tragedies. I'm the common factor in all of these events, though, which makes it difficult to convince myself that I'm not the reason why everything keeps falling apart, over and over again. And when those thoughts creep in, poisoning my mind like they are tonight, refusing to let me sleep, fear gets the better of me.

If I dream of a beautiful life with Silver, I'm gonna fucking jinx it. There won't be a little house with a music room for us. There won't be little yard for Nipper. Silver will go away, just like everyone else has gone away…and I'll be left all alone.

*She loves you, Alex. She isn't going anywhere. She's here, you fucking moron. She's* here.

The words I repeat in my head like a prayer should reassure me, but they don't. Because there's another voice, not quite as loud but far more insidious, whispering inside my ear at the same time.

*Yeah. Yeah, she is. But for how fucking long?*

∼

"Whoa, man. What the fuck is that? Didn't know they made jock straps in extra small."

Monday morning brings with it a hail of fresh snow and yet another indoor practice session for the newly named Raleigh Rebels. I'm half-dressed and glowering at the inside of my locker, wondering why the fuck I'm still doing this to myself, when Zander appears out of the showers, towel wrapped around his waist, scrubbing a smaller towel through his wet hair. He lunges forward, grinning like a moron, attempting to flick my boxed-up junk, but I give him a look so evil that even he can't mistake the warning: *Do it. Go on try. I will fucking kill* you.

"Whoa now, Susan!" He dances back a couple of steps, putting himself out of reach. "No need for any of that. Someone got out of the wrong side of the bed this morning."

"Fuck off, Hawk. I'm not in the mood."

"Yeah." He props himself up against the lockers, crossing his arms over his chest, his eyes scanning me from head to toe. "Yeah, I can see that," he muses. "Your pretty girlfriend not putting out or something?"

I slam my locker door, growling low in my throat. "Don't you fucking *dare.*"

"Okay, okay, man. Fuck. Calm yourself."

"Calm isn't on the agenda today." Grabbing my gear, I turn away, showing Zander my back—something he explicitly taught me not to do in juvie. Showing someone your back in an environment like that is way worse than shoving your middle finger in their face. It means you don't respect them, don't consider them a threat. And while Zander is most definitely a threat, what with his close ties to Giacomo, I sure as fuck don't respect the bastard. I set my shoulder pads down on the bench, flaring my nostrils as I wrestle the brand-new jersey Coach Foley tossed at me when I entered the change rooms over the hard plast—

*Hold up.*

*What the fuck is that?*

"You're still pissed about your dad. And I get it, Alex. I should have fucking told you that I knew him—"

I bend at the waist, squinting at the jersey material that's half stretched over my pads, as if narrowing my eyes at it is somehow going to make the small embroidered patch on the right-hand shoulder disappear.

"You need to stop being such an asshole, Alex. When are you gonna let bygones be bygones?"

"You still working for Monty?" I ask distractedly.

"Wouldn't be here if I wasn't," he replies.

"You still mixed up with the Dreadnaughts?"

"What do *you* think?"

"Then you're still mixed up with Giacomo. I'm not interested being friends with my father's fucking spy." I yank the football jersey off of my shoulder pads and shove past Zander, forcing a path through the other guys who are getting ready for practice, heading for Coach Foley's office.

"You don't just walk away from the Dreadnaughts, asshole!" Zander calls after me. "Don't be such a shit, Alex!"

I knock on Coach Foley's door, waiting a second before pushing it open. Inside the small office, still crowded with Coach Quentin's trophies, framed awards and weird bobblehead knick knacks, Coach Foley sits behind the desk, scribbling furiously onto a game-play whiteboard. She looks up at me and rolls her eyes dramatically. "Lord. Don't start. Just say thank you and move on."

"Thank you? *Thank you?*" I wave the jersey in the air, scowling at the *'captain'* patch that's stitched onto the fucking sleeve. "I'm not team captain. I'm barely on the damn team."

Coach Foley groans, slowly capping her whiteboard marker and setting it down on the desk. She leans back in her chair, her expression displeased. "You *are* captain, Moretti. I made you captain."

"You can't do that. I didn't apply for it. None of the other guys voted me in—"

"*Ha!* Hah hah hah!" Coach Foley's fake laughter is loaded with sarcasm. "Oh, poor kid. You seem to be under the illusion that we have some sort of high school football democracy going on here. There is no application process. The shit-for-brains douche bags out there in that locker room don't get a goddamn *vote*. I decide what the team's called. I decide who captains the team. I decide when you morons eat, shit, sleep and fart. Now go finish getting ready. If you boys aren't in the gym in the next five minutes, I'm going to adjust the thermostat and make you all shower in cold water." She picks her marker back up and returns to her game plays.

I don't budge. Coach Foley sighs loudly when I take a step toward her desk, dropping the shirt in front of her. "You can't just force this on me. I don't have the time. Plus, in case you missed it, I really don't give a shit about this team. You're better off picking someone else."

"You *will* give a shit about the team," Foley fires back. "You'll care very much when we start winning games and people notice you. You're late to the game, Alex. Literally. Any player here worth their salt has been made a scholarship offer. It's February. Your high school career ends in approximately five months. A good football player is gonna have a hard time finding a place at a college at this late stage. You're gonna have to be excellent if you want a scout to notice you now."

"*What?* What makes you think I want a football scholarship?"

Coach Foley spreads her fingers, showing me her palms. She's acting as if she's exasperated, but shit. She doesn't get to be annoyed. *I'm* the one who's annoyed. "Your grades are amazing, kid. Don't get me wrong. Somehow, amidst the knee-deep horse shit you've been wading through since you enrolled at this school, you've come out of the other side academically smelling of roses. But your criminal record? That stinks like dog shit. Honestly, I couldn't quite believe half the crap in your file when I flicked through it the other day. Your grades alone aren't gonna be enough to secure you a place at college, and I think it'd be a shame to waste—"

I shake my head, trying in vain to understand what the hell is going on here. "Aren't you, like, a *substitute*?"

Coach Foley smiles. "I sure am. See. Proof! You *are* one of the bright ones."

"You don't need to waste your energy on me, okay. I'm sure you have other things to worry about. I've got my shit handled."

"That why you were fighting with the other new kid last practice?" she asks. "Because you've got your shit handled?"

"I was fighting with him because he's *annoying*." Goddamnit. I shouldn't have to tell her this. If she's so fucking observant, then she must have noticed that all by herself.

The woman behind the desk laughs softly under her breath. "I'm not trying to interfere in your life, Alex. But it's my job to help you kids out when I can, right?"

"No. It's your job to teach us how to play football."

Coach Foley beams at me, rocking back in her chair. "Excellent. That's exactly what I'm doing. You're team captain until I say otherwise. Now, if you don't mind, I have some things to take care of before we kick things off, and we're both running out of time."

"I don't think you're hearing me—"

"I don't think you're hearing *me*, Mr. Moretti. This is non-negotiable. Principal Darhower wants you booted from Raleigh. You're an annoying reminder that Jim's star pupil turned out to be an ugly shit stain on the school's shining reputation. If he could get rid of Silver, don't think for a second he wouldn't. But *she's* a model student. Now people know what she's been through, folk in this town would revolt if she was suddenly no longer welcome here. Darhower's hands are tied. You, however…you're an unknown entity, covered in tattoos, and you *shot* someone for Christ's sake."

"Jake! I shot Jake because he was about to *hang*—"

"You think any of that shit matters? Really? You could have shot

Pol fucking Pot and it wouldn't make a blind bit of difference. One foot wrong and your days at Raleigh High come to an abrupt end. That's just how it is. So, you get to be captain of the Rebels, and you get to shine on the field and in the classroom, and you get to make me look good by doing it, with a smile on that handsome face of yours. Whether you meant to or not, you ousted the last king of Raleigh High. Now you've gotta fill his shoes, or you've got to start thinking about all of the amazing jobs you'll be eligible for once you've dropped out and gotten a fucking GED instead of graduating. *Now go and put that uniform on.*"

It feels like I'm walking to the gallows when I enter the gym. Twenty-eight pairs of eyes bore into me, some of them resentful, some of them confused, some of them outright incredulous. I wanted to keep myself occupied when I decided to rejoin the team. Keeping my mind busy meant less time for me to brood and stew over Ben. I wasn't looking for this kind of responsibility, though. Most of the team worshipped Jake like he was a god amongst men. They rallied around him, spending the night outside the hospital, boycotting his arrest after he tried to kill Silver. I put a bullet in their glorious leader, and not a single one of them looks impressed by the fact that I've now stolen his role as team captain.

Well, actually that's not true. *One* player seems amused by this bizarre turn of events.

"Hope you've got health insurance, bro," Zander says, slapping me roughly on the back. "I'm gonna say the odds of you making it out of this practice session alive are pretty low."

Zander's been really, really fucking wrong in the past. He was just about as wrong as he could be when he made the call not to tell me about his connection to my father. This time, though, it kinda looks like he might be right.

He grins his frustrating grin at me through the grill of his helmet. "After you've been such an outrageous prick, I should let the wolves have at you, Moretti. Don't sweat it, though. I got your back."

## 20

## SILVER

"Oh my god! What happened to your face?"

The library's closed at lunch for some kind of faculty meeting, so I've reluctantly had to settle on eating in the cafeteria. I nearly topple off my chair when I spot Alex walking across the loud cafeteria with a loaded tray in his hand and a vivid, massive purple bruise developing on his jaw.

He grimaces as he sets down his tray on the table, seating himself opposite me. Before he can explain how he ended up with such a huge welt on the side of his face, Zander arrives dressed in a ridiculous preppy sweater and chinos, brandishing a tray of his own. He sets it down next to Alex's, and my jaw drops even lower when I see the black eye and the split lip *he's* sporting. "The football team tried to dethrone their new ruler," he says, his tone way too chipper given that his lower lip is still oozing blood. "They don't seem to like him for some reason," he adds. "God knows why."

I drop my plastic fork, slumping back into my chair. Alex's expression confirms Zander's outlandish comment—yes, he really has been made captain of the football team. "You've *got* to be kidding me."

"Coach Foley is insane." Alex glares down at the enormous mountain of food in front of him. "She said it was the only way I was getting accepted into college. Clearly, she wants me dead, though."

Wow.

Just…*wow*.

"Hey, Silver. Alex. New guy, whoever you are. Mind if I sit with you?" Suddenly Halliday's standing next to me, clasping a brown paper bag in her hands, looking a little anxious as she eyes the open space on the bench next to me. A moment of uncomfortable silence hangs in the air where I just stare up at her, so stunned that my brain ceases to function. When that moment becomes too uncomfortable to bear, I snap out of my daze and shunt over on the bench, making room for her. "Oh. Uhhh. Sure. Yeah. Why not."

She exhales, her shoulders relaxing, and I realize that she was nervous. She thought I was going to say no. "Cool. Thanks." She sits, unwrapping her lunch, and Alex's dark gaze punches holes in the side of her face the entire time.

I kick him under the table. When he looks at me, my meaningful stare passes along a stern message: *Hey. Be nice.*

"It's okay. You don't need to rein him in," Halliday says quietly.

Damn it. I didn't think I was being that obvious.

"I was…fucking *horrible* to you, Silver." Halliday struggles with the words. Her guilt feels like a fifth member of the group, looming over our table, demanding all of the space and leaving none for the rest of us. "I was a bad person. I know that. Things should never have gone the way they did. Kacey was…well, she was Kacey. And I was so selfish. I let myself fear her more than I loved you, and that was…that was…" Her eyes are shining, and the end of her nose has gone pink. I know from experience that it only ever does that when she's about to cry.

She didn't apologize for the way she treated me when she asked if I would visit Zen at the hospital with her. I didn't expect her to, somehow. When she spins to face me, remorse all over her face, her hands fiddling fretfully with the tassel on the zip of her purse, and she says the words—

"I'm so sorry, Silver. I know saying sorry's never gonna be enough to make up for the way I was…but I *am*, okay. I'm really sorry. And I missed you. I missed my friend. I don't deserve it, but I hope we'll be able to be friends again. Proper friends. The way we should have been before."

—I find that I can't bear the sincerity or the cautious hope flickering in her eyes. I want to run away from it all as fast as humanly possible and pretend that it isn't even happening. "It's okay. It's fine, Hal. You don't need to apologize."

"Like hell she doesn't," Alex growls, stabbing his fork in her direction. "She loved you. She trusted you, and you let every single person in this school believe she lied about being raped, when you knew for a fact that it was true. You could have told the truth. At least some of the assholes in this school might have given her story credence if you'd come forward and told Darhower what you saw that night."

A pit of agony burns in the center of my chest, spreading out, out, out, making it hard to breathe. I love Alex for what he's doing; he's standing up for me when no one else would, and I could hug him for it. But I also really, really need him to stop. I can't do this now. I can't do this here. "Alex—"

"No, he's right," Halliday says, nodding firmly. "I know what I did was worse than Zen and Melody. I found you covered in blood. I saw the state you were in. My statement could have made a difference, but I was a coward. It's a little late, but I'm figuring out how to not be a coward now. High school makes us into the worst versions of ourselves, but I'm trying to do better."

"I say you forgive her," Zander says cheerily, popping a fry into his mouth. "Looks like she means it. And she's so pretty. I hate to see a pretty girl cry."

Alex pivots on the bench, glaring at the guy sitting next to him. "Why can't you ever just shut the fuck up, dude? For real. This has nothing to do with you."

Halliday looks like she wants to crawl under the table and die quietly, where no one will be able to see the life wilt out of her. I get where Alex is coming from. I'm not going to be able to just snap my fingers and forget everything that's happened since Jake dragged me into that bathroom. I'll never be able to forget it. But I think…I think I will be able to forgive Hal. Maybe not today, or tomorrow, or next week even. But a day will come, probably soon, when I don't look at her and only see all of the times she sneered at me over Kacey's shoulder as the Sirens shoved past me in the hallway. I'll see the silly, quirky, sweet girl I used to burn around Raleigh in the Nova with. I'll be reminded of all the good times we've had, instead of all the painful, sad, angry moments, and the hurt of the past year will eventually soften. Until then…I'm willing to try.

I catch Alex looking at me in my peripherals and I know he's worrying about me. This is a lot, after all. He's seen me at my worst. He's held the pieces of me together when I've fallen apart, and some of that heartbreak *was* Halliday's fault. I'm not used to having someone look out for me, and it's making my eyes prick like crazy.

"How about we just focus on the fact that you're the captain of the football team now," I say, clumsily changing the subject. Finesse has never been my strong suit. The less time we sit here, stewing in tension and guilt, however, the better. Halliday smiles meekly at me—a silent thank you for taking the pressure of her. From the smug smirk on his face, Zander's perfectly happy to divert the course of our conversation in Alex's direction. I can already tell that the guy has plenty to say about Alex's new role and can't wait to aggravate him some more. Alex, on the other hand, plunges the tines of his fork into his lasagna and spits out a string of curse words so colorful that the nerds sitting at the table next to us all trade terrified looks.

I don't blame them. Alex is an intimidating guy even when he's silent, expressionless and minding his own business. Irritated and giving his emotion free rein, my beautiful boyfriend is so savage and menacing that it's a miracle the nerds don't pack up their laptops and flee the cafeteria like a flock of startled lemmings. "I broke Travis McCormick's middle finger," he states icily.

"You should have seen it." Zander chuckles. "The moron thought he could take on our boy all by himself. He was stupid enough to flip Alex the bird, and then…*crack.*" Zander mimes something snapping in two. "Fingers aren't supposed to stick out at a ninety-degree angle. I haven't seen anything that gross in a while."

"And then he smacked you in the face? That's where you got the bruise?" I ask. Alex looks over my shoulder, at the wall behind me. When I duck to the left, attempting to make eye contact with him, he shakes his head, looking up, suddenly intrigued by the paintjob on the ceiling.

"No. That was from after." His voice is too light. Too airy. Clearly, he's trying to skirt around a piece of information that he doesn't want to part with. Unluckily for him, Zander's all too happy to fill in the blanks.

"Kyle, Lawrence and Naseem tried to take him down and stamp on his head when Coach Foley left to take a call. One of them landed a punch. Kyle? I think it was the Kyle kid. That's when I jumped in and joined in the party."

"Yeah, you didn't need to. I had the situation under control."

"He really did," Zander says, around a mouthful of burger. "He punched Lawrence so hard the fucker's probably *still* seeing stars. Hey, man, can you shoot me over that ketchup?"

Alex grumpily snatches up the bottle of tomato ketchup and slams it down in front of Zander. The guy looks a little surprised, like he was expecting Alex to tell him to go fuck himself. "Thanks. Anyway, he cracked Lawrence's head so hard, I think his helmet split in two. And that Naseem kid looked like he was about to run crying out of the gym when Alex dodged his right hook and kicked his knees out from underneath him. I would have left Alex to take care them by himself, but then three other assholes started throwing their weight around, and I decided to lend a hand. One against three's pretty manageable odds. One against six? Even *you're* not that good, Moretti."

Alex and Zander have a unique relationship. I say relationship, because *friendship* just doesn't feel right. Alex lets Zander speak to him in a way that would have him ripping someone else's arm off, no doubt about it. He also looks like he's on the verge of beating Zander within an inch of his life at other times, too. Their dynamic's so complicated that I feel like I'm suffering from whiplash whenever the two of them are together.

Alex pulls a face, shoving his tray away, his food stabbed at, poked and prodded, but otherwise untouched. "You should have let them kick my ass," he says grimly. "Break a few bones. That way Foley wouldn't be able to force the captain's badge on me."

Zander closely inspects a fry, holding it up to the light like it might contain some secret hidden message inside of it. "Friends don't let friends get the crap kicked out of them, homie. Unless they're being released from juvie and you don't want to suffer through a bullshit emotional goodbye with them. In that situation, it's perfectly acceptable to bribe another inmate to lynch them unexpectedly, so said friend doesn't want to speak to you ever again."

Alex rolls his eyes. Next to me, Halliday opens up the brown paper bag she brought with her to the table, gingerly offering it out to me. I already know what's inside. The smell hits me before I manage to take a peek. Halliday always used to make lemon bars for her brother's bake sales. Three or four times a year, I'd show up randomly at her place, conveniently 'just in the area,' and Halliday would have to make an extra batch of lemon bars to replace the ones that I inhaled.

She must have planned out coming to sit with me today. She labored in her kitchen last night to make these, and the whole time she must have been freaking out about what I was going to say to her. She probably pictured me grabbing a lemon bar and smashing it into her face, soap opera style. She has an overactive imagination like that. I take one from the paper bag, giving her a small smile in return.

Okay, so this feels weird, and not entirely uncomfortable, but…as I look around the cafeteria, I notice something remarkable. People are talking to one another, laughing over memes, gesticulating wildly as they laugh and chatter. They're all engrossed in their conversations, and their late math assignments, and their crush that's sitting on the other side of the room. None of them are looking at *me*.

For the first time in a very long time, I, Silver Parisi, am not sitting on the outside, looking in. I'm just another random student at Raleigh High, and that feels fucking incredible.

"This is nice," Zander says, winking at me from across the table. "You and blondie are sharing sugar. Alex hasn't tried to kill me in *well* over five minutes. I don't wanna get ahead of myself over here, but I'd go so far as to call this progress."

## 21

## ALEX

*Monty: Come by the bar tonight. This doesn't need to be a thing, kid.*

The first night I worked at the Rock, I was shown how to clear the waitress's stations. I was shown how to operate the POS and ring in orders. The bar tenders gave me the lowdown, explaining how they'd tip me out well if I herded people to drink at the bar instead of the floor sections. And at the end of the night, after busting my ass, making sure I did exactly what I was told, Monty ushered me into his office, where a bald guy with a moustache was lying unconscious on the floor in a pool of his own blood, and he educated me on what my job would involve *after* the bar had closed and the punters had all left for the night.

I was to be the errand boy. The bag man. I was also the guy who did most of the heavy lifting. Turned out the guy with the moustache was missing a couple of fingers thanks to the pair of pliers Monty kept in the top drawer of his desk. As he sat behind a bank of screens, scrolling through security footage, he lit up a cigarette and tasked me with collecting up the guys dismembered fingers and putting them in a Ziplock baggie filled with ice.

"Couldn't do as he was told," he'd said, blowing a smoke ring and then poking his finger through the middle of it. "*Mack here knows he's supposed to make a drop on Tuesdays. If he doesn't make a drop on Tuesday, we run low on product for the rest of the week. I don't wanna be scrambling to keep customers happy just because one of my employees can't follow simple instructions or get up off his lazy ass to do his fucking job. You understand, right, kid?"*

At the time, I nodded, kept my mouth shut, and put Mack's fucking fingers into the Ziplock without flinching. I recognized the situation for what it was: a test. Monty had wanted to apply a bit of pressure, to see how I'd react to the sight of such flagrant blood and violence. What he hadn't realized was that *I'd* used that evening as a fact-finding mission, too. I learned a lot as I listened to him talk.

Monty reached down into hell and plucked me out of the darkness. He saved me from being assigned to yet another shitty foster care situation that was bound to go bad, and I was seriously fucking grateful for that. But I quickly discovered that he had a vindictive side. He didn't like being disobeyed, and he didn't like the people he considered his property acting like they had a mind of their own. When someone did that, it inevitably ended in bloodshed. Almost immediately Monty established himself as an unforgiving benefactor, whose punishments were nothing short of swift and ruthless.

It's with this knowledge in mind that I formulate a three-word response to Monty's text—one that I know is going to irritate the hell out of him.

No. Fucking. Way.

I like my fingers. I like the way they're attached to my fucking hands. I need them to play guitar and make Silver come. And I didn't just forget to make a run on a Tuesday. I handed a bag that was very precious to Monty over to a man who Monty apparently hates. God knows what was really in that stupid fucking bag, or why half the criminals in the state of Washington were trying to get their hands on it. Honestly, I don't even think Monty knew what was so valuable about it. He just knew that everyone else wanted it, and he was willing to do whatever it took to make sure he got it before anyone else could.

I fucked up his entire powerplay, and for that Monty's gonna want my head on a stick. He can tell me 'this doesn't need to be a thing' as many times as he likes. This is most definitely a thing for him, and if I'm stupid enough to step foot inside his office, I might as well resign myself to the fact that I won't be leaving with the same number of appendages that I walked in with.

My cell buzzes in my pocket again as I hurry down Main Street, hiking the strap of my gig bag a little higher on my shoulder. I'm not interested in Monty's response, but I check the phone anyway, more out of habit than anything else.

**Silver: You nearly here? I'm two seconds from walking out…**

I smirk to myself, imagining the anxious look on her face. She makes a point of radiating this unstoppable, self-possessed, fierce attitude all the time, but every now and then I get to see an uncertain side of her and it's frankly fucking adorable. It makes me want to wrap her in cotton wool and protect her.

**Me: Arriving any second. Cold feet?**

She replies immediately.

**Silver: FROZEN**

When I enter the diner, rushing in out of the cold, the bell above the door jangles, announcing the arrival of a new customer to the five or six people seated in the booths. Silver looks up from her phone screen, her nerves giving over to relief when she sets eyes on me. The black Billy Joel t-shirt she's wearing looks new; I don't think I've seen it before. Her thick, gorgeous hair is down for once. She's wearing a touch of make-up, too—just a little lip gloss and some mascara. Evidently, she made an effort to look presentable before she left the house, which makes me feel shitty since I definitely did not.

The ripped jeans and the plain black t-shirt I snagged from my clean laundry pile two seconds before I ran out of the apartment just now have seen better days, and my zip up hoody has gotten so thin that it barely counts as an extra layer of clothing. For the first time, I regret not making more of an effort to look good for a girl. I make a mental note to order some new threads online. It'd be quicker and easier to just bite the bullet and head to Bellingham to pick some stuff up from a store but fuck that noise. Shopping makes me break out in hives.

"Hey." Silver slides over in the booth, chewing on her thumb nail. I dump my guitar on the opposite bench next to hers, then sit my ass down beside her, taking hold of her wrist and forcefully guiding her hand away from her mouth.

"They serve food here, y'know. No need to resort to autosarcophagy."

"What the hell's autosarcophagy?"

"Self-cannibalism. People are weird as fuck."

Silver whimpers, grimacing as she slumps against me, hiding her face against my chest. "I think I have tennis elbow," she groans.

Running a hand over the back of her head, petting her, I disguise my smile in the waves of her hair. "No, you don't."

"Yeah, I do," she argues.

"Try again, *Argento*."

She pinches my side, growling like a feral tiger cub. "Fine. Mom asked me to look after Max. Sounded important. If I don't head over to her place now, she's probably gonna lose her job."

"You really think I don't know your mom's still in Toronto? You can quit mumbling weak excuses into my t-shirt. They aren't gonna get you anywhere. We told Cam we'd do this, so we're doing it. End of story."

Across the other side of the diner, Harry spies us sitting in the booth and waves, beaming from ear to ear. He makes a beeline for us, carrying a gargantuan basket of fries. "This is gonna be great, kids," he says, setting down the food. "We haven't had live music here since Wesley Daniels quit playing the harmonica on account of his asthma."

I like Harry. He's the kind of guy to include me when he calls a group of teenagers *kids*. It makes me feel wholesome, which is really fucking entertaining. Wholesome is something I have *never* been. He'd probably come up with another less generous name for me if he knew the fucked-up, dark shit that goes on in my head. Or the fucked-up, dark shit I do to the sweet, innocent-looking girl sitting next to me in the booth, for that matter.

I reward his endearing naivety by giving him a genuine smile. "We're honored that you'd have us."

"Actually Harry, I'm so sorry to do this to you, but I'm not feeling we—"

I clamp my hand over Silver's mouth, widening my smile. "Don't listen to a word that comes out of her mouth. Silver's been stuck down by a bout of nerves. She's gonna be fine once she gets up there and starts playing."

Silver groans through my fingers, which makes Harry frown worriedly. "You're sure? I mean, you don't have to play if you don't want to. It's not a problem. If you don't think you can do it, the juke box is fine."

I'm not planning on uncovering Silver's mouth but she sticks her tongue out, wetting my hand, and it feels fucking gross, so I release her. "*Parisi*," I warn. "What's the big deal. You've played for me before. Your students, too. There's no one here."

She casts uncertain eyes around the diner, nervously plucking at the hem of her t-shirt. Finally, she adopts a resigned expression, snagging a fry from the basket in front of us and shoving it into her mouth. "Fine. I'll play. But if I smash all of these fries and then throw up all over the stage, I will not be held accountable."

Harry accepts her terms surprisingly quickly. "You're a star, Silver. Your dad's gonna be so proud."

"Urgh, no! You didn't *invite* him?"

"Of course I did. He's your biggest fan, sweetheart. I also told Heather and Debra from the wool shop. And Ms. Jones from the school said she'd try to pop by. I know a couple of folk are still busy with work and whatnot, but I'm expecting quite the crowd after five. I have some Pepto in the back if you need it."

He makes a sharp exit from the table, leaving before Silver can change her mind. She shoots daggers at me, feigning annoyance, but I know the truth: the prospect of playing in front of a large group of people is terrifying the shit out of her.

"How the fuck are *you* not freaking out right now?" she demands sulkily, jamming another fry into her mouth.

"I don't give a fuck about any of these people. I could give two shits if they like me or my playing. This is a low stakes game. The only person's opinion that matters to me is yours, and I've already played for you. As far as I'm concerned, these bastards can all go fuck themselves."

She thinks about this for a second. "So…you don't care what my *dad* thinks? His opinion of you isn't important to you? Not even a teeny, tiny bit?"

Okay, so she has me there. I guess I care about Cam's opinion. Just a teeny, tiny bit. I don't like admitting it, though. Shrugging, I plant a kiss against her temple, *hmm*ing. "I suppose it'd suck a little if he thought I was a hack. Won't stop me from getting up there and playing, though, *Argento*." Leaning down a little, so that my mouth is right next to her ear, I whisper my next words carefully. "If I suffered from performance anxiety, I wouldn't have fucked you in front of a room full of people, would I, *dolcezza*?"

She shivers, like she's remembering the night we descended into the basement of the Rock and gave in to our basest desires. It wasn't such a long way for me to fall from innocence—I've been a depraved bastard for a long time now—but for Silver that fall must have felt like skydiving without a fucking parachute.

Her eyes are feverish, her cheeks flushed when she pulls back and looks up at me. I'm addicted to the sight of Silver when she's turned on; the hitch of her breath in her throat and the way she licks at her lips like she'd suddenly kill a man for a glass of water makes my dick hard every single time. A second ago, she was afraid of what was going to happen when she took her seat up on the tiny, low stage in the corner of the diner. All it took to distract her and banish her worry was the mention of my hard cock inside her.

I really am *that* fucking good.

"You look pleased with yourself." Silver brushes her fingers through the front of my hair, and it's my turn to shiver now; I lose my shit every time she touches my scalp. I can't help it. I wonder if she knows how utterly powerless I am against her whenever she touches me like this. "This is nothing like fucking me in front of a room full of people, though," she says.

"What, you think playing a guitar is scarier than a bunch of people watching you get penetrated?"

She laughs, blushing deeply. God, my little Silver Parisi. *Mine.* She has no idea how fucking beautiful she is. She shyly feeds herself a fry, trying to hide from me behind the curtain of her hair. "I laid my body bare for people to see then." She takes a second, thinking. "I know it sounds stupid, but…when I play, it feels different. I'm laying my *soul* bare. And that's almost as intimidating as you are, Alessandro Moretti."

With a careful touch, I sweep her hair back behind her ear, removing the shield she put up to disguise her embarrassment. "That doesn't sound stupid. It makes sense. You're a fucking legend, though. You make that guitar weep when you play it. People are gonna lose their minds. And…side note, I am not intimidating. I'm *misunderstood*."

"Hah!" She covers her mouth with the back of her hand. "You do know that you terrify people, right?"

"Only the ones who piss me off."

"You nearly made Halliday cry at lunch yesterday."

"Yeah, well. She pissed me off. I like Halliday. Sounds like she's dealing with her own shit at home, too. She had a hand in making your life a waking nightmare, though. It's gonna take more than a couple of pieces of cake and a few tears to make up for that."

"Should I make her walk barefoot across hot coals?" She raises an eyebrow, the comment a clear dig. She thinks I'm being too hard on her remorseful friend. Silver's still a good person, though. Somehow, against all the odds, she's still trying to see the good in other people, to give them the benefit of the doubt, whereas I'm more of the opinion that people are dog shit assholes who need to bleed in exchange for a second chance.

"She's not Kacey," Silver says quietly, dipping a fry into her milkshake. "Halliday's softer. Not as resilient. If this were Kacey trying to worm her way back into my good graces, then it'd be a different story. You know what I think?"

*Eternally. Always. The inside of that beautiful head of yours intrigues the living shit out of me. I'm embarrassed by how much time I spend thinking about what goes on in there.*

I clear my throat. "Sure."

"I think you should probably take a leaf out of my book and go a little easier on Zander. He's really trying to make things right with you."

My smile wants to shrivel up and die—the mere mention of Zander Hawkins will have that effect on a guy—but I fix it firmly in place. "He's got a thick skin. He can take it."

"Probably," she agrees, leaning her head against my shoulder. "But he'll give up one of these days. He'll stop trying, and then what? I guess you've just got to ask yourself…aside from the fact that he paid someone to try and shank you, and he knew who your father was when you guys met, do you think he really *was* your friend? If you do, then you should probably forgive him and move on before you lose him altogether."

∽

Silver

Over the next thirty minutes, people filter slowly into the diner. My stomach roils, churning, and I begin to regret joking about throwing up on the stage. Why the hell did I agree to this again? What was I thinking? I've spent the past year trying to convince people not to notice me, not to stare at me, not to draw attention to myself, and now I'm purposefully putting myself front and center, asking the members of Raleigh to do exactly the opposite.

This is all Dad's fault. If he hadn't made out like we'd be doing Raleigh some sort of community service by helping Harry, then I'd be curled up on Alex's couch right now, watching television.

Alex leads the way across the diner. He sets up my guitar for me, mic-ing it so that the sound will play through the large speakers Harry's set up on either side of the little triangular stage that fits snuggly into the corner at the back of the diner. I watch him, my fingers tingling like crazy, adrenalin prickling all over my body. Fuck, I won't be able to play at all if I'm shaking this much.

I keep my back to the people taking up their seats in the booths, around the tables, and at the counter, trying not to panic every time the bell above the door rings out and someone new arrives. Alex seems completely oblivious to the amount of people who have braved the weather and come out on a work night just to watch us play. He's even and calm as he tells me to sit on a stool and he sets up the mic that I'll be introducing the songs into. I'm seconds away from bursting into tears when he asks me to say something into the mic to test the sound level.

He nearly drops the mic when he looks over and sees me the state I'm in. Placing his hands on the tops of my arms, he ducks down so that he's level with me. "Whoa, whoa, whoa. You're really *this* freaked out? We can walk out of here right now if you like. My place is thirty seconds across the road. We'll be locked inside the apartment and the door will be bolted before anyone even realizes we've made a run for it."

I let out a breathy laugh. "Harry'll never forgive me. Look at all the people who came. He's going to double his takings tonight…"

There really are a lot of people here. They're ordering coffees and hot sandwiches, chattering quietly to one another in their little groups, but their chairs are all turned toward our dark little corner, angled so they can get a better view of the mystery musicians who'll be performing here tonight.

"Recognize anyone?" Alex mutters, casting an indifferent glance over his shoulder.

Slowly, I nod. "Halliday brought her little brother. They're sitting at the counter. Dad's a couple of seats down from them. Why the hell does *he* look so nervous? He's not the one standing up here on a stage." His face, anxious though it may be, is reassuring. He's trimmed the beard that was starting to look a little scraggly back to a reasonable length of stubble, and he's wearing a button down shirt underneath his down jacket, which completely breaks his new *I'll-never-wear-anything-smart-ever-again-because-your-mother-can't-make-me* dress code. A dress code I fully endorse. The dark grey material suits him, though. I'd never tell him to his face, but he actually looks quite dashing.

I continue my sweep of the diner, looking for familiar faces. "Harriet Rosenfeld from school's here."

Alex smirks, unraveling a long cable and plugging it into the back of an amp. "Ahh. The trumpet player. Aren't you glad you agreed to give me lessons instead of palming me off on her? I could have been playing *'Reveille'* up here with her tonight..."

"I didn't *agree* to give you lessons. You gave me no choice. Oh god...is that...?"

Alex looks up, following my line of sight, and his hands go still on his guitar. "Yeah, it is," he clips out. "I haven't spoken to her since she came to the apartment. She's been calling..."

On the other side of Harry's, weaving her way through the crowd, Alex's social worker, Maeve, looks like she's trying to find somewhere to sit. She spots a vacant seat at the bar and grabs it quickly...right next to my dad.

"Well." Alex clears his throat. He looks unhappy all of a sudden. Maeve shouldn't be here. To Alex, I'm sure she's an ill omen. She delivered the news that changed his life forever. That must have been so hard for her. It wasn't her fault. Ben's death had absolutely nothing to do with Maeve, but to Alex, every time he looks at her, I'm sure all he hears is her voice saying the words over and over again...

*'I'm so sorry, Alessandro. Truly, I am. But...there's been an accident. It's your brother. Ben...oh god, I'm sorry but* Ben's dead.'

At the counter, Dad turns and smiles at Maeve, and something uncomfortable twists in my gut.

"Alright, kids. I think that's it." Harry appears next to the stage with two cokes and a couple of glasses of ice for us. I'm one hot second away from asking if he has any tequila but then I check myself. Harry's old school; he wouldn't serve alcohol to a teenager even if he did have a liquor license. Also, Dad wouldn't approve, and he'd be mad that I'd asked one of his friends such a dumbass question. "I think everyone I invited has arrived," Harry says cheerfully. "I'm not sure what you two are planning on playing but some of the locals have made a few requests. Easy stuff. Y'know, Eric Clapton. The Eagles. I love Hotel California myself."

Alex pulls a face. I think he's trying to smile but it's coming across all warped and twisted. "We're not playing Hotel California, Harry."

The old man brushes off Alex's refusal like he saw it coming a mile away. "Okay, okay. No problem. I bet you guys have got it covered. We'll all just sit back and enjoy the show. How about that?" He hurries away and stands behind the counter, not waiting for a response.

Alex hands me my guitar, then sits himself down on a stool three feet away from mine, putting the strap of his own instrument over his head. He seems a little grim now, as if Maeve's presence has thrown a spanner in the works and destroyed the playful mood he walked in here with. "You ready?" he asks. His eyes are hard as jet when he looks at me, but then they soften. "You're gonna be amazing. I already know you are. Just play. Don't worry about any of them and I'll do the same, okay?"

Taking a shallow, shaky breath, I nod. "Okay."

My fingers move to the strings of my guitar, knowing exactly where they need to be without any assistance, and I pause, repeating the same phrase again and again inside my head. *Please don't fuck this up. Please don't fuck this up. Please don't fuck this up.*

And then I begin to play.

The notes come haltingly at first. My fingers do what they've been doing for years, gliding up and down the frets, my other hand slowly plucking at the strings as they're supposed to…but I can't seem to move past the intro of the song, pedaling over the same notes, Travis picking the same strings in a loop.

Out of the corner of my eye, I see Alex positioning his hands, ready to come in. When I fail to move past the same cycle of notes again, he speaks softly beside me, so only I can hear him. *"Respira e basta.* It's okay. Just breathe. Show them how bright you shine, *mi amore."*

The music comes unstuck immediately, my fingers breaking the cycle. I don't even know how it happens, but the sound of Alex's voice is enough…

*Landslide* by Fleetwood Mac flows out of me, the first line of the song already out of my mouth before I even realize that I'm singing.

I do *not* sing.

At least not in front of people. *Never* in front of people. This is something I do by myself, alone, when I'm sure no one can hear me. My father, Mom, Max. Not even Alex. I've never even *hummed* in front of him for fear of embarrassing myself.

*"I took my love and I took it down..."*

Oh shit. Oh shit, oh shit. What am I doing? My own damned fear paralyzed my senses and I just reacted, just did what came naturally, and it's too late now. I can't just...*stop*. I'm on fire, my cheeks burning, my body shrinking, like I might be able to fold in on myself and just disappear...

*"Climbed a mountain and turned around..."*

*Just breathe, Silver. Just breathe.* Alex's words ring in my ears, reminding me to fill my lungs, which is a good thing because I'm about to fall off my chair any second now. I daren't turn my head to look at him. If I do, I won't be able to keep going.

He was supposed to join in with me, playing a harmony along with the music, but he never comes in. His guitar remains resolutely silent next to me, and all I can think to myself is holy fucking shit, what if he thinks I'm the worst thing he's ever heard?

Line after line I sing, my voice soft, lacking the power and confidence that bolsters it whenever I'm in the Nova on my own, or in the shower. Still, I hit the notes one after the other, emotion slipping into the lyrics, and before I know it, I'm lost. I'm on a journey with Stevie Nicks. I feel her pain. It's *my* pain, and it bleeds through as each word leaves my mouth.

I dare to look up from the spot on the floor in front of me—the same spot I've been staring at since I slipped up and started to sing— and there, on the other side of Harry's my Dad is on his feet, a hand pressed against his expensive grey button-down shirt that he wore here for me tonight, and he's looking at me like he doesn't even recognize who I am.

Oh my god. I've never seen him look so shaken and so...*proud*. My voice cracks, an ache burning in the back of my throat, but I keep on singing, too afraid to stop now. *"Can I sail through the changing ocean tides..."*

It's as if a spell has been broken when Alex finally begins to play. I almost sob with relief at the sound of his guitar joining in with mine. I don't feel quite so alone with him playing along, and the deeper, earthier texture of the music he plays compliments the light, brightness of my own. The rest of the song is easy because he's with me every step of the way, every note and every rise and fall in the melody. When I pluck the last string, the song coming to an end, a wave of release comes crashing down over me, and it feels as though a breath I've been holding for a very long has finally been set free.

The crowd gathered inside Harry's sits in silence, staring dumbly at us. They're so quiet you could hear a pin drop. And then, from the counter, a single clap…

Dad.

He claps again. My eyes meet his, and I can't bear it. I have to look away. It's just too much. All too much. Applause, loud and raucous erupts inside the diner, the patron's meals and warm drinks forgotten about as people slap their hands against the tables and stamp their feet against the floor.

I nearly have a heart attack when I feel a hand land gently on my shoulder. Alex faces his back to the crowd, the way I did earlier, and he whispers into my ear. "Marry me, *Argento*."

"*What?!*" Leaning sideways, I try to look at him, but he places his hand against the side of my face, preventing me from turning. I laugh, too high-pitched, too adrenalin-soaked to react any other way. "Very funny. Sit down, Alex. We need to play another song before I lose my nerve."

He takes his other hand and places it on my other cheek so that he's cradling my face. Now he lets me turn to him, away from the crowd, so only I can see *his* face. His eyes are burning with emotion, fierce and determined. His expression is more serious than I've ever seen it before. A jolt of alarm squeezes at my heart. "*Marry me, Argento,*" he breathes. "Say yes to me before I lose my fucking mind. I can't live another fucking second in a world where you haven't promised to spend the rest of your life with me. I fucking can't." He shakes his head, rubbing his thumbs against my cheekbones, his eyes so bright that he looks a little mad.

"Alex—"

"*Yes*, Argento. *God damnit, do it. You've gotta say yes.*"

## 22

## ALEX

The last place on earth a girl should be proposed to is Harry's fucking Diner, in front of a bunch of strangers. I didn't plan on proposing at all, but the moment Silver opens her mouth and starts to sing, I see her in that music room she talked about, dust motes spiraling on the air, and she's bathed in sunlight, happy and perfect and *home*, and I want to give her the dream life she painted on the cabin so badly that it actually fucking *hurts*.

People often wonder how they'd react in a war type situation. When gunfire's ripping through the air and shells are exploding all around them, shaking the ground beneath them, will they fall apart, or will all of that chaos galvanize them? I've never had to wonder that. I know war. I've lived through it nearly every day of my life. I'm used to the sky falling down and the ground renting open where I'm about to place my feet. I've never let the chaos and the calamity get the better of me.

Love, on the other hand? Hah. It's taken *love* to finally break me. I never could have seen Silver coming. There was no warning. No shot across the bow. If there had been, I could have braced myself for what was right around the corner, but instead she took me out like a goddamn sidewinder missile, blowing a crater in my chest a mile wide. There's no surviving her, I know that much. When the first line of *Landslide* came out of her mouth and the sweet sound of her lilting voice hit my ears, it was like a bomb going off in my *soul* and any lingering thoughts I might have had about waiting to ask her this question went up in smoke. It took all of my willpower not to stop her from playing halfway through the song, so I could drop down on my knees and beg her to be mine right there and then.

"*Yes*, Argento. *God damnit, do it. You've gotta say yes.*" I know how crazy I sound. I also know that Harry's is perhaps the least romantic place in Washington, and this should be happening somewhere far, far nicer, and there should be a ring, and a million other things should be different, and I should have been a better guy and asked Cameron for permission first...*wait. God, what year is this? Do men still have to ask for permission to propose? Cameron's gonna fucking* kill *me. Why...why hasn't she said anything yet?*

I search Silver's face, looking for some clue that might tell me what she's thinking. Her expression is so stunned, though, that I have no idea what she's going to say. My heart is a tense fist, refusing to beat...

"Timing's pretty spectacular, Moretti," she whispers.

Behind us, the crowd's starting to get restless. They've begun talking amongst themselves, which isn't necessarily a bad thing. I need a goddamn moment. I need three. I need for Silver to give me an answer before my head fucking explodes. "*Argento*," I growl. "Are you afraid of a life with me?"

"No."

"Are you afraid of what people will say?"

She shakes her head, sucking her bottom lip into her mouth.

"Are you afraid of loving me?"

She's unyielding when she shakes her head again, firm and sure of herself. "No, Alex. I could never be afraid of that."

I fight to keep my voice level when I ask my final question. "Then what *are* you afraid of?"

Her eyes, pale and cool, like the crisp sky over Lake Cushman, are so clear and brilliant as she looks up at me. My stupid heart gives one painful, urgent squeeze, my ribs pinching like I'm being crushed inside a vise...and finally she answers.

"I'm not afraid of anything, Alessandro Moretti. I'm happy. I'm happy...because I'm going to be your wife."

I figured I'd be able to breathe again if she said yes. But she hasn't actually said yes yet. I close my eyes, desperately trying to keep my shit together. "Silver. Tell me. Say the actual words. I need to hear them out loud, right fucking now."

"Yes," she whispers. "Yes, of course I'll marry you."

Holy...

Fuck...

All of the frantic, nervous energy pours out of me like water spilling through my fingers. She said yes. She actually said *yes*? I open my eyes, leaning my forehead against hers, and she reaches up, holding me by the wrists. A powerful, delirious electricity passes through us and the room falls away.

I forget that all my life, all I've known is war. In this moment, with time standing still and everything changing, everything evolving, everything *Silver*, all I know is peace.

"Uhhh…kids? I know I'm not exactly paying you or anything, but do you think we might be able to get another couple of songs?" Harry asks, hovering by the front of the stage. "People are starting to get antsy and we've run out of the Philly Cheesesteak. If we could distract folk for a few minutes while Cliff runs to the store for some supplies, I sure would be really grateful."

Because she's a better person than I am, Silver eventually drags her gaze away from my face to look at the poor bastard. I, on the other hand, continue to stare at her like she's the answer to every single question I've ever fucking asked.

"Sure, Harry. Sorry, I—we—uh—we just got a little sidetracked," she says. I reiterate, I like Harry, he's a genuinely good guy, but right now I could open-hand slap him for interrupting us. All I want to do is pick Silver up and carry her out of here, away from all the noise and the prying eyes that are boring into my back. I don't want to share her. I don't want to share this moment.

"Just half an hour," Silver tells me, as if she can read my mind and knows how badly I suddenly *need* us to get the fuck out of here. "Thirty minutes and we'll make our excuses."

"Too long," I rumble, shaking my head.

"Too *bad*," she whispers, smiling, her eyes alive with excitement.

"Don't worry. The second we're done playing, I'll drag you out of here and across the road myself."

Grudgingly, I let her go and sit my ass back down on my stool. The people in the crowd fall quiet, their conversations petering out as they realize we're about to start playing again. This time, I don't wait for Silver to strum her guitar. I get in there first with the opening chords of a song that isn't on our set list. I don't even know if she knows the song, but I want her to hear it. I want her to hear *me* sing…because she isn't the only one who's been hiding her voice.

Just like Dermot Kennedy's, my voice is rocky, deep and bottomless. A little raspy and rough around the edges. I belt out *'Power Over Me'*, the emotion present, right where it needs to be. I'm not a gun at fingerpicking like Silver, but this was a piece of music I mastered a long time ago. My fingers skip over the strings, the music flowing out of me like I've just opened up the veins at my wrists and the words are pouring out of me like my very own life force.

Silver sits still like I did when she played *Landslide,* her guitar resting mute on her lap. She avoided looking at me when she performed, but I do the exact opposite. I *only* look at her. Definitely not the best way to connect with an audience, but so fucking what. I don't care about connecting with any of them. Silver is my event horizon. My point of no return. Everything else is just white noise.

She's so beautiful, my fucking soul hurts.

I don't pause after I'm done with the song. I go straight into the next number on the list we drafted out, needing to keep the momentum going, and Silver joins in. We play a run of old numbers that the crowd sings along with, but we remain quiet. For our finale, we play *Barton Hollow* by The Civil Wars, and by some unspoken agreement Silver and I sing together, knowing that it's only right, our voices rising and falling in unison, weaving together perfectly, and the haunting song renders the people in the diner utterly silent.

The final discordant note of the song is still ringing out across the diner when I get up, take Silver by hand, abandoning all of our equipment, and I drag her out of the building, into the darkness, and the night, and the rain…

…and we run.

## 23

## ALEX

Silver gasps as I shove her up against my bedroom wall. I'm careful not to lean my weight against her, conscious of her sensitive ribs, but she pulls me closer by the front of my t-shirt, giving me an open-mouthed smile. "I'm not that fragile anymore, Moretti. I'm healed up just fine. You can take the gloves off a little."

We're both grinning like maniacs, drunk and high and stupid on the fact that I just posed a crazy question and she said yes to it. We don't know what this new accord between us means for our future, no one can know what fate has in store for them for certain, but we both know the pact we just made in the diner is monumental and will change our lives forever. The apartment's filled with a buzzing energy that makes me want to howl at the moon or tear my clothes off and throw myself into the lake, or jump on my bike, open the throttle and go faster than the wind. I *need* so badly right now. I need so many things. I need to feel. I need the adrenalin fizzing in my bloodstream. I need more oxygen than I seem to be able to coax into my lungs. I need Silver most of all.

"Only thing I'm concerned about taking off are your clothes," I tell her. "Get rid of them. Get rid of them all. I want you naked on that bed in three seconds, or I'm gonna end up tearing through that Billy Joel shirt with my fucking teeth."

Silver's perfect mouth is swollen and red from the rough kiss I landed on her the moment we were through the apartment door. With dazed, unfocused eyes, she scans my face, picking over my features in a way that makes me want to tear her pants down, put her over my knee and spank her bare ass until it's red raw for such blatant insubordination. I growl, the rumble vibrating in the back of my throat, and Silver's pupils dilate even further.

"*Wolf*," she accuses, eyeing the tattoo of the wolf on the back of my hand. "You're a fucking savage, aren't you."

Oh, she has no fucking idea. Not even the first clue. I consider racing outside and howling up at the night sky again, knowing just how good the bite of the cold air will feel on my skin. I choose to stay here, towering over my beautiful wide-eyed prize instead. "Silver, you're gonna scream so hard for me, the whole neighborhood's gonna hear about it."

I rub her bottom lip with my thumb, slowly using it to open her mouth. I push it inside, up to the first knuckle, and a dangerously wicked glint flashes in her eye. She's going to bite…

"Ah, ah, ah." I tut under my breath, pretending to disapprove. "Only wolves get to bite. And you…you're not a wolf." She hisses, surprised, when I quickly dip down and sink my teeth into her neck, applying just the right amount of pressure to make her squirm.

"I…could be a…wolf," she pants.

I shake my head, hiding in the crook of her neck so she can't see my teasing smile. "You're a kitten, *mi amore*. A soft, cuddly, gentle kitten." This is *so* far from the truth—she's as fierce as a wolf, any day of the week—but it's fun to tease her.

"Oooh, you are asking for trouble!" She pushes me away, planting her palms against my chest and firmly shoving. It's barely enough force to shift me at all, but I willingly give her a foot. Just one. She's still trapped in the circle of my arms as I rest my hands against the wall above her head, using it to brace myself. I find a lust-filled defiance dancing in her blue eyes. "You're lucky I'm feeling forgiving, or I might have shown you just how sharp this kitten's claws are," she informs me.

Holy fuck, I *want* her to show me. A little demonstration would be much appreciated. There'll be time for that later, though. First, I want to make her melt. I want to kiss and lick and knead and palm her until she's pliant and obedient. And then I want to fucking eat her alive. "Reckless," I accuse, grabbing one of her tits through her shirt and squeezing possessively. "Better think through your words before you start making suggestions like that. I might get carried away."

The tip of her pink tongue darts out to wet her lips, and my cock throbs painfully in my pants. She has no idea what she does to me when she performs these seductive little actions. That's why they're so fucking arousing. Lots of women lick their lips, pout, and flutter their eyelashes flirtatiously, running their fingers suggestively across their cleavages, but that kind of sexual assault is gross to me. Way too contrived and obvious. When Silver wets her mouth with the tip of her tongue, she does it because her heart's beating out of her chest, and she's nervous, and thinking about me kissing her. And *that* makes my dick harder than concrete.

She's stronger than any girl or woman I've ever met. She's stood in the face of pain and humiliation, when others would have been brought to their knees. She has the heart of a lion. She's stared down death and refused to quail at the sight of it…and yet with me, she can be vulnerable.

We undress each other, ripping clothes over each other's heads as she stumble down the hallway to the bedroom, tripping as we kick out of our shoes. My hands ache, longing to touch her, as she shimmies the thin lacey fabric of her panties down her thighs and lets them drop to the floor.

Breathless, I go to her, placing my hands on her hips. She gazes up at me, and a surge of desperation punches through me, making my head spin. If someone had told me a year ago that I was going to meet a girl and fall for her so hard that I asked her to marry me within a space of a few months, I'd have laughed in their faces. I'd never have believed it. I'd have immediately regretted my impending rashness ahead of time and done whatever I could to prevent it. I'm not that guy anymore, though. Regret is the furthest thing from my mind. I want everything now. Our future together. Our lives, unspooled before us, filled with twists and turns and unexpected surprises. I can't wait to see what happens next.

Her hair is so wavy and beautiful in the pale moonlight that floods in through the window. Like porcelain, her bare skin is so smooth and flawless. I feast on the sight of her tits, the heavy curve of them begging me to cup their weight in my hands, and it takes every ounce of patience I possess not to fuck her where she stands.

Even with its scars, *because* of its scars, her body is perfection. It's been abused, beaten, violated and broken in places, but it's beautiful in every way. Her back holds her upright and strong, unafraid. Her hands, held loose by her side, are capable of creating the most haunting music. Her eyes, the color of winter morning skies over the Walker Forest, are defiant, and proud, and brimming over with intelligence.

*She said yes...*
*She said yes...*
*She said yes...*
*She said yes...*

"On the bed, *Argento*." As though she's some kind of dream, a figment of my imagination, it feels like if I don't do something to claim her right now and physically anchor her to this reality, she'll evaporate into smoke and I'll lose her forever.

Silver sets herself down on top of the duvet, her hair spilling around her head, her coral-pink nipples peaked and begging for attention. She reaches out a hand to me, and common-sense demands that I run to her instead of walk.

The bed dips as I climb up onto the mattress, positioning myself next to Silver. I give myself a second to survey her from the crown of her head to her toes, ravenously devouring every detail of her. Her ribcage rises and falls unevenly, her breath coming in staccato bursts. "God, Alex. The way you stare at me makes me feel like I'm burning up."

My mouth hitches up in one corner, a pleased rumble building in my chest. I take my index finger, running the tip of it over the flat of Silver's stomach, satisfaction warming me when she shivers at my touch. I trail my solitary finger down, circling her belly button with it, grinding my teeth together as I venture even lower.

"You want me to put out the fire?" I ask her. "Or should I stoke the flames?" I trail my index finger to the left, over the crease where her leg meets her hip, and she bucks in answer, her ass jerking upward off the bed.

"I'll literally scream if you stop," she whispers, frustration coloring her words. Her need for me is addicting. Her eyes follow my hand, watching it as it skates across her skin, her cheeks a flushed shade of red that seems to glow hotly even in the dim light. I trace my finger lower still, tracing it lightly over the very apex of her thighs now, right where the petite slit of her pussy begins. Normally, I wouldn't give a shit if Silver waxed her pubic hair or let it grow naturally, but I'm glad her skin is bare for tonight at least. I want to see every inch of her. I want to spread her apart and see how the champagne pink of her flesh deepens to darker shade of rose. I want to witness just how turned on she is by the slickness of her cunt.

I hold the pad of my thumb against the lips of her pussy, knowing that if press down a little, guiding my finger a tiny bit lower, she'll yield to me, giving me access, and I'll have her gasping in seconds; I can already feel the small, hard pebble of her clit beneath her skin, swollen, just waiting to be rolled and rubbed until she breaks apart for me.

"You want my tongue, *dolcezza*? You want me to fuck you with my fingers while I lick you?"

Her eyes shutter closed. She lets her head fall back onto the bed, her fingers twitching reflexively, like she needs something to hold onto. "God...yes. Please, Alex. Please."

I lean over her, arching my body over hers, anticipation making my blood surge faster through my veins. She's fucking spectacular. I'm going to take my time over this. I'm going to make her tremble and shake until she can't take it anymore...

My tongue makes contact with her skin, just below her belly button, and the clean, lightly floral fragrance of her floods my senses. I try to bite back the harsh snarl that climbs up the back of my throat, hoping to soften the sound, to make sure I don't come across like a wild animal that's about to tear her apart. I fail epically, though. "Open," I demand. "Feet up. Bend your legs. Let your knees fall open. I want unrestricted access."

"Alex—"

"Do it right now or I'll arrange you how I want you myself."

She stutters out a shallow moan, but she slowly moves, placing her feet flat against the bed, letting her knees fall out so her pussy is exposed to me, not a part of her hidden from me. Her flesh is just as wet as I'd hoped. Pink, and plump and beautiful. From the hood of her clit to the opening of her pussy, she's slick, her flesh ready and begging to be licked clean.

"I want your come on my tongue," I growl, nipping the inside of her thigh with my front teeth. "I want you to come so fucking hard I feel you pulsing around my fingers, Silver. Are you gonna give me what I want?"

Her hips buck away from the bed again, her movements urgent and desperate. "Ye-yes. Fuck. Oh my god, Alex."

"You need it, don't you? You're desperate for me to make you come."

"Yes. Yes. Yes," she pants. "Please."

I haven't touched her. I'm so close, she can feel my hot breath on the most intimate, private parts of her body; I can tell by the way her skin has broken out in goosebumps. She reaches her hands down, digging her fingers into the inside of her thighs, like the crescents of her nails gouging into her skin will relieve some of the pressure building between her legs. She whimpers, sounding pained, and my protective, possessive side roars in my ears. "Don't worry. Shh, *tesoro*. It's okay. *Ti faro stare bene. Lo prometto.*" She has no idea what I'm saying, no idea that I'm reassuring her, swearing to take care of her. But she doesn't need to hear me say it. She *knows* I'm going to do it, no matter what.

I take hold of my dick, squeezing the tip, shuddering as a wall of pleasure rocks through me. I allow myself five torturously slow strokes before I get onto my knees and I fall between Silver's legs. She cries out, fisting my hair, as I sweep my tongue over her, tasting and exploring every part of her, her thighs tightening around my head as she loses control of herself.

Focusing on her clit, I get to work, making sure she feels every flick I administer with the tip of my tongue. I use my fingers, pushing one, and then two digits inside her, pumping them slowly, bringing her to a boil as her pleasure mounts.

I love fucking Silver. Being inside of her is a religious experience.

This feels better, though. Being selfless, doing something purely for her and only her, fills me with a deep sense of gratification that can't be beaten. Nothing in this life brings me more pleasure than making her come with my fingers and my mouth. *Nothing.*

She shakes, vibrating so hard, I almost have to hold her down on the bed. With her thighs still gripping my head, I can hear my pulse churning in my own ears. Fuck, the taste of her, the smell of her, the frantic way she angles herself up to me, giving me access to her pussy —it fucking turns me on more than I can stand. I rock into the mattress, unable to stop myself, my dick throbbing as I drive it up into the twisted bed sheets, and it feels so good that I groan, my breath heavy, into Silver's thigh.

Again, I roll my hips, the tip of my erection rubbing against the bed, trapped between my body and the mattress, and a mindless, depraved animal urge tells me to keep going. I stop myself, forcing myself to hold back. But only just.

God, I need her. I need her so fucking bad.

Sliding my fingers into her, I stroke up and toward myself in a beckoning motion, searching for the one spot inside her that will make her fucking implode. It doesn't take long to find it. I brace, locking my arm around Silver, making sure I have a tight hold on her, and then I apply the slightest pressure…

"Oh! Oh god, oh god, oh god!" Silver's back tries to arch away from the bed, but I have her expertly pinned down, holding her in place. "Alex! Alex, I'm gonna—"

She's still, tensed, muscles locked up, straining against me. I continue to lick and lave at her, sucking gently at her clit, knowing precisely how intense that's bound to feel with a monster of an orgasm creeping up on her. In seconds, Silver bears down, her pussy tightening around my fingers just like I wanted it to, and she lets out a high-pitched wordless scream that echoes around the bedroom.

She shudders, trying to bring her knees up to her chest, trying to roll away from me, but I bury my face deeper into her pussy, feasting on her, driving my tongue up inside her until she can't take it anymore and she's pulling me from between her legs by my hair.

"Alex! Alex, holy fuck! God, stop, I can't…I can't…I can't…"

I relent. Takes a lot of doing, but I manage. I sit back onto my heels, surveying the mess I've made of her, filled with a ruthless pride. She's struggling to breathe, fighting to pull air down into her lungs. Her face is beet red, not to mention her neck and the top of her chest. With her eyes still rolled back into her head, her mouth a little open, her arms and legs splayed haphazardly on the bed, she looks like a girl who just got her ass handed to her by a gold medalist in the orgasm Olympics.

"*Silver.*" My voice is filled with warning. Almost menacing. I can't fucking help it, though. Seeing her like this…I'm hanging onto my self-control by a very frayed thread.

Silver opens her eyes, looking at me, her pupils so blown that her irises are nearly gone altogether. "More," she whispers. "Fuck me, Alex. God, I want you to fuck me so bad."

My balls tighten, sending a powerful wave of need chasing up my back. I wasn't planning on holding back. Maybe giving her a minute to recover, perhaps, but with statements like that coming out of her mouth, I'm well and truly fucked.

I descend on her, taking her in my arms, cradling her in one arm, holding her head off the bed, while I support myself with the other. "Tell me if it's too much," I warn her through gritted teeth. "You say the word, and I'll fucking stop."

She gasps, her eyes going wide as I slam myself up inside her.

"Oh…my…god…" she whispers.

I fight to hold myself still for a second, to give her a chance to get used to the feeling of me inside her, all the way to the hilt, and it's the hardest thing I've had to do in a very long time. Her pale eyes are locked onto me, staring into my soul in the darkness, and it feels as though one more piece of puzzle is clicking into place. The moment's laden with tension, our breath caught in both our throats, as we stare at one another…

Her fingers lightly trace the side of my face. "I love you," she whispers.

"I love you, too, *cara*. You're my entire fucking world."

The exchange is soft, and gentle, and sincere. I mean it more than I've ever meant anything in my life. Silver leans up to kiss me, her eyes still open, refusing to break away from mine, and I slowly pull back, sliding out of her. A moment later, I drive myself forward, crushing her to my chest, and she moans into my mouth.

"Hold me tighter. *Please.*"

If I hold her any tighter, I'm going to rebreak her ribs. I understand what she's feeling, though, because I'm feeling it, too. I need to get closer to her. I need us to become one being, one entity, one heart and one soul. She wraps her legs around my waist and rocks against me, angling her hips up to meet mine, then pulling me back down, asking for even more of me, and my mind goes blank.

She feels…she feels so fucking good. I—

Holy…

…*shit.*

I go slowly for as long as I can, but soon Silver's scratching at my back and fisting my hair again, sinking her teeth into the top of my shoulder. I hiss through my teeth, reveling in the pain, and I give her what she so desperately needs.

I fuck her like my life depends on it, and each time I slam myself into her, thrusting my cock as deep as it will go, Silver peppers my neck and my face with kisses, pleading me for more. When we come, we come together, riding out a long wave of pleasure that seems like it will never end.

## 24

## ALEX

"Well if this isn't a damning picture, I don't know what is." I wasn't expecting to run into anyone. I was only planning on jogging down the fire escape and grabbing the cable for my cell from the Camaro, but when I fling back the apartment door, preparing for the cold, Cameron's standing there, his hand raised, about to knock.

He assesses me, eyes skating up and down my body, plainly unamused by the fact that I'm next to naked and only my thin boxers are covering my junk. "I'm assuming my daughter's in there," he says stiffly.

"Uh, yes?" Thank fuck I actually put on the boxers. I wasn't going to bother. The parking lot behind the hardware store is obscured from the street and isn't overlooked. I've made the mad dash down to the car naked before, when I've needed to grab something quickly. I only changed my mind because Silver threw my underwear at me and ordered me to cover myself.

Cameron's mood is almost as stormy as the night we broke into Weaving's pool house and he pulled out a motherfucking gun. He rubs a hand over his stubble, looking back down over his shoulder at the Parisi's van that's blocking me into my spot. "Put some fucking clothes on and come meet me down by the car, Alex. I need to talk to you."

"Should I arm myself?" I'm only half joking.

Cameron doesn't smile. "Hurry up. It's cold and I have a headache the size of fucking Texas. Tell Silver you're going out to grab some food or something. Chinese. She loves Chinese." He turns and walks down the metal fire escape, his boots clanging on every step, and it dawns on me that Cameron's about to finally give me the *'stay the hell away from my daughter'* speech. What else could he possibly want to talk to me about, when he's shown up on my doorstep wearing *that* murderous expression?

Back inside, Silver frowns at me from the bed. Holy fuck, she looks so damn good lying there, wrapped in nothing but a sheet. "That was quick," she says.

I kick my way into my jeans and snatch up a t-shirt, hurriedly getting dressed. "Figured I'd run out and grab some supplies for us since I'm up anyway. You want Chinese?"

She flops back against the pillows, groaning loudly. "Oh my god. You read my mind. Have I told you how much I love you recently?"

Socks go on next. I nearly eat shit as I balance on one leg, trying to shove my foot into one of my sneakers without undoing the laces. Silver laughs at me under her breath. Once the task is accomplished, I kneel on the edge of the bed, kissing her firmly on the mouth. "You haven't told me in at least five minutes," I say softly.

She bumps my nose with the end of her own. "Well I do. Very much, Mr. Moretti. Come back soon. I need your naked body back in this bed."

My dick would be rock hard if she'd said this to me any other time. Cameron's looming presence outside seems to have rendered my cock incapable, though. Goddamnit, this is gonna suck.

I give her another kiss, this time on her forehead, and then I hurry out of the apartment, grabbing a hoody and pulling it on as I run down the fire escape towards the van. No sooner am I sitting in the passenger seat than my temple is bouncing off the window, pain splintering my skull apart. Stars explode in my darkened vision, lighting up the inside of my head.

"You're lucky I'm not more like you," Cameron snarls.

*What...the...actual...?*

I hold my hand to my face, staring dumbly down at the flecks of blood that stain my palm when I lower it again. He hit me. Cameron fucking *hit me.* I gape at him, trying to make sense of what just happened.

"Don't look at me like that," Cam hisses. "I thought about taking a pair of secateurs to your balls."

*"What the fuck are secateurs?"*

"Does it matter? They're sharp. You wouldn't like them. Put your seatbelt on."

"What the fuck! I'm not putting my seatbelt on until I know that you haven't *actually gone and lost your fucking mind."*

I'm fizzing with anger. I can't help it, not that I should have to. Cameron belted me hard enough to ring my fucking bell and then some. It hurt way more when my head smashed into the fucking window, though. My temple feels like someone just took a sledgehammer to it.

"If I *were* more like you, both your legs would already be broken, I'm betting," Cam says. He tries to pretend that he's just rubbing his hand over the top of his thigh, but the way he's flexing his fingers suggests he probably hurt himself almost as much as he hurt me when he lamped me. "Tell me something." He turns sharply, gunning me down with a vicious glare. "Have you ever killed anyone?"

"What? *No!* God, can you stop being so fucking crazy for one second? You're not the fucking Godfather."

"Have you been present when that boss of yours has killed someone?" he asks.

*No, of course I haven't, Cam.*

This is what I'm a second away from saying. I close my mouth on the lie I was about to tell, quickly looking away. Fuck, it hurts to clench down on my jaw but it's the only thing keeping me from losing my shit right now.

Gary was the last man I let hit me like this. When I was young and smaller than him, there was nothing I could do *but* let him hit me. The moment I was strong enough to retaliate, I threw my punches as hard as I could manage, and I didn't hold back. I was hit plenty of times in juvie, too. Not once did I allow someone to get away with the infraction unpunished. My body wants to launch a counterstrike of epic proportions against the man sitting next to me in the driver's seat... but I can't allow that to happen.

He's Silver's father. I like him more than I thought possible. And... well, he kind of owed me a jaw-rattler. I've hardly been subtle when it's come to Silver. I've disrespected his home, and him in turn, with some of the shit I've done to his daughter under his roof. I don't blame him for wanting to tan my hide. Fuck, I totally deserve a beating, I guess. That doesn't stop the fire in my veins from demanding I grab him by his fucking throat and choke him out until he stops breathing.

"I don't work for Monty anymore." I grit the words out between my teeth, the coppery tang of blood coating my tongue. "I quit working at the Rock. I'm not gonna be around that kind of shit anymore."

"Oh, yeah?" Cam doesn't sound convinced. Sounds like he thinks I'm fucking stupid. "And your pal Monty just waved a hand in the air and said, 'Cool, see you around, man. Nice knowing you.' Is that what happened? He wasn't even slightly concerned that the guy who's been cleaning up his messes for him the past god knows how long just... doesn't feel like doing it anymore?"

I don't say anything. I'm not accustomed to being spoken to like this. Not even by Monty. Cam hisses angrily under his breath. He turns the key in the ignition, and the van grumbles to life. He reverses back out of the tiny parking lot way too fast, not even bothering to pause and check for on-coming traffic before he veers out onto the road.

He drives down Main Street, muttering furiously to himself. It's not until we're pulling into Raleigh High's parking lot and he's cutting the engine again that he quits muttering and speaks to me properly. "I wanted to be the cool dad, y'know. I was doing all kinds of shit when I was Silver's age, so I figured fuck it. Better that I know what she's up to. Better that I know where she is and who she's with. I've never once judged you, Alex. Most fathers in my position would have shot fucking first and asked questions later. But I gave you the benefit of the doubt. I thought...Cam, it's gonna be fine. They're just kids, figuring out their shit—"

"God...you're making it sound like I knocked Silver up and fled the state, Cameron. I love her. You know I love her. You knew we were...having sex..." I say, awkwardly tripping over the last two words. "She's not just some—"

"OF COURSE I KNEW YOU WERE HAVING SEX!" he roars.

Stunned, I immediately shut the fuck up.

He smashes his fist into the steering wheel, and the van's horn lets out a surprised *meep!* that sounds patently fucking ridiculous. "I didn't care about that," he says, panting a little too fast. "I wasn't fucking thrilled about it. Don't get me wrong. No father's stoked to know that their only daughter's no longer a—never mind. The sex thing...whatever. But you did something far worse tonight, Alessandro Moretti."

My head's spinning. Throwing my hands in the air, I try to figure out what his deal is, but he's making it fucking impossible. "Cameron, I don't know what you think I've done, but—"

"Do you think I'm stupid?" he asks, shaking his head angrily. "Is it the glasses? Do they make it seem as though I can't fucking see, Alex? 'Cause I hate to break it to you, but that's what they're there for. They make things pretty damn crystal clear, even from across an average-sized diner." He pauses. Takes a slow, tense breath. And then he lands a blow that rocks me way harder than his right hook. "You asked my seventeen-year-old daughter to marry you, didn't you, you little fuck?"

*How?* How can he know that? No way Silver would have told him. She made me promise to come with her to break the news. She hasn't left my side since we fled the diner...

I stare at him, trying to figure out how any of this has come to pass.

Out of nowhere, Cameron's anger disintegrates. He sags back into his seat, letting his arms fall to his sides. "A silence like that's gonna betray you every time," he murmurs. "Doesn't matter, though. Not really. See, I know my daughter, and I know what it feels like to love someone the way she loves you. I can see it in her eyes. The way she looked at you after you whispered in her ear..." Again, he shakes his head; he can't seem to stop repeating the motion. "I knew what you'd done the second I saw that look on her face."

A sour, bitter knife twists in my chest. I should have seen this coming a mile away. "What? So, it's one thing letting your daughter date the bad boy for a little while, when she's young and wild, but another thing entirely letting her saddle herself with him for the rest of her life?"

I wait for his confirmation. It's obvious, for fuck's sake. He's been tolerating me since I rolled up on my bike and now he's done playing at the 'cool dad,' as he so eloquently put it. He's going to put his foot down, and he's going to try and take her away from me. And the very worst part is that there's nothing I can do about it. I won't come between Silver and her father. I *won't* do it. It would be the most selfish thing I've done.

Cameron heaves out a heavy, dejected sigh. For a moment he says nothing, gazing blankly out of the windshield, but then he rubs his hands over his face and speaks. "Do you really think I see things so black and white? This has nothing to do with you, asshole. This is about *her*."

Well, that's a surprise. I chew on that for a beat, trying to level out my frustration. "You don't think I'll make her happy?"

He laughs, frustrated. "I'm sure you will. But this isn't the life I envisioned for her, Alex. Married at seventeen? You say you're too smart now but trust me. You'll end up with kids before you know it, before either of you really know how the hell to be adults yourselves, and that'll be it. She'll end up getting a practical qualification at night school because it'll help her get a steady, reliable job. And you'll do your best, too. I know you will. But fuck..." He trails off, closing his eyes, and the flash of pain that crosses his features stuns the shit out of me. "It makes for a small life, Alex. Making do. Getting by. Doing just enough. I want so much more for her than that. She deserves the biggest life imaginable. She's supposed to be an astronaut or a fucking explorer in the Amazon, not a goddamn admin worker."

Inhaling a steady breath, I cross my arms, letting my chin rest on my chest. "I want her to fly, Cam. I'm never going to clip her wings. Being *married*—" Shit, why is that so hard to say out loud to him? "—won't mean she can't chase down her dreams. I'm never going to stand in the way of the things she wants."

"Easy to say. But twenty years down the line, when you're both turning forty and all you've done is get by, then what? Are you gonna do something stupid and have a fucking affair? What then?"

Oh…

Damn.

This isn't about Silver and me. Scratch that. I suppose it *is* about us…but it's more about Cam. He married Silver's mom right out of high school. They were kids themselves when they had Silver. He told me himself, back when I lived in the trailer, that he'd packed his bags and nearly moved across the country the very same day she was born. But he'd stayed in the end. They'd been happy. And after it all, Silver's mom had destroyed their marriage by sleeping with another man. She'd grown bored of her safe, comfortable, predictable life and she'd done something that had hurt Cameron in the worst way possible. From his point of view, it's happening all over again, only this time it's Silver giving up her freedom too soon and too young. It's Silver who'll be hurt down the line when I grow frustrated with our safe, comfortable, predictable life, and now he can't bear to watch.

So, he did something about it instead. He got me in his car, punched me in the face, and now he's holding me hostage at the school for some reason. "Cam. Come on. I'm not going to do that to Silver. Ever."

"You're *seventeen*, Alex. You don't know what you're going to do next year, let alone in twenty."

Fuck him for that. I don't like hearing the accusation or the condemnation in his voice but losing it at him isn't going to prove anything. Instead, I manage to keep a cool head. "You're right. I don't know what I'm going to do next year. I don't know if I'll go to college, or if I'm gonna get a job, or…I don't know. But what I'm certain of is Silver. If she goes off to Dartmouth, I'll be sitting in the car right next to her with all my shit packed up, too. She wants to disappear off into the Amazon? I'll take my malaria pills like a good boy and make sure she doesn't get eaten. And, shit. If she decides she wants to be a fucking astronaut and go into space, I'll figure that out too somehow. Whatever direction she decides to head in, and for as long as she *wants* me by her side, I will be there, taking every step with her. And our life won't be safe, or comfortable anyway. She's full of music, and laughter, and light, Cam. How can anything ever be predictable with Silver around?"

Inside the school, a light goes on in the main hallway. Cameron clenches the van keys in his fist, loosening his grip and then tightening it again. We both sit for a while, staring at the rectangle of light coming from inside the school, cutting through the dark, and I wait for him to say something.

It takes a long, *long* time.

Finally, he reaches into the inside pocket of his jacket and pulls something out. He turns it over in his hands—the small maroon box with the gold fleur-de-lis embossed in gold on the top—and then puffs out his cheeks, slapping it into my chest.

"What's this?" I ask even though I know precisely what it is; the box feels like a burning hot coal in my hands.

"It was my grandmother's."

"I can afford to get her a ring, y'know. I have plenty—"

"Yeah, yeah, I'm sure you do," Cam interjects grumpily. "But this was supposed to go to Silver when she got engaged. It's special. During the war, my grandfather helped to pass messages through the Dolomites to the allied forces. He bought that ring in Switzerland and he carried it with him for three years until he could get back to my grandmother. It has a good story. There's a happy ending attached to it. It's the kind of ring that should be worn. Better than some soulless new piece of jewelry from Zales."

"I have better taste than *Zales*." It's offensive that he'd even suggest such a thing. I may be a guy, and I may have neck tattoos and look like I could give a shit about women's jewelry, but I'd never walk into a chain store and buy a generic ring for the woman I wanted to marry. I would have bought Silver something that reflected her—something unique and one-of-a-kind.

When I open the box that Cameron thrust at me, the ring inside is exactly that. The stone isn't a diamond. It's a blushed color of pink, clear and bright, and it catches what little light there is in the van, refracting it beautifully. The design isn't as traditional as I thought it was going to be. It's feminine and truly special, but... "The setting's silver?"

Cam grunts. "There was a war on. Precious metals and stones were rationed just like everything else. Even in Switzerland. My mother asked if she could get it remounted for my grandmother back in the seventies, but that idea went down like the Hindenburg. My grandmother turned to her and said..." Cam turns to me, echoing the woman's words, "*This* is the ring I said yes to. I wouldn't change it for the world. As far as I'm concerned, *silver is far more precious than gold.*"

Huh. Too apt to be a coincidence. Silver's an uncommon name for a person. I get the feeling that a little piece of her great-grandmother's story was passed down to Cam's daughter when she was gifted with that name. I nod, snapping the box closed. Silver *is* far more precious than gold.

"You're not going to try and stop us, then?" It could be the recent head injury, but I'm completely confused.

Cam laughs down his nose—one doleful, resigned huff of breath. "You're never gonna hurt her. You're never gonna cause her pain. Not even for a minute."

These are statements, not questions. Still, I respond as though they are. "I'd rather fucking die."

"Then, no. I'm not gonna try and stop you. What would be the point? It's too late for any of that. I swore I'd always give Silver the life she wanted, and she's made her decision. She's chosen a life with you. And at the end of the day...a song can't be unsung, can it, Alessandro?"

I grimace down at the box, a little twisted up inside over the sound of that name coming out of his mouth. He's done it to rile me up a little. He knows only Silver can call me Aless—

"Alex."

"It's fine. I don't care. You can call me whatever you—"

"No, *Alex!*" He hits me in the top of my arm, and a low growl builds deep in the barrel of my chest.

"I swear, man. That was your last free shot. If you hit me again, I'm gonna fucking—"

He grabs me by the arm and shakes me. "Shut the fuck up. *Look!*"

Shocked by the urgency of his tone, I look up as commanded, following his wide-eyed gaze out of the windshield, back toward the school. The light's still on in the hall like it was before, but...now there are three people standing on the steps that lead up to the main entrance—the figures of three men.

I lean forward, squinting into the dark. The identities of the three men become apparent all at once, and a cold, vile sensation descends on me. "What in holy fucking shit is *this*? Can I borrow your glasses?"

A deep, throaty rumble fills the car; in the driver's seat, Cameron growls like a feral dog that's just cornered in a cage. "They're broken," he replies. "They have to be. Because I can*not* be seeing this right. That's Principal Darhower. And that motherfucker from the DEA. And that—" Cam says, choking on the words, "Is someone who should *not* be breathing free fucking air."

## 25

## SILVER

Orange chicken doesn't even take an hour and a half to cook from scratch at home. I know from many, many experiences (no, I am *not* proud of myself) that it takes less than twenty minutes to order, wait for, and collect said dish from the Imperial Dragon over by the post office, so I begin to get a little worried. I try to call Alex, but his phone's sitting dead on his bedside table. He was going out to get his charger when he suddenly came back into the apartment, talking about supplies and Chinese food, and then he left without even plugging it in to power up.

I'm getting ready to call over at the diner—maybe Alex went there to pick up the guitars and all of the gear we just left sitting there after our performance—when he creeps in through the apartment door like a criminal trying to sneak past a guard dog.

From the kitchen, I peer out into the hall, folding my arms across my chest. "Alex, what are you doing?"

"*Figlio di puttana!*" He puts a hand out, bracing himself against the wall. His dark, wavy hair looks like he's run his hands through it a thousand times, and his eyes are...wait...

"Alex, *why the hell do you have a black eye?*" I rush toward him, reaching up for the swollen, bruised contusion on the side of his cheekbone. "Oh my god, your eyebrow's split open. What the hell happened?" Less than two hours. He's been gone less than two hours, and he still manages to find trouble.

He grimaces when I touch my fingertips to the cut just above his left eye, sucking in a sharp breath. "Well, the black eye's courtesy of your dad."

I can't have heard him right. "What? My *dad*?"

"Turns out he's really fucking good at putting two and two together. Did you know that about him?"

"I spent most of my childhood trying to pull the wool over his eyes unsuccessfully. Yeah, I know that. What are you talking about?"

"He knew I asked you to marry me. And he wasn't very happy about it."

I step back, covering my mouth with both hands. "Oh, shit."

"Yeeaahhhh."

Quickly looking him up and down, I scan for any other injuries. If Dad figured out what we did tonight, then he wouldn't have left it at a black eye. He would have gone for castration, no doubt about it. "Are you okay?"

"I'm good."

"Then...what's with the sneaking in? And what's with the weird look on your face?" He really does look weird, like he's holding a swarm of bees inside his mouth and they're stinging him repeatedly, but he can't let them out.

"I thought maybe you were asleep. I didn't want to wake you."

"It's nine-thirty and you promised me Chinese food. Why the hell would I be asleep? Alex? Hey, what's going on? What is it? What aren't you telling me?"

The look on his face is really beginning to freak me out now. He was smiling when he left the apartment, but now he looks like the world went ahead and ended on him. My nerves are shot to hell when he reaches out and takes hold of my hand, guiding me into the bedroom.

"Alex?"

"Sit down, *Argento*."

"Why? God, just spit it out. I'm about to have a goddamn nervous breakdown."

"Just sit down a second. I need to think."

He looks like his nerves are fried. Pacing up and down the bedroom, he chews on his thumb nail, breathing heavily. I sit on the bed, pulling my legs out of the way of the path he's wearing into the area rug, tucking my knees under my chin. The waiting is fucking killing me but rushing him isn't an option.

Following him with my eyes from one side of the room to the other, my mind races. Something's happened. Something terrible. I can't figure out what, though. Sadly, the worst things that could ever happen to Alex actually did happen recently. His brother fucking died. He can't be trying to brainstorm a way to break up with me; he only asked me to marry him four hours ago. Hopefully it's going to take a lot longer than that for him to get sick of me. Which means this can't be about him. So that means...

Oh.

It must be about me.

A sharp pain begins to throb behind my right eye—forewarning of an epic headache. For Alex to be this wound up, whatever this is about has got to be bad.

"Is it Dad?" I ask quietly. "You were just with him. Is he hurt or something? Sick?"

Alex shakes his head, eyes briefly meeting mine before he looks away again. "No. No, Cam's fine. Well...he's pretty worked up, but..."

"About us? Getting married?"

"No. Christ." He stops abruptly, dropping into a crouch in front of me at the end of the bed. His hands are like ice when he reaches out for me and threads his fingers through mine. He's wearing that look that people get when they know they're about to say something that's going to shatter someone's world into pieces. "Cam's upset because... he drove me to the school. He wanted to talk. When we were done, we realized there were people standing on the steps outside."

"Okay. Sometimes they have teacher training after the students leave, right? Or a janitorial crew might have been—"

"It was Darhower," Alex says, cutting in. "That DEA prick was with him. And so was..." He blows out, hard.

"If you don't spit it out, I'm gonna scream. For real. I can't take it anymore."

"Jacob." His voice cracks on the name. "*Jacob* was with them."

I blink, and then I blink again. Alex is out of focus. My vision sways and warps like someone just dosed me with acid. "I'm sorry. Did you just say Jacob was outside the school? *Jacob Weaving?*"

Alex nods, worry pulsing off him in waves. "I had to wrestle your dad back into the car and drive him home. That's why I was gone so long."

"Dad got out of the car?"

"Yeah. I think he would have tried to kill him if I hadn't grabbed him first."

Everything is so muffled, like wads of cotton wool are blocking my ear canals. I can't quite… seem to understand…

Frowning, I narrow my eyes at Alex. "That's not possible, though. Jacob's in prison. They took him away. They have so much evidence. Your witness statement. The photos of Zen. All of the charges they slapped him with for helping his dad. It can't have been him. It must have been someone else."

Alex winces. "Cam made a couple of calls as I drove him back to your place. Sheriff Hainsworth said he couldn't discuss the matter, but one of his deputies called back a couple of minutes later. She heard the Sheriff and said it wasn't right, what was happening, and that we… that *you* deserved to know what was going on. Apparently…" Alex looks off to the left, staring, his mouth slightly open, as if he doesn't really know how to proceed. "Apparently the DEA are dropping the charges against Jake. His dad cut a deal with that Lowell fucker and said he'd give them the names of five big drug smugglers if they lessened his sentence. Jake won't be held responsible for anything he did while working for Caleb. The rape charges still stand, but they've let him out on bail until his hearing."

Unwittingly, my hand moves to the base of my neck. Fuck, the rope is still there, tightening around my throat, cutting off my air supply. "What about the attempted murder charge?"

Alex lets out a tight, scathing sound. "Dropped. They've replaced it with an assault charge instead, which is absolute fucking bullshit. Your dad thinks that they lowered that charge as part of Caleb's deal with the DEA as well."

I hug my knees even tighter, staring at the floor. "So…that's it. They just let him out?"

Alex huffs, his head hanging low. "Yes."

"And…if he was at the school, then what does that mean? They're just gonna let him come back? Like nothing fucking happened?"

"I don't know. Darhower yelled across the parking lot, but I didn't exactly get a chance to stop and speak to him. I was too busy trying to get your dad to calm his shit."

"I can't imagine that," I say numbly. "*You* trying to calm *him* down. I'd have thought it'd be the other way around."

"Believe me, *Argento*. I wanted to peel the bastard's fucking face off the moment I laid eyes on him. Darhower and Lowell were there, though. It would have been a one-way ticket to jail for me if I'd even spat in their direction. They can't watch over him twenty-four seven, though. He'll find himself alone at some point, and when he does, I'll be ready and fucking waiting for him."

This is so, so bad. Alex's rage is unparalleled. He's simmering with it—it won't take much for him to bubble over. We've been through this already. If he hurts Jake, it'll be the end of the line for him. And he won't just hurt him this time. He'll kill him. And then what? I only get to see him a couple of hours a week? For the next thirty fucking years? He'll be fifty by the time he's released from prison, the best years of our life together gone. Jacob will still have fucking won.

I'm not stupid enough to tell Alex not to hunt him down, though. It'd be a waste of breath. He saw me hanging from that rafter with a rope around my neck, and *I* saw the fear and the pain on his face when he thought he was going to lose me. Jacob has to pay for what he did, and Alex won't rest until he sees it come to pass. But there has to be another way.

Slowly getting to my feet, I sniff, surprised to discover that I'm crying.

"Silver?" Alex whispers.

I step around him, picking up my bag from the floor by his bedroom door. Inside, I hunt down the small card, still tucked into the zipped interior pocket. It's a bit rumpled and dog-eared on one corner, but the number's still perfectly legible. I hand it over to Alex, knowing that I'm handing over a piece of my soul with it—a piece I will gladly sacrifice if it means that Jake finally gets his just desserts.

Alex scans the card with quick, assessing eyes. "What's this?"

"The doctor who treated me…I think her boyfriend might be the kind of guy you pay to make people disappear." The words don't sound real coming out of my mouth. They sound like something someone else would say, reading off a script in some kind of movie. Things like this don't get spoken about in real fucking life. I barely feel any connection to the statement at all. Instead, crazed laughter bubbles up the back of my throat, spilling out of me in bursts, like deranged hiccups.

Alex frowns at the card. "A hitman? You think your doctor's boyfriend is a *hitman*?"

"Yeah. He had a weird name. Zeus, or Zane, or—"

His head snaps up. "Zeth? The guy who gave this to you was called *Zeth*?"

"Yeah. That was his name."

Shaking his head, Alex stares at me incredulously. "No…fucking…way."

## 26

## SILVER

"For the fifteen hundredth time, this isn't up for discussion."

Dad's on the warpath. He hasn't stopped ranting about injustice and corruption since I woke up this morning. He nearly mowed down an old woman on the drive over to Raleigh because he was gesticulating too wildly and didn't notice her step out into the road.

"I'm not gonna stand by and allow that boy to come back to school, Silver. No. Uh-uh. No fucking way. Their position's utterly untenable. Well, I have no idea what their position could possibly actually *be*, but it isn't going to fly. If Jim Darhower wants to bow and scrape to a family in disgrace, then he's gonna have me to contend with. Not to mention the rest of the parents, when they find out that the principal of the fucking school is okay with a fucking rapist murderer rubbing shoulders with *their* kids."

"Jake didn't actually kill anyone," I mumble under my breath.

"We don't know that! How are *we* supposed to know that?" Dad screeches. "For all we know, Jake's murdered a bunch of people and his sycophant parents covered it all up. Man, it makes me fucking sick that Caleb Weaving can still wield this kind of power from behind prison bars." He smashes the heel of his hand into the steering wheel, baring his teeth. *"It isn't fucking right!"*

Suffice it to say, I didn't want him to drive me to school this morning. I didn't want him anywhere near this disaster of a situation, but there was no talking him down. He swore he was going to keep a calm head, but he'd broken that promise before he even hit the end of the driveway. "You're cursing too much," I tell him. "Darhower isn't even going to agree to see you, you know that, right? You're supposed to make an appointment. And you look *insane*, Dad. He's gonna take one look at you and be afraid for his life."

Dad does look terrifying. His hair's standing on end, his glasses propped at a weird angle on his face, and there are dark circles under his eyes. He didn't go to bed last night. He was still waiting up for me when I came in just before midnight, and he refused to sleep. He prowled around the house, banging cupboard doors, slamming around in the kitchen, generally being a pain in the ass, and when I came downstairs at seven thirty this morning, he was ready and waiting for me at the door with the Nova's keys in his hand, blue murder written all over his face.

His expression has only worsened on the drive across town. "He's gonna see me," he grits out, swinging the car into the school parking lot. "And he'd better not tell me that that little fuckboy is gonna be allowed to come back and attend classes, or I will burn the place to the fucking ground. So help me, God, I'll do it."

∾

"I understand your concern, truly I do. Now, I know this situation isn't perfect, Mr. Parisi, but we have to face facts. Raleigh High is the only school within thirty mi—"

Perched on the very edge of his seat, my Dad cocks his head to one side, leaning in closer to Darhower. The principal doesn't know my father as well as I do; he doesn't know that my old man is about to go nuclear. "Let me just lay this out for you, Jim. So you can see it from an impartial perspective...because I'm giving you the benefit of the doubt here. I'm sure the only reason you're even considering this *ridiculous* course of action is because you're way too close to this. A student at this school has raped not one but *two* girls. That we know of. He broke into my house and kidnapped my daughter. He then brought her here, to this school, where *you* have been tasked with ensuring the safety of our children, and he brutally beat her. As if that wasn't bad enough, he then put a fucking noose around her neck and attempted to hang her from the rafters of the school's gymnasium. Government officials charged this same boy—"

"Those charges have been dropped, Cameron."

"I DON'T GIVE A FLYING FUCK IF THE CHARGES HAVE BEEN DROPPED!"

I've never seen Dad's face go purple before. Not even when Mom told him about the affair. A vein pulses in his temple, fit to burst. I reach over and place a hand on top of his clenched fist, but my plea for him to take it down a notch goes unnoticed.

"Government officials charged this same boy with some pretty serious offences, including but not limited to smuggling, coercion, assault and battery, theft—"

"This really isn't helpful—"

"Shut the fuck up, Jim. This piece of shit has broken countless laws and hurt more people than I even know what to do with. Did you know that Zen MacReady tried to fucking kill herself, Jim?"

"I know Zen's parents thought it would be best if she took some time to recuperate at a facility. They said her nerves—"

"And what about the pregnancy, huh? Did you know that that poor girl is stuck with a horrendous decision now, because one of those assholes actually got her *pregnant*?"

Darhower's face turns ashen, the color draining from his cheeks. "No," he mutters. "No, I didn't know she was pregnant."

"Well, she is. What are you gonna do if she decides, even though she was violated repeatedly by those sick fucking assholes, that she can't face having an abortion on top of everything else? Are you going to expect her to come back to this school, too? And make her walk the halls with Jacob Weaving sneering at her swollen belly every time he passes her on the way to class? What the *fuck* is wrong with you?"

"Cam—"

"No, *Jim*. If that boy steps foot inside this school, there *will* be consequences."

Darhower looks at me, a skittish, brief glance that says a lot. He hates that a student's parent it talking to him like this, and he hates that I'm here to witness it. In fairness, I really wish I wasn't. He puffs out his chest, drumming his fingers against his desk. "Threatening me is ill-advised. I'm sure Karen heard that."

"So what if she fucking did? Karen's a good person. She's probably drafting up her resignation letter as we speak. I can't imagine for a second that she'd want to continue working here, for a man who'd let something as heinous as this happen on his watch. I'm gonna be frank, here. You're gonna call whoever's been charged with watching over that bastard Weaving, and you're gonna tell them to keep him faaaaaar away from Raleigh High. If you don't, I'm gonna drive myself over to Bellingham and I'm going to visit every single newspaper and news station I can find, and I'm gonna lay this mess out to them the same way I just laid it out to you, and I'm gonna see what they think of it. And when I'm done in Bellingham, I'm gonna drive to motherfucking Seattle, and I'm gonna do the exact same thing there. I'm gonna give them your personal address. I'm gonna give them your cellphone number. And then, when I've got everyone good and riled up, I'm gonna remind them of the shooting that took place here not that long ago, and the very stirring speech you gave to my kid about how you were gonna do fucking better—"

Principal Darhower is visibly shaking as he rocks back in his chair. "To what end, Cameron? What good would any of that do? Stirring up painful memories is only going to hurt—"

"I don't care who it hurts," my father hisses. "I care about my daughter and the shit that she's been through. Now you make that call right the fuck now, while I'm sitting here in front of you, or I swear on all I hold dear, I am quickly gonna become your worst fucking nightmare."

## 27

## ALEX

Muffled chatter leaks into the hallway, spilling out from the gaps underneath the classroom doors as teachers mark off their students one by one. I should be in my own home room, grunting out a response when *my* name is called out, but my perfect attendance record is irrelevant now. Maeve and Rhonda might leave a voicemail, griping about my decline in fucks given, but frankly I couldn't care less. I have an itch that needs to be scratched, and it isn't the kind of itch that'll just go away on its own. Left unchecked, this itch will turn into a full-blown obsession, liable to cause some serious trouble.

From around the corner, footsteps, quick and urgent, echo off the walls, growing closer. I take a step back into the recessed doorway to the men's bathrooms, willing the shadows to hide me. It's only that Mr. French is heavily distracted when he comes into view, lasering in on the door opposite me, that he doesn't notice me lurking in wait.

He raps briefly on the classroom door but doesn't wait before steamrolling in. I get a brief snapshot of students sitting at their desks, faces turned up to Mr. French as his hushed voice disturbs their morning ritual. "Ah, Ms. Jarvis. Sorry for the interruption. I need to see Jacob Weaving."

The door closes, blocking my view of the intrigued faces beyond and stealing away the sound. I bounce on the balls of my feet, impatience running rife in my veins. Any second now. Any second...

"THIS...CAN'T DO THIS...FUCKING BULLSHIT!"

Only half of Jake's outraged shout is audible through the classroom door, but I get the gist of it. He's making a scene. I paint the mental picture—Jake, sitting behind his desk, oozing swagger, smug as the obnoxious prick he is, planning out how best to taunt the girl I love with his presence. Then, Jake suspicious, wondering why he's being beckoned out of class already, when the day hasn't even started. Jake, asking questions, demanding answers. And now, losing his fucking mind when that poor bastard French tries to 'manage' him.

"NO! I'm not...anywhere. I... is my right! The cops... sorry you ever... hands off me, you..."

I smirk into the collar of my leather jacket like the sick motherfucker I am. Inside the classroom, there's a scraping of chairs and a stifled shout. Loud clattering follows, and the sound of Ms. Jarvis' shrill voice rising into a startled yelp. A second later, the classroom door opens, and a confusion of sound and movement pours out. Jake stumbles—Did French just *push* him? My god, has he been a secret badass this whole time?—catching hold of the doorjamb for balance. His bag skates along the ground in front of him...and comes to a stop right at my feet.

Jake's eyes travel from my Stan Smiths all the way up my legs, my stomach, my chest until they reach my face, and a look of abject hatred twists his features. "What the fuck are *you* looking at?" he snarls, snatching his bag up from the floor.

Yup. Nothing's changed. He's still the same arrogant cunt he was before he got locked away. You'd think becoming intimately acquainted with the inside of a jail cell would have humbled him a little. Some guys rot in that environment, though. The vilest things about them, their anger, their prejudice, their vitriol, fester in the dark, and when they step out into the light again, they have become the very worst possible versions of themselves. I didn't think Jake *could* get any worse, but seems as though I was wrong.

"Looks like you lost some muscle, Jake. Most people pack it on in prison." I can't help it. It's in my nature to want to destroy this evil cocksucker. I want to take hold of something serious and sharp and drive it up underneath his ribs until I hear his breath turn wet and crackling. I want him to experience a paralyzing level of pain that will make him *beg* for death. A verbal jab won't come anywhere close to satiating my need for violence, but unfortunately it's going to have to do.

An ugly sneer contorts Jake's face. "Getting shot'll have that effect," he snarls. "I spent weeks on a hospital ward because of you. You're lucky I didn't die."

"Lucky?" I step out of the bathroom doorway, my mouth turning down as I pretend to consider this. I don't stop walking forward until I'm good and right in his face. He smells like laundry soap and expensive, fancy cologne—some ultra-masculine scent that probably has a name like *'Victory'* or *'Warrior'*. I can still smell the metallic, unpleasant, desperate odor of prison on him, though. It's a smell like no other and takes a long-ass time to fade. "Luck's subjective, I guess. Personally, I would have felt a little luckier if you'd bled out and expired—"

"Moretti, what the hell are you doing out here? Get to class!" Mr. French storms out into the hallway, his face a livid shade of red. I almost pity the guy; he wasn't built to handle this kind of situation. He trained to become a teacher, not a glorified bouncer, tasked with dragging wayward teenagers across school grounds. From the looks of him, his grip on this situation's weak at best.

I flash a stark, hostile smile at Jake, staring him down, before taking a healthy step back, holding my hands up in the air. "Just saying hello to an old friend."

"You're so fucked. You know that, right?" Jake thunders. "You don't know when to play it smart. I'm *out*, Moretti." He holds his hands out, posturing as he looks around, proving his point. "I'm out, and I'm not going back. My old man's taken care of everything. There's nothing you or that cunt girlfriend of yours can d—"

"NO!" Mr. French roars, grabbing Jake by the scruff of his shirt. "Absolutely not. No chance. That is not a word I will tolerate. Get moving. *Now.*" He shoves Jake, who hardly even moves. Baring his teeth at me, he pointedly ignores the teacher.

"Wait and see, Moretti. Your precious social worker can vouch for you all she wants, but you're on borrowed time. Dad's going after Monty. How long do you think it'll be before that stupid motherfucker turns *you* over to the feds, huh? They know about the drugs and the guns. They know all about your little midnight deliveries. And who have you got, huh? You think your dad's got enough pull to negotiate a deal for *you*, asshole? Hell no. I know all about your old man and he's a fucking dumb, drop out loser, just like his son."

I mean to throw the right hook in my head, but somehow the imagined action fights its way out into reality. My fist connects with a satisfying crunch, and a stunned, laughably hurt expression flickers over Jake's features before he staggers back, tripping over his own feet and landing hard on his ass.

The classroom door's still open. Jake looks over his shoulder, his eyes wide with embarrassment as the students, who have all been watching on, look away, suppressing smiles and whispering to one another. None of his brainwashed football buddies are here. No, the students sitting at the desks are mostly girls. Once upon a time, they would have had his back. They would have urged him to get up and return the hit. Now, they look disdainfully down on the boy they used to worship, and their message is clear. Even I can hear it, silently screamed, as one by one they all avert their eyes.

*We know what you did. We know what you did. We know what you did.*

"You saw that, Mr. French. You were witness. He attacked me," Jake spits, scrambling to his feet. He turns to the other students. "You all did!" he rages. "My lawyer's gonna want witness statements from all of you!"

No one says a word. Ms. Jarvis appears in the doorway. She refuses to meet Jacob's furious gaze. She looks to me for a second, and—what is that in her eyes? Condemnation? Commiseration? Looks more like gratitude—before she slowly swings the classroom door closed.

"Fucking *bitch*," Jake hisses.

"Enough!" Mr. French grabs Jake by the arm, jerking him toward the exit. "This is over. Time to go, Jacob. One more word out of your mouth and I'm gonna have to have you forcibly removed."

"By who?" he snorts, ripping his arm free. "You really think you can take me? You're pathetic, French. You couldn't fight your way out of a wet paper bag. You're gonna tell them what Moretti did to me or my father's gonna sue you for every penny you have."

"That shit won't work on me, asshole. I'm flat broke, and besides, I doubt your daddy's feeling very litigious. He's got more important things to worry about. Now get the hell out of this school before I call the cops."

Jacob runs both of us through with a viciously sharp glare. "You think this is gonna last? Seriously? I'll be back before the end of the week. You'll see. Yeah, you'll fucking see."

He charges for the exit, pausing halfway down the hall to piledrive his fist into a locker door, his shout of rage loud enough to wake the dead. More amused than upset, I realize that it's my locker he's just dented, and I begin to laugh quietly under my breath.

"I mean it, Moretti." Mr. French pants, his shoulders hitching up and down, probably from the adrenalin that's just hit him square in the chest. "Get to class. I swear on my dead grandmother's grave, I am *so* sick of this shit."

## 28

## SILVER

"He *didn't*."

I snap off a piece of Red Vine, digging my fingernail into the red, gummy candy. "He *did*. And then he insisted on walking home in a rage instead of just taking my car."

"Wow. I can't picture your dad going full psycho like that. He's always seemed so…un-provoke-able," Halliday says, inspecting her split ends. Zander hums, laying down on the backseat of the Nova, sticking his booted feet out of the open window. Gradually, he seems to be surrendering his preppy disguise and his true colors are bleeding through. He's still sporting a button-down shirt, but his chinos are gone, traded out with semi-smart looking black jeans. I'm guessing by the end of the week he's gonna be rocking a band tee, and the clean-cut image he's been trying to project will be gone completely. "I can totally see it," he says, prodding a finger at a small hole in the fabric of the Nova's roof.

"Don't rip that." I fix a disapproving stare on him in the rearview mirror. He drops his hand to rest on his chest.

"I saw how crazy Papa Parisi got when that prick hurt your dog. He lost his shit at the vet's. Makes sense that he'd go nuclear on Darhower at the thought of Weaving anywhere near you again."

Halliday dips her head, squinting harder at the spiky ends of her hair; I haven't mentioned her very obvious reactions every time Zander opens his mouth to speak, but it's becoming hard to hold back. She either has a thing for him or she's terrified of him, one of the two.

The wind moans across the parking lot, shaking the stand of trees that lead down to the dell, making their boughs dance. My heart damn near skips out of my chest when I see the dark figure, shoulders hunched up around his ears, jogging toward us across the cracked black top. Alex pulls a face when he sees that Halliday has claimed his spot in the passenger seat. He mumbles unhappily under his breath as he wrenches the rear door open, slapping Zander's feet out of the way as he slides into the car.

His cheeks are red from the cold, his dark eyes bright, hair a little tousled, and I suddenly resent the fact that there are two other people in this car. I want him all to myself. I want him some place dark and quiet, where I can unwrap him slowly like the gift that he is and savor every tiny, quirky detail of him. He smirks at me, catching the edge of his lower lip between his teeth, and pinpricks of heat tingle across the top of my chest.

"Gross," Zander states. "If I'd known swooning was on the agenda, I would've brought something to vomit into."

"*Move*." Alex shoves at his legs, trying to push him further over. "If any part of you is touching me by the time I take off my jacket, you're gonna wind up bruised."

Zander rights himself in his seat, sitting up properly. "Oh, we can be matching," he says, poking a finger at the purple shadow that's rising on Alex's cheekbone. "What happened? Lemme guess. You walked into a doorframe."

Quick as lightning, Alex grabs Zander's finger and bends it back, growling. "The fuck's wrong with you? Do you have *no* sense of self-preservation?"

Oh my god. Now I know how my parents felt when I used to brawl with Max on the backseat. "Just behave, both of you, or I'm gonna turn the heating off."

Zander wrenches his finger free, shaking his hand out, silently mouthing the word, *fuck*. "Don't worry, *Argento*. This is how he shows me that he loves me."

Alex thumps him hard, giving him a dead leg. "Only I get to call her that."

I have to take control of this situation now, before things get out of hand. "Zander, what did you wanna talk to us about?" I hold up the ratty piece of paper I found in my locker after History, showing him the scrawl of his own handwriting, which reads:

**Group chat.**
**Lunch.**
**Muy importante.**
-Zander

I wasn't sure who he'd meant by group—presumably just me, Alex and himself—but he didn't object to Halliday's presence when he got in the car. Zander snags the note from my hand, tucking it into his jeans pocket as though he's planning on reusing it later. "I heard about the Weaving situation last night when I was working at the Rock."

Alex clenches his jaw, turning to look out of the window; the very mention of the Rock is uncomfortable for him.

"Monty's pretty pissed at you, man," Zander continues. "He wants a sit-down. Things are getting ugly with the Dreadnaughts. I'm not sure how long I'll be on task at Raleigh, casing the place for your boss."

"He isn't my boss anymore."

"Don't be such a baby. Just go and talk to him for fuck's sake. Things aren't as bad as you think they are."

Tension fizzles in the air as Alex twists, turning a cold scowl on Zander. "Is this seriously why you dragged us out here? To try and play peacemaker between me and Monty?"

"No. That's just a side note. A *by-the-way*. Do with it what you will."

"Great. I'll shove it up your ass."

"*Alex.*" I thump my head against the headrest, rolling my eyes. "Just get on with it, Zander. I'm starving."

"All right, all right. Monty was talking to some DEA Agent last night. Some smarmy fucker called Lowell." Alex sits up in his seat like he's been electrocuted. He keeps his mouth shut, though, letting Zander speak. "Monty told Lowell that Jacob wasn't his concern anymore, so long as Caleb went down. He's obviously got some kind of his own deal going on with the feds. But what he said after Lowell left was surprising. He told Casey, one of the Dreadnaught boys, that there's an informant in the club. Someone who's been slipping information to the feds for years. Said he finally had proof and there was gonna be hell to pay."

Alex frowns. "Informant?"

Halliday pivots, twisting around in her seat to face the boys. This piece of information seems to have piqued her interest. "What kind of informant?"

"A long-standing one," Zander says. "I asked Casey about it afterwards, and he said back in the day Monty served three years at Washington State for armed robbery. Someone threw him under the bus. Cut themselves a deal and disappeared into thin air. Apparently, Monty's had his suspicions forever, but last night he seemed pretty sure of himself. Now there's gonna be some reshuffling at the club 'cause of whatever the DEA told Monty. I hung back at the club house after they closed up for the night and low and behold, Q showed up with—"

"My dad," Alex says grimly. He looks askance at Zander. "Right? He showed up there with Jack." He's resolute, like after all this time the pieces of a complex puzzle are falling into place.

Zander nods. "Q knows your dad's been informing. I think he's been supplying him with information to pass on to the DEA that'll benefit the club, one way or another. He warned Jack that Monty was gonna be coming after him for real this time. Your dad said he wasn't gonna leave Raleigh with you still in such close proximity to—"

Alex lashes out, smashing his fist sideways into the car door. The sudden movement makes Halliday yelp, jumping out of her seat. Alex shakes, wound extremely tight. I think he's gonna repeat the action and hit my car again, but he lets out an uneven breath instead, grinding his teeth together as he looks at me. "Sorry," he says. "That fucking *asshole*. You can tell him not to stay here on my account. What does he think's gonna happen? I'm just gonna drop everything and leave Raleigh with him? He's fucking delusional."

Panic grabs me by the shoulders and shakes me. I see it all play out: Alex forgiving his father; life here becoming untenable; Alex showing up on my doorstep in the middle of the night to tell me that he has to go away, that it's for the best, that I'll be better off without him...

*Not gonna happen, Silver. He'd never do that to you, and you know it.*

The thought is upsetting, though. Life was one long nightmare before I met Alex. Yeah, things have been absolutely crazy since I met him. Tragedy has nipped at our heels, dogging our every turn, but at least he's been there, right by my side. Losing him...well, it doesn't even bear thinking about.

"He doesn't just want you to come with him," Zander says, exhaling as he leans his head against the window next to him. "He wants you to set up a new chapter of the M.C. with him. Be his vice president."

Alex's reaction is priceless. His mouth drops open and he lets out a rattle of laughter that bounces around the inside of the car. "No offence, man," he says. "But I'd rather choke on a dick than join a motorcycle club. I'm done with old men thinking that they can manipulate and use me for own their own ends. My life's my own. I'm not gonna let anyone pull my strings again. Especially not fucking Giacomo."

"Figured you'd say that."

"Why are you even telling us this? Q's gonna be mad as hell when he finds out you spilled club intel."

Zander shrugs, pressing his hands to his chest as he straightens out his already creaseless shirt. "Ahhh, y'know. There have been spurious rumors that I'm a bad friend floating around lately. Thought I'd knock that one on the head."

A loaded, wordless exchange passes between Zander and Alex.

*See. I* do *have your back.*

*Yeah, yeah, all right. You've made your point.*

I haven't had any dealings with the Dreadnaughts. However, I've seen a couple of the club's members at the Rock when I've hung out there with Alex, and they don't look like the kind of men you want to cross. Zander could get into very real, serious trouble for telling us what he knows. Like, kneecaps shot out and fingers cut off kind of trouble.

Alex rewards Zander with a grudgingly grateful look. "Thanks, man," he mumbles.

Zander could use this opportunity to be an asshole. It'd be easy to shoot off some attitude after all the grief Alex has given him. He chooses not to. Rather, he gives Alex a perfunctory smile, slapping him on the shoulder. "While we're on topic, there is something else."

"What?"

"Giacomo figured you weren't gonna be interested in the role he's picked out for you, so he came up with a plan."

Alex bristles. "What plan?"

"The most timeless plan there is. You want the guy, then you go target the girl, right? He's hired someone to go after Silver…and I'll give you three guesses who he's picked for the job."

## 29

## ALEX

I'm going to fucking kill him. Going after me is one thing, but putting a mark on Silver 'cause he knows he'll never get what he wants any other way? My worthless father's really crossed the line this time. He's going to regret he ever even thought about stepping foot inside Raleigh town limits.

I'm going to bide my time. If I go after him guns blazing, I'll only end up tipping my hand. He'll realize his plan's been leaked and concoct a backup. He'll scramble to regain the upper hand, and that could lead to all kinds of reckless behavior.

Back in the car, I thought Zander was going to tell us that my father had hired *Jake* to pursue Silver. He probably wouldn't have had to pay the psycho to do it, after all. He'd have done it for free. But no...he tapped Zander for the job. In his words, *"You can get the closest, my man. Charm her in the parking lot at school or something. Tell her you're a champion cunt eater. Girls pretend that they're all embarrassed when you try to stick your head between their legs, but they love that shit just as much as we love getting our cocks sucked. And I've* never *turned down an opportunity to get my cock sucked."*

I nearly knocked Zanders teeth down his throat when he told me that. Wasn't his fault, but the idea of him propositioning my girl made me want to eviscerate him right where he stood. He'd waited until

Silver and Halliday had gone to cheer practice before he'd told me that ugly piece of the story, which was good. If he'd disrespected Silver by repeating my father's repellant suggestion, I don't think I would have kept my shit together. Not because I'm worried that she might have been offended; thanks to Jake's campaign of hate at Raleigh, Silver's heard much worse. No, I would have been ashamed that a man who would say such a thing was actually related to me, and the same blood flows through our veins. If I could drain every last drop from my body and somehow still draw enough breath to protect her, then I'd do it without hesitation.

Football practice goes about as well as can be expected. The entire team collude to make me suffer, but they picked the wrong fucking day to pull that shit. I'm just itching to break something. A helmet. A record. A rib or two. By the end of the hour-long debacle, two of my teammates, die-hard Jacob Weaving minions, have been benched with injuries that were very satisfying to inflict, I hold the title for most completions in a Raleigh High practice game, and vengeance is *still* burning hot in my chest.

I want to rain down fire and brimstone on Giacomo Moretti's head, and I want to laugh like a madman while I'm doing it.

Outside, Zander walks with me to the Camaro and hops into the passenger seat without bothering to ask if he's welcome. My reservations have reservations where he's concerned, but Silver's words of advice have been ringing in my head ever since she said them: *You should probably forgive him and move on before you lose him altogether.*

I would have had a very different experience in juvie if Zander hadn't been around. He showed me the ropes and made the infinitely slow passing of time more bearable. He just took a number of cage-rattling hits that were unquestionably meant for me in that practice game. And there's no doubt about it that as president of the Dreadnaughts MC, Q will do more than kick him out of the club for telling me my father's plan to jump Silver. That incursion will probably land Zander in a shallow grave just off the five if anyone finds out about it. Q's been feeding my father information to pass along to the DEA, which means he's a valuable asset to him. If Zander shared information that in turn compromised the club, then he signed his own death warrant. It doesn't matter how big or small the transgression, clubs like the Dreadnaughts have a zero-tolerance policy and an equally swift and merciless system for meting out justice.

"Where's Silver?" Zander asks, fiddling with the radio dial. I resist the urge to slap his hand out of the way.

"Teaching. Guitar lessons."

"She's good, huh." He pulls a Subway footlong out of his bag and opens it, showering the Camaro with crumbs. My vision flashes red, but I bite down hard on my tongue, refusing to gripe about the mess. Zander gives me a wolfish smile, knowing just how badly I want to yell at him. Wordlessly, he offers me half of the sub.

"What is it?"

"Steak and cheese."

I grunt, taking it from him.

"I saw you guys play at the diner together," he says, taking a huge bite out of his half. "You were *both* good."

That's surprising. I didn't see him show up at Harry's. Didn't see him sitting at any of the tables or in the booths either. I wasn't exactly paying attention, though. I had other things on my mind. "Thanks," I say stiffly.

"You never told me you played when we were in juvie."

I shrug, taking a bite of the sandwich, hoping he'll move on and talk about something else.

"There was a guitar in the common room. Two of them, actually. Why didn't you ever play them?" he asks.

I chew. And I chew. And I chew. Eventually, I have to swallow, and Zander's still sitting there, waiting for an answer. Fucker. I struggle for a moment to figure out how best to explain, shuttling the St. Christopher around my neck up and down on its chain. "Music's personal, man. To me, anyway. If I'd picked up one of those guitars in that place, I would have sullied it. I wasn't myself in there. I wanted to leave that part of me outside of the gates. And…music makes me feel free. Playing in there would have made me feel even more trapped than I already was."

I wait for the mockery. This is an easy opportunity for him. I basically just handed him my ass on a silver platter, just begging for him to ridicule me for being a little bitch. Zander does nothing but nod, intently studying his steak and cheese sub. "I get it. Makes sense.

You've got a talent, though, dude. You should definitely share it more often. Now that you *are* free and all."

Compliments about my playing have always made me break out in hives. I smash the rest of the sandwich, occupying myself with the act of eating. When I'm done, I start the engine and I say no more about my musical abilities. *'Whole Lotta Love'* by Led Zeppelin comes on the radio, and Zander turns it up as we pull out of the school parking lot.

"Where we headed?" he asks. I get the impression that our destination doesn't really matter to Zander. He's just content to be moving.

"The Rock," I tell him, in a clipped voice. "It really *is* about time I paid Monty a visit."

## 30

# SILVER

I still get paid if a kid's parents cancel a lesson.

When I arrive at Gregory and Lou's place, Dr. Coombes hands me three twenty-dollar bills, folded in half, and informs me that both the boys have come down with a stomach bug. I try to give him his money back, though. Honestly, I wouldn't charge him for the boys' lessons at all if I could get away with it. I'm wracked with guilt every time I teach them, knowing what I know. Their mother was fleeing *my* mom's workplace, after seeing Mom half-naked with her legs spread on her boss' desk, when she careened through that intersection and was smoked by another vehicle. If she hadn't seen her friend so flagrantly cheating on her husband, she wouldn't have been driving that recklessly. She'd probably still be alive. By extension, I feel somehow responsible for Gail Coombes' death.

"No. I respect your time, Silver," Dr. Coombes says. "You set aside an hour to teach a lesson, so I'll pay you for it. It's only right."

I object, but it's no good. He makes it impossible for me to refuse his money, which makes me feel like a fucking monster. I get back in the car with a sinking, oily, unpleasant feeling swirling around in my stomach.

Halfway home, I notice that I'm being followed.

Dread begins to churn like a piston below my ribs.

Way too close, riding my tail, the truck is black and gleaming, its windows tinted out, making it impossible to see who's behind the steering wheel. The vehicle's expensive. Must have cost a pretty penny. I only know of one family who'd be able to afford a truck like that. Caleb Weaving's assets were all frozen when he was arrested, but it sounds like he's been negotiating all kinds of bullshit agreements with the powers that be. If he could swing getting Jake released after everything he did, then it stands to reason that he could also arrange for at least some of his vast fortune be made available to his wife and son.

*"You've gotta be* kidding *me."* There's no one in the Nova to hear me but it had to be said. Technically Jake isn't breaking any laws by following me across town, but the way he shadows me, moving from lane to lane, taking every turn I take, is an intimidation tactic for sure.

My heart jackrabbits in my chest as I reach for my phone and pull up Alex's number. By the sixth ring, I realize that he isn't going to pick up. Shaking all over, I call Dad instead.

"Hey, kiddo. What's up? Thought you were teaching the Coombes boys?"

God, he's only just calmed down after he found out Jake had been released. This is gonna send him flying off the handle again. "I'm being followed, Dad. I think it's Jake."

Dad's voice is as icy as the seventh level of hell. "Where are you?"

"On Court Avenue, about to cross, uh…Lederman."

"You're close to the hospital. Go straight there, Silver. Run every red light if you have to. I'm leaving the house right now. I'll meet you there. Stay on the phone, kiddo."

"Okay."

I'm still trying to tell myself that I might be overreacting as I take a left and gun the Nova's engine, speeding in the direction of the hospital. The truck takes the same left, speeding up, inching dangerously close, though, bursting that idea like a bubble.

*He's going to run you off the road. He couldn't break you when he fucked you. He didn't break you when he tried to hang you. Now he's gonna force you into a ditch in the rain, and Alex is going to lose you in the exact same way he lost Ben, and…*

*God, stop! Just fucking* stop!

I silence the panicked voice in my head, forcing it to be silent. I need to think. The hospital's still three or four miles away. Between here and there, there isn't much of anything, just one long, winding stretch of road bracketed by tall trees. The occasional house, set back from the road. There's nowhere for me to go but straight. Behind me, the truck's engine roars and the vehicle surges forward like a leashed dog, pulling at its chain.

"Fuck. *Fuck, fuck, fuck.*"

Where the hell is Alex? Where the hell *is* he?

The skies are clear now, but it rained all morning. The temperature plummeted at some point this afternoon, and now the roads are slick with ice. I come heartstoppingly close to skidding off the road when I take a corner a little too quickly. The car coasts, swinging wildly through the turn, and for one horrible moment the brakes do absolutely nothing.

*This is it.*

*This is it.*

*This is when I fucking die.*

The truck's horn blares out like some sort of warped victory cry. Only…the Nova's wheels gain traction, biting into the blacktop, finding purchase, and suddenly I'm tearing forward again.

*Focus. Drive. Just fucking* drive*. You've got this. You can do it.*

It takes forever to get to the hospital. I pull into the parking lot, drenched in a cold sweat, the Nova's wheels screeching as I burn toward the familiar sight of Dad's silver van. The truck follows after me, right on my tail.

I come to a jarring halt next to the van and Dad climbs out, brandishing a gleaming black weapon in his hands.

"Holy fuck! DAD!" I scream, but he doesn't hear me. He's fixed on the menacing black monster that's barreling right for us.

CRACK!

CRACK!

The sound of the gunshots splinter the air apart. My mouth hanging open, I twist, watching as the truck tears past us, two massive bullet holes blistering the paintwork of the rear passenger door. I'm fear personified as I wait for the truck to come to a stop…

But it keeps on going.

Rocking wildly as it performs a wide turn, the truck narrowly misses a parked Prius as it peels out of the hospital parking lot, back the way it came.

Holy...fucking...*shit*.

I lean forward, pressing my chest up against the steering wheel, suddenly incapable of holding myself upright.

"Silver. Hey, open the door, kiddo. It's okay, he's gone." Dad raps on the window, peering anxiously in at me. It takes a second to wrangle my limbs into some sort of order. They don't seem to want to do as they're told. The moment I've unlocked the door, Dad's there, helping me out of the Nova, pulling me into a bone-crushing hug.

"You *shot* at him," I say breathlessly. "You, like, really *shot* at him."

"I know. I know. Come on, come here and sit for a second. You're trembling." He's still holding the gun in his hand. I feel the coolness of the weapon's unforgiving steel against the back of my neck as Dad guides me to the back of the van, opening up the back door so I can sit on the trunk's ledge.

"That motherfucker's pulled his final stunt," Dad seethes, flustering over me, tucking my hair behind my ears, out of my face. "I'm gonna fucking *kill* him."

"Sorry to interrupt, friends."

Dad and I both jump, startled at the voice that speaks behind us. I'm teetering on the brink of a heart attack when I look around, and there, leaning up against the Nova in the bruised purple dusk, is the guy who gave me his business card, Dr. Romera's boyfriend, the guy Alex named Zeth.

Oh...*fuck*.

He might not be wearing a suit and a tie, but he looks every inch the mafia kingpin as he coolly assesses us with dark, intelligent, albeit emotionless eyes. "I'm in the market for a weapon," he says airily. "That one looks pretty average but I'm not picky."

Dad stiffens, glancing down at the gun in his hand. "What the hell are you talking about? I'm not giving you my g—"

Zeth pushes away from the car, taking a casual step toward us. "Registered, is it?"

Dad's face pales. Oh lord, he never registered his gun? Is that thing even *his*? It looks like the one he used to keep in a shoebox in his closet, but then again I only really saw it in stolen peeks through the cracked lid of a shoe box.

"You just shot that thing at a moving vehicle in a public parking lot," Zeth muses, running his tongue over his teeth. "The powers that be don't tend to like that kind of shit. An' I'm betting they're on their way here as we speak. I suspect I might be doing you a favor by taking it off your hands, Cameron."

Dad narrows his eyes suspiciously at the guy. "How do you know my name?"

Zeth huffs in a bored manner, staring off into the dark stretch of forest on the other side of the parking lot. "Better for you if you just hand it over, friend. I'd hate to have to take it from you."

A knot of worry tightens in my stomach. "Give it to him."

"*Silver—*"

"Just give him the gun, Dad. Please. Let's get rid of it and get the hell out of here."

Dad looks at me like I've lost my fucking mind, but he gingerly steps forward and hands over the weapon, placing it in Zeth's outstretched hand. "Good man. Now get your daughter home before five-oh shows up."

Dad stabs his finger after the truck. "That bastard was trying to hurt her. We need to report that to the police."

A terrifying smile spreads across Zeth's face. "I think you're better off leaving that matter in my hands, too. Don't you think, Silver?"

I say nothing. But as we drive away, Dad following closely behind me, chattering incessantly on the phone to keep me occupied, I think it to myself:

Yeah. Maybe the whole Jacob situation would be better off being dealt with by a man like Zeth.

## 31

# ALEX

The sound of shattering glass fills the air.

On the other side of the altar, the name given to the bar by the Rock's most loyal patrons, Paulie the bartender blanches at the very sight of me, the glass he just dropped lying in pieces on the polished mahogany in front of him. "Alex," he says nervously. "Where've you been, man? Monty was planning on sending out a search party soon."

"Yeah, I'll bet he was." It really was only a matter of time before Monty came looking for me. I've relied on his arrogance up until now, knowing that the bastard expects me to come crawling to him for forgiveness, but that plan had a shelf life. At some point, he would have gotten tired of waiting and sent someone out to drag me back here by the scruff of my neck like the misbehaving stray dog that I am.

"He know you were planning on swinging by?" Paulie's voice is abnormally high-pitched. He's freaking the hell out because he likes me, he's a friend, and he knows I've just strolled on into the lion's den without a thought as to what was going to happen once the door swung shut behind me.

But I have given it thought. Plenty. I know exactly what I'm gonna do, and how, and Monty's gonna sit there like a good little boy and listen to me while I speak. "Don't worry, dude," I tell Paulie. "I got this covered."

I head for the door through to the back, but Paulie calls out after me. "Hey, hold up. You're probably gonna need this." He moves quickly, sloshing some amber liquid into a glass, which he slides down the bar toward me. The shot glass comes to a stop a foot away. I down the raw tequila—the *puts-hairs-on-your-chest* kind—wincing at the heat that burns all the way down my throat. I then place the glass back down on the bar, upside down.

"Thanks, man."

"I'd say yell if you need me, but…"

I smile tightly, nodding. Yeah, I'm on my own with this one. There's nothing Paulie can do for me without getting his ass fired or shot. "No worries. Like I said. I've got this covered."

Unusually, the door to Monty's office is yawning wide open, throwing light out into the dark corridor. I stop in the doorway, leaning against the jamb, watching with mild interest as Monty scrambles around on his hands and knees inside, looking for something on the floor. He goes rigid when he sees my Stan Smiths in the doorway. Without hinging back, he laughs gruffly, letting his head hang down between his shoulders. "Wondering when you were gonna develop some balls," he says. His voice is light but also edged with acid. When he sits back, he's brandishing a dagger-sharp smile that makes me wish I'd brought a knife with me, too. He gets to his feet, whatever he was looking for on the floor forgotten about. "Come on in, kid. We've got some stuff to talk about, you and me."

I hate that my heartrate kicks up a notch. Thankfully it doesn't show on my face or the way I hold myself. I developed the ability to hide my thoughts and feelings a long time ago, when I was just another unwilling participant in the foster care system. I sink down on the chair I always sit in, opposite Monty's. The old man watches me like a hawk as he takes a seat himself. So fucking stupid. I could have caved in the back of his fucking skull while he was scrabbling around on the floor just now if I'd come here for that.

"I gotta say, I'm a little hurt, Alex." He leans an elbow against his desk, propping his chin up on a fist. He looks like a bored student, only half paying attention in class. "You and me...I thought we were friends."

I slouch back into the chair, shoving my hands into the pockets of my leather jacket. "That makes two of us. Looks like we were both wrong, huh?"

Monty pulls a sour face. "What the hell's *that* supposed to mean? You forget...I helped you, kid. I made sure you weren't dumped in another foster home. I gave you a place to live, didn't I?"

"Sure. But you didn't do it out of the kindness of your heart. You saw an opportunity and you took it." I rub a hand at the back of my neck. "That first day, when I asked you why you were helping me, you said you owed my father a debt and helping me was how you were gonna settle it. I guess you were telling the truth, but when you said debt, you really meant *revenge*, didn't you?"

Monty's eyes narrow to slits.

"Giacomo fucked you over. He left you to rot in prison while he disappeared off to Mexico or wherever and got fat on good food, booze and women. So, when you saw his son was close by, within reach, and you could just reach out and *take* him..." I cant my head to one side, arching an eyebrow. "Feel free to stop me if I'm getting any of this wrong."

Monty flashes me his teeth. "Costa Rica."

"What?"

"Costa Rica. While I was rotting in prison, your dickless father was living it up in Costa Rica. Did he tell you he got married again? I'm not a hundred percent on the dates, but I'm pretty sure your mother was still alive then. I s'pose Jack figured if he was in a different country then getting a divorce wasn't really important."

My hatred for Giacomo was a bottomless well before. I didn't think it could get any deeper. Turns out I was wrong. He *married* another woman, while my mother was still alive? Fuck's sake. Marshalling my expression, I make sure Monty doesn't know that this little piece of information has affected me as much as it has. "So, Jack was a thousand miles away, getting laid in the sun. When you got out of prison, he was still in the wind. And then I show up out of the blue, like some sort of gift-wrapped godsend, just begging for you to swoop in and manipulate me, getting me on side. What was the plan, Monty? Were you gonna *steal* me? Was I supposed to worship you like the father I never had? Or was I supposed trust you implicitly, think you only have my best interests at heart, and then you were gonna drag me in front of Giacomo and plaster my brains all over his living room wall, just to spite him?"

Monty laughs, shrugging carelessly. "Honestly, I didn't really give it that much thought. I suppose I would have done whatever hurt your father the most. Trouble is, Giacomo found out you were working for me pretty quick. And…I'm gonna let you in on a little secret now. Just between you and me, okay?" He cups his hand around his mouth, leaning closer to me, whispering like we're co-conspirators. *"He didn't really care."*

Now, this? This isn't a surprise to me. I don't need to master my emotions this time, because it's no less than I expected. Yes, Giacomo wants to steal me back from Monty now. Whatever half-baked plan he's cooking up to start his own chapter of the Dreadnaughts involves me in some way, but it isn't because my father cares about me. It's because he needs something from me. I haven't figured out what that could be yet, but I'm sure it'll become obvious sooner or later. He's probably got a cerotic liver and he needs half of mine, for Christ's sake. If that's the case, then he's gonna be sorely out of luck. I wouldn't piss on that man if he was on fire. "If you're expecting me to burst into tears, then I'm gonna have to disappoint you," I say, rocking back on my chair. "Don't you know me by now? I couldn't give two shits if Giacomo didn't break his neck in his race to Raleigh to come save me from you."

Monty thinks about this. He scratches at his chin, worrying at his stubble. "Let me ask you something, Alex. You think that girlfriend of yours would look pretty sliding up and down a pole out there? I prefer my girls to be a little curvier, but your Silver's got that doe-eyed innocent look about her." He pauses, waiting for my reaction. I'm willing to bet he's already getting ready to yank open the top drawer of his desk so he can grab the gun that he keeps there. I'd be a fool to explode on him, even if his question has got my blood simmering. Chewing on the inside of my cheek, I meet his gaze, adamant that I won't be the first to look away. "You have a lot of stupid people working for you, Monty. Like...*a lot* of stupid people."

Bemused, he taps his index finger against his desk. "Is that so?"

"I think you like 'em that way, to be honest. Stupid people don't think for themselves. They don't ask questions, because they're too dumb to think of them. They don't plan ahead, either. Me, though... I'm not stupid. I have plenty of questions, but I'm smart enough not to ask them. I compile them, one after the other after the other, and I spend a considerable amount of time hunting down the answers on my own time. And yeah, I plan ahead. Way, way, way ahead."

My hand is already closed around the thumb drive in my jacket pocket. Slowly, I take it out, laying it down on the desk in front of me, keeping my hand pressed down on top of it.

Monty waves his hand in a derisive gesture. "What's that supposed to be?"

"This is a record of every time you've ever asked me to do something for you. Dates. Times. The amount you paid me. The people you asked me to hurt. It's a pretty damning dossier, really. Or it would be, if it fell into the wrong hands."

"Ho ho ho, kid. You have no idea how bad fire burns, do you? You play with shit like this and you're bound to get hurt." Monty shakes his head, a broad smile taking over his face, his eyes bowed into crescents. He looks at me askance, drilling into me with his faded blue irises, and I can see just how badly I've irritated him. "That doesn't prove anything. You realize that, right? Anyone can make up a list of names and dates."

"But when those names and dates lead down dark alleyways, to bags filled with blow and smack, things begin to get interesting, don't they?" I counter. "I'm not sure which department to take this to first. The DEA seem to have taken leave of their minds, but maybe the ATF would be interested in the contents of this thumb drive. Could be the regular cops would like to know this stuff. How many times has the Sheriff come sniffing around this place, looking for something to hang you over?"

"You're not very smart at all if you can't see that that information hangs you as well as me, boy."

I roll my eyes, groaning loudly. "I'm a fucking minor, asshole. And you are technically still my legal guardian. Coercion's a real thing. What judge is gonna prosecute a kid that some wannabe crime lord snatched out of the hands of CPS to use as his own personal whipping boy?"

Monty does the math on this. I watch as he runs the numbers and weighs in his head how likely it'll be that I will walk away from all of this unscathed. With my record and the fact that I recently fucking shot someone, the odds aren't exactly in my favor. There's a chance that I'm right, though. Either way, even if I do go down or I don't, Monty knows that my testimony and the information on this thumb drive pretty much guarantees that he'll be looking at some hardcore jailtime. "You wanna go back inside because of another Moretti, Montgomery?" I ask, tapping the end of the thumb drive against his desk.

If looks could start fires and bring about the end of the world, then I would be facing down the apocalypse as Monty scowls at me from across his precious fucking desk. "What the hell do you want, kid?" he hisses.

Oh, this is an easy one. I already have my demands prepared. "No fall out for handing over the bag. For me, or Silver, or Silver's dad, or anyone else."

"And?"

"And you figure out how to get Zander cut from the Dreadnaughts."

"Why the hell would he want to leave the club?"

"Does it matter?"

"I suppose not."

"Lastly, I want your help."

"Jesus, kid, your asking price is getting kinda steep," Monty growls.

"I'm pretty sure you'll be happy to lend a hand with this part," I tell him, rolling my eyes. "I want Giacomo gone. I want him out of Raleigh. Preferably out of Washington. I don't care if he winds up behind bars or in the fucking ground. I just want him *gone*."

Monty sucks on his teeth. "You'd ex out your own father?"

"I'll kill anyone who poses a threat to Silver, Monty. And that includes you. Now pick up that cell phone of yours, Boss. I believe you've got some calls to make."

"Made it out alive. Gotta say I'm impressed."

I told Zander to stay in the car, but I honestly expected him to have vanished by the time I came back outside. He's never been very good at doing what he was told. However, when I head back to the Camaro, he's sitting in the driver's seat, racking up a monster of a joint on his lap.

"Move," I command.

"I'm an excellent driver. Why don't you just relax and I'll—" He stops talking when he glances up and sees the look on my face. *"Fuck's sake."* Mumbling to himself, he slides across the bench to the passenger's side, careful not to dump out his weed in the footwell. "You're a walking cliché, Moretti. A teenaged bad boy who doesn't let anyone else drive his muscle car? Come on. You're better than that. Don't be so fucking obvious."

"I let Silver drive my car," I reply, slamming the car door behind me. "I'd let Cam drive it, too, probably."

"Then why can't I?"

"Because it amuses me to fuck with you," I answer, snatching the joint he's just finished rolling from his hands and pinching it between my teeth. "Light," I say, holding out my hand. Zander slaps his Zippo into my open palm. The weed hits hard, a pleasant numbness traveling down the back of my neck as I hold it in my lungs for a second.

It's been nearly a year since I smoked pot, but the comfortable buzz feels both familiar and enjoyable. One toke's all I need, though. I pass the joint back to Zander, exhaling twin jets of smoke down my nose.

"Should I assume that your dad's no longer a concern?" Zander asks, his voice muffled by the thickness of the smoke in the back of *his* throat.

Starting the Camaro's engine, I slam my foot down on the gas pedal, peeling out of the parking lot. "He's still gonna be a problem. So will Monty, one way or another. I figure I've bought myself some time, though. Oh, and by the way, you're no longer a Dreadnaught."

I can feel Zander staring at me. "What the *hell* are you talking about?"

"You're done with them. And you're done with Raleigh. Time you went back to Bellingham, man. No sense in both of us being caught up in this bullshit."

Zander's going to object. I'm prepared for it, but he's barely shaped the sound of his first *no fucking way, man,* when a black truck with tinted windows comes hurtling around the corner toward us. For a split second, we're both on the same side of the road. The tinted-out windows hide the unquestionable surprise of the driver behind the wheel. I have nowhere to go. The only thing between the Camaro and the forty-foot drop into the ravine beside the road is an already dented guard rail. It won't hold us if we hit it. We'll go straight over the side and tumble down the sharp slope, rolling every time the car bounces off the rockface.

Somehow, inside the smallest fragment of time, an eighth of a second, no more, I understand how Ben felt right before Jackie went careening off the road. My language is a little more colorful, but I'm sure his thoughts were exactly the same, too:

*Man, I really don't wanna fucking die.*

The black truck swerves, struggling to get back on its side of the road in time. It makes it, but only just. The murdered-out vehicle clips the Camaro's wing mirror, ripping it off the car, sending it bouncing down the road behind us in a shower of twisted metal and shattered glass.

"God...DAMN!" Zander yells at the top of his lungs. "What the *FUCK!*"

My hands are shaking, and it feels like my heart's about to burst, but I manage to keep on driving. "D'you see 'em?" I say through my clenched teeth.

Zander doesn't need to ask what I'm talking about. He nods, bracing himself against the dashboard as he leans forward, taking in an uneven breath. "The bullet holes? Two of 'em, right in the middle of the door. Kinda hard to miss."

Back in two thousand and fourteen, Raleigh was voted number one safest town to live in in all of Washington State. Harry has the newspaper clipping framed on the wall at the diner to prove it. Monty might have been cultivating his little criminal empire here for a while now, but he's low key about it. Most of Raleigh's residents have never even seen Montgomery Cohen the third's face. This isn't the kind of town where trucks speed around corners on the wrong side of the road, shot up with bullet holes.

No, this, somehow, some way, is related to *me*.

It's then that I notice the missed calls from Silver.

# 32

## SILVER

I barely have any nails left by the time Alex finally shows up at the house. Zander's not with him anymore, probably dropped off at Salton Ash Trailer Park. The Camaro's tires kick up gravel and old snow as Alex burns up the driveway. He parks next to the Nova, not even bothering to kill the engine before he jumps out of the driver's seat and races to the porch steps to the house, where I've been sitting out in the cold, waiting for him.

"You okay? You hurt?" His hands are frantic, patting me down, searching out hidden injuries. I've already told him via text that I'm okay, but obviously he needs to check for himself.

"I'm fine. I'm okay, I promise. Nothing actually happened. I was just scared, that's all. Dad…god, if Dad hadn't come and met me…"

Alex's expression hardens, his nostrils flaring. "Where is he?"

"In the kitchen."

Alex nods, getting up and heading inside. I follow him in, already prepping my speech about how neither Alex nor my father are allowed to go off half-cocked on some stupid *bring-down-Jacob-Weaving-plan* again. It was sheer luck that neither of them ended up shot by one of Caleb Weaving's security guards last time. Alex doesn't even make the suggestion, though. Dad keeps his hard liquor in the cupboard above the oven. When he sees us coming down the hallway, he takes an extra two low ball glasses out and sets them down next to the one he's already taken out for himself. Alex prowls up and down the length of the kitchen, brushing his hands through his hair over and over again as Dad decants a double shot of whiskey into each glass. When Dad gives Alex a glass, he grunts out a thanks and knocks the amber liquid back in one go.

Dad takes Alex's glass away and hands him the half full bottle instead. "It's official. I'm the worst parent in the world," he says. "I must be the only father in the state of Washington who lets his underage daughter drink fucking Bruichladdich." I take the glass he offers me, wincing down a sip of the whiskey, feeling a little better as the alcohol blazes a path down my throat. "I'm putting the house on the market. We're moving to Chicago," Dad mutters. "It's safer in fucking Illinois than it is here."

Alex laughs, the sound brittle and harsh. "They're not kicking us out of Raleigh, Cam. None of us. This has always been your home. It's my home now, too." He laces his fingers together behind the back of his head, interlocking them at the base of his skull. "This can't go on forever. The cops are gonna find something else on Jake, and he's gonna get sent down again. My father's gonna disappear. Monty's gonna scrub me from his memory. Everything's gonna go back to normal. The end."

I think it hits him at the same time it hits me; all of this madness and chaos *is* the norm. Things have been this way, fraught with danger and heartbreak, for a long time now. It'd be unusual if life settled down and things actually *stopped* falling apart. He rubs his face with both hands, sighing out a long, unhappy breath. "You were a badass, shooting after that truck, man," he says through his fingers. "Good thing you gave Zeth that gun, though. He's unpredictable. I've heard too much about him to think he's not tapped in the head."

My dad picks up a butter knife from the kitchen counter and distractedly digs the blunt blade into the pad of his thumb. He'd been making a sandwich earlier when I called him in a panic, and now there's a pool of melted butter on the chopping board. "This is gonna sound pretty rude," he says, staring, sightless, out of the window that overlooks the Walker Forest. "But I am honest to god looking forward to the day you both leave for college. At least then I'll only have to worry about you getting wasted and flunking your exams like everyone else."

## 33

## SILVER

"So. You two are a regular Bonnie and Clyde power couple, huh?" Zeth eyes the whipped cream-topped strawberry milkshake sitting on the table in front of him with a level of malevolence that should have shattered the glass by now. He's wearing a plain black sweater with a tiny hole in the neck. Worn jeans. A pair of black boots. Nothing about the way he's dressed sets him apart from the weekend lunch crowd at Harry's, but the energy radiating off him is powerful enough to make the people in the booths surrounding us subconsciously all lean away from him without realizing it. Like Alex, there's a sharp-edged, wicked kind of electricity to him that makes people nervous.

Beside me, Alex dumps yet another sugar into his coffee, viciously clanging the spoon around inside his mug as he stirs. I already know he isn't going to drink the piping hot black liquid. He takes his coffee black. The empty sugar packets, discarded on the table next to the laminated Harry's menu, are a sign of his agitation.

"For the record, I think this is a terrible idea," Alex growls unhappily.

Zeth sighs down his nose, slouching back into the bench seat on his side of the booth. "Agreed. I had a date with an eighteen-month-old."

I vaguely remember Dr. Romera mentioning that she had a kid. Can't seem to wrap my head around the fact that this guy might be someone's father, though. He seems too hard. Too distant. I'd say I can't imagine him changing a baby's diaper, but I totally can. He'd have the job done quickly, with frightening efficiency, in under five seconds flat.

"I can handle this Weaving situation myself," Alex says. "I don't have a problem putting the motherfucker down."

Zeth's mouth twitches. I think it's a sign that he's amused. "You already shot the kid once. You have a list of motives to bury the bastard longer than your arm. The cops would have you in cuffs before you could blink. And your girl doesn't want you locked up for the rest of your life. Am I right?"

He's hit the nail on the head. There's no way Alex can be the one to take down Jake with the cops already watching him like a hawk. He'll be the first person they suspect, no matter what, and they'll throw the book at him this time. He's on very thin ice as far as the law is concerned. It won't take much for Alex to wind up with a lengthy prison sentence on his hands. His life will effectively be over. Still, he's absolutely hating this. Like, *hating* it.

In an attempt to break the staring contest that's taking place between Alex and Zeth, I gingerly ask, "How much do you normally get paid for this kind of thing anyway, Mr...uh...Mayfair?"

Zeth's eyes glide over to me, cool and assessing. "I have no idea what *this kind of thing* is, Miss Parisi. I run a boxing gym in Seattle. If you're asking how much the monthly membership fee is, then our prices are available on our website."

"You have a *website*?"

He huffs out a solitary laugh. "No. No, we do not."

"Why are you even still here?" Alex asks. "You got your bag back. You have a life in Seattle by the sounds of things. Isn't it time you were thinking about leaving town?"

Zeth's eyes come alive with interest as he sits up and leans closer to us across the table. "You thinking about running me out of Raleigh, kid? You should make up your mind. One second you want me to kill someone for you. The next, you want me gone. I don't deal well with mixed signals."

I look around nervously, hoping to god no one heard him just say that. "Maybe we shouldn't talk about killing people," I hiss. "No one said anything about *killing* anyone."

Zeth casually leans back, slouching in his seat again. "So, you just want me to break a couple of bones? Knock out some of his teeth? Put the fear of god into him?" His tone is mocking.

"We want to know about the deal Jacob's father made with the DEA," I say. "We want to figure out a way to make sure Jake's punished for all the terrible shit he's done. Legally."

Zeth pulls the straw out of his milkshake, wiping the pink cream from it on his napkin, then slides it into his mouth. He chews on the end of it thoughtfully. "Could tickle him too, if you like."

Oh god. This is not going well. "Look, you were the one who said I was better off leaving the Jacob situation to you when you took that gun from my dad earlier."

I wait, studying his face, watching for some sign of emotion, but none appears. "I did say that, didn't I."

"If you're just gonna be unhelpful and rude then Alex is right. You probably should just go—"

"Easy, sweetheart. Easy now." Zeth pulls the straw out of his mouth and uses it to point at me. "Would you call in a demolitions expert to knock down a partition wall?"

"Uh...probably not."

"I'm not the kind of guy you hire to accomplish what you're looking to accomplish, sweetheart. I'm definitely not the kind of guy you hire to accomplish things legally, either. But that's all irrelevant, 'cause I didn't come here to be interviewed. I'm not looking for work. Like I said...I run a boxing gym in Seattle."

I'm glad we're in public. If we weren't, I'm pretty sure Alex would try and kill this guy. He's turned a threatening shade of purple. "We're wasting our time, *Argento*. Come on. Let's get the fuck out of here."

"No need to get bent out of shape," Zeth quips. "I have a personal interest where the DEA's concerned. This Lowell guy...what do you know about him?"

Alex sets his jaw. "That he's an asshole who's probably gonna wind up dead. The DEA are the ones prosecuting Caleb Weaving, but this guy's trying to clear Jake's name. He wants to discredit Silver. I think he has links to my father, too."

Zeth shrugs a shoulder, turning his head to look out at the unfriendly, wet night on the other side of the window. Down Main Street, the trees, still trussed up with sparkling Christmas lights, sway and shake as the wind howls toward the north. "Wherever Giacomo Moretti goes, trouble soon follows," he says mildly. "If Jack's around and there's a bad smell in the air, it's a safe bet that he's causing the stink." Zeth inhales, abruptly turning back to face us. His eyes flicker first to me, and then to Alex, and then he's on his feet, pulling a wallet out of his jeans pocket. "All right, then."

He lays a twenty-dollar bill down on the table and begins to walk away.

"All right, then?" I call after him. "What does that mean, *all right, then?*"

The guy pauses, closing his wallet and stuffing it into his back pocket. "Means I'll see what I can do," he says gruffly. "In the meantime, stay the hell away from Weaving. And Lowell if you can help it. Better for you if you just lock yourself in that big old house and don't come out 'til spring."

He goes, and with him goes the tension that's been leaching the life and color out of the diner. Next to me, Alex grips hold of the teaspoon in his hand so hard he bends the metal. "What's that saying?" he grumbles through his teeth. "Better the devil you know? Well, I don't trust any of these shady motherfuckers."

## 34

## SILVER

"Don't forget, students. Our 'James Bond: Spies and Villains' evening is fast approaching. This Friday, dust off your slickest suits and your sparkliest dresses and join in the revelry at Raleigh High's senior prom! Tickets will be on sale until Wednesday afternoon. Remember, those of you whose academic records prevent them from attending prom, there's still time to bring up your GPA with some extra credit assignments. Visit your counselor today and—"

I smirk as I head down the hallway toward History. Principal Darhower's assistant, Karen, is usually as quiet as a mouse. She has a hard time making eye contact with you when she speaks to you, and any time she has to deal with a student's parents, she blushes furiously. She sounds like a *Good Morning America* presenter when she voices the announcements over the new PA system, though. You can practically hear her Hollywood smile being transmitted through the shitty, crackling speakers.

A group of guys hover outside Jacob Weaving's locker, even though their hallowed leader is still banished from school grounds, thanks to my father's recent hysterics; all of them members of the football team, they glare hatefully at Alex, as he approaches from the opposite direction. He stands almost a foot taller than the other students in the vicinity, who are all bustling, jamming presentation folders and books into their backpacks as they hurry to make it to their first class.

My heart skips a little at the gentle upward tilt of Alex's mouth when he sees me. Brushing his thick, wavy hair back out of his eyes, he alters his course so his path will cross mine, and reality seems to shift and bend. I'm never going to get used to this. Never. Alessandro Moretti, somehow, bizarrely, miraculously, amazingly, is mine. He loves me. Him, with his smoldering, *I'm-gonna-set-your-whole-damn-bed-on-fire-and-to-hell-with-the-world* attitude, and his mind-blowingly handsome face, and his intricate, beautiful artwork that covers his body…all of him is mine. I don't think that's ever going to make sense to me.

When I stop in front of him, not giving a shit that we're causing an obstruction to our fellow classmates, or that the football team jocks outside Jacob's locker are still drilling holes into the side of Alex's face, he huffs softly under his breath, allowing the smallest suggestion of a smile to form on his face as he brushes his fingertips over my cheek. "Damn, Parisi. I don't think you're ever gonna stop being the most beautiful thing I've ever laid eyes on," he murmurs.

I lean into his hand, briefly closing my eyes, enjoying the warmth of him, just for a second. "Funny. I was just thinking the same thing."

He hooks his index finger through the belt loop of my jeans at my right hip, tugging me closer to him. Close enough that he can dip down and whisper into my ear. His hot breath makes me shiver as it skates over the skin of my neck. "I'm not beautiful. I'm a handsome bastard. And don't you forget it," he growls.

Goosebumps break out on my arms and over the entire expanse of my back. "Cocky," I accuse, angling my head back just enough that I can make eye contact with him. "You're very sure of yourself, Mr. Moretti. When the hell did your ego get so damn big anyway?"

His dark eyes glimmer with pleasure as he tugs on my belt loop again, closing the small gap between us so that our bodies are flush. "The day you agreed to marry me," he whispers. "If a girl as stunning, smart, kind, and brave as *you* is willing to get hitched to *me*, then I must be pretty fucking amazing, right?"

I shove him in his chest, laughing. "Maybe I just pitied you, 'cause I knew how heartbroken you'd be if I said no."

"Well, that's true. I would have been fucking devastated if you turned me down," he says. His eyes are still full of mirth, but his expression becomes a little more serious as he takes me by the hand, pulling me into the little alcove next to a water fountain. "Seriously, though, *Argento*. You don't need to follow through on this if you're not ready for it. My mom married Giacomo so quick, she had no idea who he really was—"

I hold up a hand, pressing it against his chest, cutting him off before he can wander too far down this road. "I know exactly who you are. And I want to marry you more than I've ever wanted anything, so stop talking right now before I begin to worry that *you* don't want *me* and I have a panic attack, okay?"

Alex leans back against the wall—all six foot three of him pure muscle, arrogance, and vulnerability, hidden behind a wicked smirk. He works his hands beneath the hem of my t-shirt, his palms burning into my bare skin as takes hold of me just above my hips and grips me tightly. "Does that mean you're gonna go with me to this stupid fucking prom thing, then?" he asks. From his tone, you'd think this was an off-the-cuff remark, but I know Alex. I know that he's probably been stewing on this question ever since he arrived at Raleigh High this morning. He's acting way too casually about the question for it to really be of no concern to him.

Trying not to laugh, I marshal my features into a stern expression and look him in the eye. "I don't know. Senior prom's a big deal. I think you're supposed to make some kind of grand gesture when you ask a girl to be your date to such an auspicious event. Y'know…jump out of a plane and land on the school field, holding a placard or something."

"You're not serious," Alex deadpans.

"I think Gareth Foster's organizing a flash mob in the cafeteria at lunch for Stacey Jones."

He's gone a little pale. "I don't really think synchronized dancing is a good idea, *Argento*. You'd lose all respect for me."

"Maybe you could read a poem about how awesome I am in front of the entire year?"

"Or maybe you're fucking with me," he answers, arching an

eyebrow suspiciously. "Seeing as how you'd glue my mouth closed before you'd ever let me do that."

I do laugh now. "All right, all right. You got me. No outlandish prom invitations required here. I think it's safe to say I'll happily be your date to every party and event from here on out until the end of time. Gotta say, though…I'm surprised you even want to go to prom."

He rolls his eyes dramatically, leaning his head against the wall behind him. "And why's that?"

"Prom goes against everything you stand for."

That crooked smile of his makes another appearance. In a heartbeat, he's spun me around, pressing my back against the wall, and his lips are mere millimeters away from my own. Now that the prying eyes of Raleigh High's student body have been blocked out by the tumbling dark waves of his hair, he lets himself smile fully—a cautious, secret smile that feels wonderful pressed against my mouth when he kisses me. He leaves me breathless and stupefied when he inches back a little. "And what, pray tell, do I stand for, Silver Parisi?" he whispers.

"Non-conformity. Anarchy. Chaos. Mayhem in general." I reel off the list, still reeling inside my head, too. Fifty years down the line, a kiss from this man will still send me spinning out of control, I already know it.

"Looks like you *do* know me," Alex says quietly. "You're right. I never once thought I'd willingly signing up to go to a high school dance, but…y'know what, *Argento*? Prom's *normal*. It's a rite of passage for a girl in high school. I don't want you to skip it just because I'm a salty bastard who hates everyone and everything in this world apart from you. You deserve to witness the entire, ridiculous spectacle. And…more than anything, you deserve normal. After everything you've been through, and all the shit that's still not resolved…you deserve one night where all you have to worry about is what dress you're gonna wear, and if you're gonna be able to dance all night in your skyscraper heels. So yeah. Prom. We're doing it. And it's gonna be the best night ever, because I said so. The end."

"The end?"

"Yeah." He nods, as if that has sealed the deal and finalized the whole thing. The steely look in his eyes says he'll brook no argument on the matter…which is actually fine by me.

I haven't even contemplated prom. Even with all of the posters and the notices and the announcements being shoved down our throats at every turn, actually buying a ticket and attending the event seemed so preposterous that it never crossed my mind. Now that Alex has lodged the seed into my mind—buying a dress, and dancing with him in front of everyone, and just getting to spend the night together as two teenagers in love? Shit, that sounds pretty spectacular to me.

## 35

## ALEX

A shrill blast of the bell signals that class is about to begin, and Silver kisses me quickly before darting off into the crowd. I make it three steps past the row of lockers, heading for the science block, when I notice Zander leaning against the scuffed and scratched metal of a locker door, idly staring at his fingernails. He pretends to start when he notices me standing in front of him.

"Fancy seeing you here," he says, beaming. I groan, hurrying past him, but the persistent fucker falls into step alongside me.

"If you're about to give me shit for asking my girlfriend to go to prom with me, then don't bother, okay? I'm not embarrassed about it, so there's no point cobbling together any cutting one-liners."

"Dude! I'd never mock you for wanting to show Silver a good time. I think it's highly commendable that you wanna take her to prom. I was thinking about asking our lovely Billie Halliday to go with me, for your information."

"I don't think Halliday'd be stoked about your using her stripper name outside of the Rock, man."

"Duly noted. Duly noted. You're completely right. That wasn't cool. I take it back." Zander spins to avoid a gaggle of freshmen girls who are loitering at the bottom of the stairwell, staring at us with eyes the size of saucers. "If I was about to admit that I'd accidentally overheard your conversation—"

"You were eavesdropping, Hawk." I thunder up the stairs.

"If I was about to admit that I was *eavesdropping* on your conversation with Silver, then the whole prom invitation would hardly be the most surprising element of whatever I had or hadn't overheard, now, would it?" Zander muses.

I pause mid-step, turning around to face him. Suddenly, I realize why he's following me like a lost fucking dog. He heard our conversation. He overheard all of it.

Fuck.

Zander grins, slapping me on the shoulder. "I'd say congratulations, but from what I've seen of the holy order of matrimony, *commiserations* might be more appropriate. Still, what the hell. I say go for it. Follow your hearts and your hormones and all that other weird shit. Now…have you thought about dates? Venues? Themes? I'm gonna need as much information as possible."

Horror courses through every inch of my body. This…this is a fucking nightmare. No one was supposed to know about this. Not yet anyway. And especially not *Zander*. "Why the hell would you need as much information as possible?" I ask in a worried tone. Worried, because I already know the answer…

A broad smile splits his face apart. "Well, how the hell am I supposed to perform my duties as best man if I'm left out of the loop?"

# 36

# SILVER

It's tough to concentrate in History. I mentally cycle through my wardrobe, weighing the pros and cons of every single dress I own before coming to the conclusion that I need to buy something new for the occasion.

A year ago, I wouldn't have bothered panicking over my clothing options. It would have been a futile exercise. Kacey would have monopolized all the sirens' time, making us give her feedback on the dresses she picked out for herself. Once she'd selected the perfect little number that hugged her curves and emphasized her tits, she'd have picked out our dresses for the rest of us—dresses that were still nice and still worked well for our body types, but that were also not quite right somehow. A little too long, or a little too tight, or a little too gaudy. It was our job as Kacey's minions to make sure our shortcomings highlighted just how perfect she was by comparison. With Kacey now gone, the knowledge that I can wear whatever the fuck I want is a dizzying breath of fresh air.

Class ends, and I'm still floating in a daze as I traipse out into the hallway. I'm so distracted by prom plans that I don't register what I'm seeing for a second. It's the awkward silence that's pressing down on the hallway that initially brings me back into myself, and then it's the weird way that all of the other kids in the hallway are all looking in the same direction, their bodies angled toward the same focal point.

Next to the door that leads to Raleigh's south exit, Zen MacReady stands, staring down at her feet, clutching a folder to her chest; it looks like she's trying to use the binder as some sort of shield to fend off the incredulous, suspicious glares of her former subjects.

Once upon a time, you could spot Zen a mile away by her hair. Either in a teased-out afro, or braids, or some wild, outlandish color, Zen's hair always made her stand out from the crowd. Courtesy of the cat fight she had with Rose Jimenez outside the front of school, her hair's all gone now, though. The red beret she's wearing obviously covers the top of her head, but it can't hide the shaved sides of her head.

Timidly, she pushes away from the wall, navigating a pathway through the frozen forms of our classmates, her eyes diligently glued to the floor.

"*Bitch*," someone hisses under their breath. A male voice. A voice filled with malevolence.

"*Whore*."

"*Lying cunt*."

A wall of heat rises from the pit of my belly. It begins as a small flame of anger, licking at my insides, but quickly my temper fans that flame and it becomes a roaring inferno, raging through every part of me.

This should *not* be allowed to stand.

Day after day, I endured this kind of treatment, and nobody did anything about it. Just like they are now, the guys and girls I grew up with stood by and observed as I was humiliated and publicly shamed. Well, I won't stand amongst them. Not today. Not ever.

Quickly, I break through the forming crowd and slip my arm through Zen's. Her automatic response is to flinch at the contact. When she looks up and sees who's dared to take her by the arm, however, her fear subsides.

"Silver. You don't—I don't expect you to—" She gropes for the right words, but I already know perfectly well what she wants to say to me.

"I know. I don't have to stand up for you. I shouldn't have to, either. I reckon I've been dealt enough abuse to last a lifetime. But that's the whole point, isn't it? *No one* should have to deal with this shit. And what kind of hypocrite would I be if I stood by and let these assholes do this to someone else?"

Zen gives me a weak, broken smile. She's sorry. I know she's sorrier than she's ever been before in her life. Now that she's experienced just how foul this kind of treatment tastes, she knows what it must have been like for me to endure it day after day, week after week, and she doesn't like it one little bit. "I wanna be invisible," she whispers, so softly only I can hear her. "I just want to be no one. I just want…to *disappear*."

How many times did I say that exact same thing to myself? I couldn't count that high if I tried. It was all I repeated to myself inside my head for months. That desperate wish seared itself into my very soul. I smile sadly as I take a deep breath and begin to guide Zen down the hallway. "If you become a ghost, they win," I tell her. "If you make yourself small for them, it'll never be enough. They'll demand that you make yourself smaller and smaller still, and they'll cheer you on as you do it. You can't hand over victory to them like that. You have to raise your head, lift your jaw, look them in the eyes, and tell them *no*, Zen."

"I did tell them no." Zen's voice breaks. She's referring to Jake, Sam and Cillian, and the night they assaulted her on the concrete beside the Weaving's family swimming pool. The cops showed me the photos of Zen trying to fight the boys off when I was in the hospital. I witnessed the fear on her face; I saw how hard she was trying to fight them off. She probably screamed *no! stop!* until her throat was raw and bleeding. Her panic must have excited Jacob and his monstrous friends to the point of frenzied madness.

"Just because it's hard, doesn't mean you can ever *stop* saying it, Zen. It might be easier to just give in, shut your mouth, lie down and let the wolves pick over what's left of you. Do that and it'll be so much harder to get back up again, though. These assholes on the football team are never going to let up if they think you're weak. You stand up to them and you take their power away from them."

Zen doesn't look cheered by my instructions, but she makes an effort to stand a little taller. She even lifts her gaze from the floor, though she stares straight ahead, doing everything in her power to avoid making eye contact with anyone. People begin to turn away, shuffling off in different directions, heading for their next classes. Three guys grouped together on the left-hand side of the hallway stay firmly put, though. I don't really know them at all, but I know their names. Kyle Braiding. Lawrence Davis. Naseem Khatri. They're part of the *Jacob Weaving is God* fan club, founding members, if memory serves, and from the cuts and scrapes on their faces, they're also amongst the football players who tussled with Alex and Zander recently.

Kyle leers at Zen as we walk by them, eyeing her loose sweatshirt like she's actually wearing provocative lingerie. "Damn, MacReady. I always knew you were smoking, but shit. Jake showed us those shots of you on his phone. I nearly came in my pants on the spot. Ain't no point in hiding away those luscious curves now, girl. We all seen what you workin' with."

Zen digs her fingernails into my arm, her body tensing. "Ignore him," I whisper. She tries to quicken our pace, urging me to hurry forward, but I hold her back. I make her walk at an easy, regular speed, refusing to give Kyle or his friends the satisfaction of watching Zen scurry off, afraid.

"God, this was a mistake," Zen mutters, her voice riddled with anxiety. "I shouldn't have pushed to come back to school so quickly. Mom said this was a stupid idea, but I wouldn't listen…"

Last time I saw Zen, she was laid out on a hospital bed, tagged and drugged, and it didn't seem like she was close to being released any time soon. Clearly, I was wrong. There's a story here—I have a lot of questions. I don't even know how to broach the topic of her pregnancy—but it's going to have to wait for another time. Right now, all that matters is that we get out of here without her breaking down in front of the football team. "You did the right thing. It's gonna be okay. Come on. Let's just get you to class."

Zen's shaking from head to toe as we walk past the guys. We're successfully past them and I'm beginning to think we're free and clear of their bullshit…for *now*…when something hits me in the shoulder, really hard. Dark brown liquid showers all over the place, soaking my shirt and my hair, drenching Zen at the same time. It splashes in her face, running down her neck and soaking into the collar of her sweatshirt.

For a horrible second, I worry about what kind of liquid we've both just been soaked with—I saw on the news that a woman in L.A. was recently attacked and had a bucket of piping hot diarrhea dumped over her head—but then I see the dented Coke can on the floor at our feet, still spraying fizzed up soda out of its partially cracked opening, and I'm overcome with relief.

*It's just Coke, Silver.*

*It's okay, it's just Coke.*

The thankful reassurance that I plays out in my head quickly morphs into something angrier, though.

*They threw a can of Coke at you, Silver. They threw a can of fucking Coke at you.*

"Ahhh, sorry, ladies. Didn't see you there. I was aiming for the trash can," Nassem jeers. "Don't worry, though. There are plenty of witnesses around. No need to go running to Darhower and crying rape or anything."

I see red.

I don't really see anything at all.

One second, I'm helping Zen dab the soda from her face and her shirt, and the next I'm flying across the hallway, lifting my fist…

Suddenly, a menacing roar fills the corridor, and I'm no longer standing on my own two feet. I'm being lifted in the air, spun around, set back down again…

…and Alex is hurling himself at the group of football players.

It all happens so quickly. A startled scream splits the air behind me. People collide into one another in their desperate attempts to get out of the way. Kyle looks stunned for a split second, before he's lifted from his feet and Alex has him pinned against the wall.

"Alex, no!"

My shout goes unheard.

Alex pulls back his fist and I watch as he drives it forward in slow motion, slamming it into Kyle's face.

A dull *crack* fills the air, and Kyle's head makes contact with the wall behind him. That's when Lawrence and Naseem seem to realize that there are more of them than there are of Alex, and they fall on him, pulling at his shirt, dragging him off their friend.

I can only watch, horrified, as the three jocks tear into Alex. It's simple math: three against one. My boyfriend stands to get his ass kicked. Kyle seems a little dazed, as he throws a punch at Alex and misses. Lawrence has better aim. His fist makes contact with Alex's jaw. Naseem plays it safe and lands a winding punch to Alex's gut.

It seems, fleetingly, that Alex is about to hit the deck, but when I see the fury on his face, it becomes clear that that just *isn't* going to happen. Alex isn't the type of guy to go down in a fight. He's the type of guy who'll doggedly remain on his feet no matter how hard he's hit, until someone rings his bell hard enough for him to lose consciousness. I don't want it to get that far, though. The last thing I want to see is Alex knocked out on the ground.

"Hey!" I step forward, but Zen grabs my wrist, preventing me from getting too close to the melee. The three jocks are oblivious to me. Alex isn't. The whites of his eyes show as he finds me amongst the madness, and his steely warning drills into me: *don't come any closer, Argento. Keep back.*

Kyle hits Alex square on the jaw. He shakes his head, as if he can shrug out of the pain and the disorientation. It doesn't look like it works, though. With Lawrence and Naseem now holding Alex by either arm, an already shitty situation begins to look even worse.

Kyle staggers back, grunting as he hefts back his arm, swinging for Alex's face...

Oh god.

Come on. Please, no.

How many times do I have to watch the guy I love being hurt because of me?

I flinch, my breath lodged in the back of my throat, alongside another pleading cry. I can't work it free. It's jammed there, unable to get out. Kyle lurches drunkenly, too far away to land his punch...

...as Alex wrenches himself free of Lawrence's grasp. In a predatory, swift movement, he dips, pivots his hips, rises again, and grabs Lawrence by the side of the head. The crowd sucks in a communal breath as Alex digs his fingers into the other guy's shaggy hair, reels him in, and then smashes his head into the lockers.

"Holy shit," Zen hisses. "Did you see that? His eyes rolled back into his head. He's out cold."

Sure enough, Lawrence *is* out cold. His eyes are open, staring up at the ceiling. Kyle and Naseem exchange a glance that spells trouble—their outraged that Alex has KO'd their boy. Naseem steps forward first. The hallway suddenly becomes stiflingly hot. It's as though the walls are pressing in on all sides. Smirking like this entire fight has boiled down to this moment, Naseem eyes Alex like he's about to give him a taste of his own medicine. My boyfriend laughs softly under his breath, eying him dubiously, though.

"One more step, Nas. Just one more."

"And what? You can't take me *and* Kyle, asshole. Jesus, you really do think you're god's gift, don't you?"

Alex answers with a subtle twitch of his mouth. It's as close as he's ever going to get to smiling in front of Naseem. "You *were* warned. One step closer and you'll—"

Naseem steps forward.

In a blur of arms and smudged black clothing, Alex flies at him. Naseem braces, ducking a little to take the brunt of Alex's weight as he crashes into him, but he's massively underestimated Alex's strength. He goes down. Alex grabs the front of his shirt, pulling the guy off the ground to meet his fist, which he pulls back and unleashes again and again, until the asshole falls limp, his head lolling back.

"Darhower!" a girl cries on the far side of the knot of people. "Darhower's coming! Get the fuck out of here!"

The crowd breaks, scattering like a bunch of cockroaches across a kitchen floor. Students flee in every direction, tripping over one another, pushing each other out of the way as they attempt to distance themselves from the fight. Alex lowers his fist. He also drops Naseem, letting him fall to the blood streaked linoleum beneath his feet.

Curses under his breath, Kyle braces himself against the locker door beside him; looks like he's still winded from the very first hit Alex landed on him.

"Go on and get to class, Silver," Alex says grimly, clenching his jaw.

What the…? Of all the ridiculous things he could say to me right now, this tops the charts. "I'm not going anywhere. Neither's Zen. We'll tell Principal—"

His nostrils flare. Shaking his head, he steps over Naseem and gently tugs me toward the rear exit of the building, urging me to move. "Come on, *Argento*. If Darhower's shitty to you, even remotely shitty, then I'm gonna lose my temper and hit the fucker. This is already bad enough as it i—"

"What the *hell* is going on?"

Fuck.

Too late.

Principal Darhower's enraged voice booms down the hallway as he draws closer. Sounds like he's already clocked the two kids lying on the floor, and Kyle leaning awkwardly against the lockers, with Alex and me standing right in the middle of the carnage. It's too late to go sneaking off now, even if I wanted to.

I turn just in time for Darhower to arrive. He places his hands on his hips, pushing his suit jacket back, disbelief etched into the lines of his face. "Heaven help me, but I thought this week was gonna be it," he huffs. "This week, I figured things would be normal for once. Quiet, even. Hah!" His small snatch of laughter makes me jump. "I'm delusional. What is it, what's the saying?" He clicks his fingers, urging the phrase he's looking for to reveal itself to him. "Repeating the same act over and over and expecting a different result…that's the definition of madness. Well, I must be out of my fucking mind, because I really did, once again, let myself believe that you two weren't going to cause any more trouble. Yet here we are…*again*…"

"Alex was defending us," Zen says, stepping forward. Her voice sounds strong. Her attitude—the way she's set her jaw and is looking Darhower dead in the eye—is night and day from the anxious, scared demeanor she was rocking not five minutes ago. "These idiots threw a can of soda at us. They were threatening us," Zen announces, everything about her tight and controlled. "I was scared. You know. *For the baby.*"

*Whoa!*

*What the* fuck? Did she just say that out loud? I jerk back, startled by Zen's statement. I'm not the only one surprised by what she's just said, either; Darhower pales, his cheeks turning ashen white. I can only image the looks on the faces of the students around us who didn't run, because I can't tear my eyes away from the man in the wrinkled suit standing five feet away.

"I—y—wha—" Principal Darhower's mouth opens and closes a number of times before he breaks eye contact with Zen and looks briefly down at his feet while he gathers himself. He wasn't expecting her to bring up the fact that she's pregnant. Not in a hallway full of people. *I* wasn't expecting her to bring it up, either. Darhower kneads the back of his neck, pressing his fingertips into his skin like he's attempting to ease a sudden pinched nerve. When he looks back up, he's wearing a tight, unfriendly smile.

"Y'know what? I should suspend the lot of you. Send you home and demand your parents do something about this...this *mayhem*. It'd be a complete waste of time, though, wouldn't it? You're like goddamn wolves. I can't handle a second more of this, I swear. Ms. MacReady, get yourself to the nurses' station and get yourself checked out. We wouldn't want any harm to have come to your *baby*. Once she's finished, you three idiots drag your asses over there and get seen, too. Lawrence Davis, were you *unconscious* just now?"

Lawrence has woken up and has gotten to his feet while Darhower's been ranting. "No," he lies, shaking his head blearily. "I was fine. I was just..."

"Don't even bother. Just make sure you don't have a concussion, and then get the hell to your next class." You can practically see the fumes billowing out of his nose as he turns his attention to Alex and me. "You were so sweet and easy when you were a freshman, Silver. I swear to god, puberty is a curse sent from the gods to punish *me* specifically. And you..." he says, narrowing his eyelids to slits as he considers Alex. "The day you were foisted onto this school was a bad day indeed. Honestly, I literally pray at night that you all graduate with flying colors, purely so there'll be no chance of you repeating your senior year. At this rate, I'll be in an early grave before June. Get out of my sight."

Alex arches a cool eyebrow at the principal, his dark eyes sharper than razors. "No suspension? No threats?" he asks. "Don't you want to finally expel me from the school?"

That is what Darhower's wanted for a very long time. This, right here, is plenty of cause to expel Alex from Raleigh, and Maeve wouldn't be able to save his ass this time.

Darhower's lip curls up. "I've learned the hard way that getting rid of you isn't as easy as it sounds. Enjoy prom. Enjoy what's left of your senior year. Just do me a favor and keep the hell out of my way, boy."

## 37

## ALEX

You're expected to look smart in court, but I've stood before judges and juries in a t-shirt and jeans every single time I've been dragged up onto a dock. I haven't given a single fuck about the impression I'm supposed to give them. Those uptight stiffs, perched on their benches, heard the charges against me and immediately made their decisions about me and the kind of person I was. In their eyes, I was a criminal. A waste of space. A piece of shit that didn't deserve to share the same oxygen as them. I always knew that a collared shirt and a tie wouldn't do much to sway them when it came down to it, and so I dressed accordingly. No sense in being uncomfortable for nothing.

Tonight marks the very first time I've ever worn a suit. It's black and tailored, and the woman in the store cooed over me like a fucking psychopath when I tried it on in the store. She told me I was the most handsome guy she'd ever fitted. Yet all the while, she made sure to avoid looking at the ink that covers half of my body, fussing nervously around the tie clips and the cufflinks, watching me out of the corner of her eye like I was about to burn the place down to the ground with her still inside the building.

I straighten out the thin black pencil tie I just fastened around my neck, and for a moment the guy staring back at me from the bathroom mirror doesn't look like me at all. He looks like someone who might have a promising future ahead of him. I can see him accomplishing lofty goals and making something of himself, and that is frightening as fuck. Because failing is easy. Being the guy everyone expects me to be—that tearaway thug who'll never amount to anything but trouble—is the path of least resistance. Working to be better, to be more, is a much harder path to walk. If I convince people I'm a good man, there's a solid chance that, at some point, I'll actually end up letting them down…and that possibility, especially where Silver's concerned, is unacceptable.

*Then don't let her down, asshole,* I tell the guy looking back at me in the mirror. *Give her the life she deserves. Keep her safe, and never,* ever *hurt her.*

I already know I'm not gonna hurt her. I might not be the perfect husband but fuck me if I don't damn near kill myself trying to be. For her.

I walk away from the mirror, feeling like I've entered into some kind of contract with the promise of the man I might become, and I feel strangely optimistic about the whole thing.

As tradition dictates, Cameron opens the door to the Parisi household. I've knocked, even though I'm perfectly comfortable with walking through the front door unannounced these days. It's prom night, and I want Silver to get the whole experience. Wouldn't have been right if she didn't hear the boy who asked her to be his date arriving on the doorstep, as she checked her hair and straightened out her dress.

"Mr. Bond, I presume?" Cam says, putting on a thick non-descript Eastern European accent. He waggles his eyebrows as he looks me up and down. "Prepare to die. Mwahahahaha!"

"I don't think any of the Bond villains were vampires, old man," I tell him, skirting past him into the hallway. "You ever even seen a Bond movie?"

He folds his arms over his chest, arching an eyebrow at me suspiciously, like this is a trick question. "No. You?"

I shake my head, laughing softly. "Guess I haven't."

"We should probably rectify that. Have a movie marathon or

something. I don't think we count as real men until we've at least seen the Connery years."

I lean back against the wall next to the mail stand. "You asking me on a date? 'Cause you should know, I'm already seeing someone."

"Hah hah. Very droll." He clears his throat, his expression turning serious. "I'm supposed to tell you to have my daughter home by midnight now. And tell you to keep your hands to yourself. Seems a little futile now, since she already agreed to marry your sorry ass. You *should* still keep your hands to yourself, though," he adds on the end. "I don't condone your hands anywhere near my daughter, just so we're clear. If it were up to me, neither of you would be allowed to make physical contact of any kind until you're both at least thirty."

"God, Dad, please stop talking." Silver's standing at the top of the stairs. It's an undeniably cliché moment—Cameron giving me his fucked up, messy version of 'the talk' while I wait by the door for the girl of my dreams to appear. But fuck it. I don't give a shit, because Silver looks like she *is* a dream. Her hair's loose and wavey, styled to look like it hasn't been styled at all. She's wearing hardly any makeup, maybe just a touch of mascara and some lip gloss, and she looks fresh and vibrant. And her dress…it hits me that I've never seen Silver in a dress before. She lives in her jeans and t-shirts just like I do. The little black number she's wearing isn't your typical prom dress. It's a little edgy, and short, and the long expanse of her legs instantly makes my dick hard. Awkward, since Cam's standing four feet away.

The shoulders and the top of the dress that covers her cleavage is made of some kind of lace that sparkles and catches at the light as she hesitantly begins to come down the stairs. "What do you think?" she asks, running her hands over the material.

"Beautiful."

*"Beuuulful."*

Cam and I say it at the same time. We look at each other, and Silver's father coughs uncomfortably, clearing his throat. "Right. Screw you guys for growing up and leaving me here at home on my own. I'm gonna get the camera."

"No! Jesus. Dad, we don't need embarrassing prom photos. We're both covered in bruises."

We are, too. They're fading fast—a few of mine are fresher than others—but you can still see them if you look close enough. Cam doesn't give a shit, though.

"Uhhh...yeah. You have to have embarrassing photos taken. How else am I gonna remind you how dumb you looked in thirty years, when fashions have changed and everyone's wearing bell bottoms again?"

He ducks into his office, and Silver races down the remaining steps, grabbing hold of me by the suit jacket. "Come on, let's bail before he manages to find the Polaroid."

I scoop her off her feet, holding her up against me for a moment, placing a long, smoldering kiss on her lips. No tongue. I just hold her, lingering as I enjoy the sensation of her pliant lips, until she begins to melt against me. I love kissing this girl so fucking much. Each and every kiss I steal from her is a gift I don't deserve. Cameron clatters, dropping something in the office, and his hissed, "*Shit!*" echoes out into the hallway.

I release Silver, setting her back on her feet, pleased with the fact that her pupils are so blown they've almost swallowed her irises and she looks dazed as hell. I know I have an effect on her but witnessing it with my own two eyes makes me inordinately smug. God, she's so fucking beautiful, it feels like my insides are on fire. With a light touch, I skim the palm of my hand over her hair, humming softly under my breath. "Let's give him the moment, *Argento*. He's your dad. He should play his role in this whole prom debacle, just like we do."

"Urgh. Fine." She pretends to be annoyed, but a pleased light dances in her eyes. I think she loves the fact that I consider Cam from time to time. He bursts back out of his office, brandishing a DSLR like a weapon, as if he knows his daughter was planning on making a run for it. "Stand by the painting," he orders. "And I know this is gonna be painful for both of you, okay, but I'm gonna need you both to smile."

Once the obligatory modeling shoot's over with (yes, we both smiled), Cam lets us leave. Silver gasps when she hits the end of the path that leads to the turning circle in front of the house and sees our ride for the evening. "Alex! What the hell have you done?"

Shrugging, I suddenly feel out of sorts. "I thought about renting a limo for the evening and having someone drive us to the school, but I couldn't make myself do it. So Cam gave me the keys to the Nova, and…well…" I gesture to her car, as if the sight of it alone is all the explanation she needs. The gleaming new cherry red paint job speaks for itself. She can't see the brand new chromed out engine block from here, though. Or the newly upholstered leather seats.

"Oh my god. Alex, this is…" Silver covers her mouth as she heads for a closer inspection. She bends, marveling at the new interior, shaking her head. "This must have taken you forever."

I grunt, kicking the toe of my new, polished shoes against the curb. "Hate to admit it, but Zander might have helped out. Just a little." They make TV shows about car restorations like this. Zander and I worked way faster than any of those hacks could have. We didn't eat, and we didn't sleep. We went through a couple of cases of PBR afterward, but that didn't count.

"I love it," Silver whispers.

"You're not sad that we got rid of the black?"

"No way! The red is to die for."

"So…you're telling me you wanna take this thing for a test spin? Or would my queen like *me* to chauffeur her to the ball?"

"Are you kidding me, Moretti? Gimme those keys. I'm driving."

~

Silver

I'm still spinning out over the car when we walk into Raleigh High. The whole school has been decked out and decorated, with silver, gold and black balloons all over the place. Karen, Principal Darhower's assistant, is dressed in a sparkling blue floor length gown that's transformed her from dowdy admin worker to glamorous Bond girl; I almost can't believe she's the same woman. She ushers the arriving students into the gymnasium, taking our tickets and telling us to line up for the school photographer, who's taking shots of everyone in front of a huge black and white shutter design—one of the most iconic James Bond images ever created. Students stand in the open circle, back-to-back with their dates, making finger guns and posing goofily as their pictures are taken. Thankfully Alex sees the look on my face and leads me right past the whole mess, guiding me to the punch table.

"Doubt it's been spiked yet," he says morosely. "Still. You want some?"

He fills up a red solo cup for me, pouring one for himself, too. Zander arrives before either of us have managed to taste and see if anyone has covertly added any tequila. "This party sucks," he announces, pulling unhappily at the black tie around his neck. He's wearing a suit that rivals Alex's—also black, with a slight metallic blue sheen to it. He almost looks as handsome as the guy standing next to me. Almost.

"The music's terrible. They've already played Diamonds Are Forever a thousand fucking times. They're gonna run out of Bond theme songs before ten at this rate."

The gym's packed with kids in over the top dresses and suits of every color and style. By one of the massive PA speakers, Micha Williams is wearing a pale grey suit and a bald cap, with a stuffed white cat jammed firmly under his arm. Obviously, he chose the villain route and came dressed as Blofeld. My respect for him triples on sight.

"Some of the jocks have been hitting rails in the bathroom. There was a fight in the parking lot. One of your fellow cheerleaders broke a heel, Silver, and Darhower kicked a couple out for fucking in the janitor's closet. You guys haven't missed much. I'm feeling a little robbed. Bellingham's prom would have been far more exciting than this snooze fest."

"If you'd transferred back there like I told you to, you could have gone," Alex reminds him.

Zander pulls a face. "Graduating from Raleigh looks a lot better on college applications. And besides, you would have missed me too much."

For once, Alex doesn't volley a snarky retort back at him. He sighs heavily instead. "Where's Halliday?"

"How should I know?"

"Uhh...because she's your *date?*" Alex replies.

I still can't believe Zander asked Hal to come to prom with him. I definitely can't believe she said yes. Under Kacey's rule, Halliday would never have agreed to come to a major school event with a guy like Zander. Goes to show how much things have changed around here.

"Fine, fine, you're right. I should probably go find her. She's so fucking hot tonight, she's probably got eight guys hitting on her right now, anyway. Maybe I'll have to defend her honor and knock a few of 'em out." He sounds way too excited by the prospect.

On our own again, Alex offers me his hand as the song changes to something upbeat and bouncy. "Oh boy. You wanna dance?" I ask.

He's devilishly handsome as he smirks, slowly shaking his head. "I only have one dance in me, *Argento*, and I'm saving it for another day. No, I wanna steal you away for a second, if that's all right with you?"

His dark eyes burn into me like brands, intense and fierce, and my heart backflips. Jesus Christ, the way he looks at me is too fucking much. "Lead the way."

There are chaperones guarding the fire escape at the back of the gym, so we have to lie to Ms. Gilcrest and tell her we're heading to the bathroom in order to leave. Before I know it, Alex has set off at a jog, laughing, dragging me along behind him down the hallway. When we arrive at his locker, he places his hands on my shoulders, positioning me so that my back's up against the cool metal. It's much calmer here; gentle strains of music from the gym float down the corridor, but it's quiet enough that I can feel my own pulse thundering in my ears.

I never thought I'd get to have this. Prom was a rite of passage I thought I wasn't going to get to experience. After everything that's gone down over the past year, I assumed I'd be boycotting the night, curled up on the sofa at home in my sweats, shoving popcorn into my face as I watched a movie while everyone else partied the night away. Alex made this possible, though. He made me want to come here tonight, to be by his side. He's made prom perfect.

"Close your eyes, Parisi," he says, dipping down to bury his face in the crook of my neck for a moment. His hot breath skates over my skin, and the back of my neck breaks out in goosebumps.

"Shit, Alex..." I close my eyes, reveling in the feel of him pressing up against my body. I want him to kiss me properly. I need his mouth on mine. His hands on my naked flesh. If Darhower hadn't already booted a couple out for screwing on school property, I'd be trying to find the closest janitor's closet myself right now. Alex looks so good in his suit that my immediate response is to try and get him out of it.

He pulls away, taking his heat with him, and I ache from the lack of him.

To my right, I hear the ticking of a combination lock being opened, and then the creak of his locker door as he opens it up. Silence follows. I can't even hear him breathing.

"Alex?"

"I asked you to marry me in a diner, *Argento*. A fucking *diner*. I asked you without a ring, because I couldn't hold back a second longer, and I've felt pretty terrible about that ever since. So…no, wait, not yet. Keep them closed." He laughs shakily—an adorably vulnerable sound. "Cameron gave this to me a while ago, and I've been waiting to give it to you."

Oh, shit. Oh…my god. He's giving me a ring? My cheeks flame, blood rushing to my face. I can't…even…think straight. I need to open my eyes. I *have* to open them. As if he can sense that I'm losing my battle to obey him, Alex places a hand over my eyes, blocking out my vision.

"I wasn't waiting for the right moment," he whispers. Jesus, his mouth is so damn close, I can feel the brush of his lips against mine as he speaks. "I was waiting to give you time to think this through properly. I wanted to give you a chance to change your mind. And now that you've had the opportunity to process all of this, what I'm truly asking of you, I'm going to ask it of you again, Silver Parisi."

I whimper as he removes his hand. He leans away again, and I'm left feeling like I'm about to slide down the lockers and collapse to the ground.

"Open them, Silver. Open your eyes."

"I—" Now that I know what's happening, for some reason opening my eyes has become an impossible task.

"Silver. *Look at me*," Alex says.

Slowly, I crack my eyes, and everything blurs for a second when I see him, on both his knees at my feet. The small velveteen box in his hands is open, and inside it, shining brightly against the blue, plush material, is the most beautiful ring I've ever seen. The huge stone at its center is a stunning coral pink instead of diamond white. The setting is silver.

"I don't think you're supposed to get down on both knees," I whisper.

"Getting down on one knee's supposed to be a sign of honor and respect. One knee's not good enough for you, *Argento*. I'll always be on both for you, worshipping you, honoring you. Please..." He's deadly serious as he looks up at me. Serious, and hopefully, and desperately vulnerable. "Say yes again and take the ring."

I'm blinded by the sheer force of the love that hits me. It's incredible, like nothing I've ever experienced before. I cup the side of his face in my hand, brushing my thumb over the ridge of his cheekbone. "I didn't need time, Alex. I knew the very second you asked me in that diner. You made me so ridiculously happy. So, yes. For the second time, yes, I *will* marry you."

He tries to hide away his quietly pleased smile, but I can see it in his eyes. Before he can get up, I drop down to my knees, too, joining him on the floor. "I worship you, too, y'know. I've been too shy to say it in the past, but...I think you're pretty cool, Alessandro Moretti," I say, teasing him.

"Pretty cool, huh?" He laughs, rolling his eyes to the ceiling. "Okay. I s'pose I'll take it."

We're both just nervous, I think. Because the asking part is intense, yes, but the taking the ring out of the box part, the sliding it onto my finger part is even more intense. Alex's hand shakes as he plucks the ring from its cushion; he pauses, blowing out down his nose, and the shakes stop just like that. He's steady, solid as a rock as he gently takes my hand and slips the beautiful ring onto my finger.

Once it's done, Alex sinks back onto his heels, like he's relieved he didn't screw up. "It was your great-grandmother's," he says. "Cameron told me it was meant for you all along."

"And *you* were the one who was supposed to give it to me."

We kiss like the world is ending, and neither of us really cares.

## 38

## SILVER

Halfway back to the gym, I realize I haven't got any lip gloss in my purse and Alex just kissed all of mine off. "Go on ahead. I'm gonna go back to my locker really quick."

"You planning on shoving the ring back in the box and hiding it under an algebra text book?" Alex jokes. Sounds like there's a hint of real concern in his voice.

"Absolutely not. I don't want to hide it. And I don't care who knows about us either. I'll make an announcement on the PA in between Bond theme songs if you like?"

He smirks at that, squeezes my hand and gives me a quick kiss on the temple. "Take too long and I'll have to come find you, Mrs. Moretti."

A chill runs up and down my spine at that name. A good chill. One that makes me smile so hard it hurts. "A little premature, there, don't you think?"

"Oh, Silver. Don't you know me by now? I'm *never* premature."

I'm still laughing to myself, my heels clicking loudly against the linoleum, as I hurry back to my locker. I open up the lock and pull the door open, already reaching insi—

An avalanche pours out of my locker, small scraps of paper fluttering and flying everywhere, tumbling out onto the floor.

"Oh my god." I smile, bending to collect one up from the floor. Alex must have arranged this. It must be part of his second, albeit unnecessary proposal. Turning the small shred of paper I've just collected over in my hand, I expect to read something sweet written on it. One of a thousand 'I Love You's Alex must have slipped through the grate on the locker door, only…

*Silver Parisi: most likely to suck dick for a dollar.*

"What the fuck?"

I pick up another, and then another.

*Silver Parisi: most likely to contract syphilis.*

*Silver Parisi: most likely to cook meth.*

*Silver Parisi: most likely to fuck your boyfriend behind your back.*

I'm too shocked to process what this is for a second. And then it all comes rushing back to me in a tidal wave of horror—months ago, the day I saw Alex for the very first time. I was in detention. Jake had been there. And I'd been tallying up the nominations for the Raleigh High yearbook's *'most likely to'* taglines for the student photos.

I was hurt by the litany of insults my fellow classmates had written about me. There were score upon score of them, each progressively worse than the last. They'd cut, sharp as knives, every time I'd read a new and awful suggestion for the yearbook.

There had been one nomination that had repeated itself over and over again, as I'd trawled through those never-ending ballots. One that had made my blood run cold. It's as cold as ice in my veins as I scoop up a handful of the scraps and find the phrase repeated here, too, over and over again.

With horror coursing through me like a river, I realize that I'm all alone in the hall.

I take off, running in the direction of the gym, stumbling, rolling my ankle, as a sharp jolt of pain fires up my leg. Cursed heels. I kick them off, discarding them, sprinting as fast as I can back toward the gym.

"No running, Ms. Parisi!" Karen calls, as I dodge around the 007 photo booth.

I don't stop running. I barrel forward, scanning the packed gym for a sign of Alex, and when I see him standing by the far wall, talking to Halliday and Zander, I run even harder, shoving through the crowd, deaf to the irritated shouts of the people I slam into.

Alex, so dashing in his suit, dark hair swept back out of his face, pales when he sees me flying towards him. He stops whatever he was saying to Halliday. "Hey. What's wrong?"

In my attempt to hand them over, I drop most of the yearbook ballots I brought with me. Alex grabs one of them, though, and quickly scans the scrawled black in on the paper's surface.

*Silver Parisi: most likely to die on prom night.*

"What the fuck is this?" he asks, his eyes suddenly sharp, boring into me. "Where did you get this?" He reads two more of the ballots, a dark, palpable fury pouring off him like heat.

"They were in my locker. Hundreds of them."

"I don't understand."

Fighting for breath, I try to order my thoughts enough that I might be able to explain further and tell him their significance, but a low chorus of chatter sweeps across the gym. Alex looks up, Halliday and Zander mirroring his confused glance across the room...and that's when I see him. See *them*.

Wearing a suit as black as midnight, his blond hair slicked back, and amused cornflower blue eyes skipping over the faces of Raleigh High's senior year, Jacob Weaving enters the gymnasium. And on his arm, dressed in a sequined gold dress with a plunging neckline, walks Kacey fucking Winters.

## 39

## SILVER

"This isn't real. This isn't real, is it? I'm seeing things." Halliday's high pitched, question parallels the racing thoughts screaming loudly in my head. This isn't real. There's no way this is actually happening. It just can't be. But Jake and Kacey look more than real, as they head into the crowd. They look like royalty, and they've come to claim their prom crowns.

"Last time I saw that bitch, she shot me," Alex snarls under his breath. His hand moves to the point where, beneath his clothes, the bullet from Leon Wickman's gun pierced his skin and came damn close to taking his life. "Why the fuck would she come back here? And why would he be stupid enough to think he'd be welcome."

The music continues to play. People carry on dancing. Conversations, muted and confused, proceed, even though two of Raleigh High's most notorious ex-students have just waltzed into the building like they have every right to be here.

"I've gotta go," I rasp out hoarsely. "I've got to get out of here. Now." It was one thing being here, in this place, where I nearly had my neck broken, to celebrate prom with my friends. But I can't suffer *Jake* to be here and keep my shit together at the same time. I'm about to have a panic attack. Jake put those ballots in my locker. Jake, with Kacey's help. This stinks of her brand of evil.

Alex takes me by the arm. "Okay, it's alright. Come on. I'll take you home." He leads the way, cutting through the crowd, giving Jake and Kacey a wide berth. I stumble after him, my legs numb and unresponsive. How can Karen have let the two of them in? She's quiet and shy, but Ms. Gilcrest's a stickler for the rules. She wouldn't allow two non-Raleigh students to attend a school event like this. Even if they did used to be enrolled here. Not unless...Darhower expressly told her they were to be permitted entry.

Something hot and nasty churns in my stomach.

God, Dad was right. Back in Darhower's office, he'd called the guy out over the speech he gave to us in this very gymnasium. After the shooting, he promised us he'd do better. He swore he'd never be so complacent again, and that our safety would be his number one priority. How quickly those promises went flying out of the window. It took all of a couple of weeks for him to fall neatly back into the Weaving family's back pocket. Jacob's father's still manipulating him, pulling his strings all the way from behind his prison bars. He must be paying Raleigh High's principal one hell of a lot of money to get him to sign off on something like this.

Suddenly, the small, ever-present, flickering flame of anger that's been burning in the core of my soul for the past year kindles and roars to life, becoming a seething inferno.

This isn't right.

No fucking more.

This—Jacob showing up at prom with Kacey—might be the smallest of his offences, but it is the straw that finally breaks the camel's back.

If I run away now and flee the school, he wins. He gets exactly what he wants, and I am so fucking sick of Jacob Weaving winning, when what he really needs is to be punished.

"Alex? Alex, wait."

Ahead of me, Alex halts, looking back at me over his shoulder. He checks I'm fine first, and then he peers over the tops of the heads of the other students, searching for and locating Jake and my ex-best friend. He is a storm front, ready to break and crash down upon the people who have caused me pain. The dark, foreboding look in his eyes makes even me want to shrink away from him. One word from me, and he'll unleash hell on these people. He'll make them hurt, and he'll make them beg for mercy, and he won't stop until I decide he's done enough.

He's fought too many of my battles for me, though. It's about damn time I fought them for myself.

"I changed my mind. We should stay. I'm sick of that bastard getting his way, every single time he acts out. We'll just ignore him."

Alex gives me a *look*, one that shows he thinks I've lost my mind. "Silver—"

"Seriously. It'll be okay. We'll let him hold court and do his thing. And Kacey can fluff her feathers and preen all she likes. The best thing we can do is to stand our ground and have a good time, no matter what."

"Have a good time? With him breathing down your neck? You're sure?" He's understandably doubtful. If I were him, I'd be doubtful, too. I've made up my mind, though. I won't duck and cower for anyone anymore, and that includes the guy who raped me.

I was born in this town. I have as much right as anyone else to be here tonight, and if I have to tolerate veiled threats against my life and make sure I have eyes in the back of my head, then so be it. I *will* enjoy prom if it's the last thing I do. "Yes, I'm sure," I tell him.

Alex's conflicted expression turns to one of resolve. "All right, then. Mission: Enjoy Prom is a go. Just keep me away from that fuck, or I'll end up knocking a couple of his molars loose, yeah?"

"Okay."

Alex stays true to his word and refuses to dance, but luckily for me, my old dance partner is here. Kacey never danced so much as strutted around, tossing her hair and jutting out a hip every once in while. Zen could dance, but she always chose to mimic our supreme leader. I could always count on Halliday to hit the dance floor with me, though. At parties, she'd move with wild abandon, throwing her arms in the air and bouncing on the balls of her feet, pulling out cheesy moves when she felt the need, not caring what she looked like or what anyone thought. She only cared that moving her body in time to the music felt good and it made her grin from ear to ear, and so she always let herself go.

Tonight's no exception. She whoops as we jump and laugh

together, dancing our hearts out in the center of the gym's dance floor. Her floor-length, black, extraordinarily slinky dress is a little restrictive and prevents her from performing some of her trademark moves, but she doesn't let that stop her in the slightest.

After a while, I stop thinking about Jake and Kacey, and I just… dance. It feels incredible. Halliday's blonde hair swings around her as she spins, and she looks like she's about to float away from sheer happiness as we crash into each other, laughing at the top of our lungs.

I'm so glad I let her back in. Things are never going to be exactly the same as they used to be, but this, right here, is a moment of joy, and I miss sharing moments of joy with Hal. We used to have them on a daily basis.

"God, could they be any more obvious," she pants, as the song dips. She looks over in the direction of the boys, who are both leaning with their backs against the wall closest to us, watching us with a fevered energy in their eyes. Not one word of conversation passes between them. Both Alex and Zander are fixed on us, as if we're the only two girls in the room.

I laugh when Alex raises a questioning eyebrow at me. I know what that eyebrow means. He wants me naked in a dark room, with his teeth gouging into my skin. The dirty little freak.

"They love us," Halliday purrs, amusement dripping from her words. "They love us, and they want to marry us. God help them, poor souls."

I fight the urge to laugh. "Uhh…" I'm not the girl who runs around, squealing, holding out her hand for everyone to accidentally notice the gargantuan rock flashing on her ring finger. I'm not even the girl who secretly whispers her news into her friend's ear. I'm the kind of girl who says nothing and acts as though everything's normal, until someone finally notices the fact that she's wearing an engagement ring all on their own.

Halliday's not the most observant person usually; she's always away with the fairies. She must be on high alert tonight, what with Kacey prowling around by the refreshments, glowering at us out of the corner of her eye, though. She sees the look on my face, and then somehow manages to put two and two together. She looks down at my hand and takes an exaggerated step back, clutching her hands to her chest.

"Oh my *fuck*. What? What the fuck is *that* on your finger, Silver Georgina Parisi? Get the hell out of town. Is that an *engagement ring?*"

Sweet lord. She's practically yelling. I'm too scared to look around and see if anyone heard her. "Shh! Yes. It's an engagement ring."

"God, I wish I'd convinced Zen to come tonight. She should be here for this. Wait, how the hell did *this* even happen?" Halliday squeals again, even more high-pitched and excited.

"He asked. I said yes." It'd be cool if we could keep this conversation simple and move on as quickly as possible, but I know Halliday better than that. She's going to want details. The minutia of an event as colossal as a proposal is bound to be very important to Halliday "He was very romantic," I offer, hoping that alone will be enough to stave off her questions.

"How romantic? What did he say? What was he wearing? What were you wearing? Oh, shit, I think I'm about to have a heart attack."

"Take it easy, girl. One thing at a time. Remember to breathe..."

"Huh. Would you look at this," a chillingly familiar voice says. The sound of it reminds me of knives being sharpened, their edges honed to vicious points. "How small-town trailer park of you, Silver. Hitched before graduation. Suppose I shouldn't be surprised. You always were just so...*basic*."

Kacey Winters is standing right behind me.

If I turn around now, I'll come face to face with her, and I'll be forced to look her in the eye. No doubt I'll be forced to endure more of her cutting remarks, too. The excited smile that was plastered all over Halliday's face a moment ago has frozen into some sort of horrified rictus of panic. She looks like Kacey's turned her to fucking stone.

"Well? Aren't you going to say hello, Silly? It's been a while. Haven't you missed me?"

Slowly, I pivot on the point of my heels, dragging out the movement, wishing with every part of me that the Ice Queen of Raleigh High will somehow have disappeared by the time I've rotated a hundred and eighty degrees. Unfortunately, my wishing does no good. She's there all right, standing in front of me in all her manicured, blown out, plucked, buffed, and polished glory. Her jet-black hair is longer than it was before she got shipped off to Seattle. And she looks skinnier. So skinny that her cheekbones protrude too far out of her face, creating hollows in her cheeks. It wouldn't be a good look on most people, but Kacey, with her porcelain skin and her cool eyes and her rosebud mouth it makes her look annoyingly chic. Old habits die hard; she must have been sticking her fingers down her throat again.

I look her in the eye and take a weary, tired breath. "No. I haven't missed you, Kace. No one here's missed you. Take a look around. Does it look like Raleigh High fell apart without you?"

I'm just being honest, but I see the stab of hurt in Kacey's eyes. I've touched a raw nerve. Such a fucking narcissist. She can see that life went on without her after she was banished from Raleigh…and she fucking hates it. From the disgusted scowl she sends Halliday's way, she also despises the fact that her minion made friends with me again, the moment her back was turned.

"So this is why you stopped replying to my texts?" she spits. "Because you were busy sucking up to the school whore? Pathetic, Halliday. Really fucking pathetic. I thought you kept better company. But then again, I guess you're used to hanging out with whores now that you are one too, right? Dancing at the Rock? I mean, aren't all of those strippers essentially prostitutes?"

Attacking Halliday and calling her a whore, for trying to keep a roof over her family's heads? That is *not* okay. "Shut your nasty mouth and fuck off, Kacey. You're tiring. You're *so* fucking tiring, and we've had enough. Being your friend was a literal prison sentence, okay? And we've more than served our time. You're irrelevant now. Your bitching and your catty jabs are just boring. So…go away."

Pure, cold, distilled hate shines brightly out of Kacey's cool blue eyes. "You think now because you've got yourself a hot bad boy fiancé, you're untouchable, Silver?" she says. "You think your loser trailer park boyfriend somehow makes you better than us? Than *me*?"

"Alex has nothing to do with this." It takes all of my strength and then some to stop myself from rising to her comments. She's baiting me, trying to anger me, but I have more control over myself than that. I know what Alex is worth, and so does he. That's all that matters. "I'm not better than you because of who I'm dating. I'm better than you because I'm not a venomous, cold-hearted, disloyal bitch who turns on her friends and hurts everyone around her, because she's afraid that they might somehow outshine her."

Kacey runs her tongue over her teeth, like she's trying to get a bad taste out of her mouth. With a dawning sense of realization, it occurs to me that our little spat is being observed now. The music's still blaring out of the PA speakers, but the dancing has stopped. My classmates, once subjects who suffered under the bootheel of Kacey Winters, have all gathered around and are listening intently to what's being said.

I don't give a fuck what they hear. I don't give a fuck about their opinions, or who's side they're on anymore. None of that matters. Only the truth matters. I won't keep it to myself. It's time it all came out, every ugly, uncomfortable detail, and then maybe there would be an end to this bullshit.

"Tell me, Kacey. What was it that Sam Hawthorne said to you that night?"

"What the fuck are you talking about?" she scoffs.

"You know what I'm talking about. The night of Leon Wickman's spring fling party. I was standing outside in the dark and the cold, *bleeding*...I was waiting for my friend to come and help me, but..." I shake my head. "You didn't come to help me, did you? I saw you through the window. Sam Hawthorne said something to you that made you so angry. And when you came outside, you weren't my friend anymore. You'd decided I was your enemy, and I didn't deserve your compassion."

"YOU *WERE* MY ENEMY!" Kacey roars. "You wanna know what Sam said to me? Fine. All I ever heard come out of my father's mouth was, *Silver's such a nice girl, Kacey. Why can't you be more like Silver, Kacey? Silver isn't failing math, is she, Kacey? Silver's so goddamn smart, Kacey. Why don't you get Silver to help you, Kacey?* Silver, Silver, Silver all the fucking time! I could never understand why he insisted on banging on and on about you all day long. And then there it was. Sam told me that my father had actually been banging your *mother*. She was the reason why my parents split up, though my poor mom never found out who the other woman was. She sure as hell wouldn't have let me hang out with you if she'd known."

"*What?*" What the actual fuck is she talking about? My mom never had an affair with Mr. Winters. She had an affair with her boss at work. Kacey doesn't know anything about that, though. Aside from Alex, no one knows about that.

"You heard me. Your mom seduced my dad when we were thirteen. I saw her coming out of the guest house once, but he told me she'd come looking for you. I didn't think anything of it, but that's where they used to meet up. They'd fuck in there while my mom was at work."

"No. No way. Sam made it up. How the hell would he know anything about my mom and your dad?" I'm telling myself this, pleading with myself to believe it. Sam *had* to have made it up. But a worried part of me is scared that it might be true. "He just said that to turn you against me, Kacey. And look?" I hold my hands up. "It worked. You let a boy rape me and get away with it because you believed a lie. And then you decided to *date* that boy!"

"God, you're the liar. You fucked Jake because you *wanted* to fuck him, and then you cried about it afterwards 'cause you didn't want anyone to think you were a slut. But you are a slut, Silver. *Just like your mom.*"

So this is what it's like to see red; my entire vision turns crimson, darkening around the edges. I've never been so angry that my blood feels cold in my veins. It feels like I'm frozen and carved out of ice, from the roots of my hair all the way down to the soles of my feet. Alex takes my hand, muttering reassuring words under his breath, but my ears aren't willing to listen. I'm too livid to be soothed, even by him.

"You're fucking insane," I snarl. "You're so desperate to be the best, to be looked up to, and have everybody falling at your feet, that the moment someone pays someone else a compliment, you paint a fucking target on their backs. Maybe your dad was just sick of your shit. Maybe he just thought it would be fine to ask your friend to help you with some math tutoring. Maybe he simply didn't like the way you were behaving and thought you'd benefit from an attitude adjustment. What does it matter? I was your *friend*, and you threw me away like I was garbage, Kacey. You're vapid, and cold. And you're never going to find anyone to love you. How can you, when you don't even like yourself?"

She glowers, stung, her cheeks flooding with color. So unlike Kacey Winters, the Ice Queen, to ever show emotion. It was always beneath her to let anyone visibly ruffle her feathers, and yet here she is, very ruffled indeed. She's so fucking predictable.

*Love me.*
*Worship me.*
*Praise me.*
*Look up to me.*
*Treat me like your fucking god.*

The moment her layers are stripped back and her insecurities are revealed, she's no longer special and she knows it. She's just as afraid, and tired, and scared, and fucked up as the rest of us. A seventeen-year-old girl, affecting a level of calm she doesn't possess, pretending that she has even the slightest control over her own life, when in truth she's confused and spinning dangerously out of control.

"Jesus, just fuck off and die. *Please.* Do everyone a favor and expire already. We're all so over of the Silver Parisi show." The venom in her voice is toxic. It's there on her face, in the way she's leaning toward me like she's desperate to lash out and hit me but she doesn't quite know how; Kacey's always been far more efficient at hurting people with her tongue than her fists.

Her words only have an effect on me now because of the yearbook nomination ballots that just came tumbling out of my locker. She really does want me to die. She's not just saying it, attempting to wish me away, out of her life. She hates me so badly that she wants me dead and buried in the ground. That kind of ice-cold hatred is enough to make anyone's teeth chatter.

Perfectly timed as ever, Jake decides that now's the right moment to saunter over, absently toying with an olive in between his teeth. He sucks it into his mouth, winking at me as he chews. He's the type of guy who's comfortable in a suit. He wears the expensive-looking cloth like it's a second skin. Looking me up and down, he does nothing to hide his disdain at my outfit. "A dress? Brave of you, Silver. I was expecting you to show up in a hessian sack. Something with a little more material?" he sneers.

Alex bristles beside me, his anger palpable at such close quarters. This kind of confrontation is exactly what I wanted to avoid. We were supposed to be having a good night. Supposed to be keeping to our side of the gym, minding our own business. It would have been fine, too, if Kacey hadn't noticed Halliday checking out the ring on my finger.

She clearly still hasn't forgotten about it, either. Glaring at it pointedly, her mouth twisted into a sour pout, she pops out a hip, arching a sculpted black eyebrow, and announces out loud, for everyone to hear, "Come on now, baby. Tonight's a special night for Silver. She's just agreed to become Mrs. Trailer Trash. Shame her loser fiancé couldn't afford a proper ring. Looks like it came out of a fucking gum ball machine."

A chorus of titters and awkward laughter travels from one side of the crowd to the other like a Mexican wave. All around me, seniors avert their gaze, avoiding making eye contact with me as they hide their smiles. They react this way because they've been conditioned. Kacey lashes someone with a cutting barb, and our classmates all respond in kind, giving her the reaction she so craves. It's a fucked up symbiotic relationship that I thought had ended the day Leon Wickman bled out on the rough grey carpet in the Raleigh High library.Seems as though people here are all too willing slip back into old routines, though, acting out the roles that are expected of them.

They can laugh and smile all they want. They can mock me until the end of time. It wouldn't matter if Alex had bought my ring from a gum ball machine for all I care. I'm wearing my grandmother's ring. It's legendary in the Parisi family. I don't think even Alex realizes that the stone, mounted in the simple yet elegant silver setting, is a pink diamond, and one of the rarest stones money can buy.

Gram used to tuck me into bed at night sometimes, and I'd beg her to tell me the story of how her parents fell in love and survived the war. And at the center of my great grandparent's story, was the beautiful ring I'm lucky enough to be wearing on my finger. I wouldn't trade it for anything.

I'm about to fire off a retort to Kacey's shitty comment, when I notice the stunned look on Jacob's face. His full lips are parted, a glass lifted halfway to his open mouth, and his cornflower blue eyes are wide, doubled in size. "What the fuck is that?" he sputters, staring at the ring. "You can't be fucking *serious*."

"As a heart attack," Alex growls, stepping in front of me. He's stood his ground, letting me handle the situation until now; I know he held back in order to try and rein in his anger, but Jake's shocked statement has tipped him over the edge. With bared teeth, he prowls forward, a biblical rage burning in his dark eyes. "It kills you, huh? You wanted her so bad, you took her against her will. And when you couldn't break her, you decided you'd do the next best thing and kill her. You failed at that too, though, Weaving. Silver's stronger than you, and you know it. You're never going to best her. And you're never gonna fucking own her, either. She'll never belong to you now."

What the hell's happening here? Jake's eyes shine, wet and glassy looking. He downs his drink, swallowing down the whiskey in his cup —I can smell the powerful, sharp tang of it on his breath from where I'm standing. His nostrils flare as he puffs and blows like a wild, angry horse. Out of nowhere, the cooler-than-cool attitude he was affecting when he strolled over has vanished and he comes alive with fury. "Stupid fuck. You think you own her 'cause you slipped a ring on her finger?"

Alex pushes out a sharp bark of laughter, loud over the pounding music. "That's the difference between you and me, isn't it, Jake? I've never tried to own her. I want her to be free. You only wanted to crush her to your will, regardless of how you accomplished it."

"God, back off, Trailer Trash," Kacey groans. She studies her nails, angling them under the white lights that strobe on and off overhead. She can feign boredom all she likes, but I can see that she's sizzling mad from the impatient, repetitive tapping of her heel and the way her mouth has flattened into a straight line. "The grown-ups are talking, okay? You're embarrassing yourself. You'd be better off keeping your dirty mouth closed, sweetheart."

Oh, shit. Alex is three seconds from exploding like a goddamn IED. On the outside, he's perfectly calm. Anyone would be forgiven for thinking he was absolutely fine. He isn't though. Not even close. I take his hand, as he took me by mine before, and I try to get him to look at me, but it's no good. He's too far gone to be reached.

"*You*," he says quietly, addressing Kacey. "I'm confused by you. You're so *weak*. There's absolutely nothing remarkable about you. You're uninteresting to look at. Below average intelligence. Your obsessive struggle for power has ranged well past the border of pathetic and you've now officially hit pitiful territory. Somehow, you're still trying to best the girl who adored and doted on you, even though you know you can't. You know you lost to her a long time ago. You know she's better than you in every way imaginable, and yet… you keep on trying. He calls her Second Place Silver," he says evenly, jerking his chin in Jake's direction, "but in your heart, you know she's first place. She's all he cares about. He can never love you as much as he hates her. She consumes his entire fucking being, doesn't she? He's so determined to despise her, that there's hardly any room left inside his head for you at all. You're *always* going to be second place." Taking a measured step forward, he tips his head to one side, shaking his head slowly, like he feels sorry for her.

"I get what it's like to feel worthless, Kacey. You're right. I lived in a trailer park, and I come from poor stock. That doesn't really set a guy up to excel in life. I see all of the things I used to hate about myself in you, and my heart breaks for you. But I swear to god," he says, leaning into her face. "Call me Trailer Trash again, and I'll make you wish you'd never been fucking born. I don't care if you're a girl. I haven't forgotten that bullet in the library, Winters. Now, you close *your* mouth like a good little girl now, or I'll happily slam my fist into it."

Kacey pales. The haughty expression on her face fades and dies as she shrinks into herself a little. "You wouldn't. You wouldn't hit me. Your dumb masculine pride wouldn't let you."

"Oh, believe me. You grow up in the places I grew up and things like pride are a luxury you can't afford. Do not doubt me. I'll break your fucking neck if you piss me off again. And if you do or say anything to hurt Silver, then god help you, Kacey Winters, because only he will be able to save you."

"All right, senior students of Raleigh High! Is everybody having an amazing time?" An overly cheerful voice on the PA cuts over the top of the music. The DJ stops the track, and a strained quiet falls over the gymnasium. No one's paying attention to Susan Foyle, class president, who's apparently commandeered a microphone from somewhere. All eyes are on Alex and Kacey. All eyes are on me and Jake.

"It's that time of the night, guys! The votes have been counted, and the candidates have been weighed. I'm delighted to announce that this year's Raleigh High prom king and queen have been selected by you, the people, and we are ready to unveil their identities to the world!" Susan claps enthusiastically up on the stage. No one joins her.

At any moment, this place is going to go up in flames. The tension's so thick, you could cut it with a dull knife. Jake grabs Alex by the suit jacket, pulling him close. I can see his mouth working, hard words being spit out of his mouth as he snarls something at my boyfriend, but I can't hear what he says, because Susan starts speaking again.

"Okay, okay. Not quite the response I was looking for, but hey. Tradition is tradition, people, and we are still excited to have our Raleigh High senior coronation. If everyone could please look this way, we'll call our new king and queen up to the stage and then everyone can get back to dancing. *Yaaaaayyyy!*"

Poor Susan. She's trying to inspire some sort of excitement in the crowd, but her Raleigh High pep is falling on deaf ears. Alex shoves Jake away, a hard, murderous light in his eyes. He turns his back and walks away from the other guy instead of hitting him, though. Alex isn't going to try and kill Jake in front of two hundred witnesses. Thank the fucking lord.

"It's okay. It's over," he whispers, ducking down to place a kiss against my cheekbone. "Come on. Let them parade themselves around in front of everyone all they like. I wanna get you a drink."

Whoa.

The deadly, quiet rage that was oozing out of him just now has gone. I've never seen such an immediate turnaround in him before; it's miraculous that he's suddenly so calm. "Really?" I search his face, looking for any tell-tale signs that he's about to lose it and start throwing his fists, but when his eyes meet mine, all I see is frustration and weariness.

"Yeah. Come on. We've had enough of this shit to last us a lifetime. Zander's got some tequila in a flask somewhere. We should find him."

"Okay. Sure."

Kacey still looks stunned, white as a sheet, as Alex pulls me away through the crowd. I don't look back at her, or at Jake, as we walk across the gym, cutting a path toward the emergency exit.

"First things first," Susan projects through the PA speakers. "I'd like to thank everyone for helping to decorate the school for tonight's event. These things take work, and we'd have been lost without you guys—"

"Get on with it, Susan!" someone yells in the crowd. "Get off the fucking stage!"

Susan blushes furiously, shuffling a bunch of pages in her hands. She obviously wrote an entire speech for tonight's proceedings, and she'd planned on more time with her audience. With crimson cheeks, she flicks through the pages, her hands shaking nervously. "Okay, okay. I get it. This is a party. We all wanna get back to the festivities. In that case, let's proceed to the matter at hand. Our prom queen this year didn't win by a landslide. In fact, just to make the rest of you girls feel a little better, she only won by three measly votes. Honestly, we were a little surprised when we finished the count. Anyway, anyway…I'm getting side-tracked. This year's prom queen…" Susan looks around, searching for someone. "Can I get a drumroll, please?"

"Here." Alex hands me an engraved silver flask, smiling softly. "I'm sorry, *Argento*. I shouldn't have let that bitch get under my skin. Take a hit of this. Should make you feel better."

Since there's no live band in the gym, the DJ obliges Susan and plays a drum roll for her, while I place the mouth of the flask to my lips and tip it back, wincing as the liquor sears the back of my throat with a welcome burn. God, I fucking needed that.

I still have a mouthful of tequila when Susan's chirpy, high-pitched voice blasts out of the speakers again. "This year's Raleigh High prom queen is none other than…*Silver Parisi!*"

I spray tequila at the back of Micha Williams' head, splattering his bald cap with liquor. What the fuck did that girl just say? "No. Uh uh." I shake my head, turning to Alex. I'm panicked. Totally, utterly and desperately panicked. "No. I'm not the fucking prom queen."

Alex laughs a little as he holds his hand out toward the stage.

"Seems like your fellow classmates have all voted otherwise, *Argento*. Better not keep your public waiting." He is fucking loving this.

"Haven't you seen Carrie?" I hiss. "If I take one step up onto that stage, I'm getting drenched in pig's blood."

"You honestly think I'd let that happen? You don't think I've already made it very clear that nothing bad is to happen to you tonight, on pain of very agonizing death?"

"Come on up here, Silver! Where are you?" Susan booms into the microphone. She's already got the damn crown and a bunch of red roses in her hand, and she's scanning the faces of the people in front of her, looking for me. "Get up on the stage, girl! Come up here and claim your crown!"

"I'm not claiming shit. No fucking way." I attempt to back away. The emergency exit's only a couple of feet from me, and the chaperones who were guarding it before are nowhere to be seen. Wouldn't be that hard to make a run for it, slam through the double doors and flee barefoot out into the night. Alex has other ideas, though. I crash into him, my back colliding with his chest, and I suddenly have nowhere to go. It's like trying to go through a brick wall.

"No way, Parisi. This is your 'fuck you' moment," he whispers into my ear. "This is the moment you get to look down on every single one of these motherfuckers and let them know that you're still standing strong. They voted for you, for fuck's sake. Doesn't matter how many votes you won by, either. They chose you. So, go take that fucking crown. It's yours, damn it."

It's a nice thought, that there are actually people at Raleigh who want me to be their prom queen. I just can't swallow the idea, though. Even if there are people here who feel badly about how they treated me, they wouldn't vote for me as their prom queen. It makes no sense. I don't trust this moment, and I don't think I should get up on that stage.

Alex is so damn adamant, though.

I look back at him, and there's a devilish, wicked smile on his face that speaks volumes. "You did this, didn't you?" I hiss. "You rigged it so that I'd win."

He shrugs nonchalantly. "I might have accidentally found out that Kacey was planning on coming back tonight and claiming her crown.

It sounded like a vulgar display of power. I might have fiddled with the votes a little to make sure she didn't get what she came here for. Now seriously move. Kacey's head looks like it's about to pop."

God, it does. She's gone so red, her usually perfect, creamy, flawless skin is all blotchy and uneven. If she could only see herself now, she really would explode.

My feet carry me to the steps that lead up onto the stage. I'm numb down to the very roots of my soul as Susan shoves the flowers at me and places the crown firmly on my head. It's all so damn surreal…

I've never imagined this moment. Never. Kacey was always going to be crowned queen of prom, there was never any doubt. The fact that I'm standing up here in front of the whole school instead of her is bewildering. I can't make any sense of it.

The round of applause that follows my coronation sounds real enough. There are even a couple of loud whoops and catcalls, cheering out my name. Zander and Halliday, by the sounds of things. Horrified, I realize that there's no way Alex would ever have doctored the votes to make sure he was crowned prom king alongside me. It's just not his style. Which means…

Oh god, no.

Surely not Jake.

God, please no, not Jake.

Susan beams at me as she holds the microphone up and makes the second part of her announcement. "My fellow Raleigh Rebels, tonight we have not one but two surprises for you! Our prom king is also an unexpected surprise, but one I personally could not be happier with. It's my great honor to share with you all that our new prom king is none other than my friend Gareth Foster!"

Gareth Foster?

Captain of the Chess Club?

*Gareth Foster?*

What the fuck?

I should have known Alex wouldn't put me in a position that brought me anywhere near Jacob. He *did* doctor the votes for prom king, and he *didn't* give himself the crown. He gave it to the captain of the chess club, a nerdy guy, who was perhaps the person least likely to be nominated. It's so bizarre and so sweet of him, that I almost don't mind as Gareth comes bounding toward me across the stage and plants a wet kiss on cheek, screaming, "Hey! Wife For The Night!"

Oh boy. This is gonna be interesting. Bemused, I try to hunt down Alex's wretched, grinning face in the crowd but typically he's nowhere to be found.

## 40

## ALEX

"Outside. Fifteen minutes. Just me and you. Let's end this once and for all, Moretti. Unless you're too chicken shit to face me without your girlfriend 'round to protect you."

The words Jake spat into my ear were filled with violence. They still ring inside my head as I hurry out of the emergency exit, glad that I slipped out unnoticed as Silver ascended the stairs.

She's going to hate me for this. She might never forgive me for what I'm about to do, but there's only so much a person can take, and I've just about had enough. Not for myself, but for her. She's stronger than me. I don't think there's an end to the amount of abuse she can take if she has to, but I can't stand by and watch it happen anymore. I've allowed it for long enough. It's time I stood up and finally said enough on her behalf. I should have done it a long fucking time ago.

Snowflakes float in the still night air, hauntingly suspended in place as I follow the channel of footprints that have cut a path through the labyrinth of looming snowbanks covering the basketball court behind the school. There's no wind to speak of, but the cold still knifes through my suit, sinking its fangs into my bones. The sky's clear overhead, and the waxing gibbous moon—a shining smudge of light in the vast, sweeping midnight blue—casts long shadows from the naked trees.

There's death in the air and I can feel it. It tries to seep inside me, just like the cold, as I hurry around the back of the gymnasium, keeping a sharp eye out for Jacob. The prick has no honor. I expect him to jump out of a fucking tree and lynch me—it's definitely his style—so I'm surprised when I turn the corner around the building and there he is, waiting for me in an open clearing. His hands are in his pockets. Fog clouds on his breath when he opens his mouth and speaks.

"Well. Didn't think you were this stupid, Moretti. Gotta say I'm surprised."

For fuck's sake. What an asshole. "You got me all wrong if you think I'd ever be afraid of facing you, man. You're nothing special. I've taken down bigger guys than you and I didn't even break a sweat."

"Nah." Jake shakes his head, laughing as he looks down at his shoes. His hands are still in his pockets. "Nah, I know you're not worried about facing me. I didn't mean that. I meant that I didn't think you'd be stupid enough to come out here on your own."

Snow compacts, creaking under the soles of boots, as two...no, three other guys come into view, appearing around the other side of the gymnasium. My old friends Kyle, Naseem and Lawrence. Jesus. What did I just tell myself as I walked out here? Jake has no fucking honor. It's no surprise that he told me to come out here alone, and yet made sure he'd have an entire crew of guys with him. This is on me; I should have known he'd never have the stones to go toe-to-toe with me in a fair fight.

"Coward." I toss the word to him like a pebble, but Jake flinches like I hurled a boulder at his face. He recoils, scowling deeply, as his friends come to stand by his side. They remind me of hyenas, laughing moronically, skulking through the shadows to stand behind their pack leader.

"I'm not a coward," Jake snaps. "I've dealt with shit you can't even imagine."

"Right. Sure. Daddy confiscate your Ferrari? You actually had to buy groceries and make your own lunch once? Tough life, Jake."

His grimace deepens. With the moon casting warped shadows across his face, he looks like a grotesque gargoyle, eyes sunken and cheeks hollow. "Having a drug runner and smuggler for a dad's not as fun as it might sound," he says. "Thugs and criminals at the house every night of the week. I've seen people beaten. I've watched people get shot and die on my living room floor. I listened to my mother cry herself to sleep every night between the ages of seven and thirteen. Nothing in my house was easy, you dumb piece of shit."

"Aw. Condolences." I laugh scathingly down my nose. "Sounds like a fucking summer camp to me, but hell. What do I know? I had to watch my mother blow her own brains out when I was six, so I'll never know how hard it must have been for you to hear your spoiled, rich, Percocet popping mommy sniffle into her pillow when she went to bed at night. Must have been hard. Christ, you really do think you're the only person in the world who's ever had to deal with hardship, don't you? Well your brand of hardship looks an awful lot like privilege to me. I've literally been fucking *tortured*, and I never used my shit as an excuse to hurt and defile people weaker and more vulnerable than me. Only a sadomasochist does something like that."

Jake chuckles, winking at me playfully. I want to ram my fist into his fucking face so hard that his skull bursts like a motherfucking balloon. "Ahhh, Alex. You been speaking to my therapist? You and he sound an awful lot alike. Y'know, you're brave, I'll give you that. You're about to die, but you're not about to let a small inconvenience like that prevent you from saying whatever dumb shit is on your mind, huh?"

The hairs on the back of my neck stand to attention; there's someone behind me. I sense their presence, even if they're light on their feet and I can't hear their footfall crunching in the snow. Terrible at keeping his cards close to his chest, Jake's eyes flit to the right and briefly lock into something over my shoulder, confirming that my odds just took an even bigger nosedive. Four against one was pretty bad; I'm guessing it's more like six against one now, from the smug, shit-eating smile on Jake's face.

I have better reflexes than most people. I was eight years old and still living in the group home for boys when I learned how to hone my senses so I could tell whenever someone entered or exited a room. Takes me a moment, but I pinpoint the location of the guy closest to me, about four feet directly behind me. The other guy, the one hanging back, seems less sure of himself and hovers by the gymnasium wall, about ten feet away.

I'm a proficient fighter, more than able to take down two or even three dudes who are a lot bigger than me, but six? That's gonna be difficult. Still, no point in giving Jake the satisfaction of making this easy for him.

"I feel so fucking sorry for you, man," I tell him.

"I beg your fucking pardon?"

"You heard me. I pity you. I pity you, because just like Kacey, you've lost." I say it matter-of-factly.

Jake's lips pulling back, exposing his teeth as he slowly walks toward me. He'd never fucking dare to approach me if his boys weren't following his every move. "NO!" He barks out the word like a military general issuing an order. "You're the loser, Moretti. *I* haven't lost. I'm the fucking winner. I'm *always* gonna come out on top. Don't you see? These are our lots in life. I was born to be great. You were born to shovel shit and fail at every turn. *You* don't get to feel sorry for me!"

Jake may have stepped off the ledge and surrendered his self-control, shouting for all the world to hear, but not me. I'm calm as can fucking be. "You hate her *and* you love her."

"What?"

"You're in love with Silver. And you're so fucked up and broken that this is the only way you know how to let all of that emotion out from inside you. You love her, so you lash out at her, and you try to break her, because that's what your father did to your mother. And that's the only kind of love you've ever known your entire fucking life —the kind that really fucking hurts."

"Quit trying to psychoanalyze me, asshole. You're way off base. I hate that girl. She's the worst thing that ever fucking happened to me. She's a lying fucking cunt who can't keep her legs closed. End of fucking story."

Smirking, I begin playing out how this thing is going to go in my head. Jake's gonna throw the first punch, because he's going to want to demonstrate his superior strength first. Kyle, Lawrence and Nas won't be far behind him, though. He'll have told them to back him up as soon as the shit hits the fan. They won't give me time to hit the guy back before they're on me, tearing into me, trying to pull me apart.

I can take Kyle down without too much hassle. The other boys are big and strong, and certainly pose a considerable threat, but they're not smart. The second Kyle's decommissioned, they'll tuck their tails and run. Lawrence will probably have enough courage to stand his ground, but the fucker's on steroids. He's too big not to be. He's slow and cumbersome, and I'll have him on the ground in a few seconds flat. Once he's on his back in the snow, taking him out will be fairly simple. I just need to make sure he doesn't try and lock his legs around my torso—

"Damn, Alex. Cogs are whirring away, huh?" Jake spins his index finger in a fast circle, mimicking a spinning wheel. "I admire the optimism. You're hoping that you're gonna get out of this. I hate to break it to you, but you're not. Let me break this down. I'm gonna break some of your bones. I'm gonna have these boys hold you down while I shoot you in the stomach, the way you shot *me* in the stomach, remember? And then you and I are gonna hang out for a while. I'm gonna take great pleasure spending a few hours with you somewhere nice and quiet, just so I really get to soak up the experience of you writhing in immense pain. And when I'm bored of that, the guys behind you? Those fine gentlemen are gonna drag your carcass out into the Walker Forest, and they're gonna tie you to a tree. Won't be long before the wolves scent the blood on you and come looking to feast. I hate to miss that part, I really fucking do, but it's better if I'm here when prom ends. Gotta have an alibi, right? Not that anyone will ever find your remains. Everyone will think you simply proved them right by bailing on your girl here and skipping town. No one's gonna look too hard for you, Alex. You're your father's son, after all. Bailing is what Morettis do best."

The guys behind me are much, much closer. I can practically feel them breathing down my neck. I glance back over my shoulder, curious to see who else Jake's managed to talk into participating in this messy affair, and I have to say I'm shocked by who I find standing at my back.

My money was on another couple of guys from the football team. Maybe some of the less athletic members of the Jacob Weaving fan club. I sure as shit wasn't expecting to find Monty and Paulie creeping up on me.

"You've gotta be fucking kidding me," I groan. *"Paulie?"*

"Sorry, dude. Nothing personal. Maisy's pregnant. I can't afford to lose my job." Paulie and I have been friends ever since Monty took me in and I began working at the Rock. Admittedly, not the very best of friends, but the amount of tequila this guy's poured for me over the past year could drown a small nation. He works his mouth—looks like he's chewing on the inside of his cheek—as he comes to stand beside Monty.

The old man doesn't look remorseful in the slightest; his long hair's pulled back in a tight ponytail, which has always symbolized that he means business. His eyes flash like razor sharp steel, his quick intelligence working overtime as he looks me up and down with a disappointment on his face. "I could have gotten over the bag, kid," he says. "Eventually. You might have lost a finger, but fuck. What's a finger or two between friends? The way you came steamrolling into my office like King Shit, though? That kind of reckless behavior's worrying, son. It points to more reckless behavior down the line, and I don't operate well knowing that a threat like that exists. You could bring my whole operation down with one careless word. You gotta go. I'm just sorry it had to be like this. I coulda made it a little easier if you'd just come to me, but…"

He is so full of shit. The way he's talking, you'd think he was Mother fucking Theresa and he was brought here against his will. Monty's always been a vindictive cunt, though. He's enjoying this just fine. He'll sleep in his bed tonight, untroubled by a guilty conscience.

"Looks like you got over your spat with the Weavings, then?" I don't really care who Monty has or hasn't mended fences with. Now that he's here, I'm not walking away from this alive. I've seen Monty murder indiscriminately. He's not a seventeen-year-old high school jock with a mean streak. He's a seasoned criminal, and he knows precisely what he's doing. He's not about to fuck this up, and he will not hesitate to put me down.

"Q wouldn't hand over Giacomo," Monty provides. He knows perfectly well that I've wanted your father's head for a long time now. He wasn't willing to give him to me, so that was that. You know how this business goes. One week, you're a Capulet, the next you're a Montague. I don't know what to tell ya, kid."

I overestimated the strength of Monty's ties to the Dreadnaughts. Or I underestimated just how much Monty hates my father. Either way, I'm fucked.

"I admit, I was a little unsure about working with your old boss," Jake says. "But Lowell's got him on a leash, right, Montgomery? Lowell promised to turn Giacomo over to him if he did as he was told and took care of you for us. Looks like your old man's career as a CI is in the gutter. I gotta say, I'm surprised at how perfectly all of this is working out."

"You really think Silver's gonna believe I just got on my bike and rode off into the night without her?"

"I don't care what she thinks. It won't matter. I have *plans* for her. She won't be causing trouble for me soon enough. And when she's learned how to be a good, obedient little girl and she knows how to please me, I might just let her suck my dick from time to time. Don't worry, she's gonna be so fucking grateful of the attention—"

No.

Fucking.

Way.

Fire ignites in my chest, roaring to life.

I've remained calm throughout all of this, but the moment Jake starts talking about Silver, I'm done for. How am I supposed to keep a clear head when the images he paints with his words are so dark, disturbing and royally fucked up? Without me here to keep her safe, Jacob *will* get his way. He'll find an opening, all he needs is one, and he'll snatch her again. He'll secret her away to some underground bunker, and he'll keep her there for months, abusing and raping her over and over again until she finally cracks and gives him what he's so desperately desired all along: her submission.

He'll be careful. He'll be protected. He'll make sure he's never caught, and no one will find her body, either. They'll think she ran away to find *me*. Fuck!

It's futile, but I run. I charge at Jake with such a furious rage in my belly that all I can taste is copper and acid and pain. My ears are muffled, like they're stuffed up with cotton wool. My heart's seized—I can't tell if it's beating too fast or not beating at all. All I know is that it hurts, a crippling, sharp agony spreading across the front of my ribcage.

I drop my shoulder, planting it right into Jake's stomach, and I crash into him with the force of a battering ram, tackling him to the ground. Dead men don't usually charge the living. Jacob likely thought I was going to drop to my knees, piss my pants, and start begging for mercy. I am, if nothing else, a constant source of disappointment, though.

Jake's kicking and throwing his fists before he even hits the ground. He *uffffffs* out a hard exhale when his back hits the compacted snow but manages to land a jab to my ribcage. I don't feel any pain. I feel nothing but rage. It sweeps through me like fire across a lake of gasoline, and I become a crazed, burning thing that cannot be stopped.

Jake screams, shouting out sounds that might be people's names. I have his head in my hands, and my thumbs are digging into his eyelids, gouging, and gouging.

I fall sideways, hitting the deck so hard that my vision splinters for a second. Everything's black and red, and the light from the moon blazes too, too bright. I can't breathe. I can't fucking breathe.

I've got to get back inside the gym.

I've got to get back to Silver.

Someone's got an arm around my throat.

It's Paulie.

His boots kick and scramble against the snow as he struggles to subdue me, but I'll be fucking dead before I stop fighting.

"Alex, man! Alex!" he cries. "Go easy, for fuck's sake."

I won't be going easy. I won't be going at all. I have to fucking get out of here. The stars in the night sky overhead flare, turning to blazing torches, blistering the dark mantle of the heavens, and my pulse begins to throb urgently in my ears.

Relief rushes me—Paulie's grip around my windpipe momentarily loosens—and I seize the opportunity, pushing up with my legs and slamming all of my body weight back against the bartender's body. He cries out, a single weak howl of pain, and then Jake's standing over me, wiping a trickle of blood from his nose with the back of his hand.

He's breathing hard, his blond hair stuck up in every direction, and there's snow on the sleeve of his suit jacket. "Fucker ripped my blazer," he complains. "Get out of the way, asshole. Let me take care of him. You're making it worse."

"For heaven's sake, just get the job done already. Take the gun," Monty says somewhere off to the left.

*Find Silver.*

*Get the hell up, Alex.*

*Get off your ass, get inside, and find Silver.*

The voice is insistent, but I can't obey. Naseem and Lawrence have finally entered the fray; they pin me down against the ground, leaning all of their weight against my chest as I kick and lash out like a deranged animal. They flinch away from me as I land blow after blow on them, which makes it hard for them to hold me in place, but then Paulie's back, grabbing hold of me from behind, cursing angrily into my ear.

"Broke my nose, A. Not cool. Really not cool."

How the fuck does he expect me to behave? He wants me to lie still and docile as a lamb while Jacob and his dickhead buddies execute me? I almost laugh at the absurdity of the hurt in his voice. Paulie yelps again when I drive my elbow back hard, right into his stomach.

"Fucking idiots," Monty snaps. The toes of his scuffed boots come into view. Then: the sound of something metal spinning, something clicking, something snapping into place. It's the sound of the chamber of a gun being checked and flicked closed. "Take the fucking thing before I shoot the bastard myself. Kids were way tougher in my day, I swear. There are four of them and one of him, for crying out loud. Shouldn't be this hard."

Above me, Jacob's face shutters in and out of view as I wrestle for freedom. His mouth pulls down, his hatred pouring out of him so viscerally that it looks like it's choking *him*. "Gotta show him a little love first," he sneers.

The first time he kicks me, I still don't feel anything. He drives the toe of his shoe into my ribs, and suddenly it's daylight and my ears are ringing. The blinding brightness fades, just in time for the second blow. Lawrence and Naseem release me, scrambling back out of Jake's way, but then he's barking orders at them, his voice cracking as he hollers at the top of his lungs.

"Do something! Kick him. Hurt him. Fuck him up, you pussy fucks. Jesus, you want me to hold your fucking hand or something?"

The pain begins to seep in as more feet drive into my body. I slowly begin to feel each sharp, crushing impact, until, out of nowhere, I'm hurting so badly I can't even think around the lightning firing up and down my body.

Oh...

...*shit.*

Through the blur of black pants and Italian leather shoes, I see something that makes me fall still in the churned up snow.

It's...

It can't be.

It's Ben.

The little boy sits down on the edge of the clearing, crossing his legs underneath him. His dark eyes, so similar to our father's, bore into me, filled with confusion. *"Why don't you make it stop?"* he whispers. His lips don't move, but I hear his voice as clear as a struck bell inside my head. A tear streaks his cheek, and then another, and then another. *"What are you doing, Alex? Make it stop."*

"I...can't..."

*"You're not even trying."*

I *am* trying, though. I've fought so hard, I'm exhausted. My limbs are unresponsive now, heavy as lead weights. They remain thrown out over my head, no matter how hard I will them back to my sides.

*"You didn't save me,"* Ben whispers, slowly laying down in the snow. He settles himself on his side, so that he's mirroring my prone position on the ground. It looks like he's curling up to die. *"You have to save yourself. For me. For Silver."*

He opens his mouth and blood pours over his lips, thick, and black, and frightening. Panic wells up inside me, my body convulsing...

And still the blows keep on raining down.

They're never ending.

Jacob crows, bringing his foot down on my shoulder, and an

explosion of pain detonates down my arm and across my back. I try to hold the pain at bay, but it's impossible, and I roar through my teeth.

"All right! ENOUGH!" Monty bellows. "Any more of this and someone's gonna come out and find us. You've had your fun, kid. Pull the trigger and let's get the fuck out of here, or you're on your fucking own. You hear me?"

I pull and pull and pull, trying to suck some oxygen down into my lungs, but my diaphragm is frozen, spasming with pain.

The edges of my vision fade to black, and everything narrows to a point.

This…this is really fucking bad.

I always knew I was going to die a violent death. I'm not surprised. I just wish I'd had a little more time to turn shit around is all. With a little more time, I might have been able to distance myself from this kind of world. I could have moved out of Raleigh and taken Silver with me. We could have made a life for ourselves. Most importantly, even if she'd cast me aside and left me ruined in the dirt, I could have at least gotten her somewhere *safe*…

I look back to the spot on the snow where my brother was a moment ago…and he's still lying there, his eyes closed, his lips tinged blue…

God, I failed him. And now I'm about to fail Silver.

What a stupid, pointless, unforgiveable sin.

"Ready, Moretti?"

Somehow, I muster enough energy to look up at Jacob. The gun in his hand, the one Monty must have just given him, gleams black and menacing in the moonlight. It looks every inch an instrument of death. It's with some sense of irony that I realize it's the same gun Monty used to give to *me* to take out on my midnight runs.

"You really should have minded your own business, Moretti," Jacob says blankly. "I really did think we were going to be friends."

He places his finger on the trigger.

He pulls.

## 41

## SILVER

I think my toes are broken.

"Checkmate in five moves. Such a fucking amateur." Gareth shakes his head, wrinkling his nose in an attempt to wriggle his glasses back up the bridge of his nose without using his hands. "I mean, what kind of competition is that? Michael Kilroy was Bellingham's best player. He was their *team captain,* and I beat him in less than three minutes. I'm not one to brag, but seriously, I really showed him who was boss."

He steps on my foot again as he clumsily maneuvers me into a spin, and I nearly eat shit right in front of everyone. I would never have danced with Gareth in a million years, but the prom king and queen dance is a Raleigh tradition, and pretty much mandatory. Plus, Gareth looked so damn excited that I felt a little bad trying to worm my way out of it.

"Oh, and how about this!" he exclaims. "I heard you got into Dartmouth! Guess where I'm going next year?"

From his gaping, wide-eyed grin, it's fairly obvious where he's going. "Dartmouth?" I pretend to be remotely interested.

Nodding, he kicks my shin as he stumbles over his feet, nearly ending up in a heap on the floor. "We can tell everyone, Silver, *we* were king and queen. No one'll believe us. I mean, what are the chances?"

"I know. Pretty surreal," I agree, vacantly skipping from person to person in the crowd, still looking for Alex. I haven't seen hide nor hair of him since I got up on the damn stage and, more worryingly, I haven't seen Jacob either. I should never have come up to claim the crown. For starters, I didn't even want it. And now I'm beginning to feel like this entire thing is some sort of distraction…

For three long, tortuous minutes, I dance with Gareth, biting my tongue every time he steps on me. As soon as the music ends, I give him a quick high five instead of the kiss he was leaning in for, and I make my way back out into the press of bodies that are packed into the gym.

I find Halliday pinned up against a wall with Zander's hand up her skirt and his tongue down her throat. She blushes like crazy when I tap her on the shoulder, coughing to get their attention.

Zander's hair is a messy halo around his head. His eyes are glazed over, pupils blown wide open as he smiles suggestively down at me from his six-foot-one vantage point. "Look who it is. Raleigh High's very own Prom Queen. If you're wondering how to get in on this action, it's really simple actually. All you gotta do is ask."

"Really?" I cross my arms over my chest, arching an eyebrow at him. "You're hitting on me?"

"I don't see the problem," he quips. "We shared everything in juvie."

"I'm Alex's *fiancé*."

At that, Zander goes extremely pale. "Actually yeah, now that you mention it, on second thoughts he'd probably be pretty pissed. Maybe you shouldn't mention that I said that. What's up? How can we be of totally non-sexual, completely unromantic service to you?"

"I can't find Alex. Where is he? I've been looking all over for him."

Zander looks confused. "Huh. Haven't seen him in a while. I assumed he was watching you dance with that nerd, plotting out how he was gonna kill him."

"Uh…oh," Halliday mutters, tucking her hair behind her ears as she extricates herself from the cage of Zander's arms. "Uh, shit. I saw him going outside before. Things got so tense with Jake and Kacey that I figured he just needed to get some air or something. He hasn't come back in?"

Sick to my stomach, I scream at myself for being polite and dancing with Gareth. I should have made sure I had eyes on Alex before I did anything. He seemed to cool down so quickly before. I'd thought he'd just put Jake out of his mind, but obviously I missed what really happened.

*Shit.*

Alex went after Jake the moment I turned my back and looked away.

"Come with me," I command. "We need to find him. I have a *horrible* feeling about this."

Halliday leads the way. Instead of guiding us toward the gym's main entrance, she heads for the emergency exit I considered fleeing out of earlier. No one notices as she pushes the bar and the door opens a crack, just enough for the three of us to slip out one at a time into the cold. The moment I take my first step outside, my heel sinking right into the snow, a blood curdling cry pierces the night and my blood runs cold.

"What the hell was *that*?" Halliday asks. Zander and I trade glances; *we* know perfectly well what it was. Unlike Halliday, we've both heard the sound of a person in extreme pain before. We both know that a strangled cry like that, one that sounds so similar to a tortured animal, can easily come from a human being if they're suffering enough.

I don't stop and wait for them. I rip my shoes from my feet and I take off, flying in the direction that horrific cry came from with fear clawing at my insides. The snow and ice feels like it's burning the soles of my feet, it's so cold, but I don't stop. A maze of pathways cut through the snowbanks the cover the basketball court behind the gymnasium. I pick the first pathway I come to and I run along it, as fast as my legs can carry me.

My lungs are on fire, my heart surging like a piston as I come upon…fuck! A dead end.

"ALL RIGHT! ENOUGH!"

The yell comes from the right. It sounds so far away and so close at the same time, distorted by the huge swathes of snow that rise high above my head on either side of me. This is madness. I'm never going to find my way to Alex in time. Behind me, Zander yells my name. "Stop! Fuck, Silver, wait! If you get hurt, Alex is gonna put me down." He almost barrels into my back when he rounds the corner, Halliday right on his heels.

"I need to get over this snow! Help me!"

Zander shakes his head. "No way. You can't climb this shit. It's rotten, you'll fall straight through."

He's right. The snow is old and loose, clumped together in chunks. The moment I try to climb up the side of the snowbank in front of me, my bare foot pushes straight down, catching on a sharp branch that slices into my skin. This won't work. We need another plan. There's no other way to get across the basketball court, though.

"Ready, Moretti?"

The voice sounds closer this time. Way closer, even though it's far quieter than the shout we just heard. Zander's head whips around, his eyes narrowing into slits. "I'm not joking around, guys. You really gotta wait here." He takes off, sprinting in the direction of the voice… and of course I am right behind him.

I'm not hanging back, waiting on the sidelines to see what happens, when Alex needs me. No fucking way. Zander skids as he comes to a fork in the pathways, chooses the left path, then changes his mind and goes reeling down the one on the right. The soles of my feet scream in pain—I'm not sure if it's from the cold or if I've torn them open on the ice and the gravel compressed into the snow. All I know is that it hurts, and I have no choice but to keep on moving.

We turn a corner, and then another, and then there *are* no more corners. We stumble out into an unexpected clearing, and there, in its center, Alex is lying on his side, staring off into space as Jacob Weaving extends his arm and aims a black, sleek gun at his head.

*NO!*

The scream never makes it past my lips.

Fog clouds on my breath as my lungs empty. It feels as though I've been kicked right in the solar plexus and every single one of my ribs has just been shattered.

Alex…

Alex is going to die.

There's no time to do anything. I'll never reach him in time. It feels as though the very air itself is trying to hold me back as I take off across the clearing toward my boyfriend. Jake's finger hovers on the trigger. He hasn't even noticed me, racing as fast as I can toward him. It wouldn't make a difference if he did. My only thought is to get to him before he can pull that trigger and end the life of the guy I love. I have no idea what I'm gonna do once I get there.

Jacob sneers.

"SILVER, NO!"

Behind me, Zander's desperate yell echoes up and up, louder and louder each time it repeats itself. I witness the moment Jacob makes the decision. I see his index finger slowly begins to squeeze the trigger...

And there, behind him, a dark figure emerges from the shadows.

For a second, I can't make sense of what's happening. The figure's a blur, nothing more than a dark smudge against a sea of white. Then the edges of the newcomer begin to sharpen, coming into focus, and I see the weapon he's holding in his hands. He raises the gun, aiming it directly at the side of Jacob's head, and a bright flare of light erupts from the muzzle.

Jake's head rocks violently to the side.

The sound comes after.

*CRACK!*

A fine red mist sprays into the air, debris shooting off in every direction.

Oh...my...*god.*

Whatjusthappenedwhatjusthappenedwhatjusthappened...

I screw my eyes shut, dizzy and nauseous.

Thum...

Thum...

Thum...

My pulse is so weak, like my heart is barely beating at all. When I open my eyes, Jacob's on his knees, his eyes rolled back into his head...and then he topples over, limbs slack, falling sideways into the snow.

Half of his fucking head is missing.

It feels like it takes forever to happen, but in reality, Jacob drops to the ground like a stone. In the distance, a flock of birds explode from a dark stand of trees; they scatter in every direction, wheeling and zipping through the air, scared by the loud report of the gun as it echoes out over Raleigh.

Jacob's utterly still. His body doesn't twitch. No weird convulsing like in the movies. *Because there's nothing of his brain left,* the logical part of me says. The shot took out the contents of his skull, spraying it onto the snow in front of me. There are no synapses left to fire. No nerve endings to shoot off random, confused messages as the life inside him sputters out and dies. Jacob was brain dead before he even hit the floor.

He's gone.

He's fucking dead.

"Wha...?"

I can't tell what's real right now.

I'm too dazed. I look up, and it takes a long moment to understand that Detective James Lowell is moving toward me across the snow, stepping over Jacob's mangled head, lowering a gleaming silver gun to his side.

"Silver? Ms. Parisi, are you okay?"

I blink at him.

"Silver? Look at me. Are you hurt?"

He has me by the shoulders. The gun's still in his hand, and he presses it against my bare arm, the muzzle pointing up toward the sky as he ducks down, peering into my eyes, looking concerned. "You shouldn't be out here, kid."

"Hold on. Hold on! *Wait!*"

The sound of the panic in the cry behind me snaps me out of my shock. I'm falling. I come back into myself with a sharp, unpleasant jolt that feels like I just hit the sidewalk after slipping from the ledge of a ten-story building.

There are people everywhere.

Three of the Raleigh High football team are scrambling in the snow, whimpering, clinging to one another as they stare in horror at the pool of blood spreading in the snow around Jake's ruined head.

Zander and Halliday are standing stock still, taking in the chaos to my right...

And, weirdly...

My *doctor* is prowling towards Alex's old boss with a gun in her hands.

Monty shakes his head, his grey hair coming loose from his ponytail as he backs away from her. "Listen. There's money. A lot of money. The bar, too. You can have the bar. I was thinking about retiring, anyway—"

As if by some weird trick of the light, Zeth coalesces out of nowhere, like the very shadows themselves merged together and gave him form and life. I've never seen anything like it before; one moment there's only the ink-black darkness, and then there he is, all murder and death, with the biggest silver gun I've ever seen in his hands. He lovingly caresses Dr. Romera's cheek, shaking his head. "There she is. My angry girl. Hate to make you break a promise, though. You save lives. You don't take them."

His hand whips up and he fires the gun. I brace for the sound. The gun's so massive, I expect an earsplitting bang, but there's nothing more than the dull thud of Montgomery Cohen the Third's body hitting the snow. A rifle suppressor. A regular silencer wasn't good enough for the weapon in Zeth's hands. He literally needed a *rifle* suppressor to mute it.

A commotion breaks out as Zeth and Dr. Romera approach the three guys on the football team. I can't even muster up a single fuck to give about them. All I care about is the dark, still form lying on a patch of ice ten feet away. Jacob didn't shoot Alex, but he's far too still.

Oh god. Oh god, no, why the hell isn't he moving?

Detective Lowell says something to me, but I shake myself out of his grasp. I reach Alex, skidding toward him on my knees, and for a terrible heartbeat, I see the way he's staring up at the sky and I think he's fucking dead.

And then he blinks.

"Weird...night." His voice breaks when he speaks. Wincing, he tries to roll onto his side, but it seems to take his breath away, so he slumps back into the snow. I quickly help him, lifting his head and placing it carefully into my lap.

"I'm hallucinating, right?" he says, his eyes searching for and finding mine. His face is a patchwork of bruises, forming rapidly underneath his skin. His lip's split open, as is his left eyebrow, and there's a gash on his temple, but he seems fairly alert. The vine tattoos around the base of this throat shift as he swallows. "*Lowell* shot Jake?"

A strangled laugh wells up and spills out of me, anxious and too loud. "Yeah. Yeah, I have no fucking clue what's going on. Are you okay?"

He nods, slowly lifting his hand and taking hold of mine, squeezing it reassuringly. "Of course I am."

"You don't look okay."

He smiles. Thankfully all of his teeth are still where they're supposed to be. "Wow. *Rude.*"

"If he's smiling, then he's definitely concussed as fuck," Zander says. He drops down next to Alex, peering over him suspiciously.

Shock sets in all over again as Zander fusses over Alex. The weight of what's just happened finally begins to hit me, and my calm starts to slip away from me.

I just watched two people get shot.

My boyfriend's in pieces.

*Again.*

How the fuck are we getting out of *this* shit fight unscathed?

Zeth appears opposite me, crouching down, forearms on his thighs, his hands hanging loosely between his legs as he dips his head, trying to make eye contact with me.

"Sometimes the job's way bigger than you think. Sometimes you do need a demolitions expert after all," he says.

"And...what about that?" I ask numbly, eyeing Jacob's body. God, this is so weird. He was a monster. A creature made of nightmares, who posed such a threat to me and those I love not five minutes ago. And now he's this fake-looking, mangled, empty vessel. Now, he's nothing at all.

"Don't worry about that," Zeth rumbles. "I'll get this cleared up. I know a guy."

## 42

## ALEX

"Where the hell is he? No, no, I'm not his father. Look, lady, I'm going into that hospital room whether you like it or —I need to see if he's o—thank you. Yeah, well, you can report me to security. I don't care."

The door opens, and Cameron blazes into the room like a meteor, coming in hot. He's panting and he looks like he's ready to physically fight someone. Curled up in the armchair with her legs dangling over the arm rest, Silver doesn't even stir from her slumber when he father bursts into the room. I smile, because he's just so ridiculous sometimes. "And you're normally so good with people," I say, pouting. "Weird that she wouldn't let you in."

In fairness, the woman sitting at the nurse's station outside my room is terrifying. Silver had to lie and tell her she was my sister in order to gain entrance to my room, which is kinda awkward now, since the nurse saw Silver kiss me on the mouth about half an hour ago. God knows what she thinks is going on between us.

"Still alive, then. That's nice," Cam observes, planting his hands on his hips. "It's all over Raleigh. Jacob Weaving's dead? Wha—?" He shakes his head, as he looks up at the ceiling. I know exactly how he's feeling, because I'm feeling the same way: confused, exasperated, lost for words. "What the fuck happened?" he asks. "You guys went to prom, for fuck's sake. And somehow that motherfucker winds up with his brain splattered all over the basketball court? I swear to god..."

I'd laugh if I could, but it hurts too much. Besides, it's not really funny. It *is* typical, though. Of course Silver and I weren't going to be able to make it through a dance at Raleigh High without the world blowing up in our faces.

I explain what happened as best I can, shrugging through the parts when Agent Lowell showed up and shot Jake, and Cam listens without saying a word. When I've filled in the details I have to hand, he sighs, kneading the back of his neck with his fingers.

"Why did you go out there with him in the first place?" he asks quietly. "You had to know—"

"I figured I could take him. And I just wanted it to be over. Silver had been through enough," I tell him. That's the only real explanation I can give him. It was time for the situation to be dealt with properly, and I really had thought it would turn out differently.

"Aren't you sick and tired already of looking at yourself in the mirror and seeing so many bruises? All of the time, Alex. You look like a goddamn punching bag," Cam says morosely. "Dr. Romera said it's a miracle they didn't break your jaw."

"Yeah, well, it kinda feels like they did, so..." I open my mouth as wide as I can, stretching out my jaw, and it hurts like a motherfucker. I should just leave it be, but I can't help myself. Propped up against what feels like a cloud's worth of pillows in a rather sexy hospital gown, I know that the body-wide numbness I'm feeling right now is a short reprieve. They gave me the good pain meds when they wheeled me in here, but it won't be long before they wear off, and I won't be taking any more. I'd rather be sharp in my head and suffering than fuzzy and fucked up like I am now. "As for the bruises, there won't be any more. I promise. I'll be healed up and out of here in a couple of days, and that'll be it. No more fighting. No more conflict. No more drama. I've decided, I'm gonna bust my ass and get a spot at Dartmouth. It's what she wants, and I'm gonna give it to her."

This makes him laugh. "Wow, you must be super fucking high if you're talking about college."

"*Soooo* high," I confirm.

Cam looks at his daughter, passed out in a set of scrubs Dr.

Romera gave her, and wipes his hand over his face. "I can't say I approve of you going after Jake on your own like that, but it makes sense. She's been through so much. I probably would have done the same thing."

"Of course you would. You love her." A rush of tingling euphoria crests in my chest as another wave of the meds washes over me. For a moment, I feel really fucking good, like I just dumped a whole heap of MDMA down my throat. "Have the cops shown up?" I ask. It's inevitable. I've been waiting for them to roll in here *en masse* and start with their questioning. It's standard protocol to interview people, naturally, but someone *died* tonight. There'll be an investigation without a shadow of a doubt. I'll be interrogated and harassed until they somehow make Jake's death my fault. And I can hardly defend myself by saying I went out there to shake hands and bury the hatchet with the dude. I *was* gonna fucking kill him.

"Don't worry about the cops," Cam says. "Apparently, this whole nightmare's gonna be handled by the DEA directly."

Jesus. I don't know if that's better or a million times worse. Nothing's really making much sense right now. "Can you do me a favor, man?" I ask, my voice hoarse.

"So long as it doesn't involve breaking you out of this place, then sure. You need to stay here overnight at least. You took a pretty bad beating."

I've had way, way worse. How fucked up is that? I just smile brokenly at Silver's dad, though. "Get her outta here, will you? I'm so sick and tired of her being pulled back to this place. It's fucking depressing. And she wouldn't say it, but it makes her anxious."

Cam nods, studying the girl asleep on the chair. Cameron and I have very little in common, but the fact that we'd both do anything for Silver makes us more alike than either of us would care to admit. "Yeah. I reckon I can do that," he says.

She doesn't even wake up when he lifts her into his arms and carries her out of the hospital room.

∽

It's somewhere in between very late and very early when my next visitor arrives. He enters the room at around four thirty in the morning, carrying a Styrofoam cup and a brown paper bag full of fast food. Lowell's hair is all messed up, and there are dark shadows under his eyes but he's alert—sharp, in a wired, hyper focused way that happens to people when they drink too much coffee. Or take way too much speed.

I've been waiting for him.

He doesn't say anything until he sits himself on the chair by the bed, pulls a burger out of the paper bag, removes the lid from the Styrofoam cup, dumps a sugar into the acerbic-smelling black liquid inside, stirs it, and has himself officially situated.

"I had this sister," he says. "I always used to look up to her. She was a lot older than me. Our parents thought she walked on fucking water. No matter what shit was going on at home or whatever, Dee was always in charge and in control. She never lost her cool." He takes a big sip from his coffee, raising his eyebrows when he realizes it's too hot. He swallows regardless. "Our dad was a fighter pilot. And then he joined the police force when he came out of the air force. Natural progression, everyone said. He was a hard guy to live with, but Dee knew exactly how to handle him. She got away with murder. Me, on the other hand? I was a major disappointment. Never good enough. I couldn't put a single foot wrong. Denise was accepted into the DEA and she was his fucking hero, serving her country. I joined the DEA, and I was a lazy, worthless piece of shit who couldn—"

"Hate to interrupt." I shift uncomfortably in the bed, wincing. "But I'm a little messed up at the moment. Any chance we could save the family history for another time? Y'know…go grab lunch and really get into it. Bring out the photo albums. Everything kind of hurts at the moment, and I'm struggling to care about the Lowell family dynamic, fascinating thought it sounds."

The agent shoves the burger into his mouth and takes a monster bite. Wiping his mouth with the back of his hand, he mumbles around his food. "I'll paraphrase. Dee was a bitch. She got too caught up in the job and went off the rails. Your friend Zeth there—"

"We're not friends."

"God, can you just shut up and listen for five seconds? Zeth was her white whale. You read Moby Dick, right?"

I raise my eyebrows.

Detective Lowell takes this as an affirmative and continues. "She could never pin that motherfucker down, and it drove her mad. She broke protocol. Completely lost it. I won't bother with the details, but the Weavings? They were my white whale. The whole fucking family."

Huh. I wasn't expecting that. Ever since he showed up in Raleigh, the DEA agent's been by Jacob's side. He's been on him like white on rice. Jake was so sure that Lowell was in his back pocket from the way he was talking before he pointed that gun at me. Not to mention the way Lowell went after Silver, trying to make out like she concocted the whole rape plan and made up the entire attack that happened at Leon's.

"So you went rogue to catch your white whale, too?" I surmise.

Lowell bites. Chews. Swallows. "There are a lot of rules when you work for an organization like the DEA. They can be a little restrictive. I'm good at..."—he shrugs— "...*bending* those rules from time to time, if it means I get the job done in the end. The higher ups wouldn't like it, but hey. What they don't know can't hurt 'em, right?" He finishes his burger in four bites and immediately takes out another one. "Didn't like having to treat your girl like crap there, dude, but it was a necessary evil at the time. You feel me?"

Am I supposed to nod or something? Tell him his bizarre and unorthodox way of doing his job is all right by me now that Jake's dead? Fuck it, maybe it *is* all right by me. He put a bullet hole in Jake's skull, and he saved my fucking life. It's all over. Silver won't even need to stand up in court now, which is fucking huge.

"The Weavings drove my grandparent's farm out of business when I was a kid. They tried to salvage what they could of their livelihood once Caleb and his crew began forced sales in the area, but it was impossible. The Weavings ruined them. My grandfather ended up committing suicide to avoid the debt and the shame. So you could say I've had my eye on that asshole my entire life. Can I tell you something?" he says, leaning in close.

"I feel like you're going to anyway."

"I watched all the pieces fall into place with the Weaving case, and it was obvious what was gonna happen. Caleb was going to wriggle his way out of that shit. No doubt about it. And that asshole's son of his was gonna walk, too. Too much power and money changing hands. Give it another couple of months and both of them were gonna be released with no recourse for their actions. I wasn't gonna have that. So yeah. I made Jacob trust me, and the *moment* he gave me justifiable cause, I put that fucker down like the dog that he was."

Wow. Stone. Fucking. Cold. I hated this guy from the moment I set eyes on him, but looks like I had him wrong. Honestly, I have no clue *what* to make of him now, but shit. Jake's dead. That's all I fucking care about.

"I took care of the paperwork." Lowell slumps back into the chair. "You and your girl, you're free of all this shit. My way of saying sorry for how strong I came on. You can go about your lives and wash your hands of the whole business."

Glorious, glorious relief. It feels so much better than the drugs coursing around my system. We're *free*? That feels…damn, I can't even describe how good that feels. "And what about you? What about Caleb? He's gonna be out for blood when he hears you shot his precious boy in the head."

Lowell smiles, absently drumming his finger against the arm of the chair. "Oh, yeah. Caleb. Heard this morning that there was an incident at the prison. Not sure what went down really. Some kind of fight over a toothbrush. Caleb Weaving was stabbed in the neck in the prison yard. Didn't make it. Very unfortunate turn of events."

Very unfortunate indeed. I can tell the guy's super broken up that Jake's father avoided justice by bleeding out on the snow in a prison exercise yard. He looks positively distraught right now.

Hah.

"And Zeth? What about him? He shot Monty."

"Actually…" Lowell frowns. "I know nothing about Monty. There was only one body found at the scene. And…I've never met Zeth Mayfair in person. If I did meet the guy, I'd probably have to kill him."

I know perfectly well what I saw. And from the odd, secret smile on Lowell's face, he knows what I saw, too. This is the line he's sticking with, though, and I'm not going to argue with him if he wants to give Zeth a free pass. For some unknown reason, the guy helped us out…and I'm grateful to him for that.

# 43

# ALEX

Two Months Later

Emancipation's a powerful word. It holds an ocean of power within its five syllables. For a long time now, it's been a word that has taunted and eluded me. It's held me back from so many things, because it was always out of reach. But today, a sunny spring day in April, I have finally been granted my emancipation, and it feels oh-so-bittersweet. I'm free today, because today is my eighteenth birthday.

"You know, I had the whole thing planned out," I say, staring up at the sky. The wind's still a little cool, but the sun's out. Wispy, thin clouds slowly float from one side of my vision to the other, forming and disintegrating before they can even properly come together. Cirrus clouds. My favorite kind. "We were gonna drive all the way down the PCH to San Diego. Our first Moretti boys' road trip. I was gonna take you to the aquarium there. We were gonna swim in the ocean and ride bikes on the strand by the water. When we got back, I was gonna take you to the pound and I was gonna let you pick out a dog to bring home with you. To our house. Fuck, I hope you know…"

*How perfect it would have been.*

*How well I would have taken care of you.*
*How badly I wish I could change this.*
*How much it hurts when I even* think *your name.*

I swallow hard, clearing my throat. Laying on my back in the cemetery wasn't how I'd planned to spend today. I was going to keep myself busy. Keep on moving, keep my mind occupied until the day was over and done with, but all of those plans disappeared the second the sun came up. I got out of bed before six, careful not to wake Silver, and I left the apartment, my feet guiding me here all by themselves. I couldn't have altered my path even if I'd wanted to.

"I think I always knew…in my heart…that you liked living with Jackie. I knew she was good for you, even if she was a bitch and she kept trying to come between us. And…I think I made you feel guilty for liking her. I'm really sorry about that, man. That…that wasn't fair."

When Ben first went to live with Jackie, I talked shit on her constantly. I used horrific terms to describe her that my brother had probably never even heard at that point. I called her a whore. I called her a cunt. I called her a cunt a lot, which I now regret. Jackie wasn't a cunt. She was a threat to me, as I was a threat to her. And in between us, trapped between our shared states of anxiety, anger and fear, a little boy had tried to survive while being torn in two different directions.

No matter how scared I was that Jackie wanted to take Ben from me for good, it was shitty of me to speak badly of her in front of him. He was just a fucking kid, and Jackie was truly the only mother he'd ever known. I only have a handful of faded memories of our mom, and some of them are really painful, but at least I *have* them. Ben was too young to remember her at all when she died. I hate that he didn't get to know her even a little.

"*It's stupid to be so sad all of the time. It's okay. I loved having you as my big brother. You were pretty great at it. You built the best forts. And you always knew what I should do if another kid was picking on me. You made me feel safe all the time. I liked feeling safe with you.*"

One night, three and a half years ago, after a particularly harrowing beating courtesy of my old pal Gary, I pledged to myself that I would never, ever cry again. I curled up on my side amongst the thin, dirty, bloodied blankets I slept in, and I let myself bawl. I was hurt, and I was in pain, and I was scared about what was going to happen to me, so I let myself sob into those filthy blankets, and when I was done, I said enough, no more, never again.

I broke that vow the night I read Silver's email, where she described what went down at Leon Wickman's spring fling party. I broke it again the night she was taken into hospital with rope burns around her neck. And I break it now, as well. I permit myself three tears that course, hot and quick, over my temples, into my hair, before I dash the wetness away with the back of my hand.

"I didn't keep you safe though, did I? If I had, you'd be here. We'd be halfway to fucking Oregon by now."

My younger brother's voice remains quiet in my head this time. Even my own subconscious can't think of anything to argue that point. The fact is that I'm never *not* going to feel responsible for this.

Across the cemetery, a woman bows down before a headstone, kneeling in front of it. It's still early, eight maybe, but she's dressed in a suit, ready for the day. She's probably going to work once she's done here. She's calm. Serene, even. She made her peace with the death of her loved one some time ago, and this morning's brief sojourn amongst the headstones feels more like visiting an old friend than trying to dig broken glass out from underneath her skin. I'm making assumptions by the handful, naturally, but the way she laughs quietly as she talks to her loved one sounds easy and relaxed.

It's going to be a long time before I'll be able to affect that same level of ease in front of *this* headstone.

The ground's so fucking cold. I laid my leather jacket out before I laid down on the damn grass, but the chill from the earth has managed to seep through it and into my bones without a problem. I try not to think about how cold it must be for Ben, eight feet beneath me, lying in his coffin. I try not to imagine the state of decomposition his body is in now, four months after his death. Another tear slips past my defenses, a fresh surge of pain lancing through my side, right into the center of my chest.

"Oh, fuck..." I drag in a shallow sip of air, trying to force the agony into submission, but it won't be leashed. "Fuck, I'm so sorry, Ben." I throw my arm over my eyes, blocking out the sun, pretending not to feel the fresh onslaught of tears that fall. For the first time ever, I hate myself for not believing in God. If there's no God, then there's no afterlife, and that means Ben can't hear me now. There *should* be an afterlife. If anyone deserved one, it was my brother. He was just a fucking kid—

"I find counting helps."

I jerk upright, coughing for no good fucking reason. It feels as though I just got caught doing something dirty. The woman from across the cemetery is standing eight headstones over with her purse clutched tightly in her hand. She's blonde. Forty. Forty-two. In a light black trench coat and a formal black pant suit, she looks like she could be a bank manager. With a sorry tip of her head, she looks at the carved marble behind me and sighs. "When children die, the world never seems to be able to right itself on its axis again. I'm sorry for that."

I don't know what to say. I just stare at her, willing her to leave so I can pretend like I wasn't just sobbing in public. With a cursory swipe of my hands, I scrub my face, sniffing hard as I breathe in sharply. "Yeah. Well." That's all I've got.

The woman hangs her head. "Like I said. Counting helps. In for four. Out for four. That's how I remembered to breathe for a really long time. Eventually, you'll be able to pause in between and it won't even feel like you're about to crack open." She smiles sadly again, nodding like she's fielding some pretty painful memories of her own. "Something to look forward to, I guess."

She goes. Doesn't try to talk me out of crying, alone, in a graveyard. Doesn't ask if I'm okay. Doesn't try to convince me that I should leave, or get better, or get on with my life. She continues on her way, without telling me her name or asking me mine, because our names aren't important. We understand each other just fine without them. And we both know words are pointless when it comes to this kind of hurt.

*"You should go home, Alex. Silver's gonna be worried about you."*

"I know, man. I know." She'll have woken up by now and found my side of the bed to be empty and long-cold. Bailing on the apartment first thing was a shitty thing to do, considering that she's been planning on cooking a birthday breakfast for me for weeks now, but I needed to get this out of the way. If things had been different, I'd have been on my bike this morning, sitting outside Jackie's house before the dawn, ready to take Ben back home with me, come hell or high water. He would have been expecting me. When I woke up at four this morning with this restlessness in my soul, this tremendous weight sitting on my chest, it felt like he was *still* expecting me, and to get up and eat breakfast and go about my day without going to him first? Well, I just couldn't do that…

Now that I've visited my brother and said my piece, it *is* time to get back to Silver. I take one last long, shuttered breath, trying to manufacture a little positivity for the day ahead, when I look up and there she is, walking toward me across the cemetery with a large basket in her hand.

I blink, making sure I'm not seeing things, but the image of her, dressed in blue jeans and a pretty, white, lacey top beneath her red peacoat persists instead of vanishing. She's here, in the cemetery. It's as though I've conjured her here, simply by acknowledging how badly I need her all of a sudden.

She stops five feet away, smiling gently at me. Strands of her golden-bronze hair, already lightening from the little spring sun we've had here in Raleigh, dance on the soft breeze that sighs between the headstones. With the cool early morning sun bathing her face in light, she looks stunning.

Hell. She's such a beautiful creature. This girl is beyond the realm of comprehension. She *can't* be fucking real. Most days, I'm convinced that I've hallucinated her into existence. My mother hallucinated shit on the regular. No reason why I shouldn't be following in her footsteps. I can't quite muster the appropriate level of concern when I think things like this, though. If Silver *is* a hallucination, then so be it. Let me go mad, if it means I get to spend the rest of my life with her. I will descend into lunacy, and I will go gladly. So far, my experience of madness has been sublime.

With a casual nod of her head, Silver points with her chin off to the left, sighing gently on a long exhale. "Thought about grabbing a breakfast ice cream for you from the truck in the parking lot. Then I got to wondering why anyone'd be callous enough to set up their ice cream truck in a cemetery parking lot, and I didn't wanna support that kind of shady business practice."

Holy hell. She's stunning, she's strong as fuck, and she knows how to defuse a tense, potentially awkward situation in a heartbeat. I laugh, hanging my head for a second. The last thing I want is for Silver to catch me post-breakdown, but too late to do anything about it now. My eyes are still burning, and my cheeks are likely still flushed from my crying jag. I just need a moment to regroup and separate myself from my heartbreak before I give myself over to her completely. "Pity," I say, clearing my throat. "Could have done with a Screwball right about now."

"I mean, I haven't heard Greensleeves yet. They're probably still there," Silver teases. "I felt like a Choco Taco myself, but I didn't wanna look like an insensitive graveyard tourist."

"Oh, yeah. I hate those fucking guys."

"Me too. They're the worst."

I laugh again, but the sound is strangled this time. Silver doesn't say anything. She sets down the basket she's holding next to Ben's headstone, then she quietly arranges a thick blanket on the ground, kneeling down on it as she then begins to unpack the items she's brought with her.

Three containers covered with metal foil; one thermos flask; knives and forks; plastic camping plates; and a small cardboard box that looks like it came from the bakery across the street. A cacophony of smells hit the back of my nose as I finally steel myself, finally exiting the stormy emotions that had ahold of me before she arrived. Took me too long, but I meet Silver's gaze, nodding back at her when she nods at me. She doesn't need to ask her question; it's written all over her.

"I'm okay," I confirm. "Just...tough morning, y'know."

"I do," she says, scooting to sit beside me. "I packed most of this up last night. I figured you'd wanna make a trip here and have a moment with him before you could face anything else. And I considered staying back at your place and waiting for you there, too, but I got to thinking that you might eventually need some company, so...I hope you don't mind?"

"God, *Argento*, I'm so glad you're here, I might start crying all over again," I joke. The joke falls flat though, mostly because of my miserable, borderline-pathetic delivery. Silver leans into me, resting her head on my shoulder. Like the class-act that she is, she doesn't mention the whole crying thing, even though *I* was the one to bring it up.

"I'm so sorry, Alex. This is the worst day in the world, isn't it?"

Yes. For me it is. After the day Maeve showed up on my doorstep with tragic news, and the day I watched Ben being lowered into the ground, today really *is* the worst day in the world. It should be a momentous, happy day. Birthdays are supposed to be celebrated and enjoyed, but I've been dreading today ever since I properly processed the fact that Ben was dead, and I wasn't going to be bringing him to live with me the very second I turned eighteen.

I'm so grateful that Silver's not trying to ram rainbows and butterflies down my throat right now. It would have been understandable, forgivable, even, if she'd wanted to try and spin today in a positive light and make a big deal out of it. But she *knows* me. She *gets* me. She *loves* me, and she knows today could never have been anything other than a somber affair.

I turn and kiss her on the temple, closing my eyes as I lean my forehead against her hair. She smells of flowers, and sunshine, and the laundry detergent I washed my bedsheets in yesterday when I knew she was going to be spending the night. "Do you know how much I love you, Silver Parisi?" I murmur.

"A lot," she whispers. "Almost as much as I love you."

My smile hurts, it feels so sweet. "And do you know how dark and utterly shitty my life would be without you in it?"

"Pitch black?" she guesses. "Charcoal black? Obsidian black?"

"Obsidian black, probably."

She nods wisely, as though this choice makes the most sense. "I'm glad your life isn't obsidian black. I'm glad I lighten it up just a little."

I sit up straight, shifting so that I can take her face in my hands. Her eyes skip over my features one by one, and her irises look like mercury, like shifting lightning trapped inside a glass bottle. "You don't just light me up a little. You are the goddamn sun, *Argento*," I tell her. "You give off so much heat, and life, and joy that it's fucking spilling out of me. I have more light than I know what to do with. It's just that losing him...losing *Ben*...that pain was a black hole that just kept getting bigger and bigger for a second there. I thought it was gonna swallow me whole. You kept me going, though. You gave me what I needed to cling on. And I was a shit, and I'm so sorry for the way—"

She cups her hand over my mouth, slowly shaking her head. "Despite the rumor mill at Raleigh High, you're human, Alessandro. And people break open and fall apart when people they love die. It's a brutal truth. Never try and apologize to me again, or I'll revoke your backrub privileges"

"I don't seem to recall there being backrub privileges." The words come out muffled, since she's still covering my mouth with her hand. She laughs, winking at me suggestively, lowering her hand.

"If you play your cards right, there might be backrub privileges down the line. In the meantime, I have a question for you."

"Oh?"

She looks very serious indeed. "On a scale of one to ten, how weird is it to eat a birthday breakfast in a cemetery?"

"I'm gonna say that would be a seven, but I'm also will say that I'm ravenous and I don't care how weird it is. Whatever you've got in those containers smells fucking delicious, and I think we should devour all of it right now before it gets cold."

I'm not really hungry. I just want to make her smile, which she does as she unwraps the dishes, unveiling her birthday breakfast masterpieces: chicken and waffles in one dish, pancakes and freshly cut strawberries in another, and, last but not least, bacon and cheesy eggs in the third. So much food we'll never come close to finishing it all. We give it a good goddamn try, though. The second I fork some of the chicken and waffles into my mouth, I realize just how hungry I actually *am*, and I get to work.

Ben wouldn't mind us eating at his grave. He'd wholeheartedly approve, I think to myself, as I drain my second cup of coffee from the Thermos Silver brought to our macabre early morning picnic. He would have gorged himself on Silver's pancakes until he made himself sick. Pancakes were his favorite.

Once we've finished stuffing our faces and we're so full we're groaning, Silver grabs the picnic basket, dragging it toward her. I begin to stack the dishes, thinking it's time to clean up, but Silver stops me. "Not yet. If we're breaking cemetery etiquette, we might as well do it properly. You need to open your presents," she says.

I just stare at her, a little dumbstruck.

Her smile begins to fade. "Oh, fuck. Presents are a little much. I should have gauged that a little better. Sorry."

"No, no. I just, uh…it's just that I don't think anyone's bought me a birthday present in…" I wrack my memory, trying to do the math. And then it hits me: *I haven't received a birthday present since my mother died.* That is just too fucking depressing to admit out loud, though, so I simply laugh and shrug, like it's no big deal.

Silver hesitates, as if she knows exactly how long it's been since someone was kind to me on my birthday, but mercifully she doesn't say anything about it. She reaches inside the basket, producing a small box, wrapped in blue and white stripy wrapping paper. I accept the box with trepidation. How the fuck do normal people receive gifts? How do they fucking react? What the hell do they say? Most importantly, why does this feel so fucking awkward right now?

"Uhh…thanks." God, I'm such a fucking moron. "I…the paper's cool."

Silver looks heavenward, groaning. "The paper was ninety-nine cents from the general store. It was all they had left after Christmas. Just open it up already, Moretti. I'm gonna break out in hives if you make me wait much longer."

She grumbles as I open her gift with care, peeling back the tape and unfolding it at either end instead of ripping through the stripy paper. At one point, she almost snatches the present from my hands and tears into it herself. I manage to get into the box before she has chance, though.

Underneath the wrapping paper is a small jewelry box. Amused, I hold it up, arching an eyebrow. "Bling, Parisi?"

"Argh! Open the damn box, Alex!"

"Okay, okay! Little Miss Impatient." I snap the box open, curious as to what I'll find inside. And there, on the blue velvet cushion inside, is a gold medallion. It's small—the same size as the St. Christopher I wear around my neck—but there's no saint engraved on this medallion's surface. It's a crest. One I'm unfamiliar with. I take it out of the box, inspecting it closely. Along the bottom, around the outer edge of the coin's surface, is the word '*Parisi.*'

"It's kind of stupid, I know. But that side bears my family's crest. And on the other side—"

I've already flipped it over, to find the Moretti family crest on the other side.

"I know how you feel. I know that, with your mom gone, and… now Ben too," Silver says, struggling with the words. "I know it might feel like you're alone. But you're not, Alex. *I* am your family, and *you* are mine. Parisi. Moretti. They're just words, really. Ideas. I had both our names engraved on this to show that those ideas are one and the same. We're bound together forever, Alex. Always. Two sides of the same coin."

I hold the medallion in the palm of my hand, turning it one way and then the other, battling with my emotions. I try to string a sentence together in my head, but every time I think I'm almost there, whatever sentiment I've cobbled together doesn't do justice to what I'm feeling.

I put the medallion back on its cushion briefly, so I can reach up and unfasten the clasp on the chain around my neck. Silver watches intently as I thread her gift onto the chain so that it hangs right next to St. Christopher.

"It's nothing really. Just a little trinket—" Silver begins to say, but I cut her off, crushing my mouth to hers. The kiss is long, and deep, and it burns in my fucking soul.

When I pull back, I say, "It's *not* nothing. It's *everything*, Silver. It's more than I know what to do with. Thank you. I'll die before I take it off."

We pack up our picnic, and we get ready to head back to the apartment. As we leave, I whisper a goodbye-for-now to my brother, not caring if Silver hears it. "See ya around, little man. I love you."

*"I love you, too. Happy birthday, Alex."*

## 44

## CAMERON

When you have kids, your dreams, your hopes and your aspirations are no longer your own. Every positive thing you wish for becomes a wish offered up on behalf of someone else. For your children, you pray for health. You pray that they'll be content and never suffer heartbreak or misery. As they play and you watch their personalities develop one day at a time, you hope that life will be kind to them, and you'll be able to arm them with every skill and character trait they'll need to navigate the murky, treacherous waters of adulthood. Most of all, you hope that they'll find someone to love and be loved by. For a family and a support network of their own, that will bring them joy and fulfillment. At least that's how it was for me. From the very first moment I held Silver in my arms, I knew that whatever wishes or luck I'd been allotted in this life were now all hers. Max came along, and it was only natural that his name be added to my fevered pleas for happiness and safety.

I gave up on asking for anything for myself. Seemed greedy, when I had two small people depending on me, who needed me to take care for them to the best of my ability. I never resented the fact that I've had to sacrifice most of my own dreams along the way. I'll forever keep on using up every scrap of chance, luck, and fate that comes my way on my children, too, but…tonight, I make a rare exception. I allow myself one wish, purely for me and no one else.

*God, I hope everything goes well tonight.*

The house is eerily quiet as I collect the keys to the new car from the mail stand. I hover by the front door, my palm resting on the cold, smooth metal of the handle, listening for a second to the roaring silence.

A year ago, my kids were bickering with one another, the television was blaring, my wife was hollering at anyone who'd listen, trying to find something she'd misplaced, and everything felt so alive. Now, the cavernous old house feels abandoned. So weird. It feels as though I'm a stranger here now. A ghost, haunting empty, forgotten rooms.

Outside, the evening's balmy, dusk just setting in. My favorite thing about summer: the fact that it doesn't get dark until eight in the evening. A light, playful breeze tugs at my jacket as I jump in the car and tap my destination's address into the onboard GPS. During the twelve-minute drive across town, my mind races out of control as I consider all of the things that could go wrong once I arrive.

By the time I pull up to the curb outside the small, neat little cottage set back from the road, I've almost talked myself into calling the whole thing off and driving back home again with my tail between my legs.

*"Jesus, Dad. Don't be such a coward. I thought us Parisis were made of sterner stuff?"*

The voice in my head—Silver's voice—might be a figment of my imagination, but that's exactly what my daughter would say to me now, if she were sitting next to me in the passenger seat. She'd roll her eyes, laughing at my discomfort, and then she'd find a way to bribe me into hauling my ass out of the car and up the flower-lined pathway that leads to the cottage's red front door. Silver would never let something so irrelevant as nerves prevent her from taking a step into the unknown. She proved that well enough when she packed up her room and moved across the country to Dartmouth with the guy she promised to marry. Kid always has been *far* braver than me.

Steeling myself, I glance down at my phone, checking the screen for the fifteenth time since I left the house. No cancellation texts have come through. No apologetic messages, asking for a rain check. Looks like this is all still a go…

*Come on, you stupid bastard. You got this. You're handsome. You're funny. Your beard looks fucking* amazing. *Get out of the damn car or I'm gonna kick your ass.*

As pep talks go, this one's pretty bad. The promise of a beating's obviously an empty threat, since I'm not a fan of pain and I'm hardly going to thrash my own backside, but it does light a persistent albeit small fire underneath me. Next thing I know, I'm grabbing the flowers I bought at the boutique florists on the high street from the seat next to me, and I'm getting out of the car and slamming the car door closed behind me.

*One foot in front of the other, Cam. Left, right. Left, right. Left, right. Nice work. You're not nervous at all. You're confident. You're a fucking catch. You're successful. You've got money. You've got all your own teeth… Oh, that's just great. Awesome. Well done. You've got all your own teeth. Like she'd go out with a guy who was missing—*

I'm halfway up the path, berating myself for being weird, when the front door opens and a man steps out into the fading, honeyed light. Our eyes make contact, and I nearly drop the bouquet of flowers onto the ground.

"Al—" I catch myself before I can finish his name. It isn't Alex. This man's older, with deep frown lines and a tired, sickly look to him that makes me think he drinks too much. A broad smile forms on his face, altering his features entirely so that he looks nothing at all like my future son-in-law in less than the blink of an eye.

"Yeah, we share a passing resemblance, huh?" the guy says. So this must be Giacomo. Has to be. There's no other reasonable explanation for how similar he and Alex look. Their dark hair and their dark eyes are so alike it's uncanny. The way he holds himself, like he's ready and prepared to throw a punch at the slightest provocation, has Alex written all over it. But there's something fundamentally different about this man. There's an edge to him that I don't like. I can't put my finger on it…

"You always early for a date, man?" Alex's father asks, as he slaps together a pair of leather gloves. He puts them on, frowning at me like he can't quite figure out what to make of me. "You ask me, looks a little too keen. S'posed to make 'em sweat a little, y'know."

Rocking back on my heels, I take a look around the front yard—the small yet well-manicured lawn; the rose bushes underneath the cottage window; the little yellow windmill, nestled in amongst the ranunculus and the pretty wild daisies—and I run my tongue over my teeth. "This might come as a shock to you, Giacomo...but people aren't toys. You're not supposed to play games with them or try to manipulate them. Life's far less complicated if you're straight up with people. I've found that being honest...being *yourself*...it gets you way further than if you're constantly striving for control and power over others."

Giacomo huffs down his nose, flaring his nostrils. He doesn't seem to like or agree with the statement I've just made. He squints off to the right, where a huge cruiser is parked against the curb fifty feet down the road. *His* bike, I presume. "Kids made it safe to New Hampshire, I heard," he says stiffly. "Personally, I can't see the attraction. Tying themselves to a stuffy institution like that for four years. Spending all that money on an education that'll end up being no good to 'em. Shoulda gone traveling or something. Gotten some real-life experience."

"Oh, yeah? The foster care system? Getting shot? Raped? Arrested? Nearly killed a couple of times a piece? I think both our children have had enough life experience already, don't you? Dartmouth's exactly what they need right now. It'll be good for them. They're both too smart...*brilliant*, actually...to be wasting their intellect riding around the country on a motorcycle, waiting for trouble to track them down and destroy their lives all over again." I can't get this bitter, acidic taste out of my mouth. It seems to grow worse whenever Giacomo speaks. This is the man who abandoned Alex and Ben when they needed him. He's the piece of shit who abused Alex's mother, and left her high and dry in her darkest hours. Looking at him now, I'm surprised to realize that I don't just want to hit the bastard. I want to *really* hurt him.

"What are you doing here, anyway?" I push my glasses up the bridge of my nose. "I'd have thought you'd be long gone by now. Monty's dead. The Dreadnaughts have been disbanded. Alex is gone. There's nothing to keep you in Raleigh anymore."

Giacomo wags a finger at me, a fake smile plastered all over his face. "You...you don't like me much, do you, Cameron?"

"I'd be lying if I said I did."

"Everyone's so quick to judge, aren't they? Oh, Giacomo's the bad guy. Giacomo's a piece of shit. Giacomo doesn't deserve to breathe the same fresh air as the rest of us Raleigh well-to-do's. Well, I...am officially *hurt*, Cam. Us about to become family and all. Does this mean you won't be setting a spot at the table for me when my son and your precious little firecracker come home for Christmas?"

I shake my head, looking him square in the eye. "No. You won't be welcome here."

Giacomo chuckles darkly. "Whew. You weren't kidding, huh? Straight from the hip." He twists quickly, making a finger-gun and pretending to draw it on me, using his thumb to cock the hammer and shoot me three times in quick succession. "He's too old for you to adopt him, Cameron. He's got my blood running in his veins. He's a Moretti. He's *my* son. Best you don't forget that."

God, what a bastard. He ran out on Alex when he was six years old and he never looked back. Why the hell would he bother trying to claim him now, when Alex doesn't need or want him in his life. "There you go again," I say sadly. "I'll say it one more time with feeling. *People are not toys, Giacomo.* You can't break someone and toss them aside, only to throw a temper tantrum when someone else takes interest in them. Alex *is* a man now, and you don't even know him. I'm afraid that probably isn't going to change."

Like a feral, threatened dog, Giacomo Moretti growls. "Whatever you say, Poindexter. I s'pose time'll tell. Alex ain't cut out for college. And he sure as hell ain't cut out for marriage. I'm betting your precious Silver comes crying to daddy about her broken heart before the end of the first semester. Until then, I'm sure my boy'll have his fun. We Morettis always do."

Sighing, I pinch the bridge of my nose. It's so, *so* sad how wrong he is. Truly. "The blood in Alex's veins has nothing to do with who he's become. You shove the Moretti name in people's faces like it's something to be feared. By rights, the Moretti name's something your son should be ashamed of. You're weak, and you're selfish, and you don't give a fuck about anyone else. Alex is nothing like you, though. He's brave, and he's good. He's loyal, and his capacity to love, despite everything you allowed him to suffer through, is remarkable. You might have tainted your family name, but Alex has made it shine. He's restored it to something he can be proud of. And I'll be damn proud when Silver becomes a Moretti, too, because as far as I'm concerned, it's a name that represents strength and courage. Alex might not be my son by birth. He might not even be my son by law yet, but he is one of the brightest parts of my life, and I'm *honored* to have him as a part of my family. Now, if you'll excuse me, if I hurry, I can still be early for my date."

I'm not a very brave person by nature, which is why I'm all the more impressed with myself as I stroll past Alex's father and up the path toward the cottage without flinching. I only know he's not going to kill me when I hear the growl of his motorcycle start up on the street.

Once he's gone, I lift my hand to knock on the cottage door…

…and Maeve Rogers answers with a smile on her face.

# EPILOGUE

Ivy league.

Jesus fucking Christ.

When he was still alive, Gary Quincy took great pleasure in telling me what a worthless piece of shit I was. I can't count how many times he assured me that I was never going to amount to anything, and all the while he was spewing hate and did his best to tear me down, I was scheming.

Tell me I'm worthless, and I'll make damn sure I'm worth more than you.

Tell me I'm stupid and I'll break my neck to make sure I'm way smarter than you.

Tell me I'm never going to amount to shit, and I'll rise above just to spite you.

So now, through a series of bizarre, horrific, and sporadically wonderful events, I am a fucking *Ivy League* college student. What a fucking riot.

Thanks to Coach Foley's insistent and highly annoying nagging, brutal training regime, and her amazing stubbornness, not only did I manage to get into Dartmouth with Silver, but I bagged myself a full ride, too. The woman's part psychopath, part miracle worker, and I owe her big time.

Graduation was a surreal affair to say the least. I didn't feel like I belonged up there on that stage beside Silver, and yet I fucking *earned* my place there.

Now I stick out like a sore thumb at college, just like I did at Raleigh. Only difference is…no one here really seems to care. The ink, my clothes, the way I walk and talk…none of it fazes anyone at all. And, most important of all, Silver's happy. She's more than just happy. She's *flourishing*. It's the most amazing thing; I get to watch her put down new roots in this remarkable place, and I get to watch her grow into herself.

Thanks to Cam's non-too-subtle influence, I plan on studying architectural design as my major. Silver's majoring in Space Sciences. We have no shared classes. We rush out of the door in the mornings at different times, and sometimes we're both so exhausted by the end of the day that we don't even get to eat dinner before we're passing out on the couch. The classes are hard, the workload is unforgiving, and there aren't enough hours in the day…but I'm with Silver. I could be walking through fire and brimstone and I wouldn't mind, so long as I have her by my side.

"Did you know your new friend thinks the Earth is flat?" Silver asks, taking a giant bite out of her pizza slice. We have assignments hanging over us like the blade of a guillotine, but we've taken a break to fuel up on carbs and sugar. A Hammer Horror B-movie plays on the TV with the sound muted. The air conditioner in our small yet perfect apartment whirs industriously, doing little to cool down the living room, but I'm not complaining. If it were cooler, Silver would be wearing more than her skimpy little shorts and a thin t-shirt, and I am enjoying the view far too much to bitch about the stifling heat.

I arch an eyebrow at her, jamming my own pizza slice into my mouth. "Monroe?"

She nods. Her hair's tied up in a messy bun, strands fallen loose, framing her face. Silver looks incredible when she's run a brush through her hair and she's wearing a little makeup, but she looks best when her skin is bare and she looks like she's just been fucked. Which she has. "They have a flat earther society on campus."

*For fuck's sake. Just when you think you've made a normal friend…* "And

Monroe's a member? *Monroe?* The guy with the buzzcut and the tricked-out Dodge Charger?"

Silver swallows, smiling, and leans over to kiss me. "Sorry, *passarotto*. I think he's actually *president* of the club."

"*Fuck.*"

"Back to the drawing board on the Zander replacement, then?"

I pull her plump, too-tempting bottom lip into my mouth and I give it a gentle bite, running my tongue playfully over the spot that I just pressed between my teeth. "Zander should not be replaced. Zander is a pain in the ass. I'm relieved I don't have to deal with his bullshit anymore."

Silver laughs, falling back onto the sofa. The skin around the base of her throat that was once bruised dark purple is back to normal now. Just like the doctors promised, you'd never know to look at her that she'd even been hurt. "God, you're such a liar, Alessandro Moretti. You miss having him around, I know you do."

Urgh. She might be right. I'm on the verge of admitting to myself that Zander Hawkins proved himself to be a good friend after all. It'll be a long time yet that I admit anything of the sort out loud, though. And potentially years before I tell him so to his smug, annoyingly cocky face.

"I got an email from Mom today," Silver tells me. "She bought the house in Toronto. My little brother's officially gonna be a Canadian."

"You pissed?" I know how much Silver misses Max. They've been FaceTiming with each other nearly every day, though Silver's been quick to cut their calls short whenever I come home. I think she feels bad that she's building a better relationship with her brother, even though I've told her countless times that it doesn't bother me. If Ben were still alive, I'd be talking to him twenty-four seven.

"No," she says, shaking her head. "He loves it there, and he's made a ton of new friends. I think it'll be good for him. He asked if we'd go visit him soon."

"Hah! You think you can handle spending five minutes in a room with your mother?" Things haven't been as great on the Parisi mother/daughter front. Kacey's revelation at prom that Silver's mom had an affair with her father went down like a lead balloon. Silver confronted her about it, but the woman refused to discuss the matter. In Silver's eyes, her silence is tantamount to an admission of guilt.

Silver pulls a face. She's getting better at changing the subject. "Oh! And speaking of mail, a package came from Maeve for you this morning."

I smirk at the mention of the woman's name. He hasn't told Silver yet because he's a pussy of the highest order, but Cameron confided in me that he'd had a date with my ex-social worker and they'd hit it off in a pretty big way. Apparently, they exchanged numbers at the diner, the day Silver and I played in public together for the first time, and have been texting each other ever since. I figured I'd be rid of Maeve the moment I turned eighteen, but now I'm not so sure. She's fussed over and mothered the shit out of me ever since she took over my case when I moved to Raleigh. Now, there's a chance that she could end up being my mother-in-law for real. This shit just gets weirder and weirder, I swear.

"Probably a court order, demanding we go back to our dorms and stay there like good little kids," I muse. Technically, Silver and I are not supposed to be living together. On paper, Silver's official residence is at Morton Hall in East Wheelock House. I have digs assigned on the same floor. Cam and Maeve both signed off on paperwork to prove that Silver and I have a domestic partnership, but the powers that be said we hadn't been together long enough for the administration to recognize the relationship. So, I used the money I had left over from my time working as Monty's runner to rent a small pad five minutes away from campus for us instead. We show our faces in dorms every now and then, study there sometimes, use the laundry just to put on a show for the floor directors, but we *live* here.

After we've eaten, I grab the package from Maeve, wondering what the fuck is inside it. When you age out of the foster care system and CPS is no longer responsible for your well-being, it's not like they send you a fucking certificate or anything. Much like a bad breakup, you part ways hoping to god you never have to hear from or speak to the other party ever again. I pull the thick sheaf of papers out of the heavily taped padded envelop Maeve has sent me, expecting to find official documents inside. Maybe even a bill of some kind; I wouldn't put it past the board at Denney to somehow try and charge me for the time I spent in juvie with Zander. The last thing I'm expecting to find are drawings.

Pencil. Pen. Ink. Even paint.

And they're all of my mother.


Alex,


You don't need to work in a field like mine to know that families are complicated. It's a universal and very obvious truth. People are flawed and unreliable. They hurt each other all the time, especially those closest to them, which makes the pain they cause so much worse. But you must know that even the very worst people occasionally have redeeming moments. Your father came to see me this morning. He didn't want your address, and he swore he wasn't going to bother you. He seemed quite adamant that you were going to come to your senses and track him down after all is said and done, which I really hope you do not do.

Anyway, he brought these drawings to me and asked if I would pass them on. Your mother was a striking, very beautiful woman, Alex. I've seen pictures of her, but the way your father captured her in these sketches only heightens her beauty. The sheer amount of times he drew her shows just how much he must have loved her at one point in his life.

There are so many things about your father that are ugly, but the amount of love he poured into these pictures of your mother is beautiful, Alex. You hate him, and I don't blame you for that. I kind of hate him for you, too. But that doesn't mean you can't love the art he created.

I hope everything in New Hampshire's going well for both you and Silver. Please pass on my warmest regards to her.

Sincerely,

Maeve

I feel like I'm being torn straight down the middle, furious and elated, as I leaf through the drawings and sketches in my hand. There must be at least fifty of them, on different sizes of paper, some of them on proper thick artist's stock, while some of the most detailed, lovely pieces were drawn on scrap. I turn over a drawing of my mother with her knees drawn up to her chest, a half-eaten apple held in one of her hands, her hair wild, head tossed back, her mouth open wide as she laughs, only to discover that it was sketched on the back of an overdue invoice for a Bosch Power Drill dated January 29, 1995.

The second I register the way my mother's laughing, a slew of memories hit me hard like a sledgehammer to the chest. I can barely breathe around them. My mother would sink into the deepest, darkest depths of depression and wouldn't smile for months. But when the depression didn't have its claws in her and she was gloriously herself, she smiled a lot. She laughed with her whole body. I *hear* the breathless, raucous unmistakable sound of her laughter when I look at that picture, and it makes my heart shatter to pieces.

*Don't be sad, passarotto. There's so much to be happy about. You're no longer a boy. You're a man. No, you're a* king *amongst men. You have the love of a beautiful woman. I'm so proud of you, mi amore. You're lighting up the world. Go on. Go out into the world and be great. Be the man I know you can be.*

I haven't heard my mother's voice in my head for quite a while, I realize. With a heavy dose of sadness that makes my throat throb with emotion, I think that this will be the very last time I hear it. I don't know how I know that. I just do.

"Wow. Those are spectacular," Silver whispers behind me, leaning over the back of the couch to look at the drawings over my shoulder. "Holy crap, Giacomo could have earned a living as an artist. What the hell?"

He could have. There was nothing stopping him from becoming an illustrator, or designer, or a freelance artist of some kind. He chose a different path for himself, though—a selfish path that, in the end, benefitted no one. Not even himself.

"She was so lovely, Alex," Silver says softly. "I really wish I'd gotten to meet her."

"Yeah." I run my fingers over another image of my mother, a dull ache pounding in my chest. Mom would have loved Silver. She loved anyone who knew their own mind and wasn't afraid to say what was on it. And Silver, she would have adored my mother in return. It was impossible *not* to fall in love with her.

I have so few photos of my mom. There were never many taken, I suppose, and those that did exist were lost when she killed herself and CPS took us away. I was too young to ask what was going to happen to her things. Everything my mother had owned was likely bagged up by her old landlord and taken to a thrift store. Could have been discarded in a dumpster for all I know. Giacomo certainly never came back for any of it.

These pictures are a connection to my mother that I've been missing since I was six years old. I don't give a shit that Giacomo drew them. I'll cherish them for as long as I live.

Days later, when I come home, Silver's waiting for me by the door to the apartment, and she's wearing a look of excitement on her face. She bounces from one foot to the other, clapping her hands over her mouth as I walk in.

I dump my bag at my feet, smirking at her ridiculousness. "Oh my god. You won the lottery. You're rich now and you're leaving me to become Billy Joel's unpaid intern."

"Psshh. If Billy asked me to be his unpaid intern, I'd dump your ass and be on the road in five seconds flat. I wouldn't need to win the lottery. Getting to be Billy Joel's unpaid intern *is* winning the lottery."

"All right. Noted. Noted." She's still grinning nervously, unable to keep still; I slowly walk around her, making a show of studying her closely. "Nasa called and they've invited you to become their youngest ever astronaut."

She rolls her eyes. "Do you have any idea how much studying I have to do before they'll even think about letting me near a shuttle, Alex? There's a reason why astronauts are ancient by the time they get to go up."

"Okaaay. So...your Dad told you he's dating Maeve, and you're excited about getting a new mom?"

She freezes, eyes growing wide. "*What?*"

"Never mind. Joking. I'm joking. What are you so excited about, *Argento*? The suspense is killing me."

"Go back to what you said about my dad and Maeve."

"Or you could just pretend I didn't breathe a word about that and spill your guts instead." Having circled her fully twice, I come to a stop in front of her and plant my hands on her hips, snatching her up off the ground. She squeals, wrapping her legs around my waist, her tits crushing up against my chest, and my dick begins to throb hopefully.

*God, you are never satisfied,* I tell it. Unfortunately, the universe might have seen fit to give my cock a mind of its own, but it neglected to give it ears. It doesn't listen.

Silver, so breathtakingly beautiful in the summer dress she's wearing—the material's a rich blue tone that really brings out her eyes—laces her arms around my neck, planting a delicate kiss on my forehead, right between my eyebrows. "I did something for you in the bedroom. I hope you don't mind."

"I *never* mind when you do things for me in the bedroom."

"You're so bad," she laughs. "Come on. Put me down. I wanna show you."

"You sure you wanna show me? 'Cause you're looking a little panicked right now."

"I'm not panicked! I'm just…" She shrugs, her cheeks coloring. She's definitely panicking. "I'm just hoping I haven't taken over something that you wanted to do is all." It's too damn easy to screw with her sometimes. She's goddamn adorable when she's embarrassed.

"Fuck," I rumble, butting her nose with mine. "You bought yourself a strap-on, didn't you? Kinky. I'm a firm believer that the anus is an *out* hole, but I'll try anything once if it'll make you happy."

She looks scandalized. "I do *not* want to dominate you with a strap-on. Wherever you got that idea from, you can send it right back because it's never gonna happen. Ju—for fuck's sake, come with me. We'll be here all night otherwise." She grabs me by the hand, and that's it, she's physically dragging me through to the bedroom.

There are physics textbooks and notebooks all over the bed—she's been studying hard while I was gone—but there are also plastic wrappers and cardboard packaging all over the floor, too. "Looks like you had a party in here without me. What have you been up to, *Arge*—" I stop talking, because when I look back at her, I *see* what she's been up to. Opposite our bed, dozens of picture frames have been mounted on the wall in a collage style, slotted together like a jigsaw puzzle. From plain black wood, to raw pine, to fancy old fashioned gilded gold, every single picture frame is different. Like, not a single one of them matches any of the others. Of course, inside the frames are Giacomo's drawings of my mom. But not only that. There are photos of Ben in the frames, too. Pictures I've never even seen before. Shots of him playing baseball and posing with his friends. And, oh god...there... there are pictures of me and him together, too. Selfies I took for him on his phone, for him to keep, so that he knew I was always going to be there for him.

I sit down heavily on the bed, right on top of one of Silver's textbooks.

She looks at me worriedly, covering her mouth with her hands again. "I'm sorry. I know...it's a lot, isn't it? It's like...I just went ahead and gathered up everything that made you hurt and I plastered it all over our bedroom wall. God, I'm so stupid. I can...fuck, I can take it down. I'm sorry." She lifts a picture of Ben from the wall, looking for somewhere to put it so she can take down the others, too.

"Silver, stop," I say softly.

"God, I don't know what's wrong with me. I have no idea what I was thinking."

"I love it, Silver."

"You don't have to say that."

"I know I don't. Please, just...Silver, wait, wait, wait. Don't take that down. Listen to me. *I love it.*"

She sniffs, daring to glance over at me. Her eyes look glassy, like she's on the verge of tears. Her pain is enough to have me back on my feet and hurrying across the bedroom to her. "Seriously, please do not cry, *Argento*. I'm not upset. It's fucking beautiful, what you've done for me. I adore it. I love it. I wanna keep it. It was just a lot to take in all at once is all. I just needed a beat to process it." I cup Silver's face with my hand, and she leans into my palm, closing her eyes. Sniffing, she says, "You don't talk about him. I know how much it must still hurt."

Just to prove how right she is, my chest squeezes sharply, grief tightening around my heart like a fist. Normally I'd avoid this conversation, moving onto a lighter topic, but that's the whole point, isn't it? Silver notices when I do that and she takes note. "Some days, it feels like I should shut myself away from the world and never show my face again. The guilt...the guilt's crushing. I know, I know. Before you say it, I know his death wasn't my fault. Not really. It *was* an accident. But he should have been in Hawaii, Silver. He should have been playing soccer on a beach, and instead Jackie was bringing him back to see me. I'm gonna have to live with that knowledge somehow. Some days, I *can't* live with it. It feels like I'll die from the weight of that knowledge, pressing down on me."

I take a shaky breath, pausing while I pull my shit together. "Other days are easier, though. The sadness lets up for a minute, or an hour, and I get to remember the good stuff. I get to laugh at the goofy, stupid shit we'd do together. And I think those minutes and those hours will become more frequent, the more time passes. It's fucked up, y'know. A part of me doesn't want to stop being sad. It feels like, if I stop being sad all of the time, I'm betraying him. Forgetting him."

"You're never gonna forget him. He's a part of you, just like you were a part of him. He's going to be with you for the rest of your life, no matter where you go or what you do. You'll live your life for him, and experience as many things as you can. *For him.*" The way she looks up at me makes everything come into focus. She's a lens. I look into her eyes, and everything that has been blurry and confusing for the better part of a lifetime suddenly just...makes sense. She is cool water, after years of thirst. A soothing balm, after far too much hurt.

"And soon, we're going to have a family of our own..." she says, trailing off.

I carefully tuck a rogue strand of her hair behind her ear, aching to kiss her. I hold back, though. "Hmm. A family. You're saying you actually *want* me to knock you up one of these days?"

Smiling, trying not to, suddenly shy, Silver nods. "Yes," she says quietly. "One of these days. When we're done with college, and we've learned the lessons we need to learn, I am going to want that more than anything, Alessandro Moretti. One day, we'll have a son of our own. And you are going to be an amazing father, you know that?"

Fear prickles at the back of my neck, a thousand worries and concerns trying to make themselves heard all at once. I shut them down with one quiet thought, though: Silver believes I'll be a good father, and so I will. For her, I'll be anything she believes I can be.

"A son?" I muse.

Still a little shy, Silver dips her head, but she manages to look up at me when she tells me in a firm, unwavering voice, "Yes. And when we meet him for the very first time, we will call him Ben."

## ALSO BY CALLIE HART

WANT TO KNOW MORE ABOUT ZETH, SLOANE ROMERA AND DETECTIVE LOWELL? The Blood & Roses Series is out now and available to read for FREE on KINDLE UNLIMITED!

**FREE TO READ ON KINDLE UNLIMITED!**

**DARK, SEXY, AND TWISTED! A BAD BOY WHO WILL CLAIM BOTH YOUR HEART AND YOUR SOUL.**

## ALSO BY CALLIE HART

Read the entire Blood & Roses Series
FREE on Kindle Unlimited!

**WANT TO DISAPPEAR INTO THE DARK, SEDUCTIVE WORLD OF AN EX-PRIEST TURNED HITMAN?**
Read the Dirty Nasty Freaks Series
FREE on Kindle Unlimited!

**LOVE A DARK AND DANGEROUS MC STORY? NEED TO KNOW WHAT HAPPENED TO SLOANE'S SISTER?**
Read the Dead Man's Ink Boxset
FREE on Kindle Unlimited!

ALSO BY CALLIE HART | 357

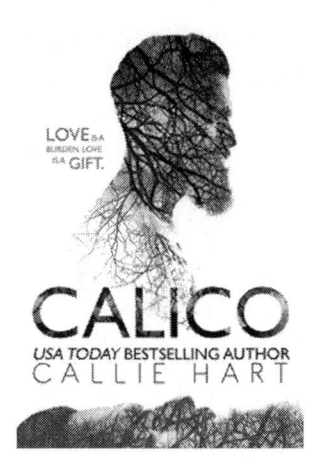

WANT AN EMOTIONAL, DARK, TWISTED STANDALONE?
Read Calico!
FREE on Kindle Unlimited

WANT A PLOT THAT WILL TAKE
YOUR BREATH AWAY?
Read Between Here and the Horizon
FREE on Kindle Unlimited!

## ALSO BY CALLIE HART

**WANT A NYC TALE OF HEARTBREAK, NEW LOVE, AND A HEALTHY DASH OF VIOLENCE?**
Read Rooke
FREE on Kindle Unlimited!

## FOLLOW ME ON INSTAGRAM!

The best way to keep up to date with all of my upcoming releases and some other VERY exciting secret projects I'm currently working on is to follow me on Instagram! Instagram is fast becoming my favorite way to communicate with the outside world, and I'd love to hear from you over there. I do answer my direct messages (though it might take me some time) plus I frequently post pics of my mini Dachshund, Cooper, so it's basically a win/win.

**You can find me right here!**

Alternatively, you can find me via me handle @calliehartauthor within the app.

**I look forward to hanging out with you!**

*Callie*
*x*

## DEVIANT DIVAS

If you'd like to discuss my books (or any books, for that matter!), share pictures and quotes of your favorite characters, play games, and enter giveaways, then I would love to have you over in my private group on Facebook!

We're called the Deviant Divas, and we would love to have you come join in the fun!

# ABOUT THE AUTHOR

USA Today Bestselling Author, Callie Hart, was born in England, but has lived all over the world. As such, she has a weird accent that generally confuses people. She currently resides in Los Angeles, California, where she can usually be found hiking, practicing yoga, kicking ass at Cards Against Humanity, or watching re-runs of Game of Thrones.

To sign up for her newsletter, click here.

# KEEP ON READING TO MEET ZETH FOR THE FIRST TIME!

In case you missed the beginning of Zeth and Sloane's story, here's your chance to read it for free now!

## SLOANE

WHEN I SAY I'M A GHOST, I'M NOT BEING LITERAL. I'm very much alive. Or at least some days I hurt just enough to know I'm still clinging onto a heartbeat. No, when I say I'm a ghost, I'm referring to the fact that people rarely see me. I'm the girl in the background. The average height, average weight, average hair color, non-event that eyes skip over instead of lingering on. I slip silently through this yawning city I live in without smiling. Without having to greet anyone for days at a time. It's been that way for the last six months. It's rare that I have to speak to strangers, and when I do it's perfunctory; people know instinctively that I'm not primed for small talk. Today is no exception.

"Here's your room key, Ms. Fredrich." The receptionist in downtown Seattle's Marriot hotel slides the plastic key card across the marble countertop. Once she's withdrawn her hand a safe distance, I reach out and palm it.

"Thank you."

Eyes down, she's stapling the paperwork created by my payment. "So…business or pleasure?" The warmth in her eyes dies when she finally looks up at me and registers the blank look I'm wearing. The smile slides from her face like butter from a hot knife.

"Business," I tell her, because nothing has ever been truer.

"Okay, well…I hope you enjoy your stay." She looks away as soon as she's done with the appropriate front desk script. She doesn't ask why I've turned up at her hotel with no bags, or why I'm only booking in for one night. Or why I've left a spare key card at the front desk for a Mr. Hanson. She doesn't ask any of that; she's not supposed to. Eli's given me a rundown of how this thing will play out, and so far it's almost to the letter. I lift my purse from the desk and head to the elevator, straightening my coat.

*Twenty-two, twenty-one, twenty, nineteen, eighteen….*

I watch the numbers light up one by one. Each disc, the size of a dollar coin, lights up and darkens in turn, and the elevator descends while I wait, patient and unblinking. There are other people waiting for the car to arrive. If this were an office building or a shopping center, I'd take the stairs; closed spaces and I aren't exactly the best of friends, but since this hotel is forty-seven floors high and I've booked a room on the forty-second floor, I'll just have to tolerate the inconvenience of their presence.

The doors slide back and I walk in first. The other hotel residents —four businessmen—are staying somewhere mid-level, and I don't want them brushing past me as they exit. It's easy to label them as mid-level guys. They're wearing mid-level-guy suits, and all four of them have mid-level-guy hair-cuts. Their accommodation is being paid for by a cost center funded by an accounting department, and accounting departments don't spring for penthouses. They spring for double rooms with en-suites that have access to the gym and not much else. No mini bar for you, Mr. Corporate.

The lift doors roll closed and I retreat within myself, pressing my back against the rear wall of the elevator car. I close my eyes, exhale down my nose. This will all be over soon, but my heart still dances in my chest all the same. The fear of being trapped, of what I am about to do, is like a coiled snake, ready and waiting to wreak havoc on my insides.

"Hey. Hey, are you okay? You're looking a little freaked out."

One of them talks to me. He thinks my panic is tied to the elevator ride, which it is, but only partially. He has brown eyes, a soft, warm color that reminds me of melted chocolate. He has dimples, too, probably twenty-three or so, around my age. He looks nice. The kind of nice I might have dated once upon a time, before…before any of that became impossible.

"I'm fine, thank you," I tell him.

"Good." The guy with chocolate eyes smiles at me. "Deep breathing sometimes helps my sister. She's not fond of elevators either."

He's so sweet. Way sweeter than I deserve, considering my purpose here today. I reward him with a watery smile—he grins back—and then the doors open, and the four of them leave. I jam my hands into my pockets to stop them from shaking. I'm alone for eighteen floors, which is better than being trapped with four strangers but still not great, and then, finally, it's my turn to alight. This hotel is much like any other I've stayed in. The only difference about it, the thing that will define it from all others in my memory for as long as I live, is that I'm here for a very specific reason: to have sex with a total stranger. And I'm doing it to find my baby sister.

## SLOANE

BY THE TIME I'm inside and my coat is hung neatly on the hook behind the door, I'm pretty much ready. I'm wearing what I've been told to wear—black lace. Eli, the private investigator I hired to help me find my sister, wasn't any more specific than that. He's the one who set this whole thing up.

"Sometimes money just isn't enough to buy what you're looking for, sweetheart. Sometimes it takes a little more… persuasion *to buy information like this. I tell you what…I'll share what I know in return for a little favor.*"

"What kind of favor?"

"You spread your legs for a paying customer and I'll tell you everything you need to know." The disgusting pig has the audacity to smile. "Oh come now, Ms. Romera. Don't look at me like that. You want to find your sister, don't you?"

And in the end, I'd agreed. He was right; I do want to find Lex, and I'll clearly do anything to make that happen. Even if I'll never be able to live with myself afterward.

Aside from the lingerie, Eli told me to bring something else with me today, something hidden in the pocket of my jacket. I take it out and put it on. The mask is a black lace number with blood-red lace edging and makes me a feel a little more disguised at least. I hit the light switch in the bathroom and rummage in my purse for the only thing that's going to keep me sane during this experience: a bottle of Valium. One of the perks of being a fifth-year resident is that there's always someone available to prescribe medication when you need it, no questions asked. The sedative's not even in my name, will never appear on my medical record. I pop one, just enough to keep me calm but not enough to make me drowsy, and then I peer into the mirror, fixing the band of my mask underneath my hair.

*You look like shit, Sloane.*

I tell myself this every time I look into a mirror these days. It may be the truth, but then again it may not. I've been staring at myself in mirrors for so long now that the reflection just doesn't make any sense anymore. Lex was always the beautiful one. I know I have a nice body. Eli said that was the only reason he was willing to do business with me, because my tits were real and I had a nice ass. *Your height might make some guys uncomfortable, but hey...not a lot you can do about that.* I focus on the dark rings under my eyes, trying to remember that this is all temporary. It's not forever. I'm a medical student after all. The body is just a machine, full of cogs and intricate parts all ticking away, working in harmony to keep you moving. Having sex is just making use of that machine, nothing more.

*You can do this, Sloane. You can do this.*

And then, not even two seconds later...

*Lex wouldn't want this for you. She wouldn't want you used and abused, selling yourself for so little.* I hate that voice inside my head. It makes it so hard to justify going through with this, but it's not as though I'm auctioning off my most valuable possession for drugs or money, or even fame and fortune like some girls do. No, I am doing it out of love. Love for Lex. Any sister would do the same.

It's been six months and I'm still no closer to finding Alexis, and this really does feel like my last resort. Eli's smart—he's given me just enough information to keep my hope alive, but nowhere near enough to risk me backing out of our little arrangement.

*Thud, thud, thud.*

"Holy shhhh—" The door. I suck my bottom lip into my mouth, trapping the curse word behind my teeth. It's go time.

Mr. Hanson will have collected his key from the chirpy concierge downstairs. I was told to expect the knock. Let's me know the guy I'm going to be sleeping with is here, and I have to wait in the bathroom until he comes to get me. I pull the door closed and for a brief second a rush of fear grapples hold of me. If I lock myself in here and refuse to come out, how long would he wait until he gets pissed off and leaves? I can't do that, though. Eli would never hold up his end of the bargain, and besides…none of this matters anymore. None of it. It's just something I have to get through.

I hear the electronic beep of the key card being accepted into the door, and the rough catch of the lock sliding back. Silence follows after that. The edge of the sink digs into the back of my legs as I remain frozen, leaning heavily against it, before I remember I shouldn't do that. It'll mark my body, and that's against the rules, even temporary marks like that.

Thankfully the drugs begin to kick in, washing over me with a muted sense of peace. A good thing, too, because whoever is out there takes their sweet time in making themselves at home. Without it, I'd have been on the verge of making a run for it by the time a knuckle raps against the door. "Come on out. Turn the light off first," a voice commands. It's gruff and full of gravel, maybe the voice of a smoker? Fucking great. I'm going to have to spend the next two hours with my tongue down a smoker's throat, and then I'm gonna have to bleach my mouth out. I turn the light off and open the door, and I'm perplexed by what I see beyond.

Nothing.

Absolutely nothing. The room is pitch black.

"Couldn't find the light switch?"

"Don't touch it. Just come here," the voice tells me. He sounds young enough, and he's alone. Not that I was expecting more than one guy, of course. Eli swore it would only be the one guy. And only this one time. I step gingerly into the room, wishing I'd paid more attention to where the furniture was positioned before I'd locked myself away. I immediately stub my toe on god only knows what and hiss with pain.

"You okay?" There's an amused lilt to his voice, which is kind of irritating. What kind of a guy gets off on a girl breaking her toes?

"Well...I can't see a thing," I mutter.

"That's the point, I'm afraid. Come here."

If I knew where *here* was, I'd probably be a little less turned around. I try again, and this time I manage to stumble to the bed without colliding with anything else. The mattress dips as I climb onto it, wondering where the hell *he* is. I'm not half as scared as I should be. In fact, I feel almost a little giddy.

"Sit in the middle of the bed with your hands behind your back," he whispers. I wonder if he's going to tie me up. That should bother me. Would bother me any other time.

"Do you need a name?" I ask him; Eli said I should ask.

A low rumble, deep and throaty, breaks the silence of the room and I realize he's laughing. "Are you offering to tell me your *real* name?"

"Eli said that's against the rules."

"Then no." The mattress dips again. He's moving, coming closer. His hot breath grazes across the skin of my neck when he speaks. "I don't need to call you Melody or Candy or some other fake-ass name. We'll just be strangers for a while. That square with you?"

"Yeah, I—I guess."

In the darkness my skin is alive. So are my other senses. My nose keeps on whispering to me, hints of mint and the ocean. Whoever he is, this guy smells incredible. Not a whiff of cigarettes on him at all, which means that voice...that voice is one hundred percent natural. I'm curious about him in the most detached way.

"You done this before? Like this?" he asks me.

"Never." My breath actually catches in my throat. I'm so spaced out that I can barely think straight, but the lack of lighting in the room is making my heart race. Maybe it's because this guy could be a serial killer. He could still be a serial killer with the lights *on*, but at least I'd have the chance to see it in his eyes and run for my life.

Mystery Guy exhales, sending another warm breath across my chest. My nipples harden even though I'm not cold. I've never experienced that before. Never. Probably because I've never been this close to a guy before. "Place your hands in your lap," he tells me.

I do it. I jump a little when I feel his hand reach out and touch my leg. "Scared?"

"No."

He laughs, and it's a cruel and wicked thing. His hands gently trail up my leg until he finds my hand, where his fingers curl around my wrist. "You're braver than most girls."

"You do this with a lot of girls?"

"Yes."

Well at least he's honest. He lifts up my hand and brings it toward himself, and stubble prickles against the sensitive skin on the inside of my wrist.

"You smell like flowers. What perfume do you wear?"

"Afresia," I tell him.

"It's clean. Not too heavy. I like it."

*So glad you approve.* I feel like giggling. His nose brushes against my wrist and then the soft touch of his lips follows soon after. The kiss is barely even there, soft and gentle, but I can read a lot from it. His lips are full and he's gentle with his mouth. That's unexpected. I fidget on the bed, wondering where this is going. Where his mouth will be going next.

"Have you ever thought about what it would be like to be blind?" he rumbles.

"Why? Are you blind?"

"No. Answer the question."

"I suppose so. Sometimes."

He guides my hand upwards and takes it in both of his, un-curling my fingers so that my palm is open. He does it slowly, running calloused fingers down the length of my own, and I can't help but shiver. It's a fairly simple thing, but the way he does it feels intimate and considered, not just grabbing and touching for the hell of it. I hold my breath as he guides my hand again, until my fingertips meet his hair, and then down to his face.

"Tell me what you think I look like," he says, his voice a resonating growl. He lets go of my hand, and I have to lean forward to reach him properly. I shimmy closer, tucking my legs under my butt so I can balance properly, and then I raise my other hand to his face, too.

His hair is short, a little stiff from the styling product he's got in there; his facial features are strong, pronounced. Jaw's
a little square, nose mostly straight apart from a slightly flattened part near the ridge of his brow. His eyelashes are surprisingly long, and his lips…I was right. His lips are full and way softer than any guy's lips have a right to be. Especially a guy with a voice like his. From the tingling pads of my fingers, I can sense this guy has the face of an angel. A barbaric one—maybe like one of those guys who did a lot of smiting back in Babylon.

"What do you think?" he asks.

"I think you're probably very attractive," I admit.

He grunts. "And what about the rest of me?"

He applies a little pressure to my forearms so that they travel down to his chest, where my fingers meet with smooth skin and hard-packed, rippling muscle. His pecs twitch as my hands brush lightly over them, and then downward. I come across three horizontal ridges in his skin that shouldn't be there, to the right of his abs spaced a couple of inches apart, and my fingers draw circles over them, trying to tease their story from them, trying to figure out where they came from. There's an untold history of violence here, written in the planes of his formidable body. He shakes a little as I explore him, probing with a feather-light touch until I've traced my way across his washboard stomach and up over his obliques. He sucks in a sharp breath and tenses when I do that, and I smile a little. I actually *smile*. This guy's ticklish. He doesn't laugh or tell me not to touch him there, but his body tightens further still when I go over the area one more time to test the theory.

I move up to his shoulders, which are powerful and strong, and I lace my arms around the back of his neck, feeling over his shoulder blades. He's huge, but I'm not really afraid of him. Of course I should be, yes, but I'm not. The valium has flattened out my fear, and besides, the way I'd imagined this, the guy was going to come in here and want to lay his hands on me; he'd poke and prod and examine every inch of me, and he'd most definitely want to see what he was paying for. So far, this guy has touched me sparingly and that was on the hand.

"Well?" he asks.

"Where did the scars come from?"

"I was stabbed." He doesn't ponder on whether he's going to answer me; he just comes right out and says it.

"Did you nearly die?"

"Yes."

"Did it hurt?"

"Yes."

I let my hands fall from his shoulders and find the scars again, one, two, three of them. They feel jagged and terrible under my fingers. "What happened to the person who did this to you?" I almost don't want to ask. Mystery Man's been unnervingly candid since we began this bizarre interaction five minutes ago, and I'm afraid his answer will finally put the fear of God into me.

"He got what was coming to him," he says softly. The bed sheets rustle when he moves, his stomach muscles contracting under my hands; when he touches my hair, tangling his fingers into it, I'm still trying to decide whether he means he killed whoever did that to him.

"I'm very particular about what I want. You need to do what I ask you without question and this will go nicely for both of us, okay?" he breathes.

A shot of adrenaline finally lights up my nerve endings—the appropriate reaction to my situation. What the hell have I gotten myself into here? Valium or no Valium, I know that sounded like a threat. I'm in way over my head, but there's little I can do about it. Besides, Alexis. *Always* Alexis. "I can do that," I whisper.

"Good. Lie on your back."

I let go of him and suddenly I feel like I'm afloat in the middle of an ocean, drowning, with no way of saving myself. The sensible, smart part of my brain that still clings onto a vague sense of self-preservation is screaming that I should probably get the hell out of here, and for the first time the wrath of Eli almost isn't enough to keep me pinned to the bed. But the thought of finding Alexis is. My muscles are jumping, ready to explode into action, when the guy gently takes hold of my right ankle.

"Did you touch yourself today?"

*What the?!* "Do…do you mean—"

"Have you made yourself come today? Have you played with your pussy?"

My cheeks heat up to an uncomfortable temperature. No one has ever asked me that before. "No. No, I—I haven't," I stammer.

"Good. Then you'll taste so much sweeter." Instead of hook-ing his fingers under the waistband of my panties and pulling them down, he draws them to one side. My legs lock up when I feel his hot breath skimming over my exposed flesh. I'm not sure what I'm supposed to be doing with my hands. This is untrodden ground for me in a very big way. When a guy gives you head, it's usually because he's done something very, very bad and needs to make up for it, or at least that's what Pippa, my only friend in the world, says. I've never had a boyfriend to treat me badly in the first place, so I've never experienced it myself.

"Do you want me to lick you?" His voice is even deeper now, laden with the promise of sex.

"I want whatever you want," I gasp. That's what he's paying for, after all. That's what's going to help me get Lex back. He grips me hard around the top of my leg, squeezing until I cry out.

"That's not the game we're playing, here. Own me, or I'll own you. And trust me…you don't want that."

*Shit.* "Y—yes, I want you to lick me."

He makes a satisfied grunt and immediately moves, pushing his way between my legs. When his tongue darts out and laps at me, my leg muscles tense up. It feels hot and…and *good*. What the holy hell? I shouldn't be reacting like this. Embarrassment prickles at my cheeks. What sort of person am I, enjoying a complete stranger giving me head? And under these circumstances? I can't help it, though. My whole body feels like it's being caressed.

His tongue moves expertly, applying a subtle pressure to my clit, stroking up and down in a rhythmic pattern that sends wave after wave of heat crashing through me. I'm just letting go, letting the tension in my arms and legs relax, when he stops lapping and sucks.

"*Fuck!*"

He doesn't stop. He growls when I push back against him, rocking into his mouth shamelessly. I've never felt anything like this before. It feels…incredible. I'm panting and moaning like an animal when he pulls away, running his hands from the very tops of my knees, down the insides of my thighs to my panties. He rips them off in one swift motion.

"How badly do you want me to fuck you?"

I'm not here because I *want* to fuck him, but it is my job to make him *think* I do; yet the lines between acting and the truth are so blurred when I murmur, "Really bad. I want you really bad."

"Spread your legs," he commands. I spread them, wondering what's coming next. The room is like a black void, so dark I can't even make out the shadow of him as he moves quickly around the bed. I hear a zip being undone and then the rattle of metal, like a buckle being undone. Sucking my bottom lip into my mouth, I wait for him to do whatever he's about to do, worryingly piqued with curiosity. He restrains my left leg first, strapping something wide and tight around it and then affixing it to the bed. My right leg is next, and then he carefully does the same to my wrists. I'm starfished on the bed and completely vulnerable. His restraints aren't the kind for show; they're the kind made to stop people from getting away, and I'm sure as hell not going anywhere. Six months ago, I might have said a prayer. Now I just whimper, half out of fear and half out of anticipation.

He climbs up onto the bed, kneeling at my side, his breath still playing across me. I tense when I feel something cold and hard press against the skin of my stomach. "Are you still a brave girl?"

"Yes," I exhale.

He doesn't reply or tell me what he's going to do. The cool, sharp object he's leaning into my skin travels slowly upwards until it's poised directly under my breasts. I gasp lungful after lungful of air into my lungs, trying to keep still, because I know what it is he's got in his hand: it's a knife. A really fucking sharp knife.

His fingertip lifts the underwire of my bra in the middle, and then in a single, clean sweep, it springs apart, freeing my breasts. He cut through my bra! This is the most exposed, terrified, exhilarated I've ever felt. My Mystery Man straddles me, and the material of his pants, rough, slides up against my sides. He lays the flat, cool edge of his knife against my right nipple, sending a bolt of panic through me.

"Don't move," he whispers. I don't move. I am the stillest still thing ever. He leans down and touches me, his hand finally finding my breast. "You're so fucking perfect," he breathes. "So well behaved." And then his mouth is on my nipple, licking and sucking, hotter than anything I've ever felt before. My back arches up off the bed, and he chuckles. "You want me inside you?"

"Yes."

"You sure? Be careful what you wish for."

I wish for death on a daily basis. I wish for pain and suffering and blood and misery upon the heads of those who took my sister. Wishing for this feels just as dangerous but somehow safer than all that at the same time. He wanted me to own him, and despite the fact that he's tied me up now, I still think that's what he wants. I brace, hoping this is the right thing, and I demand, "Do it. Fuck me now. Don't make me wait any longer."

The knife vanishes from my skin. He shifts off the bed, and I hear him undoing his pants; slipping them off; the swish of him drawing something hard over something soft. Panic sings through me again when I hear another buckle.

"Ready?"

There's no backing out of it now. "I'm ready."

And he does something I hadn't even considered. Not even for a second. He threads a loop of leather over my head—his belt—and cinches it tight. I'm in trouble now.

"Open your mouth."

"I—"

"Do it." The tone of his voice is firm yet gentle at the same time. He brushes a hand down the side of my face, a reassuring gesture —*this is scary right now, but trust me.* Trust him? I'd be fucking mad to trust him. And yet I do what he tells me to. He pushes forward and guides his cock into my mouth. I've never done this before, so I'm basically wondering what the hell I'm supposed to do now. He's rock hard and tastes clean and slightly musky…and he's massive. I can barely fit him inside my mouth. I can tell he only fits half the length of him inside before he hits the back of my throat.

"Shit!" He hisses as I suck, forming a vacuum around him. I think I got that part right. His hips rock back and he slides out of my mouth causing a wet popping noise. "Still think you want me inside you?" He knows just how big he is; he's fucking smug about it. This is going to hurt like nothing else, but I don't want him to realize I'm a virgin. Even Eli doesn't know that part. I'm sure he would have charged this guy a whole lot more if he did, and that thought just turns my stomach.

"Yes," I tell him. "Yes, I want you."

"Good. But let's do this first." He fists a handful of my hair and lifts my head closer to him, and then he pushes back inside my mouth, thrusting in and out while applying a gentle pressure to the back of my head. I writhe on the bed, surprising myself with how much this turns me on. I'm floored when he tugs on the belt strap, though.

*Floored.*

My eyes, even in the dark, see stars. I can barely breathe with my windpipe cut off and his cock pulsing in and out of my mouth. "Stay with me, okay?" he grunts.

Fear and excitement pool in my stomach. It's the same sort of sensation I used to get when I was a kid waiting to ride a rollercoaster, only amplified a thousand times. And a whole lot scarier. Between my legs, my pussy tightens as he works his hips back and forth, keeping just enough tension on the belt strap so that I can drag the tiniest amount of oxygen into my lungs.

He shivers as his erection turns granite-hard. If he doesn't stop now, I think I know what will happen. But he does stop. Breathing heavily, he withdraws and crouches down beside the bed, easing his fingers beneath the belt and loosening it. His face is so close to mine, I can feel the intense power of his gaze as he stares at me in the dark. I still can't see a thing, but maybe he has better night vision than I do.

"Your mouth is perfect," he whispers. And then he does two things that surprise me. Firstly, in the most reverent of ways, he brushes his hand against my sweat-soaked skin, sweeping my hair out of my face. And then secondly, he places the softest kiss against my forehead.

"For being such a good girl, I'm going to make you come now," he breathes. A tremor of anticipation shimmers across my skin, and he chuckles. "You're being a *very* good girl."

He climbs up onto the bed and positions himself, hooking his arms underneath my hips, hoisting me up to meet him. The position is awkward with my ankles still bound to the bed, but all thoughts of my discomfort are forgotten when he buries his face between my legs and starts sucking on my clit again.

"Ahhh!"

The sensation is too much. I can feel myself climbing, ascending higher and higher as an unfamiliar, unfathomable feeling builds between my legs. It unfurls in gentle pins and needles throughout my body, growing more and more intense…and then…

I'm screaming. Unintelligible screaming. I'd scream for God but I doubt He would approve of this situation right now, and I have no idea who this guy is so I can't scream for him, either. I just scream for myself and the fireworks going off inside my head, the inferno licking over my skin, burning me out, leaving me hollow and spent. I fall slack, trembling as he continues to sweep his tongue over and over my clit.

"Stop, stop, please," I rasp.

"Mmm, so selfish," he hums into my pussy, making me clench. "Don't forget. It's my turn." He fiddles around for a moment—*condom? Fuck, I hope that's a condom.* And then he drops my hips and thrusts into me in one fluid motion, his hands tight on my pelvis, trapping me.

*Oh…my…*

The pain is almost crippling. An uncomfortable feeling, a buildup of pressure and then a stinging release, let's me know that it's done. He stops.

"What…?" He inhales deeply. Exhales. "You probably shouldn't have kept that from me," he says softly. He sighs, as though he's disappointed in me, which is the most messed up thing ever. "Are you ready?" he asks.

My voice is a faint whisper when I reply, "Yes."

"Try to relax." He fills me up, stretches me, makes me whole. He starts off slow, gentler than I think he would have done if he hadn't just deflowered me. After a while the pain subsides, gradually transforms until I'm no longer tensing with every thrust, but leaning into it. By the end, he's fucking me like a freight train—unstoppable and raw with need. He comes so hard, he practically roars.

I don't, of course. It's my first time, and the pain just about outweighed the pleasure. My mind is too fogged to understand what's going on as he climbs off me and slides down my body. His lips caress the inside of my thigh, and I shiver as his fingers carefully stroke over my core. The touch isn't designed to excite me—it's more of an apology. He moves around in the dark, undoing my wrists, my ankles.

"You enjoy that?" he rumbles, and the depths of his voice make my legs press together.

"Yeah, I—I did." The most startling thing, the thing that makes me most sick, is that I'm telling the truth. What the hell is wrong with me?

He grunts, unthreading his belt from around my neck. The release of pressure makes me feel like I'm floating two feet off the bed.

I'm immobile as he packs up his things. I can sense him next to me pulling on his clothes. Then, when he's dressed, he stands beside the bed looking down on me. He brushes his fingertips against my cheek again, so soft it's almost not a touch at all.

"Be seeing you." He heads for the door, and the light from the hallway nearly splits my skull apart when he opens it. And there my mystery man pauses, and I catch the one and only glimpse of him I ever get. Wearing a worn leather jacket, his back to me, a black duffel bag in his right hand, he tips his head down to his shoulder. He's doesn't look back at me. He hovers there long enough for me to make out the silhouette of his profile, his dark, mussed hair, the bruised pout to his full lips.

And then he goes.

I never find out his name.

Want to know if Sloane ever meets her mystery man in the light of day? Click here to keep on reading! You can also read the entire story for FREE on KU!

# UNTITLED

Printed in Poland
by Amazon Fulfillment
Poland Sp. z o.o., Wrocław